EDEN

TIM LEBBON

TITAN BOOKS

Eden
Print edition ISBN: 9781789092936
E-book edition ISBN: 9781789092943

Published by Titan Books
A division of Titan Publishing Group Ltd
144 Southwark Street, London SE1 0UP
www.titanbooks.com

First edition: April 2020
1 3 5 7 9 10 8 6 4 2

A CIP catalogue record for this title is available from the British Library.

Printed and bound in the United States.

PRAISE FOR *EDEN*

"Instantly cinematic. A textured, thought-provoking thriller that will make you wonder what the world would be like if humans were to give it back. *Eden* is a story about family, humanity and the desire to re-experience the wonders we screwed up the first time around. Nobody is as smooth on the lettered keys as Tim Lebbon. Here, as with all his books, you are in the hands of a master."

Josh Malerman, *New York Times* bestselling author of *Bird Box* and *A House at the Bottom of a Lake*

"Smart, prescient and gripping, Tim Lebbon's *Eden* takes us, and his team of adventurers, into the dark, pulsing heart of nature, and we all get far more than we bargained for. This near future eco-thriller puts Lebbon at the top of the tree. Read it. And then recycle."

Sarah Pinborough, *Sunday Times* #1 bestselling author of *Behind Her Eyes*

"I can smell Eden, I can feel it, I can see it. But I want no part of it. Your senses will tingle and twitch as you journey through a forest of hellish life made real by Tim Lebbon's rich prose and slick action sequences. You'll be running behind the team right to the end, and then you'll want to return to the start of the book to warn them—turn back. This is horror at its best, a terrifying nightmare of nature's darkest depths ramped up to eleven, but also a love letter to adventure running, and to nature itself. Highly recommended."

Adrian J Walker, author of *The End of the World Running Club*

"*Eden* is a smart, thrilling, relentless eco-nightmare that will worm its tendrils deep into you. Let your own ghost orchid grow."

Paul Tremblay, author of *A Head Full of Ghosts* and *The Cabin at the End of the World*

"*Eden* will intrigue, delight and thrill in equal measures. Another winner from Lebbon!"

Simon Clark, author of *The Midnight Man* and *Night of the Triffids*

"*Eden* is a perfect torn-from-the-headlines biological thriller. Tim Lebbon mixes action, complex characters, and climate science into an absolute page-turner. This is why science fiction is so important! Highly recommended!"

Jonathan Maberry, *New York Times* bestselling author of *V-Wars* and *Rage*

"An entertaining, gruesome story of endurance and survival in the last wild places on earth."

Adam Nevill, author of *The Reddening*

"Against a backdrop of environmental disaster, Tim Lebbon creates a lush, intricate, mysterious and intriguing world—an Eden where anything can happen. The writing is beautiful; the story is haunting and impossible to put down. Highly recommended!"

Alison Littlewood, author of *A Cold Season*

"*Eden* is a first-rate, genre-bending thriller, a dark vision of a horrific future full of heartache and sinister atmosphere... Nobody tells stories like this better than Tim Lebbon."

Christopher Golden, *New York Times* bestselling author of *Ararat* and *Snowblind*

"Tim Lebbon destroys the world like most of us put our socks on in the morning. But this is different. The catalyst of the story is hope. The hope that humanity survives against the odds doled out by a planet that has its own plans for survival. *Eden* is *Deliverance* with the volume turned up to eleven. A breathtaking ride through the wild—the really wild—that would give Bear Grylls nightmares."

Stephen Volk, writer of BBC's *Ghostwatch* and The Dark Masters trilogy

"*Eden* is both the darkest of fairy tales and an uncompromising, often gruelling account of adaptation and survival... A relentless page-turner in which the planet bites back!"

Mark Morris, author of the *Obsidian Heart* trilogy

"Tim Lebbon gives us a near-future as terrifying as it is exhilarating, and —most frightening of all—irresistibly beautiful. Surrender to *Eden*."

Alma Katsu, author of *The Deep* and *The Hunger*

"With *Eden*, Tim Lebbon is at the top of his game. Action-packed, thought-provoking, terrifying, this is the eco horror novel by which all others will be judged."

Rio Youers, author of *The Forgotten Girl* and *Halcyon*

"*Eden* is both an eerie reimagining of our relationship with nature and a breathless page-turning thriller. Tim Lebbon has created a vivid, wild world, filled with savagery and tenderness. It will haunt you."

Catriona Ward, author of *Little Eve* and *Rawblood*

"*Eden* is the ultimate adventure race turned nightmare, pitting the hubris of human nature against Nature itself, primal and emboldened and hostile. It's a novel that could only have come from Tim Lebbon, melding a fiendish imagination with the heart of an endurance athlete... and a profound concern for the world we must all traverse."

**Brian Hodge, author of *The Immaculate Void*
and *Skidding Into Oblivion***

"A terrifying thrill ride into nature's well-deserved revenge on humans, *Eden* is a chilling warning and a fast, hard read... today's version of *The Hot Zone*."

**Delilah S. Dawson, *New York Times* bestselling author
of *Star Wars: Phasma***

"*Eden* is visceral, cinematic and utterly wild, with a disorienting tone like Tarkovsky's *Stalker* but with a far higher body count. It's another terrifying yet irresistible novel from the effortlessly talented Tim Lebbon."

Tim Major, author of *Snakeskins*

EDEN

For my good friend James A. Moore

"Self-preservation is the first law of nature."
—PROVERB

KAT

Eden seems like a good place to die. Before arriving she hoped that would be the case, but now she is certain. Even if she wasn't ready and prepared to embrace the endless sleep, darkness is all that faces her now. After what she has seen and experienced, and what lies before her, there can be no doubt.

The deep forest surrounding her sings unknown songs in voices she cannot understand. She has never been one for courting attention. The exact opposite, in fact, and that is her main reason for coming here. She came to lose herself and find some sort of peace. Instead, something has found her.

Wiping blood from her left eye, she's surprised at how quickly it's drying. It forms a crisp, sticky layer, binding her eyelid almost shut. She doesn't want to confront death with one eye closed. She winces when several eyelashes are pulled out with the coagulating mass. It smears across her fingertips and palm, and forms dark half-moons beneath her nails. She stares at it, sad for all that has come to pass. It's not her blood.

She looks up at the tree canopy and the blue sky beyond. The canopy sways with the breeze, a calming dance that seems to keep time with the natural jazz of birds and animals, and the call of something else. Higher up, shredded clouds drift by. The counterpoint makes her dizzy, but she does not close her eyes.

Instead she looks down and sees fluid shadows coalescing from the trees and drawing close, their approach celebrated by a rising cacophony of forest song. She breathes out a shuddering sigh. After the years and miles that led her here, she always believed it would be the illness that would take her in the end. Coming to Eden, she never meant any harm. She hoped to die on her own terms. She wasn't expecting something worse.

As the shadows touch her skin, she makes a fist around the delicate stem of the ghost she has found.

1

"Our aim was ambitious, our intentions pure, our hearts and minds set on one simple task: to save the world."

Ekow Kufuor, First Chair of the United Zone Council

"With everything you've done, it still amazes me that you're shit scared of flying."

Jenn acknowledged the comment with a soft grunt that she could hardly hear above the old aircraft's engines. She stared at the back of Cove's head, right hand clasping the seat in front of her, left hand crushing Aaron's. She could feel the sweat sticking their palms together and knew it was not all hers. At least if he was nervous of flying too, the pain from her vice grip would be a welcome distraction.

But Aaron wasn't afraid of flying. From the corner of her eye she could see his grin, an expression of childlike glee as he watched trees whipping by above the level of the plane's flight path.

"Jenn."

"What?"

"I said—"

"I heard you, Dad. Thanks a lot."

"That time you climbed and base jumped the Burj Khalifa—"

"You're not helping." He must have heard her blooming anger because he fell silent. She glanced to her right and across the aisle without moving her head and saw what she expected— her father, relaxed back in his seat wearing a contented smile. While the plane vibrated around them and promised to shake itself apart, scattering them all across the deep valley below, his mind was way ahead. He was always one step or one minute in the future.

"You call this flying?" Gee said from the cramped seat behind her. "Flying implies grace and control. This is more like a long fall."

As if in response, the plane dropped with a loud thud that shook through the entire fuselage, bouncing through an area of turbulence before levelling and returning to its previous state of imminent disaster. Jenn's heart stuttered and she squeezed the seat and Aaron's hand even harder. From up ahead the pilot shouted something in Spanish and laughed, the same throaty cough he'd offered when Gee had suggested that his pride and joy might be more suited to a scrapheap.

Jenn thought she'd heard something break during that last brief bout of turbulence. The sight of the aircraft before they'd boarded had almost been enough to convince her to abort their expedition and go back to the drawing board, but Aaron had persuaded her it would be safe. *I know a guy who knows this guy*, he'd said. *He keeps it looking like this to avoid any unwanted attention. That plane's like your dad—grizzled, grumpy and decrepit on the outside, but perfect mechanical order beneath the skin.*

The memory brought a nervous smile, and she glanced sidelong at her father once more. He raised an eyebrow and one corner of his mouth in response. In his early fifties, he was the most experienced explorer among them, with enough exploits to fill a dozen books, were he of a mind to write them. He sometimes talked about retirement and memoirs, but she knew that was still decades away. He'd never be the sort to sit at home watching TV, even if he had a TV to watch, or indeed a home. In a world suffocating beneath the excessive weight and waste of humanity, there were still places left for him to explore and race across; valleys and islands, plains and forests where the toxic taint of people was still slight enough to not be seen, so long as you didn't look too closely. That was sometimes his problem—looking too closely.

Her dad was still the centre of her existence, the star around which she orbited. Though Aaron had come into her life a few years ago and she loved him and saw a future with him, it was her dad she looked for whenever she found herself staring out into the big black.

There was another shout from in front. She held her breath, staring past Cove's head at the open cockpit door. The pilot seemed unable to sit still, constantly tweaking the instrument panel, gesturing from the window, talking to himself and flicking plastic dials with his finger.

"Turn it off and turn it on again!" Aaron shouted, and Jenn gave his hand a crushing squeeze that ground bones. Maybe that would cover the sound of the plane breaking apart, at least. He didn't protest.

They drifted left and right along the winding valley, and when Jenn dared to look she imagined she could see tree limbs flicked by the wings, branches broken and leaves sprayed outwards. They were so close she could have reached out and plucked fruit. Such a dangerous flight was the price they had to pay to avoid popping up on the Zeds' radar, and that was a prerequisite for them entering Eden undetected. If the Zeds knew they were there, they'd be pursued until they landed or were brought down.

Over time, the Zone Protection Force had diverged into vastly different entities from place to place, country to country. But the aspect that continued to unite them was their tenacity and dedication to their cause.

The team would still be a solid six hours' hike from the Virgin Zone's southern boundary when they landed, but this way they'd be fresh and fully supplied when they infiltrated and prepared for the dangerous crossing.

They were about to break enough laws to put them all in jail for a very long time.

"Check that out," Gee said.

Jenn looked past Aaron and out of the window again. Lit by a gorgeous dawn palette spilling over the eastern hills, the steep valley sides had dropped and opened out, and the plane's engine tone changed as the pilot guided them even lower. Despite her fear of flying, she leaned across Aaron to get a better view through the dirty, scratched window.

On the hillside close by, a swathe of trees had died. The majestic giants were bare of leaves and bleached pale, skeletons of their former selves pointing sad, stiff limbs at the sky. At the dead area's edges some trees clung on to existence, speckled both with pale death and wan, desperate life, leaves a less luscious hue compared to those deeper in the more healthy forests. It was as if someone had taken a giant paintbrush to the view and splashed an uneven stroke of grey across the hillside.

"Weird how it's not taken all the trees," Cove said. Perhaps the keenest sportsman among them, Dan Covington was also the least aware about the changes they witnessed affecting the planet. A newfound desire to learn was why he remained with them and not some other group. They took him to places most others could not, and each expedition was an education.

"Pollution's not selective," Selina said. She was seated behind Jenn's father, and for much of the trip she'd appeared to be asleep. Now she was looking past Gee at the sad scene to their port side. Though the only qualified scientist amongst them, and a passionate environmentalist and lecturer, she rarely displayed emotion about the damage to the world they so often observed. Jenn's father told her that Selina's soul was also damaged, and her tears were all cried out.

"But why some trees and not others?" Cove asked.

"Could be distribution of species. Some are more susceptible than others to pollution and changes in climate. Might be differing rock strata guiding the water table. Maybe the dead patch follows the route of a stream, a fracture in the subsoil, or pollination patterns of the local bee population. Saw a hundred square miles of dead trees in Malaysia with five spots where about fifty trees were still thriving. Someday, someone'll publish a paper on the reasons why. Doesn't matter." Selina sat back in her seat and closed her eyes again. "Just another dead forest."

"Looks almost pretty," Cove said.

"Pretty like cancer," her dad said, and Jenn caught her breath. Guilt bit in. It always did when she thought about the secret she was holding back from him.

"Mr Cheerful strikes again," Aaron said. "You should do stand up, Dylan. You should have your own motivational net channel. You could call it Dour Dylan and the—"

"Says the man sleeping with my daughter."

"Hey!" Jenn said. "That is *not* a place you can go."

"Said Jenn to Aaron, never," Gee said, and all of them laughed. Even Selina was smirking when Jenn twisted in her seat to launch a punch at Gee. He held up both fists and her blow glanced off his left prosthetic hand, leaving her knuckles smarting. He grinned and raised his middle finger at her.

"Taken your mind off our imminent fiery death, anyway," Aaron said.

"I don't know why I stay with any of you," Jenn said, settling back in her seat. She looked at her smiling father. "You're devils. Every single one of you. I'm the only non-devil person here."

"Totally without sin," Aaron agreed.

Jenn crossed her arms and feigned anger. In front of her, Cove's shoulders shook with laughter, and her fear began to ease. She could even watch the pilot going about his frantic business without expecting them to flip over and plummet into the forest at any moment.

Jenn liked to analyse a problem, pick it apart, examine its components until she had found if not a solution, then at least its cause. But her fear of flying remained a mystery. It was not the heights involved, because she was a competent base jumper, a climber, and two years ago she'd ridden a mountain bike along a ridgeline track in Mexico which Aaron had admitted made his nerves jangle. She'd beaten his time by a good margin, too. It wasn't the loss of control, because she frequently surrendered her wellbeing to other people, and not just members of their own tight team. She knew it was not the fact that this old aircraft probably wasn't considered new for the bulk of the last century, let alone this one, because she'd made a hundred fear-laden journeys in a variety of jets, propeller planes, helicopters, and even a couple of hot air balloons.

She didn't know what it was. She could look from the window and watch cars winding along roads like ants, and welcomed the views that aircraft flight paths afforded of a wide range of vistas. Yet still when an aircraft took off with her on board, her heart fluttered twice as fast as usual, her palms sweated, and a constant queasiness swilled through her torso from throat to gut. If she closed her eyes it only made matters worse.

Maybe you died in a plane crash in a previous life, Aaron had said once when they discussed her fears the day before a flight.

Yeah, right. Fighter pilot.

Crop sprayer, maybe.

"Oh man, that's just fucking lovely," Gee said.

"What?" Jenn asked.

"Left turn, Jenn," he said, face pressed to the window. "Anyone for a swim?" A narrow valley had opened beside them, curving gently away from their flight path. The river snaking along the valley floor was pale yellow in places, and here and there it threw up a confusion of unnatural colours. The chemical slicks were a flow of broken rainbows. Foam speckled the banks in cotton-wool piles and swirled on gentle currents.

"Must come from seventy miles upriver," Lucy said from beside Cove. She was reading from her hand tablet, and Jenn marvelled how her friend ever survived without her tech. She was researching a PhD in human/artificial intelligence communication, the finer details of which went over Jenn's head, and Cove sometimes joked that she was happiest in the company of a computer. Most expeditions were tech-free, and this more than any other was going to be stripped back to the bare essentials once they set out for real. Basic, streamlined, fast. "Chemical plant, officially been closed down for seventeen years."

"Officially," Aaron said.

"Money can open doors and close eyes," Lucy said. "Fucking assholes."

"So close to Eden?" Cove asked. "I'm amazed it's allowed."

"It's not," Lucy said. "Like I said, fucking asshole." The singular was very obvious. She brushed her long dark hair over her ear and half-turned, raising one corner of her mouth. Jenn stifled a giggle. The two of them shared a birthday, though Lucy was two years older, and sometimes Cove joked that they were like sisters, whispering and keeping secrets. He didn't always smile when he said it.

"We'll leave all that behind soon," Aaron said, and Jenn thought he was talking just loud enough for her to hear. On their trip here they'd passed through plenty of places where signs of pollution were rife, and crossed a coastline where global warming and a rise in sea levels were starkly illustrated by several abandoned communities half-submerged beneath the waves. It was nothing they hadn't seen many times before, and lived with for most of their lives. They'd once taken a flight across swathes of floating garbage in the Pacific so vast that some of the islands of waste had actually been given names and were home to communities of pirates, smugglers and terrorist cells. They had witnessed whole districts undermined and washed away in Old Shanghai, with millions of residents displaced to resettlement camps where hunger, crime and disease were rife. They had wandered between terrible mass graves and monuments to the million victims of the Great Alexandrian Flood, deaths that had been easily preventable if public information had been more forthcoming from governments that shied away from, or even denied, the shattering effects of climate change. Whilst scouting a trip into the Jaguar Zone with Aaron and her father—a journey they had yet to commit to—they had witnessed the devastating effects of many decades of illegal logging, burning and deforestation on the Amazon rainforest. The giant jungle had become many thousands of small, scattered woodlands.

Such memories and experiences made the anticipation of this journey even more sweet.

"Hope so." She squeezed his hand again, more gently this time. "Love you," she whispered, but he didn't reply, and she wondered if he'd heard at all. She turned from the window and stared again at the back of Cove's head, willing the flight to be over, craving the feel of grass and soil beneath her feet, the planet pressing back.

She visualised the expedition to come. It filled her with excitement. She saw forests and hillsides, abandoned towns, valleys and rivers and lakes, a beautiful place where there were no people at all.

Then she remembered her real reason for coming and wished that flying was all she had to fear.

2

"Of course, I appreciate all the good intentions behind the International Virgin Zone Accord, and I've gone down on record many times supporting the whole effort. But you can't *become* a virgin. And however successful these places might be—and only time will show and tell us that—they're still part of a world that's already been well and truly fucked by humanity."

Anthony Keyse, Green World Alliance

Jenn always loved the companionable tension between seven people who'd prepared together many times before. There was the clink and brush of kit being checked and packed, the smell of chafe cream and sun lotion, the sweet aroma of a fuel-heavy breakfast bubbling on the camp stove, the swill of water in bottles and rucksack bladders, and the nervous and excited chatter, quieter than usual, as if speaking too loud would disturb the comfortable balance they had all found.

She loved the sense of danger, too. They all did. That was why they were here, away from their families, homes and real-world jobs. They all agreed that this might be the most dangerous thing any of them had ever done.

Forest sounds muttered around them—the hushing of leaves in the morning breeze, bird song, secretive rustlings as small creatures went about their dawn tasks unseen. It was everything that made Jenn feel invigorated and alive, and a refreshing change to the rattle and roar of the aircraft.

"Thirty minutes," the woman said. She called herself Pocahontas, or Poke for short. Jenn had laughed when she'd introduced herself, but Poke's stern glare had seen the smile away. She conveyed all manner of experience and knowledge in that look, and Jenn had to respect that. No matter what she chose to call herself.

"You don't look like a Pocahontas," Cove said as he strapped a rolled bivvy bag to the top flap of his rucksack.

"So what the fuck do I look like?" Poke asked. She was sitting on a fallen tree, smoking a foul-smelling cigarette and watching them prepare. Her dad said Poke was the best fixer he'd ever met.

Jenn found her fascinating. She couldn't remember the last time she'd seen anyone smoking. She was pleased to see that the old woman was smiling, and her dark wrinkled skin, lean physique and functional clothing indicated that she was very much at home out here. The gold on her fingers and hanging from her ears showed that she still liked some of the finer things. Her hair was snow-white, and braided tight to her scalp. She had scars. Jenn wondered at the stories each one might tell.

"Maybe a Mildred," Cove said.

"Or a Whitney," Jenn said.

Poke laughed out loud, rocking back on the tree and coughing cigarette smoke at the sky. "I guess after Eden's eaten you all up, I'll change my name." She stood and walked a wide circle around them, watching them work.

The pilot had surprised them by turning around and taking off minutes after landing and disgorging them on the old road.

Jenn thought he'd have at least checked the aircraft over, but he'd seemed eager to leave. Poke, emerging from the trees as soon as they appeared, said that if he was caught his plane would be impounded, and it was his only source of income. It wasn't only people he smuggled.

She'd led them into the forest and to a clearing where she'd prepared for their arrival. The stew cooking on the camp fire made Jenn's mouth water, and she looked forward to how it would fend off the early morning chill. She had decided not to ask what meat it contained.

"Twenty-five minutes," Poke said.

"It's a six-hour hike to the boundary," Cove said.

"And?" Poke stopped close to Cove.

"So why the countdown?"

Poke looked him up and down, chuckled, then continued circling the group without replying. Cove glanced at Jenn and raised an eyebrow. He was the most beholden to gear among them. Branded labels adorned his clothing, rucksack and other kit, and he'd probably spent more money equipping himself for this expedition than the rest of them put together. She wanted to tell Poke how experienced Cove was, but it wasn't her place to stand up for him. He wasn't usually averse to singing his own praises.

"Poke's got us on a tight schedule," Jenn's father said. "Listen to her. She knows what she's doing."

Jenn noticed that Poke had stopped pacing and was staring at her.

"What?" Jenn asked.

"Nothing." Poke stomped out her dog-end and pulled another rolled cigarette from her shirt pocket. "Just wondering where the rest of your gear is."

"Lucy's already mourning her precious gadgets," Gee said,

chuckling. Lucy glared at him from where she stood next to the small pile of kit they were leaving behind. Eden was a pristine place, the oldest and wildest of the world's thirteen Virgin Zones, and Dylan had insisted that they treat it with the appropriate respect. This expedition was as stripped down as any they had ever undertaken—no hand tablets or net implants, no GPS, no satphones, no electronics or gadgets at all. It was them against Eden, and there was a purity about that which Jenn found beguiling.

"You know," Poke said. "Sciency stuff. Prods and measuring shit."

"We've got nothing like that," Selina said.

"Scales and beakers. Sample bags. All that crap."

"Got everything we need here." Gee was the first to be ready, as ever. "Hiking, running, climbing stuff. Dried food. Water purifiers. Sun block and basic medical kit. Couple of small tents, knives, some waterproof kit in case the forecast is off, and spare clothing. But not much, because we just so love to smell."

"You'll forage for food?"

"Yeah, fruit and nuts, but we won't kill anything to eat unless we have to. We run on a calorie deficit—when you're burning twelve thousand per day you just can't carry that much grub." Gee nodded at Cove. "And some of us can afford to lose some timber."

Cove gave him the finger, and Gee giggled. A thin, small man, the Canadian was probably the most determined person Jenn knew. In the six years he'd been travelling with her and her father, she'd never witnessed him shy away from any challenge, or give up. She'd seen him free-climb a sheer cliff wall no one else would try, and face up to three racist pricks on a boat in France. They'd walked away and he'd limped, but in Jenn's eyes he'd still won. Only two years younger than her father, still Gee felt something like a brother. Yet none of his determination was to do with him having only one hand. He'd never indicated it was a disability at all; in fact he seemed to like it. He hid two joints in a hollow finger.

"What the fuck do you look like?" Poke asked, looking Gee up and down.

"Your boyfriend," Gee said. He took a step closer.

"Put you on your ass," Poke said. Gee shrugged and smiled. None of them doubted her. She lit the rollie and inhaled.

"I've told you why we're here," Jenn's father said.

"I didn't believe anyone was that stupid." She looked at Jenn again, frowning.

"We are," he said.

"So who are you racing?" Poke asked.

"No one yet. We're aiming to be the first. You know this place, you know why."

Poke just blinked at him through a haze of smoke.

"Statistically and historically Eden is the most dangerous Zone in the world," he said. "It's swallowed up plenty of people over the years."

"Yeah."

Jenn's father looked around as he continued, pleased that he had everyone's attention. They'd all heard this before, but not in front of someone like Poke. Someone who could verify the things he said.

"Other adventurer racers have tried. Some vanished. Others fled Eden and melted away, attempting to assimilate back into society. It's as if the place stripped away their sense of adventure. Over the years, it's attracted a reputation as one of the most amazing places on Earth, wholly inimical to man."

The breeze fell away, the trees growing still and the birds quiet, listening.

"And to woman," Gee quipped to break the silence.

"You want to be the first group of assholes to run across Eden," Poke said, shaking her head.

"Run, climb, swim, walk, crawl if we have to," Cove said. "It's called an adventure race."

"Adventure," Poke said, rolling the word like a strange taste.

"Want to come with us?" Gee asked.

"Want to live," Poke said. For the first time she sounded serious.

"We *are* living," Lucy said. "This is being alive."

"You got a job, missy?"

"I'm researching a PhD."

"Family?"

"My parents live in London."

"Huh." Poke circled them again, smoking, silent, and they all finished preparing their kit. She kept glancing at Jenn.

"What?" Jenn asked again. She was becoming impatient. Poke might be the best fixer her father knew, she might be able to get them through security measures and into Eden, but she was a pain in the ass.

"Just thinking what a pity it is," Poke said.

"What's a pity?" Selina asked.

"Seeing you all here like this, fit and healthy, and I'm taking you into a place that'll chew you up and spit you out. Or maybe not even spit you out. You're all fucking mad."

"So why take us?" Jenn asked.

Poke nodded at her father. "Good pay." With that she ground out her latest cigarette, glanced at her watch and took the lid off the stew. "And here's some good news," she said over her shoulder. "Breakfast's ready fifteen minutes early. That's a buffer for any unforeseens."

3

Got it on good authority that this year's death toll for those attempting to enter the Husky Plains Zone isn't as published. They tell us 7. I heard it's over 150. Wasted by the Zeds. They're murdering mercenaries. Don't believe a word of this Zone Protection Force bullshit.

@PottyBonkkers

There were no unforeseens. Jenn's dad had been right, Poke was the best fixer and guide any of them had ever met. She had their route scoped out, and she surprised Jenn with her supreme level of fitness. She might have been sixty-five, even seventy, but for the next six hours she led them on a tough hike through rising temperatures and dense forest towards the place where she said they had their best chance of entering Eden.

They knew some of what to expect. Security around every Virgin Zone was tight, but the areas involved were so vast that there were loopholes for those who knew where and how to look. Poke knew very well. She wore an advanced GPS smartwatch with all manner of upgrades and a net implant behind her ear, and she had programmed it in detail for their route, time and pace. Each buzz was a signal for some form of action—march on apace; seek cover and wait for a drone to pass by overhead; jig left and pass through a culvert beneath a road; turn right and climb a small, steeply wooded slope—and Poke had each move pre-planned and memorised. She kept a strict watch on their time, slowing them down on several occasions, and speeding them up once after Aaron stopped to take a leak.

The landscape was beautiful, with forested slopes and valleys opening here and there to flower-speckled clearings, and a network of streams and creeks flowing towards some distant river. But they were never far from signs of humankind's influence. For a while they followed a road, old and fallen into disrepair now that the only vehicles to use it were occasional Zed security patrols. Weeds grew through tarmac, kerbstones were cracked and deformed from root action, and successive years of leaf fall had turned to soil in the gutters and cracks, sprouting an array of grasses, small shrubs and trees. Jenn looked forward to seeing how much more the road had changed once they were inside. Her excitement was a physical thing, a bee buzzing in her brain.

They came across a small town nestled in a shallow valley, home now only to security personnel. Passing by on the wooded hillside, they kept way down below the ridge so that they did not offer telltale silhouettes. Soon they were far enough away to not be seen, but close enough for Poke to call a halt and lend Jenn a small pair of binoculars so she could look through the trees and examine the place. Some parts of the town were abandoned and dilapidated. The few old vehicles that lined the streets sat on flat tyres, gardens had spilled from their rigidly enforced boundaries and grown wild, and the buildings looked bedraggled, with smashed windows, peeling paintwork and gutters hanging down. Several houses had been fortified, with larger steel containers parked in front yards and between buildings. Jenn guessed the steel buildings would be armouries.

"You got someone down there?" Jenn asked.

"Fuck, no!" Poke said. "I'd never trust a Zed. Bunch of fucking mercenaries."

"Then how are we getting in?" Jenn knew that once they reached the true border there would be extensive electronic security measures, as well as physical boundaries, both natural and manmade, that would make it almost impossible to infiltrate. Entering other Zones had usually involved their fixer having an arrangement with someone on the inside, either a Zed or one of numerous maintenance teams that attended the Zones' vast and complex perimeters.

"Let me worry about that," Poke said.

"*I'm* worried about it."

"No. Let me. It's what you're paying me for."

Jenn took one last look through the binoculars before handing them back. The old woman was looking at her again, frowning, troubled by something.

"Just what the hell—" Jenn began, then Poke's watch buzzed. She glanced at it and stood, waving the way forward.

"Seventy minutes, then we stop for ten," she said. "Things get complicated after that."

"What's with her?" Aaron asked as he approached Jenn.

"I don't know."

"It's like she recognises you." He draped an arm around her neck and pulled her close, kissing the side of her face before moving on. He was strong, dependable, and he'd been her solid support when they'd both raced the Marathon des Sables, a multi-day ultramarathon across the Sahara Desert. By the end of the race, she had become his support, too. They'd met that first night, sharing a tent with several other runners and also sharing stories about other races and adventures they'd experienced. One of the men had mentioned his time crossing the Siberian Virgin Zone, known as Zona Smerti, and his story had left most of them open-mouthed with awe and envy. Not Aaron. He wasn't impressed by such unsubtle boasts. What impressed him was quiet determination, the ability to weather pain, and the triumph of mind and spirit over body.

Jenn would never forget the last day of that tough race. She ran the final marathon with her feet in tatters from blisters, three toenails missing, and skin split around her lips, eyes and ears from sunburn and the effects of sand blasted into her face from a sudden storm early that morning. Crossing the line, collapsing in a heap, she'd refused help until she saw Aaron coming in an hour after her.

"My feet," he gasped as he stumbled into her, unable to stop because his mind had got stuck in one mode—keep moving forward. Later, they'd discover that he had stress fractures in both feet.

"I don't want to see your feet, ever," she said.

"I want to cut them off," he said. "Someone. Cut my feet off." He hugged her, and the closeness felt so natural, the affection growing between them as obvious as the heat and sweat and the stink of their unwashed bodies. They both cried. Their tears mixed like blood, binding them together forever. Something about that moment was magical in Jenn's mind. She'd never believed in love at first sight, but it was something close.

That's what it is, Jenn thought now as Aaron and the others followed Poke across the forested hillside. *Like she recognises me.* She was a name on the tip of Poke's tongue, a memory buried but rising towards the surface.

Only her father had ever met Poke before. By Poke's own admission, she never travelled far from this locale. That was why she knew it so well. The only reason Poke might recognise her was if she reminded her of someone else.

"Eden," Poke said.

At first Jenn saw little to differentiate the view across the valley from the landscape they had traversed over the past few hours. More trees, more hills, more valleys. Poke had brought them here on a very precise schedule, and even now she continued glancing at her watch.

"This is where it gets tricky," the guide said.

"But you've got our route planned," Jenn's father said. He had been quiet today, no doubt considering the difficulty of the task to come. They'd all been quiet, even Gee. Coming together for an expedition, they each prepared mentally in their own private ways.

"I have," Poke said.

"But still it's tricky?" Lucy asked.

Poke sighed heavily, looked at her watch one more time, and eased herself down against a tree. She massaged her knees. It was the first time Jenn had seen her displaying any sign of discomfort.

"Of course it is," she said. "Take a look. All of you. A closer look."

"What are we looking at?" Cove asked, but none of them answered. Instead, they did what their guide told them.

Jenn and Aaron stood side by side, arms touching, breathing heavily from exertion. They were used to it. Revelled in it. She could smell him, a familiar scent of heat and perspiration.

"It looks... deep," he said. He smirked, and Jenn nudged against him. But he was right. Across the valley, over a narrow river, starting on the other side and stretching into the distance over rolling hills with dark clefts that might contain anything, Eden looked as deep as any place she had ever seen.

Deep was how she described her nightmare. It was imprecise, but the best word she could find. If she was ever ill or jaded, the deep haunted her sleep and sometimes woke her in a bath of sweat. A sense of wide open space and depth, a vision of expanse and endless, unknown breadth; she had tried explaining the nightmares to Aaron when she shouted herself awake beside him, and he asked her what was wrong. Nursing a midnight coffee she'd sit propped against the wall and talk through the fears that haunted her sleep. Like all the worst nightmares, they defied explaining. No words did them justice. *It's a feeling of endless, daunting depth*, she'd said. *Like the universe has swallowed me up and forgotten about me.*

She remembered her mother holding her when she woke from more frequent childhood versions of this nightmare. She'd never needed to ask Jenn what was wrong, and Jenn never tried to explain. Her arms were enough. The strength of her, the smell, the comfort she offered when she said, *You're safe in my warm.*

As Jenn and the others stared out across the wilderness, a dreg of her recurring nightmare trailed a whisper across the landscape. A shiver ran through her and she shook it off. The view was beautiful, awe-inspiring, and she welcomed the early afternoon sun on her face and the closeness of her friends to see away any lingering fears. She had entered several other Virgin Zones, but she would never get used to this feeling of standing outside waiting to go in. At their purest these places were removed from the world, as wild as the land before apes stood on their hind legs and walked.

And Eden was special.

She felt that shiver again. Someone was watching her

watching Eden, and this time when she glanced at Poke the woman did not look away.

Jenn inclined her head slightly. "Is there water nearby?" she asked.

Poke understood her intention. "Over here."

Jenn held out her hand and took canteens from Cove and Selina, then she and Poke moved away from the others.

"What do you see?" Jenn asked, voice low, as soon as they were out of earshot.

"A woman who looked just like you," Poke said. "Same eyes. Same mouth."

Jenn's heart jumped. "What woman?"

They knelt by a stream and filled the canteens.

"Couple months ago," Poke said. She waved a fly from her eyebrow, not blinking. "She came here with a team, bit like yours but lots more gear. Not as together. They carried a few guns, other shit. Paid me for some advice, a couple of maps. A few hours of my time. Then they went into Eden."

"And did they come out again?" Jenn asked.

Poke's eyes were flat. Cold. She smelled deception and wanted no part of it. "You're keeping something from your team," she said. "That's not cool. It's dangerous. In there you need to be solid, together."

"I have reasons," Jenn said. "Please, did they come out again?"

"Not that I heard." Poke tilted her head, cigarette smoke making her squint. "Name was Katharine, but she called herself—"

"Kat," Jenn said. "My mother." She looked back towards the group, and her father standing there staring away from her into Eden. She felt the weight of unsaid things, and as ever it was a gravity holding them together, and a barrier forcing them apart.

4

"I hereby declare Eden, the world's very first Virgin Zone, closed. Closed to human interference. Closed to human interaction. Closed away from the damaging effect we have had on our planet for centuries. We give this place back to nature, in the hope that nature might find itself once again and, eventually, forgive us our sins."

Extract from speech by Ekow Kufuor, First Chair of the United Zone Council, on the official establishment day of Eden

"Seventeen minutes," Poke said. An afternoon breeze whispered through the trees, cooling the sweat on their bodies. Small branches swayed, rustling leaves. Dylan wondered what the land might be saying about them.

As usual at times like these, with the anticipation of adventure to come and the tension that evoked, Kat was on his mind. Long ago, they used to share such moments. Other than Jenn, it was the greatest thing that had once bound them together.

He missed that. He missed his wife.

Dylan hadn't seen Kat in almost nine years, or spoken to her in six. A small part of the reason for still doing what he did was to search for her. It was a passive search, a vain hope that somewhere—at a remote train station, a mountain base camp, a sodden shack in the middle of whatever jungles or wildernesses were left in this shrinking, poisoned world—he might one day bump into her. Every now and then he heard news of her having travelled through a small Andean village, or an Alaskan settlement, or being seen en route to one out-of-the-way place or another, a disparate team of athletes or explorers in tow. Their community of extreme sports and adventure racing enthusiasts, though spread across the globe and maintaining anonymity online, was surprisingly small. A passion for adventure had brought him and Kat together, and despite whatever had driven them apart—and an element of Dylan's search was to come to terms with what had caused that, too—he was pleased that she retained that love.

The day Kat walked out on him and Jenn remained the worst day of his life. Some days, he still hated her for it, because of the pain it had caused him and his daughter. But the hate sat uneasily alongside the love that would always persist.

"It's beautiful," Jenn said as she came to stand beside him.

"It always is," he said. "What did Poke want?"

"Poke?"

"She was looking at you weird."

"She's a weird old woman. You thinking about Mum?"

Dylan sighed. "Of course I am." It was rare that they talked about her, but moments like this felt unguarded and filled with potential. A time to open up.

He was certain that his daughter had communicated with Kat over the years, but he wasn't sure if she knew that he knew. If Jenn wanted to tell him—and if there was anything *worth* telling him—she'd have done so. Keeping silent must have caused her a weight of guilt, and he had no wish to aggravate that. His relationship with Jenn was precious. He loved her too much to lose her, too. Kat's leaving had fucked him up enough. He hated to think how it had affected Jenn, her mother walking out on her and disappearing when she was still in her teens. She'd grown into a smart and capable person, one of the strongest he knew. Inside, though, he knew the memory of that time must simmer and flare like a blazing ember.

Jenn seemed on edge, more than she usually was at the start of an expedition. Perhaps it was this place. Eden seemed to radiate an unknowable air, a sense of alienness that carried a strange taint and gave their surroundings a sharpness and clarity that he'd rarely seen before. The air was so clear, as if it had never been breathed by humankind.

"So what is it?" he asked.

It was not Jenn who answered.

"It's something you need to know," Poke said. "All of you."

As Dylan turned to face her, he caught Jenn staring at him, eyes wide. *What could make my girl so worried?* he thought. Then she looked at Poke and he realised there had been something between them after all.

"You promised," Jenn said to Poke.

"No. You asked. I promised nothing."

"It's Kat, isn't it?" Dylan asked, because he couldn't think of anything else that might have made Jenn look so wretched.

"She's in Eden," Poke said. "Your daughter knows."

Nobody spoke. The others had heard, and though only Selina and Cove had known Kat, they all understood.

Jenn stared at her father, sad now, begging him with silence to forgive her, or to understand. And in a way he did.

But it appeared she had lied to them all.

"What the actual fuck?" Selina said finally.

"I'm sorry, girl," Poke said. "I don't know anything about you or your reasons for wanting it kept quiet, but I do know you can't have a lie at the heart of your team. Not when you're heading into Eden. Something like that sets a seed of rot, and you spend more time and effort keeping the lie secret than you do surviving. And *all* your time, *all* your effort, is going to be taken with surviving. I've done you a favour."

"Thanks for nothing," Jenn said, but she didn't sound angry. She sounded sad.

"The lie is still there," Lucy said. "Only difference is, now we all know about it."

"Lucy—" Jenn started, but Lucy grimaced and turned away, cutting her off. The two of them were close, and Dylan wished Lucy had given Jenn a shred of support. Someone had to.

"Jenn," Dylan said. "You know I'd still have come if I'd known."

"I know *you* would have, Dad. But you would have told the team and we couldn't do it on our own. If you other guys thought we were doing this for the wrong reasons... I was afraid you'd bail."

"When were you going to tell us?" Cove asked.

"Soon," Jenn said. "When we were inside. Maybe even later today."

"So... what does this mean?" Gee asked.

"Who knows?" Selina said. "So why don't you enlighten us, Jenn?"

Jenn looked to her father for help. Dylan only frowned. He nodded. *Yes, enlighten us.*

He looked past Jenn at the landscape of Eden laid out before them. It had changed. Now, he knew Kat was here. Maybe she and her team were crawling across one of the mountains he could see in the distance, the slopes hidden in heat haze and mists, so ephemeral they might have been clouds at the extremes of his vision. Maybe she was in one of the valleys closer to them, lost in its depth, or losing herself to the wilderness on purpose. They had been apart for too long for him to pretend to know her motivations.

It seemed that he didn't know his daughter quite as well as he'd believed, either.

It was only ten weeks ago that Jenn had started pushing hard for the team to take on Eden as their next adventure. They'd talked about it many times over the years, and made rough plans, and it had certainly been on their radar. She had put instant pressure on them to come together and initiate the journey. He'd wondered if she had reached a point in her life when true danger became adventure. As her father he'd worried about that, and he'd talked to her about it. But she maintained that she was not rash in her choices, and that Eden was only dangerous to those who didn't treat it with respect. That was the difference between their tight team and some of the others they'd encountered. However exotic and wonderful the Zones were, there were still many people who perceived them simply as new, more wild personal playgrounds. Jenn had never taken that view. She already saw the Zones as another world. *Those places aren't ours anymore*, she'd say, and her eyes would light up with the sheer wonder of that idea.

"She told me she was doing Eden three months ago," Jenn said. "I didn't know when, or how, or who with. She just sent me a single text that said, *Eden is my last*."

"How long ago did she go in?" Dylan asked Poke.

"Couple of months."

Dylan frowned. If they'd gone in two months ago and made it out the other side, word would surely have spread through the small adventuring community by now. The air was heavy with heat and buzzing insects and a sick tension. It was a hand grenade thrown into the group to hear her name now, this close to Eden and the most ambitious challenge of their lives.

"What else do you know?" Dylan asked. Poke had lit another of her stinking rollies and was consulting her watch, dragging a small map across its screen. She peered at him through the tobacco smoke.

"Nothing else," she said, cigarette stuck in the corner of her mouth. She shrugged. "Saw something I recognised in your girl there. Confused me for a while 'til I put my finger on it, that she looks a lot like Kat. I'm not as young as I used to be, y'know?" She tapped her head.

"How do you know she hasn't finished the crossing and emerged on the other side?"

"I don't," Poke said. "All I know is she didn't come back this way."

"I know," Jenn said.

"*How* do you know?" Dylan was reaching for answers, and his anger was growing. Anger didn't belong in a group like this, especially minutes before they were due to begin a delicate, dangerous infiltration. They'd traversed three other Virgin Zones, this tight team of seven, and he knew they worked well together precisely because egos were kept in check; communication was smooth and unhindered by petty personal hang-ups. Sure, there were tensions, as was natural in any group of this size. But nothing damaging. Despite the lie, Dylan was their leader, and losing it in front of them now would put them all at risk.

"I just know, Dad," Jenn said. "Mum… you know I've heard from her now and then, right?"

"Of course I know." A wall of awkwardness had solidified between them, the weight that had always been there growing thicker. *This is one of those times when life changes*, he thought. He'd experienced enough of them to recognise the moment.

"Only six times since she's been gone," Jenn continued. "And each time is when she's finished crossing one of the other Virgin Zones. We talked about doing that together when I was a kid, remember? Trying to do all of them? So she sends me a picture of herself and her team, standing on a roadside or in a wood, or sitting around a table drinking. She's always looking at the camera holding up a map of the Zone with a red line through it. Like, 'done'. Sometimes she's smiling…" Jenn trailed off, aware of the silence around her. Aaron took a step closer to her and laid a hand on her shoulder, and Dylan felt a surge of gratitude for him. He'd known Aaron for five years, since Jenn had brought him into their team; he liked the guy, knew he was good for Jenn. He was waiting with the rest of them for her to finish. "And that's how I knew she hadn't finished this crossing. No picture, just that line: *Eden is my last*. A statement of intent. I've heard nothing from her about finishing Eden."

"Is that it?" Dylan asked.

"That's it," Jenn said. But he knew she was still lying. There was something else she wasn't telling them, and now that the lie about Kat had been revealed, he wasn't sure he could ever trust her again.

She knew we were coming here to follow her mother and she said nothing!

But he couldn't call her on it here and now, not in front of the others. There would still be time. If they even agreed to continue.

"So what, you wanted us to race her?" Selina asked. "Find her? What?"

Jenn shrugged. Perhaps she wasn't even certain of that herself.

"Maybe it's an invitation," Aaron said. "Like she wants Jenn to try as well."

"You knew?" Cove asked.

"No, he didn't!" Jenn said. "This is all on me."

"But why after all this time?" Selina asked.

Jenn blinked and looked down at her feet. *There's definitely more*, Dylan thought, and he vowed to ask her as soon as they were alone.

"Do you know exactly how long?" Dylan asked Poke.

Poke looked uncomfortable. She consulted her watch and tapped it a few times.

"Eight weeks, two days."

Eden was around three hundred miles across, a wilderness of forests and valleys, cliffs and ravines, rivers and lakes and marshland. Its eastern extreme was a wild, inaccessible coastline, jagged cliffs a hundred metres high bearing witness to the countless ships that had foundered on its shores over the centuries. To the north was a tall mountain range, and Eden's western border mostly followed a deep valley, more a ravine in places, where a river growled and pounded as a white-water torrent for scores of miles. They were entering from the relatively easy southern extreme, and they intended to make their traverse in less than twenty days.

Kat had been inside for almost sixty.

"She might still be in there," Dylan said.

"After eight weeks?" Cove asked.

Dylan shrugged. Cove was right to express his doubts, but that solidified the idea that she might be dead. Her and her whole team. The Zones were dangerous enough, Eden most of all, and racing across them amplified that danger, sometimes to unacceptable levels. Two years ago they had come across the remains of a team at the base of a cliff in Eritrea, broken and rotted together into death.

"We know she went in," Jenn said, "and I'm pretty certain

she didn't come out. We work from that. And it doesn't change anything we're doing."

"So is this a search party now?" Lucy asked. "Don't get me wrong, I'm pissed you lied, but that's your mother in there. We should go back to where we were dropped, retrieve our kit. I have stuff in there we could use."

"You got stuff in there not yet invented," Gee said. Dylan smiled, someone else chuckled, grateful for the levity. If it had come from anyone else but Gee it might have seemed wrong.

"Not a search party," Jenn said. "Dad?"

"Not a search party," Dylan said. "Kat can look after herself." He meant it as a statement, not a dismissal.

"We can still keep our eyes open when we're in there," Cove said.

"We will," Dylan said. "Of course. But we came here to do something, and we owe it to ourselves to get it done. First team to cross Eden. Set the benchmark. The reason we're doing it right now... I'm not sure it matters. And it's not as if any of you needed persuading. Right?"

"Right," Aaron said. "If Kat hasn't already set it."

"Hundred thousand square miles," Dylan said. "Yeah, we'll keep our eyes open."

"With respect... eight minutes," Poke said.

"We all good with this?" Dylan asked.

"No," Selina said. "Not good with it at all. I don't like liars." Dylan saw his daughter's face drop, and he knew it was time to move this on.

"But?" Dylan looked around at them all. He'd shut Selina down, and he knew he'd pay for that later. But she said no more and no one pulled out. Their team had come together and planned for this moment, pooling all their experience and expertise, investing money and emotional effort. They were in it for the long haul. "Good. Let's move."

They gathered themselves, and for half a minute they prepared in silence. Only Aaron and Jenn stood close, foreheads touching, whispering words no one else could hear. Gee jumped on the spot, psyching himself up. Cove and Lucy stood side by side, staring out across the valley at the different place beyond.

Selina came close to Dylan and he smiled at her. He didn't want this to feel awkward for her, because they had something, though neither of them really knew what it might become. They'd slept together several times, but there were always long periods between each occasion. Between expeditions Selina returned home to her lecturing position and elderly mother in Madrid, and often they'd go months with little contact. Sometimes they felt like lovers, sometimes best friends. It didn't help that he knew so little about her, other than her complete passion for the environment, and the way its continuing degradation mirrored her own frequent depressions. She was not secretive about her background, but she rarely spoke of it, and that made the present her somehow incomplete.

"Sorry," he mouthed.

"You're the team leader," Selina said, voice low. "And her father. I imagine you're more pissed than all of us."

"Let's hustle," Poke said, clapping her hands. "Like you said, it's a hundred thousand square miles, and most of it like nothing you've ever seen before. I've been in there once, and never again."

"Huh?" Dylan said. "You're our fixer."

"Yeah, and I'll get you in, if you follow me and do everything I say." She glanced at her watch again.

"We're experienced in places like this," Cove said. "We've done Green Valley."

Poke snorted. "That place is a parkland."

"We did the Husky Plains in under thirty days, independently and unsupported," Cove continued. "No one's come within five days of that, even in a race scenario. And we hold the record for Zona Smerti, too. Same team, same setup. We know what we're doing."

"No, you don't," Poke said. "You know what you want to do, but Eden might have other ideas."

"Why have you only been in once?" Dylan asked. She'd sold herself as their fixer by saying she knew everything there was to know about how to get him and his team in without being caught or detected. To be fair, she'd never claimed to know much about Eden itself. Only its borders and security measures.

"'Cause that was one time too many," Poke said. "You know what these places are set up for, these Virgin Zones. Course you do, 'cause it's people like you see them as their own playgrounds. Their challenges. Whatever. But these are places that were established decades ago and left alone, cut off from the rest of the world, leaving nature to heal itself. No humans in there. None of us, not even..." She nodded at Selina. "Scientists. That's as pure as you can get, and it still surprises me people went for it. Governments, big business, just leaving these vast swathes of land to return to nature. Sure, it had to be done. Maybe in time they'll become the lungs of the world. I guess they're our apology to the planet. But..." She sucked on her rollie and its glowing end crackled in the still air. "... it's different in there."

"Some see the Zones as our last hope," Selina said.

"Yeah, sure, humanity's last hope," Poke said. "Thing no one gets is, no matter how much we've fucked ourselves, the planet's gonna be just fine."

"Eventually," Lucy said.

"Eventually's too long for us, but the blink of an eye for nature," Selina said.

"Different how?" Dylan asked. He could see Poke's fear and didn't like it. Her toughness wasn't just a front.

"The one time I went in there, I felt something," the fixer said. "I can't call it unnatural, 'cause I think it was purely natural. Maybe it was inhuman. I dunno, but it affected me bad. Gave me nightmares I'm still having now."

"What nightmares?" Jenn asked, but Poke ignored her. She seemed almost to be talking to herself.

"There's this Jewish legend. Says that God left a corner of creation unfinished, and challenged anyone who thought themselves greater than Him to finish it for themselves. Now, I ain't got faith, or not that sort anyway. But they had something with that idea. An' if there's any place on Earth similar to what they were talking about all that time ago, it's Eden."

She fell silent. No one spoke. Then she looked at her watch. "Three minutes."

"Good," Gee said. "Too much talking. Let's burn daylight."

5

"From the very beginning, we were given no choice. We were in the way and had to be moved. Compulsory purchase orders on our land and businesses were more than fair, but it wasn't about the money. It was about being uprooted, moved, and dumped in some resettlement camp four hundred miles from home. You can shift families, but you can't reform communities. My marriage broke up. I hit the bottle. My wife committed suicide six years later. But it's all okay, because nature found its home. What about my home? What about me?"

Vasilia (surname withheld) discussing the effects of Zona Smerti,
Eyewitness: The Virgin Zone Upheaval in Pictures and Words,
Alaska Pacific University Press

If their hike from the landing site had been managed to the minute by Poke and her programmed GPS, their infiltration of Eden was timed to the second. They all carried something that didn't belong, a tension that hung between them and held them apart. Dylan didn't like it, and he'd confront Jenn alone when he had the opportunity.

That time was not now. They were committed, and Poke was about to earn her fee.

She led them away from their hillside resting place and down into a shallow ravine, following the route of a stream as it headed for the valley floor. Dylan trailed close behind Poke, and behind him were Cove and Selina, then Aaron and Jenn, then Gee and Lucy. The spacing and order of their group was no accident. Gee and Lucy moved well together, fast and quiet, and they were an ideal pairing for the team's tail. If anyone or anything was following or stalking them, they would know.

Dylan couldn't think of anyone he'd rather have watching his back. Gee had saved his life on their first race together six years before, confronting and disarming a bandit on a jungle trail in Bolivia and sending his companions on their way. He'd used only the threat of violence, backed with intense confidence and calmness. Dylan suspected it was because Gee had faced much worse in his ten years as a cop in Vancouver, but he also knew that such toughness was natural, not learned. He might have been the toughest person Dylan knew, but he carried that with an appealing humility. He didn't talk much about his past, and rarely offered the same story about how he'd lost his hand. Shark attack, infected spider bite, birth defect, Dylan had heard them all, but only once had Gee told him the tragic truth—that he'd lost his husband and left hand in a car crash. That had ended his time in the Vancouver PD, and eventually led to his new incarnation as an adventurer.

The stream carved a winding gulley into the hillside, skirting around tough rocky outcroppings, forming occasional wider pools where the slope lessened, and splashing over several small waterfalls where shelves of rock formed solid steps in the hillside. They leapt back and forth across the stream, dancing from occasional stepping stones in an effort to keep their footwear dry for as long as possible.

A few minutes after starting out they reached a branch where another stream joined from elsewhere, tumbling down a series of steep mini waterfalls and throwing a haze of refracted sunlight across the scene. It reminded Dylan of the view of the polluted river they'd seen from the plane, but this was natural, and beautiful.

Poke held up a hand to call them to a halt, then ushered them against a sheer rock wall beside the waterfalls. Dylan pressed against the surface, relishing the fine cool spray settling across his skin. It had been hot today, and as the sun dipped down the late afternoon heat was oppressive. He took a sip of water from the tube in his backpack shoulder strap and watched a small lizard skittering up the stone surface, leaping across a crack where water flowed down, disappearing into a crevice. It seemed unaware of their presence, and he wondered whether it moved in and out of Eden.

Poke looked at her watch, then glanced up, watching the skies. She lifted her hand to get their attention. Moments later a turbo-drone whispered past high above. Dylan froze, head lowered so that the drone wouldn't spot his pale face. They were well sheltered by the cliff and the mist from the waterfalls, and moments after the drone disappeared over the trees, Poke waved them on.

They followed the gulley for another few minutes, then climbed a steep bank and found themselves on a woodland track. It surprised Dylan how well used the route was, and he could see Poke's nervousness. She crouched beside the trail, they all did the same, and for a couple of minutes she listened, head tilted and mouth open.

Dylan glanced back at his team. Most of them were watching Poke, not him. He caught Jenn's eyes and smiled, and she nodded back. Kat would be on her mind, and the pressure of a lie revealed, but they had to box that up and concentrate on the near future, not the present. And not the past.

Please be alive, he thought. The idea of finding his estranged wife dead in Eden was already haunting him. The thought that she might never be found was even worse.

Poke signalled and they crossed the track, fast and low. When they were on the other side she doubled back and scanned their trail, making sure they'd left no footprints behind. The ground was dry, the wheel ruts shallow and hard. She nodded, then moved back past the team to take point once again.

As they approached the valley floor, Poke concentrated more and more on her watch. Following close behind her Dylan could just hear as her net implant buzzed with a series of pre-programmed alarms. At every signal she would pause, change direction, wait for a defined period of time, then indicate that they should move on. They passed through a heavily wooded area, and now and then birds took flight away from them, and the undergrowth rustled as the darting shapes of small mammals sought safety. Poke frowned and watched the fleeing creatures every time this happened, worried at the ruckus that might attract attention, but there was nothing they could do about it. They were a couple of miles from Eden's boundary, and these animals might still have a reason to fear humans.

Once inside, Dylan knew it would be different and he was excited to experience it again. He'd seen it before in Virgin Zones, where animals were born, lived and died never seeing or encountering a human being, other than he and his team. It was amazing how little they were feared. It was uplifting.

"Seven minutes here," Poke whispered, and she crouched down close to a large bank of tangled brambles, ferns and dead branches. "Eat. Drink." Several trees had fallen together, perhaps in high winds or a lightning strike, and the fall provided a thick barrier behind which she indicated they should hide.

"How far?" Dylan asked.

"Less than two miles. There are Zed patrols, one along soon. We'll be safe here."

"We will?" Dylan asked, but Poke didn't respond. She looked at her watch, glanced back the way they'd come, and peered through the thicket and past the fallen trees, gaze never resting for more than a few seconds in one place. She waved once at the team, gesturing that they should stay down. She seemed in control.

Dylan wondered whether Kat had come this way, had hidden behind these dead trees. Over the years, racing across other Virgin Zones, he'd often had similar thoughts, but usually they were remote and unlikely, foolish ideas rather than certainties. Here, now, it suddenly felt more solid. If he closed his eyes he could sense Kat hunkered down beside him, waiting for the patrol to pass. He could almost smell her, that miasma of her preferred sun cream and the distinct Kat aroma that he had known for so long, and which was now gone. Sometimes he caught a similar coconut scent and memories assaulted him. He took in a deep breath, but there were no coconuts here, and no memories of Kat.

They took the opportunity to rehydrate, eat, and adjust any kit that might not be sitting quite right. Cove retied the laces on his trail shoes. Lucy retied her ponytail. Gee picked at his teeth with a pine needle. Dylan knew that they were excited at the prospect of Eden, and also now unsettled by the news that Kat and her team might still be somewhere in the Zone. The idea that another team might have beaten them across was only a part of that nervousness. Yet he could also sense their confidence. Individually they were all adept at what they did, and together they formed one of the best Virgin Zone adventure race teams in the world. In a scene that existed underground, they were respected and feted more than most.

Selina was already making notes. She was the only one amongst them who expressed continual doubts about what they were doing, because the Virgin Zones were precious, pristine places, and to invade them was not only a crime in the eyes of the law, but could also be seen as a foolish undertaking from the environmental standpoint. The Zones were set up to be completely devoid of humankind. Purity was vital to their success.

Scientific curiosity trumped her concerns. Any doubts they had were countered by their commitment to honouring Eden and its reasons for existing. They would leave no litter behind. They would bury their body waste. They carried plenty of food to fuel their expedition, in the form of high energy bars, gels and dehydrated meals designed for just this sort of endeavour. They would not hunt unless absolutely necessary, and would only forage for essential quantities of berries and nuts. They carried no electronic gadgets, in case signals or electrical fields disrupted or agitated any of the flora or fauna.

Teams illegally crossing Virgin Zones were by necessity stripped back to the basics, and in Dylan's eyes that made this the purest, most human form of exploration there was left in the world.

It was also the most dangerous. If one of them fell and broke a limb, there was no calling in emergency evac. The others would have to carry them out. Injury and mortality rates were high, but Dylan prided himself on never having lost anyone.

Though they spent the bulk of their lives apart, the more his team worked together, the more they acted like a single unit. Still, the potential of an accident haunted him. As team leader there was plenty of worry and stress to dilute the sheer enjoyment and wonder of what they were doing. Physically he was probably the fittest man of his age he knew, but in some ways he was old before his time.

A click, and his alertness snapped back. Poke held one hand up, and when they all looked at her she gestured through the treefall, then pushed her hand down towards the ground. They sank lower, as if forced beneath her palm.

Dylan heard the security team long before he saw them. They were talking, joking, laughing, and that was good because it meant they didn't expect to be heard. The forest fell silent around them as birds ceased singing. He tried to see past the fallen trees and through the undergrowth, moving left and right until he had the best vantage point. As their voices grew louder, he caught the first signs of movement, flashes of colour between leaves and stalks, branches and trunks. They weren't even wearing camouflage kit.

The Virgin Zone Protection Force was formed soon after the Accord was implemented. Centrally funded with input from every country that had signed, each area's force—the security personnel became known almost universally as Zeds—soon took on its own distinct identity. In Wales close to the Green Valley Zone, Zeds patrolled the land border on horseback and rarely carried weapons, relying instead on community interaction to ensure the Zone's peace and security. In the Jaguar Zone in central Brazil, there were early instances of Zeds supplementing their income with guided incursions into the area, but also alleged involvement from some of the big cartels that were still active back then. Early cases of border skirmishes and deaths worldwide led to an overhaul of their powers, and the funding was soon diverted to various countries' militaries. Many Zeds were now ex-soldiers who'd served their time and were now earning better pay than ever before. Many opponents claimed they were little more than paramilitary forces, procuring illicit weapons to defend themselves as much as the Zones they were hired to protect.

Yet few could doubt their efficacy. Whatever their history, the Zeds around most Zones were dedicated to their cause, and highly experienced in fulfilling their purpose. Deaths amongst those attempting to infiltrate were at an all-time low, as were the numbers of people actually getting in. It had taken decades, but the Zeds had become an expert security force to be reckoned with.

Right then, Dylan felt little threat from these six people. Even when he saw one of the women carrying a rifle over her shoulder, and one of the men with a heavy holster on his left hip, he was not afraid. They appeared so confident and casual that their patrol was little more than a stroll.

The Zeds passed by and moved down the gentle slope and into the forest, voices trailing behind them. Poke was staring at her watch, and just as the final burst of laughter faded away, she raised her hand and nodded.

She stood and they followed once more. They crossed the route the patrol had taken and headed across the hillside, negotiating a series of natural steps in the ground that required them to slip and slide down steep slopes. There was a wide stream at the base of the final step, and Poke started following it. Tall reeds grew close to the water, and she weaved her way through them, twisting left and right to avoid trampling any plants.

After half an hour following the stream, Poke called a halt. They crouched below reed level and squatted on the wet ground.

"What now?" Dylan asked.

"Couple of minutes ahead of schedule," Poke said. "This next bit's the riskiest."

"You brought Kat and her group the same way?"

"Course not!" Poke said. "I never use the same route twice. Most of what I do is just get people in for a day and out again. I'd be stupid to use the same entry point."

"You know the way well enough," Cove said.

"I've recced it four times," she said. "Enough to know it well, not enough to get noticed. One minute."

"So why's this next bit risky?" Jenn asked.

"Going to attract their attention," Poke said. "You all ready to run?" She glanced them up and down, smiled. None of them needed to respond.

She moved away from the stream and they followed, and moments later she raised a hand warning them to stop. She was standing by a sawn-off tree, the thin stump ending two metres above the ground. Tied halfway up the stump was a dark brown box, the colour offering good camouflage unless you were close enough to see, or someone pointed it out. Dylan took a step closer and saw the wire just before Poke snipped it with a pair of clippers. Then she tugged something out of her backpack, unwrapped it, and dropped it close to the post. A dead chipmunk.

"That way," she said, pointing back the way they'd come. "Across the stream. Follow me."

"What have you just—?"

"Electric fence. Enough to give humans a bit of a jolt. They used to be all over the place, but a lot have fallen into disrepair over the years."

"You think they'll believe that?" He pointed at the dead creature.

57

"We've got maybe six minutes until the first robo-drone arrives," she said over her shoulder as she started running. Dylan jogged after her. "And ten minutes after that before the first chopper. So save your breath."

The stream was shallow enough to ford, and Poke had chosen a place where there were a few rocks for those nimble enough to leap from one to the other. Dylan heard a brief, quiet curse from Gee as he slipped and went in up to his thighs, but the others crossed and carried on without getting wet.

Poke ran for ten minutes along the valley floor, staying in cover as much as possible, aiming for folds in the land, an old stream bed, clumps of trees and shrubs, always on the move, always doing her best to keep them concealed. She set a good pace, and Dylan was impressed at her fitness. They kept up with ease, but by the time they stopped they were all perspiring and breathing heavily, and taking sips from their rucksack water bladders.

"Drawing their resources?" Dylan asked.

"Something like that." Poke was concentrating on the time, and she made sure they were all together before signalling again. "That way. Along the valley floor, not far now, this is when we risk detection."

"Isn't Eden really close that way?" Lucy asked, pointing up at a heavily wooded slope to the north.

"You're looking at it. But this is where they'll now be expecting us to... Just come on. Time."

Dylan nodded to Lucy and the others and they set out again. They were on the valley floor now, close to the river, and although he feared this might mean they would be visible from the air or from anyone watching from open areas on the hillsides, in reality they were well hidden. The river had changed paths many times through the aeons, twisting like a slow-motion sidewinder as it forged its way deeper through the valley bedrock. Those million-year twists and turns had left a ridged landscape of countless small ravines and outcroppings, and Poke knew her way through them.

As the sound grew of a helicopter approaching along the valley, the fixer led them to an old dried oxbow lake where trees and bushes grew in abundance. They crouched down, motionless, and two minutes later the chopper passed overhead. Dylan worried that they'd have heat sensors on board, or other high-tech methods for detecting people hiding out in the wild landscape below, but they powered past without deviation. Heading, no doubt, for the place where the snipped tripwire had sounded the alarm.

Fifteen minutes later Poke signalled a change in direction and they approached the river. It was ten metres wide and smooth flowing, with no sign of any method of crossing over.

"Welcome to Eden," she said, pointing to the other side.

"This is it?" Dylan asked.

"No fences or boundaries?" Jenn asked. Other Zones they'd entered often had distinct boundaries—fences, walls, even heavily advertised minefields.

"This is boundary enough, here at least," Poke said, nodding at the river. "Fences tempt people to climb them."

Dylan's team were breathing hard but still looking strong, and all of them stared across the river wide-eyed. He followed their gaze.

Eden. Not the largest Virgin Zone in the world, but the oldest and most famous. No one had yet claimed a crossing. Many had attempted and failed. Some had disappeared completely. He'd been considering this expedition for over three years, and now Jenn had made it their time.

From here, the trees and grasses, shrubs and ferns, hillsides and forests didn't look any different from anywhere else. But it *felt* different. Some of that was perception, because they all knew what this place was and what it meant. Some was excitement about what they were here to do, and now concern about Kat and her team, so recently vanished into this forgotten landscape. He felt a frisson of fear unlike any he'd felt before.

From this side of the river, Eden looked wild.

"How do we get over?" Dylan asked.

"Your problem," Poke said, looking at her watch again. "I've drawn some of their attention with the broken wire, but you've got maybe ten minutes before they start an aerial sweep of the valley floor. I'm going now. If you're not over there when they fly past, you'll be caught. No cover here."

"You're supposed to get us into Eden, not close to it," Selina said.

"You want a piggyback?" Poke asked.

"Guys," Dylan said, because they didn't have time for anger or argument, however justified it might be. "We're good."

"It's not deep," Poke said, and there was perhaps a hint of regret in her voice. At seeing them go? At not getting them across? Dylan couldn't tell, and right then he didn't care.

"Thank you," he said. "You'll send our kit on to our exit point?"

"Sure. Special delivery." She placed a rollie in her mouth. It stuck to her lip and swung as she talked. "Just… take care. Look after yourselves. Nothing in there will." She nodded past Dylan and across the river, and something in her eyes raised the hairs on his neck. Just for an instant, he'd never seen anyone look so scared.

He spun around to see what she had seen. There was only Eden.

When he turned back Poke was already jogging away, heading towards the low slopes leading up the valley sides.

"Eight minutes," she called over her shoulder, a waft of smoke in the still air.

"Eight minutes, people," he said. His team was already hustling to the river's edge, assessing where best to enter in a controlled manner, closing their drinking tubes to prevent dirty water ingress, helping each other down the overgrown river bank.

None of them looked afraid.

Perhaps only he had seen the look in Poke's eyes.

6

"Work? Of course it's not going to work. You can't just put a fence around a place and pretend it's returned to the wild. That's like putting a sign up on the border between two countries that says, *No foreign weather allowed*. But you've got to admire their balls for trying."

Professor Marie Joyce, Aberystwyth University

The river felt colder on the Eden side. Poke had been right, it wasn't deep, and they managed to wade across, leaning into the current and placing their feet carefully on the slippery bed. Jenn felt something brushing past her legs and snagging on her running tights, but when she reached down there was nothing there. Further across, the flow turned noticeably cooler. By the time she climbed onto the opposite bank, clasping at plants to pull herself up, her teeth were chattering and her toes were numb. The others had felt the effects too, and were clapping their hands together and running on the spot to generate heat.

When Jenn examined her leg she found a tiny tear in her tights and a scratch on her shin, a single bubble of blood forming and dribbling away.

"We need to get away from the river," her dad said. "There, into the tree cover at the base of that hill. Quick sprint will warm us up. Then we get our shit together and start the clock." The clock was actually a waterproof stopwatch, secured in his rucksack and wrapped in protective layers of plastic. He would set it ticking when they commenced the journey and stop it when they reached Eden's mountainous northern boundary. If everything went to plan, there would be another fixer waiting there to extract them.

Jenn worried about that. Poke's obvious fear of this place might not be exclusive, and she hoped the other fixer her father had employed held up their side of the bargain.

He led the way and they broke into a fast jog to warm themselves up, and also to find cover quickly. No Zeds were allowed over the border and their choppers and robo-drones were also not permitted to cross into its airspace. But if they were spotted before they found cover, Jenn wasn't sure how their incursion would be handled. The security forces at each Zone treated potential intruders differently. In the Deep Red Zone in Belarus, there were still occasional tales of summary executions.

There were more immediate worries, however. Like her mother being somewhere in here, and the tension that fact had forced between the team and her. The weight between her and her dad had always been there in some form, an unspoken shadow created by her limited contact with her mother, and her father's suspicions about it. She should have told him, but she hadn't known how he would react. He should have asked her, but she wasn't sure she'd have come clean. The photographs were sent by phone only to her and felt very personal, even though her mother never wrote anything to accompany them— no subject heading, no messages, no notes, nothing personal or even impersonal. Jenn had discovered the meaning of the first picture soon after receiving it, hearing whispers about her mother and her team breaking a record for crossing the Jaguar Zone. The photos were a celebration of success, and they spoke all the words she wanted to say. That final text had been a statement of intent.

Perhaps she should have told them everything when she'd had the chance.

"We're in," Aaron said. "We're in Eden!"

"It already feels…" Selina said, trailing off.

"Wild," Cove said. "I like it already!" He was the wildest amongst them, and perhaps the most reckless. He'd joined her parents' smaller team almost a decade ago, eager for adventure and with romantic ambitions to see the world. He'd drifted in and out of their lives, but over the past several years he'd become more focussed. He was now training for The Endless, a self-propelled round-the-world race conducted in secret, crossing some of the most inhospitable landscapes on the planet and passing through at least four war zones. The race had only been run three times before over the past two decades, and seventeen people had died taking part. Rumour had it next year's race, and the one Cove was aiming for, was the biggest and hardest yet, designed to take competitors through each of the world's thirteen Virgin Zones, even the Congolese Dead Zone.

They reached tree cover and began climbing a gentle slope, working their way deeper. Something troubled Jenn as they moved but she couldn't put her finger on it. She listened for sounds of the drones or chopper, and expected at any minute to hear a loudhailer voice calling for them to withdraw.

She enjoyed the exertion of flowing uphill, moving like a small flock of birds, aware of each other and alert. There was no breeze this afternoon, and the humidity was uncomfortable. She took a sip of water and looked around, seeing Aaron doing the same beside her. He smiled around the water tube. Beyond him, Lucy and Gee moved together, smooth and fast.

"This'll do," her dad said, and they paused close to a rocky outcropping. The rocks sprouted scattered undergrowth, and plants grew up to their waists, a mix of ferns and a bramble-like bush she couldn't identify.

Selina was looking around in wonder. She carried a small notebook in one hand, but she seemed to have forgotten it.

They sank down onto their haunches, only their heads and shoulders visible above the sea of plants. Above, the tree canopy flickered in a gentle breeze, leaves dancing in countless complex patterns. Jenn caught Lucy's eye. Her teammate glared at her, so she looked away. Every one of these people was her friend, and she hated the idea that they were angry with her. She hoped they were close enough for that anger to abate.

They listened for the sounds of pursuit. There were none.

In fact, there was nothing.

"What the fuck?" Gee whispered, echoing what Jenn was thinking.

"Nothing," Aaron said. He turned left and right, not blinking.

"I've never known a forest so quiet," Selina said.

"It's like everything knows we're here," Jenn said, and verbalising her thoughts made them all the more disturbing. The forest was silent, but not because there was nothing there to make a noise. It was the silence of a held breath, a beat between moments.

"Where are the birds?" Lucy asked. "The animals?"

"They're here," her dad said. "All around us. Look." He pointed into the branches of a nearby tree, and for a few long seconds Jenn could see nothing. Then a shape that might have been a branch elbow resolved itself into the outline of a large bird, perhaps a bird of prey. More shapes nearby moved as if echoing the flickering leaves much higher up, other birds perched silently on the tree's limbs.

"Watching us," Jenn said. "But not flying away."

"Why would they?" Selina said, and she smiled. "They don't know to be afraid of us. We might be the first humans some of them have seen, and the deeper we go, the more that'll be the case."

The idea pleased Jenn. They'd encountered similar phenomena in other Zones, but never something quite like this.

"It's like they're all talking about us," Lucy said. It was a strange comment considering the almost total silence.

"Are we ready to do this?" Jenn's father asked. He stood again, confident that they had not been detected crossing into Eden, taking off his backpack to extract the stopwatch, urging them all to prepare for the true beginning of their journey. He was a big man with a big history, and so many stories to tell, and Jenn loved him with all her heart.

"Ready," Jenn said, standing. The others stood as well, forming a rough circle around Dylan as he zeroed the stopwatch. It was an old analogue watch that he'd picked up in a bazaar in Egypt, over a hundred years old and still reliable. It had an engraving on the back in a strange language that he'd never been able to translate, and Jenn knew that made him happy. Some mysteries he liked. The mystery of his missing wife he never had, and Jenn felt a tug at her heart when he looked at her and forced a smile.

"Five…" her father said.

"God be with us," Aaron said.

"Four…"

"We're going to do it," Cove said.

"Three…"

"I want to go home," Gee grinned.

"Two…"

A final second of peace, silence and stillness.

"One." He clicked the stopwatch start button, and for a few seconds Jenn could hear the watch's steady *tick… tick… tick*.

As one, they moved out.

7

"As a Virgin Zone, Green Valley holds several important records. It is the smallest of all the Zones, taking up most of what was once Pembrokeshire and its coastline. It was established in the smallest country. It has the fewest arrests and prosecutions for infiltration each year. The initial upheaval and compulsory rehoming of three hundred thousand people was traumatic, with protest groups remaining active for a decade, and a very small element undertaking a flurry of terrorist attacks against Zone guards and the government that welcomed and supported the whole concept. But the people of Wales are nothing if not resilient, and they remain proud of their leading role in the International Virgin Zone Accord."

Extract from Our Green Grass, *Welsh Government Press*

Jenn ran.

It was what they were here for, and what she was good at. She was probably the best endurance runner among them. She'd completed fifteen mountain marathons and she was still only in her mid-twenties. She'd won two of them in her age group, but when an opportunity came to turn professional, she had turned it down. Her father nursed some guilt for that, and believed it was partly his fault, but she'd always grown angry when he mentioned it. She was more than capable of making decisions for herself, and from a young age she'd lived a life of independence and adventure, a lifestyle imposed upon her by her parents. She had never once judged them for it.

After her mother walked away and never came back, she and her father continued their unconventional life of travel and exploration, only settling for short periods of time in their rented apartment in Edinburgh. She couldn't imagine living any other way.

Jenn rarely took point when they were running because she'd set a fast pace and some of the others would be wiped out by the end of day one. Selina went first, then the others, and Lucy and Gee brought up the rear. Jenn followed close behind Aaron, so close that she could hear his heavy breathing. Sometimes she overtook him for fun, leaping around him, launching herself from rock to fallen tree, dropping ahead of him and chuckling as she took his place.

Lucy was adept at plotting their best line across a landscape. They shared one compass between them—another part of undertaking this expedition as stripped back to basics as possible—and she wore it on her right wrist, though she rarely consulted it. She loved her tech, but as part of the team she'd prided herself on becoming proficient at surviving without it, and she could tell direction from the position of the sun in the sky using her watch, the North Star on a cloudless night, or moss growing on trees. While Selina was the scientist of the group, Lucy was more innocently excited about the landscapes they passed through, and she spent an hour at each camp writing notes about their day. It was rarely discussed, but they all knew that she was writing a book about their adventures as a team.

Selina took them across the first forested hillside instead of straight up, a longer route but one more likely to conserve energy. Into the trees, the silence around them persisted, and though Jenn tried to lose herself in the rush of running, the conviction that they were being watched niggled at the nape of her neck. It was not a feeling she was inclined to doubt. Over the years she had grown to trust what Gee usually referred to as his jingling Spidey senses. On one occasion such a hunch had saved her life when a snowfield she and Aaron had been about to cross in the Andes was swept away in an avalanche. *I just wanted to wait here for a while*, she'd said afterwards as the roar echoed through the mountains and the haze of snow creaked, cracked and settled.

She would never call them premonitions. Jenn was an avowed rationalist, and she knew that often these sixth sense thoughts were constructs of a flood of micro data. On that mountainside snowfield she might have heard the distant cracks of ice shelves crumbling high above, felt the vibration of these ruptures, or seen the sudden panic or absence of creatures much more attuned to life in the mountains. Her subconscious had sent her a message, and the real sixth sense was being able to listen to herself.

She looked around as they ran, listening to the silence, searching for movement in the stillness. She began to fear that there were surveillance devices here—cameras set into trees, alarms triggered by invisible tripwires or traps, movement detectors sending signals back across the river to one of the Zeds' security bases.

"There's nothing," Aaron said, sensing her concerns.

"It's just weird," she said.

"Yeah. Got that right." He ran beside her, and as Selina edged them uphill towards a ridgeline a couple of hundred metres above, they all eased into a walk. "My balls are tingling."

"That'll be too much chafe cream," Gee said from behind them.

"Or too little of something else," Cove said. "You looking after your man, Jenn?"

"Jesus, guys," her dad said. "That's my daughter you're talking about."

"You two are related?" Gee asked, aghast. "But she's so talented, attractive, intelligent, fit, charismatic—"

"I'll kick you down the mountain," her dad said.

"Creative. Energetic."

"I'm warning you."

"Gotta catch me first, baldy!" Gee skipped past him and flicked the back of his head with his good hand, ducking down to avoid a slap and darting uphill past Selina.

They moved in silence again, but once broken, the subsequent quiet became even heavier.

"I've never been anywhere like this," Jenn said. "Dad? Anyone?"

"It's just the place getting used to us," Lucy said. "Right, Selina?"

"Could be," Selina said. "We saw this in Zona Smerti, too."

"Yeah, but this *feels* different," Jenn said.

"Yeah," Aaron agreed. "Something's off here."

"Different how?" her dad asked. Jenn could see that he agreed with her, and if it was just the two of them he'd be more open about it. In the group, he wouldn't want to undermine their confidence.

"Zona Smerti felt like somewhere that was trying to forget humanity," Jenn said. "And that's as it should be, because the Zones were created just for that. It shows they're working."

"It's amazing most of them have worked," Cove said. "You know, 'cause of people."

"Right," her dad said. He looked at Jenn. "But?"

"But Eden feels like a place that has never known humans at all."

No one responded to that, and a few minutes later they reached a low hilltop that offered a good view in the direction they'd come from, and a panorama of what lay before them. They moved across the summit without stopping, worried that they'd present a silhouette for anyone who might be watching from the boundary still only a couple of miles behind them. Then they paused below a shallow ridge, and stood silently and close together as they looked out over Eden. The wild land lay before them, vast and beautiful. Jenn blinked and wondered if she was asleep. There was a depth to the view that promised both mysteries and pain, and just as she felt a shiver pass through her, Aaron pressed his shoulder against hers.

"Looks a little like the Rockies," Aaron said.

"Yeah," she said, cautious. It had been a while since they'd had this discussion.

"Maybe now's the time. After we cross Eden, anyway. Set up that endurance racing school. Fix each other's feet to our heart's content."

Jenn shrugged, smiling. They'd talked about it, basing themselves out of Boulder, doing what they loved and getting paid for it. Setting down roots. "Maybe it is the right time," she said. "After we finish here."

Eden was heavily forested, as they had expected. For as far as they could see there was no sign of humanity, though they knew there were six towns and dozens of smaller communities that had been abandoned when the first of the Virgin Zones had been established, over fifty years before. The hillside swept down into a wide, flat valley, bordered on the left and right by high ridges and a series of peaks that led to a distant range of hills, which in turn rolled into the first of Eden's several mountain ranges. Their plan was to follow the valley and lower slopes as far as they could, and make the mountain crossing over a period of two days. At that point they would be five days into their journey.

Their routes were based on maps over fifty years old. Her father had planned it intricately, spending weeks poring over old paper maps and searching far and wide on the net for other images. The geography of the land might not have changed, but the terrain certainly would have. They'd find no roads or footpaths here, no old hiking routes or mountain trails. Jenn knew from experience that whatever they expected to discover on their expedition, they would be surprised.

"Beautiful," Selina said, and Jenn felt that dizziness again, a stretching of her air and world until her surroundings were unfeasibly large and she was small, so small that she barely noticed herself. It made her feel sick.

"You okay?" Aaron asked.

"Yeah." She took a swig of water. "Just eager to get going. Dad?"

Her dad nodded over at her. "Yep. We've barely started, why the fuck are you all standing around playing with yourselves?"

"'Cause it feels like someone else," Gee said, holding up his false left hand. His old joke brought a couple of groans, and it was Gee who led the way, laughing as he started downhill.

Behind them, the known world passed out of sight as they headed into the heart of Eden.

KAT

He was Philippe once, but he does not look like him anymore.

He comes at Kat from out of the trees, flowing with the shadows, and at first she thinks the same is going to happen to her that happened to everyone else. She only saw two of them die, but that was enough. She has considered death often over the past several years, more so these past few months, but she never imagined it like that. Never with screaming and ripping, rupturing and snapping.

Be brave, she thinks. *Be strong. It's the least you can do for yourself.*

Fond memories huddle to make themselves known, but she has become adept at shutting them away. She would not wish them to see her die like this. She doesn't want them to know.

"Come on, then," she says.

The thing that was Philippe walks towards her, using its human form but far from human. Its inhumanity was obvious even before the decay, in the swing of its limbs, the fractured gait. Now that rot has settled into its body, the change is even more severe. Its hair has dried and withered, like dead trees grown brittle. Its flesh has weakened, skin sloughed from its face, the landscape of its features tinged with echoes of toxicity.

Still it wears an expression halfway between fury and

humour, and she can understand why. The reasons have become obvious, though there was nothing any of them could do to make amends. No amount of bullets helped them. No apologies or begging changed the way things were.

She will not beg now, and even if she had a gun, she would not use it. She is happy to accept death. If only it didn't have to be so red.

Philippe stops a few steps from her. She holds her breath. The weight in her, the core that has been swallowing her for years, feels heavier and hotter than ever before. That's one good thing, at least. Against every possibility, at least she has beaten the illness.

Philippe kneels.

She frowns. He has not toyed with any of them. She's seen no joy in his and its actions, only a necessity that she believes she is growing to understand. The man and woman in those memories niggling at her would understand too, but she keeps them shut out.

"Come *on!*" she says again, but Philippe is no longer looking at her. She thinks its furious mirth is turning to sadness as its mouth drops, but then its shoulders slump too, its torso seems to sink and fold towards the ground, and it's as if the land is swallowing him whole. *It's been swallowing us all since the moment we arrived*, she thinks. An urge to run strikes her, but just as quickly leaves. There is nowhere to run to. No escape. She recognises her human crimes and accepts the judgement of this place. Exhausted, tired, resigned to her fate, she watches as Philippe starts to come apart.

His eyes close as the skin and flesh above them slips down, reddened eyeballs empty of compassion as they have been for some time, yet filled with a stranger life. He slumps to the right, shoulder dropping, head lolling. Wet sounds accompany his disintegration, and she catches a whiff of something chemical, like exhaust fumes burning in hot summer air. It's not hot today, and there are no engines within a hundred miles or more.

As his right hand turns, his fist uncurling like a dead spider returning to life, she sees what he has been holding. The stem is fine and bright green. The orchid, white and crumpled, expands, its delicate, fleshy petals peeling back to reveal the yellow and red stamen.

The orchid still clasped in Kat's hand is an old dead thing.

Philippe splits open, a wet rip beginning beneath his chin and stretching down towards his sunken groin. By the time his insides turn out his head is resting on the ground, one leg stretched out in front of him and the other hidden beneath the slouched, fallen parts of what once made him human. She hears no voice or sigh as his mockery of life leaves him. There is only wetness, a series of pops and slurps as gravity spreads him across the forest floor.

Kat's eyes go wide, and then she squeezes them shut. Her mind, open and accepting, cannot make sense of the shape and power emerging from her dead friend and flowing towards her. It is freedom and sadness, rage and strength. It is something never meant to be seen by humankind, and she does not understand what it is doing in this place.

Not yet.

But she realises that soon, she will be made to understand. Resigned to her fate, still she cannot hold back the ice-cold terror that possesses her as she feels its first, alien touch on her mind, and its initial warm caress across her left forearm.

One more time the memories huddle and push, and now she lets them in, because she can no longer protect them against this. She is eager to remember the faces of the man and woman she loves, desperately hoping that somehow, somewhere, they will see and sense this final warning she so needs to send.

Something else uses her face to smile.

8

"Russia was way ahead of us all, of course. Tsar Nicholas II created the first state-organised zapovednik, roughly translated as 'strict nature reserve', in 1916. Which makes it doubly sad that Zona Smerti seems to have been so heavily compromised by human action."

Professor Amara Patel, Natural History Museum, London

They ate while they moved. As the sun set towards a jagged range of hills in the west, Dylan began to understand why he found Eden so troubling, and everything he saw, smelled, and felt brush against his skin gave it credence.

As did Selina's enthusiasm and excitement. Usually cool and quiet, she became more animated the further they went. She saw things no one else saw, and uncharacteristically, she made her observations known.

It's all the small things, Dylan thought. *The little changes, most of them unseen, adding up to something greater. That's what makes this place feel strange.*

Selina's work lecturing in environmental science spilled over into concern at species depletion and the effects of human habitation and action. It was her passion, and the source of her frequent depressions. As they moved across the landscape she often went on ahead, so that she could pause while they caught up and spend time examining a tree or a plant, a track in the soil or a flower. She made hasty notes, then ran on with them, eyes wide with wonder at her findings.

"What have you seen?" Dylan asked as they moved down a long, gentle slope towards the wide valley floor.

"Lots of what I expected," she said. "But also lots of things I'd never imagined might be here. Plant species that all but vanished from this landscape over the past couple of centuries are abundant again. The soil's still more alkaline than it should be, but the whole place is purifying itself. Shedding itself of our touch." She vaulted a fallen tree and Dylan slowed, climbed over, and ran hard to catch up.

"Check out the old man," Gee said from behind him.

"I'm two years older than you, with a fucked knee," Dylan said.

"Stay at home next time, Grandad, and we'll call you when we're done!" Gee chuckled.

"Check out the guy with a false hand stuck up his ass," Dylan threatened, and everyone laughed.

Dylan caught up with Selina. "What else? Haven't seen you this animated in ages."

"It's like it's almost my perfect place!" Selina said, and he felt a warm flush at her upbeat tone. Her life was so saturated with facts and figures about humanity's negative effects on the natural world that such joy was rare. Teaching about this and being down about things all the time was a selfless sacrifice, Dylan often said. She called it reality.

"But you don't find it a bit weird?" Jenn asked. She jogged along beside the two of them, drawn in by their conversation.

He knew that she felt the same as him, and the rest of the group were also unsettled by Eden.

"Very," Selina said. "But wonderfully so." She ran on ahead again, overtaking Aaron and looking around as they crossed a sloping forest floor. Large spreads of brambles reached to snag on their clothing, and Dylan already had a dozen scratches across his shins and calves that bloomed small spots of blood. He didn't mind the feeling. He liked being tactile with nature and his surroundings, hands-on with the environments he passed through. Even here.

"Look," Selina said, pointing at a tree trunk. They drew to a halt around her, breathing hard, grateful for the brief rest. Even with the sun dipping towards the western hills, it was still warm.

"What am I looking at?" Jenn asked.

"Scent markings," Selina said. She crouched and moved closer, sniffing at the darkened bark, examining the ground around the tree's base. "Pretty regular."

"She's sniffing pee," Gee muttered.

"What made them?" Dylan asked.

"I think wolves."

"Huh?" Cove looked around, as if expecting to see fleet-footed grey shapes watching them from the shadows or circling them, stalking, hunting.

"No wolves here for over a century," Lucy said.

"Right," Selina said. "Yet here we are."

"Could be just wild dogs," Aaron said. "Some might've been abandoned in here when Eden was formed, and maybe they've been mating and interbreeding over the decades."

"Possible," Selina said, but she sounded doubtful.

"Wouldn't someone have had to put the wolves here?" Jenn asked. "They wouldn't just pop up out of nowhere."

Selina didn't answer. She made a few notes, then stood and looked past them into the surrounding forest.

"Let's move on," Dylan said. "Sun's hit the hills, and I want to make the far side of the valley before we camp."

The forest canopy and vibrant tree growth restricted their wider view of the landscape as they followed the gentle slope downwards, but Dylan was confident in their direction. He watched the sun, Lucy checked their compass every half hour, and they made good progress. Talk of wolves thrilled him; although they could be dangerous animals, he didn't think there would be any hungry wolves in Eden.

There were no paths to follow, and on occasion their progress was slowed by vast swathes of twisted and knotted undergrowth. They had not brought bush knives because they were passionate about damaging the environment as little as possible, so there was no possibility of hacking their way through. Instead they worked their way around, or backtracked and searched for an alternative route.

Selina didn't appear to mind such delays. She was so used to moving with the team that remaining part of their group came naturally, but most of her focus was away from them and on their surroundings. Dylan stayed close to her, enjoying watching her enthusiasm come to the fore. She seemed to accept that humankind had set itself on a downward spiral, and that people like her could do very little to arrest its descent. When she was younger, she'd told Dylan, she had lived with grand dreams of making a difference.

Whatever they had between them was shadowed by her frequent bouts of depression, a product of her studies. He helped her through as best he could, and knew she appreciated his efforts. Here in Eden, he hoped she might rediscover some of that lost youthful confidence and positivity.

As evening approached they reached the bank of a river. Dylan called a rest and they drank and ate, chewing on energy bars and gels. Cove checked that the water was potable using a pocket kit, then they filled their water bladders and popped in purification tablets. Dylan took out his map, opened it up, tried to orientate where they were. Lucy stood beside him and turned slowly left and right until the map and compass were aligned, and Dylan adjusted for some local landmarks— a hilltop in the distance, a bend in the river a few hundred metres along.

Something was wrong.

"What is it?" Jenn asked.

"Should've hit a road alongside the river," he said. He looked at his feet and brushed one foot back and forth through the long grass. The others were watching, listening.

"Eden's been here long enough to swallow up roads," Selina said. "We know that. We've seen it before, in much younger Zones."

"Yeah, but where's the river bridge?" Dylan said. He showed her the map, and after a few checks with compass and landmarks, Selina grunted.

"Yeah. Right. River bridge."

The river wasn't wide but it was faster flowing than the one they'd crossed to enter Eden. According to the map this was a tributary to that river, starting fifteen miles away up in the western hills and descending a series of waterfalls and fast-flowing sections before joining the main river six miles to the east.

"And a riverside rest stop, over there," Dylan said pointing across the water. "Restaurant, car park, few shops."

There was nothing.

"So let's take a look," Cove said. "Gotta get across the river anyhow."

They walked upriver, as close to the bank as they could. They were on the flood plain here, there weren't many trees, and it was nice to be out in the open. Dylan had always enjoyed the sound of water, but this roaring river made his feeling of subtle paranoia even deeper. Beneath its constant rumble, anything could be creeping up on them through the undergrowth.

He saw some of the others looking around as they walked. He caught Aaron's eyes. He was alert and cautious, and that made Dylan feel a little better. Aaron had a military background, and though he hadn't talked about it much to him, he had a confidence that made Dylan feel safe. Aaron blinked, frowned, and looked down to his feet.

"Found something," he said. He knelt and pulled aside some grass and trailing bramble, revealing a rusted metal post protruding a few inches from the ground. Even though they'd only been inside Eden for a matter of hours, it was a strange sight. The first straight line they had seen in this place.

"Road barrier?" Cove asked.

"Maybe. Too rusted to tell." Aaron tugged at the object. It didn't move. "Buried pretty deep, though."

"Looks like we know what's happened to the road," Lucy said. "We're walking on it."

It didn't feel like they were following a road, but as they moved upriver they saw two other objects that suggested that was the case. Dylan mistook the first for a dead tree, swathed in climbing ivy and home to a pair of squirrels perched high up watching their approach. It was only as they drew closer that

Gee pointed out the smashed bulb enclosure on top of the lamp post. It was the only part exposed, the surviving Perspex green with mould, and only the shape's familiarity made it obvious. One of the squirrels scampered up the post and sat on the protruding head, as if to mock.

"Can't see any others," Aaron said, looking back and forth along the riverbank.

"No, but there's that," Lucy said. She jogged ahead of them towards a bank of undergrowth. Large pink flowers speckled one side, and a plant with tiny blue blooms twisted in and out of the mound. It was a gorgeous natural palette, but Lucy had seen something other than the flowers. As Dylan and the others followed, he tried to make out what that was.

"How the fuck did you see that?" Gee asked. "You got some robotic eye, or something?"

"Robot heart," Cove said, a flippant but loaded comment. Lucy gave him the finger without looking away from whatever she'd seen.

"So you keeping us all in suspense?" Dylan asked.

"Look," Lucy said. She pointed to one edge of the spread of foliage, then moved her arm slowly up. Dylan followed, and saw.

"Aerial?" he said.

"Reckon so. There's an old car in there."

"No way," Gee said. He moved closer, kicked at some of the bushes, got his foot tangled and fell on his behind. Cove laughed. Aaron shoved Gee over onto his side, then helped him up.

"Come on, old man."

There was nothing to be seen. It might have been an aerial, or perhaps simply a thin, bare stem of a dead plant. It was too far into the shrubbery to be reached, and Dylan felt the sudden urge to move on. They were wasting daylight.

"We need to cross this river," he said. "I'd hoped part of the bridge might still be standing. But if it isn't, we'll have to go upriver until we find somewhere safe."

"That might take hours," Cove said. "Why don't we swim?"

"You fucking serious?" Lucy snapped.

Harsh, Dylan thought, but he let it go. "No, we're not swimming that," he said. "You know we're on our own in here, Cove. We don't take stupid risks. Keep your ambitions reined in."

"I could get to the other side and—"

"It doesn't matter that you're the best swimmer among us," Dylan said, and nothing more was needed. Cove's arrogance only went so far, and he always acknowledged Dylan as team leader. He pressed his lips together and nodded.

"Shall I lead the way?" Lucy asked.

"Follow the river," Dylan said.

Moving out, already adjusting his plans for their intended stop that first night, Dylan glanced around as they went. He was looking for signs of Kat. She'd kept herself away from him for years, and he'd never forgotten the moment she left him. It was etched on his soul.

"Only a week," she said. "Ten days, tops."

"But you've not mentioned this trip before," he said. "Not even a whisper. No maps, no discussions, no planning." He was reaching, and he knew it. The coldness had been growing between them for a long time, an inexplicable distance that somehow seemed directly linked to the almost countless miles they had run, walked, sailed, driven and flown together on their adventures around the globe. Travelling everywhere together, they had never seemed more apart. "Have you told Jenn?"

"Of course I haven't told her," she said. Dylan knew there was something more happening here, and that admission proved it. *If it was only ten days she'd have told Jenn*, he thought, but even then he couldn't bring himself to believe that Kat was leaving for good. A break, perhaps. A trial separation, enforced by a continent or two between them. But not forever.

"I don't know what's happened," he said, and for a few seconds he thought her cool exterior was going to break, and that the iciness that had built between them would clear again, opaqueness melting so that they could reach through and touch each other like they always had before. Then her face hardened and her eyes grew distant.

"A week, ten days," she said again, dismissing any hope of a discussion.

"I don't believe you."

Kat continued preparing her kit. She took her favourite rucksack, the one he'd bought her in Canada, packing it with running kit even though it was already full of memories.

"We could talk," Dylan said. "Whatever's been happening between us, we should have talked about it years ago. We can now. Properly."

"There's nothing," Kat said, and she offered him a strange, sad smile before leaving the room. Dylan never forgot that smile, because he'd never seen its like on her face before, and it made him realise she had become a stranger. He could have gone after her. Could have tried to stop her leaving their rented apartment, talked to her, begged her to wait until whatever storms had swept over her troubled mind had passed. But he let her go, and he never saw her again.

Later, he realised that her final comment probably hadn't referred to the distance that had been growing between them. As far as Kat was concerned, it was a summation of what was left of their relationship. He spent a long time struggling to understand what had gone wrong, sometimes blaming himself, sometimes wondering if Kat had been more disturbed than he'd ever understood. She must have been. She had disappeared from their lives.

He heard from her a couple of times over the next three years; brief, awkward phone calls during which neither of them had said much—her because she didn't want to, him because he had no idea what to say. And then Kat vanished from their lives forever.

Now, it seemed that she had kept Jenn in her heart. However much he tried to think around those circumstances and construct excuses for her—and however pleased he was for Jenn—that was cold. Pure and simple: cold. Though their relationship had been complicated, time would surely have dulled the sharp edges of old arguments and resentments, and he could think of nothing he'd done to merit such treatment.

Although it appeared she might have lured them here, he wondered how Kat would react if they ran into her on some forested hillside.

Try as he might, he couldn't decide what his own reaction might be.

9

Whoda thunk 6 kids in a boat could get into the Aleutian Zone? Rumours of storm=bullshit. They were fragged by the Zeds, mark my words.

@PottyBonkkers

"Hey," Aaron said. "You okay?"

"Sure."

"Feeling good?"

"Feeling strong."

"Cool. Your dad seems tense."

"Can you blame him?"

"I didn't mean—" he began, but she cut him off.

"Hey, sorry," Jenn said. "I didn't mean to snap. Let's just run."

Jenn and Aaron were bringing up the rear. Lucy was a hundred metres ahead of them, Selina moving across the flood plain like a circling bird. Cove and Gee jogged together, and her dad was alone. Gaps had opened up between them, a natural spacing that often happened when they were moving across easier terrain. It allowed for some personal space, a comfortable pace, and sometimes it was good to run alone.

Over the next three weeks there would be enough times when they were forced close together, and the opportunity to take advantage of a few moments of privacy was rarely missed. In such massive, wild, wide open spaces, Jenn and the others often experienced a unique claustrophobia once the group had been travelling for a few days or more. Cove's brashness could get on Aaron's nerves, and Selina would spend more and more time examining plants or insects on her own. Lucy and Jenn were usually tight though, and Jenn only hoped that might be the case again.

Jenn liked me-time as much as any of them. But the best me-time was with Aaron. They leapt a narrow ditch together, perhaps a dried stream or an old drainage channel beside the road they could no longer see. Their jump was almost synchronised. She loved Aaron's grace, the way he flowed with the ground and air rather than against it. He moved like a dancer, not a soldier. After what he'd told her about his time in the Israeli military, and his traumatic reasons for leaving, she preferred to focus on this dancing dream.

"Maybe she made it out and just didn't message you. Or did, and it got lost. Maybe she lost her phone or your number."

"None of which makes it easier," Jenn said. She hoped her dad would understand why she hadn't said anything. It hadn't been to hurt him. It had been to protect him.

"Your dad'll be fine," Aaron said.

"Maybe."

They fell silent for a while, simply moving together, smooth, fluid, almost without effort. When they made love it felt like this too. Aaron was the first partner she'd had who understood that. The two of them fit together perfectly.

"This place, eh?" Aaron said. They were approaching a bend in the river where the valley sides closed in and the flood plain retreated, giving way once more to heavy forest. "Feels like it's teasing us."

"Teasing?" Jenn asked. She wasn't sure what he meant by that. She felt watched, even now, but being teased was something else. It implied an intelligence.

"Yeah. Or playing with us." He sounded more serious than usual, and when Jenn glanced at him and saw his troubled features, she tripped. He reached for her and grabbed her arm, but she went down on one knee, skidding on rough ground. She felt the damage seconds before the pain bit in. Standing, she saw the small tear in her tights and the cut on her knee.

Aaron knelt and cleaned the wound with a water pouch from his belt. The others were running on ahead, and Jenn almost called out to them to wait. But something held her back. A flush of excitement and danger, a rush of something electric and cool through her veins, a sudden burst of enthusiasm about what they were doing. It chased away troubled thoughts. She was with the two most important people in her life, surrounded by friends, and doing her very favourite thing.

She wouldn't let anything ruin that enjoyment.

"Come on!" she said, pushing past Aaron. "Race you!"

She caught his concerned frown but shook it off. If this place was teasing or playing with them, she'd give it something to see.

Sprinting as fast as she could, she ignored the pain in her knee. Blood dripped from her wound and nourished Eden's wild soil. There was pain, but it didn't hinder her running. She relished it. It was a sign of her being here, and she knew that by the time they'd finished their traverse, she would have amassed a whole collection of aches and pains.

By the time she caught up with her father, he and Selina

were at a standstill. "What is it?" Jenn asked. Aaron came to a stop beside them, and then she saw.

Lucy had come to a halt further on, closer to the river. Gee was with her, pointing out across the violent waters. He turned and waved them on.

"Bridge?" her father asked.

"Let's see," Aaron said. "No way we're getting across that otherwise. The further upstream we run, the rougher it'll be." They went to join Lucy and Gee beside the fast-flowing river.

"Well, that's what's left of it," Gee said. He didn't sound his usual chirpy self.

The objects were little more than white-topped churnings in the water, splashes where the river parted around several shapes only just breaking the surface.

"That's our way over," Cove said.

"It's just a rock," Lucy said.

"No, there's something else further across," Cove insisted. "And look at the water, the smoother way it's flowing. It's shallower. There's something there."

Dylan consulted his map, and Jenn and Aaron stood close. She was panting from her burst of speed, and she knew she'd suffer for it. Endurance running was about conserving energy, not wasting it, and this was only day one. But she felt energised, and her heartbeat throbbed behind her eyes, in her ankles, across her chest, strobing the late afternoon sunlight and giving Eden a pulse.

"It's in the wrong place, but I think you're right," her father said. "It must have collapsed." Jenn could see it now, a lighter sheen beneath the water's surface where the bridge had sunk down. Perhaps it had been a single-span structure, and its feet had been swept away when the bridge deck dropped into the water.

"Earthquake?" she asked.

"Might explain some of the map discrepancies," Selina said. "Right, Dylan?"

Her father only shrugged, looking from the map to their surroundings and back again.

"At least it's still there," Cove said. "Tie me in, I'll get across first. Then I'll guide you all over."

"And when you slip?" Lucy asked.

"*If* I slip, I'll be tied on and you can haul me to shore."

"We've got to get across," Selina said.

"We can double back," Gee said. "It's too fast-moving here. We've been inside a matter of hours, we can't afford any injuries this early."

Jenn felt the throbbing in her knee and the cool kiss of air on wet blood. She would have to clean and dress the wound properly, but not yet. Not until they were across the river. She stood side-on to the others. Admitting she already had an injury, however slight, felt like a failure. She was in enough trouble with them.

"Okay," her father said. "We'll try. But if you slip and we have to pull you back in, that's it. No second attempts."

Cove grinned. "No second attempt required."

10

"You know that story about when the first atomic bomb was ever tested? About how no one involved could predict exactly what would happen, and that there was one theory that the chain reaction would continue and eat up all the atmosphere and destroy the world, but they took the chance anyway? Yeah. That."

Anon, United Zone Council

Gasping as the cool water washed around him, Cove set out along the sunken road, legs braced against the river's fast flow. Jenn and her dad fed out the fine climbing rope secured around his waist. The water rose from his knees to his thighs, then higher, and he had to lean against the water and shuffle slowly to prevent his feet from being taken out from beneath him. Jenn made sure they kept the line tight, but not so tight that it hampered him. She felt his weight through the rope, its coils scraping against her hand, his movements transmitted as ripples and vibrations. Lucy and Gee were already moving back along the bank, matching the distance he'd made from shore and ready to haul him out if he slipped.

Jenn's heart beat faster, her senses were heightened, and sweat dribbled down her sides. It was alertness, strength and control, not fear. This was what they were all about.

Cove made the other side within fifteen minutes, and as he forced his way through undergrowth and up onto the opposite bank, Jenn let out a sigh of relief. Her father glanced at her and raised his eyebrows.

"Brave bastard," he muttered.

"Or stupid?" In their expeditions, there was often a fine line between the two.

Cove tied his end of the rope to a strong tree then waved to them. "It's slippery but not too bad!" he shouted, hands cupping his mouth. "Bit in the middle is badly broken up, but the water's clear enough to see. Just take your time!"

Selina tied the rope off on their side of the river, using a thick chunk of wood as a screw to twist and bind it tight. There would always be some slack and give with a rope strung out over that length, but by tightening it as much as possible they could make it tense enough to hold onto.

Jenn went next. She clipped on with a carabiner and a three-metre length of rope. It was short enough to arrest a fall, but still long enough to allow enough slack to descend the bank, edge around obstacles, and follow where the bridge's road surface still held together beneath the river. The water was a cold shock around her feet and lower legs, and she took a dozen shallow breaths, but there was no sense of panic. She was used to the cold. Discomfort was her friend. The smell of the river was strange, a metallic tang like rain on a sunny day, sweeping away all the scents of the forest that she only acknowledged now that they were gone—the warm sweetness of pine, the dankness of wet mud, mixed perfumes from flowers. And deeper, there were smells she did not recognise.

To begin with she walked along the sunken road, left hand loose around the rope and pushing the carabiner along. Soon the submerged road surface went suddenly deeper, the water's flow greater, and she paused for a few seconds to acclimatise more fully. Moving on, she propped her legs wider apart, left leg solid against the battering flow, and edged her feet along in smaller increments. If she attempted to take a full step the water would shove her legs out from beneath her. The rope would prevent her from being swept along the river, but she had no desire for a soaking.

The river's roar drowned out everything else. She was aware of her dad, Aaron and the others watching her go, but she focussed on the water's surface, and where the flow remained uninterrupted she could see her trail shoes and the broken road. The total concentration provided an almost meditative experience. Holding the rope in both hands she shifted both feet along in turn, edging towards the far side of the river. Away from safety, and deeper into Eden. Away from a world that was familiar and closer to this strange place that no one really knew. Not anymore. Other Zones she had traversed had felt like places one step removed from the rest of the world, but Eden felt so very different, as if it was not of the world at all. It was a sobering thought, but exciting. For decades it had been claimed that there was nowhere left on the surface of the planet to explore, and all her life Jenn had sought remote, amazing places to prove that idea wrong. Today more than ever she felt like an explorer treading where no one had ever been.

Apart from my mother.

Something smacked into her right thigh.

Jenn shouted and kicked her leg to the side, slipping on the slick surface. She gripped the rope and held herself upright.

The water around her leg turned white as something thrashed beneath the surface.

She heard voices from both banks, but could not make out the words.

The thing hit her leg again and again, dull impacts that she knew could be deep, fatal wounds that the freezing water would numb until she reached shore.

I've only got a knife! she thought. That was the nearest thing to a weapon they had brought into this wild place. Hers was folded and tucked into a pocket on her belt.

Heart hammering, taking a deep breath to control her rising panic, she let go with her right hand and withdrew the knife. She unfolded it with her teeth and reached down, sweeping her hand back and forth to try and shove aside whatever was hitting her. At any moment she expected the frothing water to turn red with her own gushing blood.

She felt something slick and twisted her hand to trap it between her hand and knife. She waited for the sharp pain of teeth, but it did not come. Jenn lifted her hand from the water, making sure she brought up whatever it was away from her face.

It was a broken tree branch. Nubs of smaller limbs protruded along its length. She gasped, not realising she'd been holding her breath, and threw it downstream. She watched the branch get carried away and took a few seconds to compose herself before looking to the far bank.

Cove was a few metres into the river, holding onto the rope and coming for her.

"I'm fine!" she shouted. "Branch hit my leg." She waved him back.

Shit, she was jumpy. Breathing deeply, trying to calm her pounding heart, she concentrated on the rest of the crossing until Cove grabbed her arm and pulled her up onto the riverbank.

"Cold," she said.

"Yeah." He waved at the others, and Jenn saw past him to where Selina began working her way across.

"You fire up the stove and make a brew," Jenn said. "I'll watch out for them."

"Sure?" Cove asked.

"I'm sure!"

Cove raised his eyebrows but said nothing, and Jenn was glad when he pushed his way through the undergrowth close to the bank and slipped off his rucksack. She smelled the faint tang of gas as he lit the small stove.

Jumpy. Too jumpy. Calm down, Jenn.

Half an hour later, by the time Aaron had reeled in the rope and made it across with her holding the line, she was feeling almost normal again.

They drank coffee, and Jenn quietly attended to her cut knee with a couple of Steri-Strips. Afterwards, as they prepared to move out into the evening towards their first camp, Jenn saw her father standing aside from the group looking at the folded map.

"What?" she asked, sidling up to him. She always knew when something was wrong. He went quiet, withdrawn. He'd never been one to share his problems, and she sometimes wondered whether that was why her mother had left. He kept everything bottled up inside.

"Weird," he said.

"What's weird?"

"Something's changed. About this place. It's the oldest Zone, more than half a century, but this map should still be pretty accurate."

"But it isn't?"

He shrugged.

"So the river bridge collapsed," Jenn said. "Maybe the map was wrong when it was printed. Maybe an earthquake has changed the landscape enough so that reading the map's not so easy."

He looked up at the hillside to the west, and then north towards snowcapped mountains in the far distance.

"Maybe." And that was all he said.

It would soon be dark, and they were several miles from where her father wanted to make camp for the first night. Day one, and they were already behind schedule.

11

"Of course we've seen stuff. Weird shit. But if we talked about it, we'd be betraying the reason we race. We don't go into those places to tell the world about what we see, hear, find. It's none of the world's business."

Patrick Slater (pseudonym), British extreme sports enthusiast

"This place used to be Naxford," Dylan said. "It was a fishing village before the war, but for a while it became a munitions distribution point, serving some big factories further inland. Then afterwards, they used it for freight transport upriver and down towards the estuary. Docks, warehouses, offices, and a couple of hundred homes."

"Long way from the sea," Lucy said.

"The estuary's wide, highly tidal, so the coast down closer to the sea is changeable and liable to frequent flooding. And long before it was a fishing village—must be couple of centuries ago—it was used to ship furs, pelts and other goods from inland."

"You've done your homework," Lucy said.

"Someone's got to look after you people."

"That's all fine, but is McDonald's open?" Gee said. Lucy

chuckled, but no one else said anything. In the west, dusk painted the ridged hilltops. The slope they'd just climbed ended on a bare, rocky plateau. It had a few trees scattered here and there, but much of it was open, affording them a wide view along the valley they were following. A steady breeze blew from the east, cooling but not cold. It carried no hint of the sea that lay in that direction. The mountains many miles to the north caught the fading sunlight like burning brands.

Down at the river's edge, perhaps a mile distant, was the remains of a small settlement. From this far away it was visible only as textures—the hints of straight edges, the suggestion of blocky buildings, as if someone had laid a heavy green blanket over the whole landscape, dulling the ordered and regular impact of humanity, blunting its sharp edges. Several tall structures sprouted along the river, with gaps in between where others might once have stood company. They might have been giant trees. It was a hazy memory of what the town had once been.

Dylan wanted to be past Naxford by the time they stopped for a break and some sleep. It was doubtful there would be any habitable buildings, and it would be far safer camping in the wild. Even after less than six hours in Eden, the idea of spending more than a short time amongst evidence of humankind felt wrong. They didn't call what they did adventure racing for nothing, and in Dylan's eyes, there was nothing adventurous about spending time within four walls, however old and dilapidated they might be. He wanted the wilderness around him, a tree canopy over his head, and stars above that.

"We could skirt around it," Selina said. Dylan looked at his old map. Though he'd been given cause to mistrust it, the location of Naxford appeared accurate. The river was in the correct place, and the larger surrounding geographical features matched what he could see from the low ridge.

"It'd take some time," he said. "Tough ground west of the settlement, with steep hills, ravines." He pointed at the wooded slopes. They presented a challenge they would all relish, but right now they were also an obstacle between them and rest. The quicker they passed the old town and reached somewhere suitable to take a break, the more time they'd have to eat and ease down for a while. Recharging their batteries sufficiently was as important to their effort as spending time on their feet.

"Get some light working down there, Gee?" Aaron asked. "Maybe there's a cinema." After leaving the police force Gee had become an electrician back in the real world, working for a small company that took contracts all across western Canada, earning enough to feed his real love.

Gee looked around at the stunning views, the striking sunset. "You need a cinema?"

"So we go through," Cove said. "Come on. It'll be interesting."

"Interesting," Lucy said. "Sure."

They descended the hillside and followed the river into Naxford.

Selina and Dylan went first, moving at a steady jog. His muscles were warmed, his limbs light, his body adapting well to the efforts he was putting it through. There would come a time when he'd have to reduce the strains he forced upon it, but that wouldn't be for a good long while yet. He was used to such hardships, and marked by them. He often thought about the first time he and Selina had slept together, and how she'd spent half an hour afterwards tracing the map-lines of scars across his torso and limbs.

"A scree slope in Snowdonia, North Wales," he said as she turned his left leg back and forth, admiring the knotted mass of his calf. "I was young and ignorant, didn't know what I was doing; tried to walk down it when I should have run. It was one of those cold days where you can see your memories frozen in the air around you. Beautifully still. The world had stopped turning and I was the only moving thing, you know? Yeah, you know. So when the scree started slipping around me, and the mountain began to hiss, I froze instead of following its movement. Ankle and lower leg broke in two places. I crawled down and was found seven hours later by a group of kids doing their Duke of Edinburgh Award. They gave me first aid. I hope I helped them pass."

She trailed her fingertips across his lower stomach. "Cliff face in Belarus. We were climbing about thirty miles from the Deep Red Zone. There was me, Jenn, Kat, couple of other friends I haven't seen in a while. It was a training climb before infiltrating the Zone. It would have been Jenn's first, but we never got there. Must have been a couple of months before you joined up with us, and about a year before Kat left. Things between us were already difficult. Distant. My concentration was off, for sure, and my fitness was far from what it should have been. I was roped on to a guy called Kelvin, and when he slipped on a climb I should have held him easily. Instead, he pulled me from the cliff face and I slid down for a few metres before finding purchase. He kicked off and just had a few grazes, but I was lacerated across the stomach, thighs. Even the old fella needed seven stitches."

She held it, turning it this way and that. "Looks fine to me. Works okay, too. And this?" She dabbed her fingertips at a series of scars across his right shoulder.

"Shark attack."

"Right."

"Knife fight with assassins sent by another team."

"Sure."

He laughed softly. "Shotgun. Chilean Andes. That was with Kat. Jenn was in her early teens, still not travelling with us on our more dangerous jaunts. I'd hired a guide to arrange transport back to Santiago. We were in three Land Rovers, ambushed on a blind bend by a bunch of road pirates. The fixer did his best to talk them down, said we were UN diplomats on a fact-finding mission. The gangsters weren't interested, and it was our security who got us out of it. First and last firefight I've ever been in, and I hope I'm never in another one."

Selina touched the scars again. She kissed them.

"Now you," Dylan said, and she froze against him. Her own scars were obvious, but she didn't want to tell him about them. Not then. It was weeks later that she finally opened up, sprawled in the back of a campervan in Portugal, naked and both still breathing heavily from their second lovemaking session together. Between those two intimate moments, Dylan had been uncertain about their relationship and what it meant. Listening to her story, he still was. The sex had been hard and fast, without passion but with need. He worried that some of what she told him explained why.

"A mountainside on Baffin Island," she said, trailing a hand down across her chest, stomach, and onto her left thigh, where scattered patches of darkened skin betrayed extensive damage from frostbite.

"I was with a small team of scientists from an independently funded organisation based out of London. My university had funded my trip—they already knew by then that I liked travelling, and they were making the most of sending me places. We were researching the effects of climate change in the remotest regions of the world. We'd pitch up, stay for six weeks, take a series of measurements and samples—atmospheric, water, soil, substrata—then move on. There were eight of us, and we had eight locals helping us with transport, logistics and general survival craft. Basically we wouldn't have got where we were without them, or survived there even if we had." She fell silent, pulling a sheet over herself as if to cover the physical scars as she unearthed the mental ones. "Shit happened. Some sort of bug in the camp's water supply, one of my companions attacked by a fucking polar bear, then a massive and unforecast snowfall hit us. The perfect storm, if you like. We were all laid low with the bug, a real puke- and shit-fest all through the camp. Billy died. The polar bear guy. He died… and I never want to see anyone go like that again. His pain… he was ripped up and…" She shook her head, took in a deep breath. When Dylan tried to touch her she pushed him away. "By the time the first of us were back on our feet, the storm had put down a metre of fresh snow. It was minus thirty, and the midnight sun meant it was difficult to rest, even if we could get warm enough to try. Then the local help fucked off."

"They left you?"

"Took the vehicles with them, and all our radios and other equipment. Later, much later, after… everything, I went to track them down, make them accountable for what they'd done. Ask them why they'd done it. But no one had seen them. No one believed they'd returned. I like to think they're still out there somewhere, frozen to death in the vehicles that might have saved us all."

Dylan moved the sheet aside, insistent. She let him touch the patchwork scars on her stomach and thigh. She shivered, and he thought it was from the memories, not his touch.

"We carried on dying. After the third death, the five of us left realised we had to make our way back down the mountain and across the island. It took seventeen days to reach the nearest settlement. By then..." She smiled, but it turned into a shuddering inhalation that shook her whole body.

"Hey," Dylan said, reaching for her. She drew back again, pulling the sheet over herself once more, a flimsy barrier made solid by what it communicated. She was still on her own.

"By then, it was only me. Guy called Jose had been the last to die. We walked huddled together for warmth, then he fell and I dragged him. Must have hauled him half a mile before I realised he was dead. When I left him he was already frozen stiff. I took his clothes."

Her tale made his own scars seem irrelevant. They told chapters, vignettes. Hers told a whole story.

Selina had come on many trips with them since then. Her focus was on the nature, not the adventure. After she'd told him her tale, that second time they were intimate together, he understood why she was with them. She needed a group around her who could not only move across inimical landscapes and take her with them, but survive in those landscapes as well. Selina was as capable as anyone Dylan had ever travelled with, but her scars were fresh, freezing memories scorching her mind like the frostbite across her body.

He had known Selina for years, but hardly knew her at all.

12

"It's believed that there are wild people living in at least half of the Virgin Zones. The UZC made some attempt to remove them from the Jaguar Zone a decade after its establishment, but four of the team sent in disappeared and were never seen again. Since then the problem of wild people has been all but ignored. Some say it's too dangerous to go in and bring them out. Others say they've returned to nature and belong where they are."

Extract from an article in National Geographic

They were in Naxford before they even knew it. Wending their way through a wooded area, brambles pricking at their clothing and the sound of the river somewhere to their right, it was Selina who first noticed the change in surroundings.

"Dylan," she said. "We're here." She pointed ahead to where there were more trees, and beyond a wall of foliage that was more than it seemed. Higher, a roofline protruded above the greenery.

For some reason Dylan had been expecting what he'd seen in a couple of other Zones—a town with broken windows, cracked concrete with weeds showing through, maybe roof structures slumped or holed by new tree growth. Instead, he realised that the whole town had been subsumed by nature. Smothered by it. It was beautiful and disturbing, and it set his senses on edge.

"Let's stay close through here," he said, glancing back over his shoulder at the others. "We'll slow it to a fast walk. Could be all sorts of hidden trip hazards, holes, old basements, rusted metal. Watch out for each other."

"And ghosts," Gee said. "Don't forget the ghoulies."

"Look at that!" Aaron said. "What is that, a butterfly?"

"No," Selina said, "a hummingbird!"

"Here?" Dylan asked, but she was already moving ahead, trying to follow the fluttering creature that looked like a colourful flower given flight. "Selina, wait up!"

He went after her, surprising himself by breaking out into a grin. There would be dangers here, but there were wonders as well. Eden had them spooked, but if the beauty of the place chose to make itself known through the colours of a bird, the lush growth of flowers and climbing plants, the way in which nature had swallowed away the remnants of humankind's stark statements on the land, he was fine with that.

As more birds appeared, darting through the canopy above them, hopping from branches to walls, singing from heights that might have been treetops or roofs, Dylan realised that they had hardly seen any since entering Eden. They'd heard plenty, but now they were making themselves known. It was as if having taken control of the old town made them more confident in exposing themselves to these new human invaders. They were singing down the sun.

There was an extraordinary variety of birds, and Dylan found himself unable to name ninety per cent of those he saw. Some species he'd have expected to see in any native woodland.

Others were more exotic—the flashing greens and yellows of parakeets; the flitting ultramarine of kingfishers; the gentle hum of hummingbirds, their colours delightful and startling. Selina would know all of them. This was her realm, and it was good to see her so enthused. Hurrying to keep up with her, he heard the others following on behind.

They wound their way through the woodland, and Dylan started to perceive changes that made the old town around them more obvious. The forest floor was uneven and he had to watch out not only for knotted tree roots, but here and there were slabs of concrete, uplifted and cracked by decades of water and plant action. Moss-covered, clothed in ground creepers and layers of soil, they were home to small lizards skittering across their sun-warmed surfaces, or blending into the background when motionless. On a larger scale, buildings were now more evident around them. A tumbled church, its tower fallen and replaced by a proud new tree, emerged from the foliage. Its timber facade was rotted away, and those stone walls still standing were moulded to the random, chaotic shape of nature. Some stones were cracked and ruptured, others had been turned or even lifted by plants and trees growing around and through them. The one sign that this had been a church was a single, remarkable portion of a stained-glass window, several large pieces of glass still hanging onto the curved remnant of a timber frame, lifted several metres into the air and nursed in the branches of the triumphant oak tree. A score of large butterflies fluttered around the window in a cloud, as if attracted to the exotic colours that mimicked their own. The tree was still young, the remains of the church old. Whatever prayers had been muttered or dreamed inside were now stale and forgotten.

They emerged from tree cover into an open area of grassland, ferns and clumps of bushes. The cause of the woodland's end was uncertain. They were closer to the river now, and perhaps this had once been a vast concrete pan, a parking area for trucks and cars, and it was only a few lucky trees whose seeds found their way into cracks and were able to burrow down to the groundwater below. It was a strange thought, and Dylan experienced an unaccountable flush of sorrow at the idea of all those potential trees that had bloomed and died so that these few could survive. The emotion surprised him. His experience had convinced him that nature was neither cruel nor kind, but indifferent to such meaningless distinctions.

They grew despite us, he thought. *They found somewhere despite what we did to this place.*

Something rustled through the long grass, unseen but obvious from the lines of disturbance radiating away from the group. Rabbits, perhaps, or other small mammals startled from their feeding. High above, two birds of prey circled in opposite directions, too high for Dylan to identify, drawing a deadly figure of eight that might have been another reason for the creatures' fright.

They were jogging again now, able to negotiate the open ground easier, but their jog came to a stunned halt when they mounted a small rise. Standing on its rim, the scene below hit Dylan like a punch to the gut.

The river flowed past a few hundred metres to their right, slow and heavy, like a giant snake wending its way across this wild countryside, and there was an island beside the small town, but it was not one of stone. A ship must have been left behind when Eden was abandoned, perhaps moored in the centre of the river, or maybe docked but since broken away and drifted a short distance. It had sunk so that only part of the superstructure and deck was above water, its aft beneath the surface. It was rusted to a rainbow of deep oranges, browns and reds, and plants had taken root in a hundred fractures and cracks across its exposed mass. The river broke around and through it. The vibrant colours of a thousand exotic blooms dotted its ruined expanse. White birds floated like snowflakes, alighting and taking wing. It was beautiful.

Set along the riverside were the remains of several giant cranes. They were swathed in climbing plants, and a couple of them sported messy multi-coloured hair of shrubs and flowering creepers. Shapes frolicked, looking like flies or fleas on a corpse. A small species of monkey, Dylan guessed. There had been no such creatures in this area five decades before. Some of the metal supports had rusted and fallen away, and one of the cranes hung low and slumped towards the river like an old drunk. Their irregular spacing suggested that three or four structures had collapsed, though their view of the riverside was obscured so they could not tell for sure. The skeletons of warehouses rose from a sea of undergrowth like stark, dead reminders of the past. Sheet walling and roof coverings had mostly rusted and been blown away, leaving concrete columns and metal bracings exposed to the elements.

A flock of birds took flight from one of the cranes. They swirled and waved skyward, then started dipping and weaving above the warehouses; ten thousand starlings, perhaps a hundred thousand, all following the birds closest to them and making patterns in the air. They swooped low and came closer, their collective calling filling the air. Before reaching where the humans stood on the small rise overlooking the dock, the birds swung about and swooped back, sheeting through the air before descending onto and into one of the rotten warehouses. Once perched, they became invisible. From this distance they were too small to see on their own.

Elsewhere were the remains of buildings, none whole, all taken back to the land. Most had fallen and were little more than humps in the landscape, smothered by plant growth, decades of leaf fall turned to mulch and new soil, and pierced by trees. Others still clung onto a bare existence, roof beams or tenacious walls protruding like the clawed hand of a corpse in quicksand. Here and there were deep, dark holes where buildings had fallen into their own basements. There was a hint of water in the nearest of these holes, its brackish surface spotted with weeds and the promise of a dank, forgotten death to anyone who stumbled in.

Fifty years, Dylan thought. *That's all it takes to erase humanity.* In another fifty years nothing recognisable would remain. Buildings and docks, cranes and bridges, roads and parklands—all would be subsumed beneath the unstoppable march of nature and time.

They headed down the slope parallel to the river, passing behind the large ruined warehouses and through the centre of the old town. Naxford might have been a ruin, but at least it placed them firmly on the map once more. He would be even happier when they had made their way through and out the other side. It was a small place, but it still felt like a blot on the landscape, even though the landscape was doing its best to erase the stain. An old human place, it felt like somewhere they were no longer meant to be.

"Over there," Jenn said. "Might've been the town square."

"This place wasn't big enough for a square," Lucy said.

"And that tree's been there a lot longer," Cove said. He was right. The tree Jenn pointed at was a huge old oak, its trunk split halfway up, branches heavy and wide. It looked healthy and lush. Red squirrels quarrelled around its girth, one of them defending a hollow in the trunk and chasing away others trying to invade its space. Birds hidden in its branches sang to the setting sun. The space around the tree was open, the nearest ruin fifty metres away. Perhaps at one time, townsfolk would come and sit beneath the tree to eat their lunch.

Selina was there first. She dropped her backpack and took out a sketch pad, a real indulgence in weight and space. By the time Dylan reached her she'd started sketching. She focussed on a flush of flowering creeper around the tree's lower trunk, leaning in close to examine the pale purple blooms.

"How far behind are we?" Cove asked.

"Few miles," Dylan said. "Don't worry, we'll make it up over the next few days."

"Unless the map's accuracy's fucked elsewhere, too."

"We'll be fine." But Dylan had already considered the possibility and it troubled him. They could navigate easily enough from sight, using Lucy's compass and experience to pick the easiest and fastest line across the landscape. But there were always unknowns, and having the map as backup was meant to help them overcome any problems. If the map was unreliable, that would only make their task more difficult.

Jenn came over and sat down close to him on a rock, chewing on an energy bar.

"Dad—" she began.

"Hey, no worries," he said. "Really."

"But I feel bad."

"Don't, Jenn. Please. Just because your mother and I messed things up, doesn't mean I want you to be messed up about it too."

"I don't know why I didn't tell you."

"It doesn't matter. It wouldn't have changed anything." He took a drink, chewed on a chocolate bar, looked around. "She'd have still come here. Still lost herself in this place. And we'd have still been left with trying to find her again."

"But I know that's what you've been doing for so long," Jenn said, her voice little more than a whisper. And she was right. Dylan had always been looking for Kat, ever since she left and cut off all communication with him. Every journey he took, with his usual team or sometimes on his own, was coloured with the possibility of encountering his estranged wife. He daydreamed about meeting her ascending a mountain while he was climbing down, bumping into her in some out-of-the-way café in Australia, seeing her crossing a street in Argentina. He'd never decided how such a meeting might play out, but that didn't mean he didn't desire it.

"Yeah, well, now she's got herself really lost," he said, and looking at their surroundings he felt a sudden deep sense of hopelessness at ever finding his wife despite her being in there with them.

"Hey, Dylan, you got us booked into the local hotel?" Gee asked. While others were sitting and resting their legs, Gee was strolling around, sipping from a water bottle and eating what looked like a chocolate muffin. It was a constant surprise to Dylan how Gee managed to carry such elaborate food, and where he put it—he was the smallest and thinnest among them.

"Yeah but they don't take your sort there," Dylan said.

Gee froze.

"Right. They don't like gay men in this establishment?"

"They like them fine."

Gee held out his hands, bemused.

"You're unrefined, dickhead."

Gee gave him the finger with his false hand and continued his slow circling of the big tree they were all seated beneath.

Aaron was watching Selina draw, and for a second Dylan considered signalling him to move away. He knew how Selina liked her own space. But Selina seemed to have finished. She sat back on her ankles, smiling, her eyes alight.

"You get a lot from that," Aaron said.

"Sketching slows the world down," she said. "We usually move so fast through these beautiful places."

"With us, that's sort of the point."

"Your point, maybe." It wasn't often that Selina differentiated herself from the rest of the team. "When I'm drawing, the world in the drawing moves at *my* pace."

"You could smuggle a camera in. I'll bet Lucy could've sourced you one of those fancy new contact lens cams."

She held up her pad and a fistful of pencils, but said nothing.

"But a drawing isn't..."

"Real?" Selina asked.

"Proof," Aaron said. "You could be drawing made-up plants and animals and landscapes, but a camera never lies."

"What makes you think this pad is for anyone other than me?"

"You're a scientist," Aaron said.

"Yeah, but I'm with you guys, not other scientists." She glanced at Dylan, and he saw the shadow of memory behind her eyes. "And it's not only because you know about surviving in these places. It's about keeping it pure. It's enough for *me* to see all this. Amazing. Beautiful. This creeper, for instance. I can't identify it, haven't seen its like before. It's a parasitic orchid, but I've never seen these colours and such a profusion of blooms."

"New to science?" Dylan asked.

"Sure, quite possibly."

"You could name it after yourself," Aaron said. "*Orchidus Selinius.*"

Selina smiled. "And if I did that, took photographs and

shared them, more people would want to come and see. That's the last thing Eden needs."

"And if and when we set a traverse time, more people will come to beat it."

"People like you," she said. "Like us. Not people who'll want to cut and chop, collect and categorise."

"So you're a scientist who doesn't put the science first?"

Dylan noticed that everyone was listening now, even Gee, chewing the last of his muffin as he crouched down close by.

"Sure I do. But I have a particular vision, and an understanding that the world is moving on."

"Not all of it, surely?"

Selina looked surprised. "You don't think so? Humanity's finished, Aaron. We're hanging on by the skin of our teeth, and these places are what's going to be left behind. Coming here, we see the future."

Dylan blinked, shocked. He'd never thought of it like that. He'd always believed that inside the Zones, they were experiencing areas of the planet given back to the past, not catching a glimpse of the future of the world without them.

"Wow," Gee said. "Deep. I guess they'll allow her in your hotel, right, Dylan?"

"Right," he said.

"Yeah, sharing your master suite."

"*Definitely* time to head out," Selina said, standing and packing away her sketching materials in her rucksack. Dylan caught a couple of smiles between the others. He and Selina had never been secretive about their relationship, but neither had they talked about it in front of the group. He only wished she was open enough to talk to him about what it might become. He wished he was, too.

Maybe Kat stood in the way for both of them. Selina had

known her, and had accompanied them on a couple of earlier expeditions when Jenn was a teenager and he and Kat were still together. Perhaps the ghost of Kat's presence troubled more than just Dylan.

"Dad," Jenn said, and her voice brought him back to the present. She was standing and staring back the way they'd come, past the warehouses and leaning cranes. "There's something watching us."

13

"People think we're lying. The United Zone Council, man, they're just blind and full of shit. We tell them we need more boots on the ground, they tell us we shouldn't be in there anyway. But they're not here, on the ground, fighting the sort of bastards we're fighting. People traffickers, illegal loggers, hunters, drug smugglers, every sort of human scum you can think of, making their home in the Cape York Zone. And why? Because they feel safe in there! Because they know the UZC can't admit to another one of their little projects having failed, not after the Dead Zone fuck-up! And it's tragic, man, so fucking tragic. The things I've seen in there... the beautiful things, like nature's rebooted itself and has found a new freedom. All of it'll go to waste. The scum will sweep it away. I guess just like they have for the rest of the old world, huh?"

Cape York border guard interviewed online (identity withheld)

Whatever Jenn had seen watching them followed them out of Naxford. It kept to the trees as they left the open area around the old oak, a fleeting thing, a hint of movement. Then when they entered the woodland she kept glancing back at the shape flitting behind them. It might have been leaves or branches moving in the growing evening breeze, or shadows shifting at the behest of the sinking sun, but she couldn't shake the conviction that they were being followed.

None of them could see what it was. If they paused to look, it stopped to hide. Jenn felt as if her own shadow was stalking her.

"Coyote, maybe," Aaron said.

"Or one of Selina's wolves."

"Huh."

The shape kept melting back into the trees, as if aware that she'd seen it and eager to hide.

She wasn't sure a wolf would do that.

As they left Naxford shadows began to flood the woods around them. Jenn usually liked the way darkness fell in a forest—light losing its battle to penetrate the tree canopy; shadows seeping from low down and rising, hauling themselves out from undergrowth and up tree trunks; the air growing heavy and still, and the visible world drawing in close. Today, dusk seemed to fall with a wry smile.

She found herself jogging with Selina, the older woman falling in beside her. It wasn't often they moved together, and when Jenn glanced sidelong, Selina offered her an awkward smile.

"I knew your mum pretty well," she said.

"I know. I'm sorry about—"

"Don't worry," Selina said. "I'd have done the same. I just wanted to talk about me and your dad."

"Oh." It felt awkward. She knew about her dad and Selina, but he'd never spoken about it, and to Jenn it appeared distant, cool. Maybe just a convenience for them both. It was odd thinking of her dad having a fuck buddy.

"It came as a surprise to us both," Selina said. "And only recently, maybe the last year or two. Certainly not when your mum was still around."

"I never thought that for a moment," Jenn said, and she wasn't lying. The idea of her dad and Selina being together before her mother left had never crossed her mind.

"Good, I didn't want you to think…" It was rare to hear Selina so lost for words, so uncomfortable.

"I want him to be happy," Jenn said.

"Yes, so do I," Selina said. "Truly. And I think we will be. We're getting… closer. It's taking time, but sometimes that's for the best."

"Don't worry about Mum."

Selina glanced at her, eyebrow raised.

"She hurt him too bad. I don't think he'd ever want her back. But that doesn't mean he doesn't still love her."

"I'd think less of him if he didn't," Selina said, smiling, and for a while the two women ran together, both of them looking ahead at Dylan.

Twenty minutes later, making their way up onto the wooded slopes, Lucy called a halt.

"Something weird," she said. She had been on point, and now she raised and lowered her feet, walking slowly on the spot and making a crunching, metallic sound as each foot fell.

"What the hell?" Cove crouched and ran his hand across the ground, shoving aside pine needles, old leaf fall and trailing bramble stems. He picked something up. In the fading light it was difficult to see, so he held it up and turned it this way and that. "Some sort of nut. But hollow."

Aaron pushed past Jenn and knelt beside Cove. He took the

object from his hand and rubbed it against his tee shirt, then held it up to the dusky light.

"Shells," he said.

"Seashells?" Dylan asked.

"Bullets."

"But there's..." Lucy stepped back and forth, using her feet to brush aside more forest debris to reveal the carpet of objects that lay beneath.

"Hundreds of them," Aaron said. He stood motionless as Lucy circled him and uncovered more and more.

Jenn looked at the surrounding trees, searching for scarred trunks, stripped limbs. There were no obvious signs of gunfire.

"Someone had some pretty hefty firepower," Aaron said. "Automatic weapons, and there must have been a good few of them. A stand was made here."

"A stand against what?" Selina asked. No one replied.

"There's *thousands* of them," Lucy said.

"Dad?"

"How old is this?" Dylan asked.

"Looks old to me," Aaron said. "Shells are buried, mostly. Caked in mud and degraded." He held one up close to his face, sniffed it, turned it this way and that. "Yeah, old. Long before Kat and her team might have come this way, I'm pretty certain of that."

"Dad?"

He turned to Jenn at last.

"This isn't good, Dad," Jenn said. "What happened to the people who were shooting?" No one had an answer to offer.

"We should turn around and go back," Lucy said. She was no longer kicking at the shells. Standing beside Aaron, she was their focus of attention. She looked at Jenn. "You should never have dragged us in here."

"I didn't drag anyone, Lucy," Jenn said. "If you'd known about Mum, you'd have still come." Lucy lowered her eyes.

"This could be anything," Dylan said. "Smugglers. Drug gangs. Poachers. I don't know."

"Anything involving massive firepower is bad," Gee said, serious for once.

"What if they're still here?" Jenn asked.

"Aaron said the shells are old," Dylan said. "We've seen and heard nothing to indicate that whoever fired them is anywhere close. So whoever was doing the shooting is either dead or gone."

"Comforting." Jenn looked around, into the shadows beneath the trees. The sense of something following them had faded away. Perhaps whatever it was didn't like this place. Perhaps it remembered something.

"We've heard about stuff like this," Selina said. "Remember Cape York?"

They all knew about Cape York, used by illegal people-smugglers bringing cheap labour into Australia. One of the remotest Zones in the world, it was also the most compromised. The humans who'd compromised it had made it deadly.

"Okay, come on, we're a team," Dylan said. "We're strong together. Let's make camp, think on it, decide what to do in the morning. We can't go far in the dark."

"If we had to we could," Lucy said.

"We don't have to yet."

They had intended travelling much farther on their first day, but by the time they found somewhere to camp they had still made twelve miles from the border. It felt good leaving the site of the bullets, and also the derelict town. Jenn found Naxford a strange place. Haunted by shadows of the past, it had fallen back into the land like a corpse, allowing nature to grow around and through it and reclaim everything. The evidence of humankind that still remained was rotting, rusting and sad.

Jenn often thought about what might be left behind if humanity finally wiped itself out. Selina's comment that these Virgin Zones were glimpses of the future, not the past, had made her view them in a different way. She'd always believed that they were racing through areas that had been given back to nature, not places that nature itself had taken back. It was a fine distinction, but a revealing one.

They found a clearing protected by an overhang on a low cliff, and Cove and Lucy went about building a fire. They both tried to spark the first flame. Jenn smiled at her friends' silent competition. Sometimes the air between them simmered, but right now she couldn't make out whether it was love or hate. Probably a volatile mixture of the two. They had a tempestuous relationship, one which seemed at present to be on the rocks. But they'd been there before and recovered. Lucy often confided in her, and Jenn hoped she would again, given time. Her friend might still be angry with her, but she found that the wilderness often took the sharp edges off damaging emotions.

"Few hours," Dylan said. "Soon as dawn touches the hills we'll be gone again. A good, full day tomorrow."

While coffee brewed on two stoves, Aaron came to sit beside her.

"We'll go further tomorrow," he said. "You feeling okay? How's the knee?"

"Fine. And yeah, feeling good," she said. She nodded up at the sky. "Look at that. Somewhere like this you almost expect to see different stars." The sky had cleared and away from any light pollution the emerging starscape was staggering. He sat close to her for a while and stared, but he could read her like a book.

"Whatever happened back there was a long time ago."

"So what do you think?" She looked at him, probing. She knew he'd have formulated some ideas, even if he hadn't aired them.

Aaron sighed. "This one time just outside of Eilat we were sent to track down a border control squad who'd stopped transmitting. They'd been attacked from across the border, hit and run, but they'd put up a good..." He sighed heavily.

"Aaron, you don't have to—"

"It's fine. You asked. They'd been pinned down in an old house, and by the time we got there the battle was over, and all but three were dead. The fight had gone on for almost a whole day, and the shells scattered around... we waded through them. They sounded almost musical."

"A siege," Jenn said.

"They were fighting for their lives."

"And that place today reminded you of that."

Aaron smiled and hugged her close, trying to cast light on his story. "Hey, your dad is right, it could have been anything." But the darkness remained in his eyes.

"That's what worries me."

"It'll be better tomorrow, in the daylight. We'll get moving again."

"I guess we'll go further if Eden lets us."

"Huh." He broke a banana in two and opened a sachet of peanut butter, and they ate together in silence. After a while he leaned in close and whispered, "Maybe we'll share a sleeping bag tonight."

"Oh sure, with my dad here and everyone else around."

"Wouldn't be the first time."

"Huh."

"I'll be quiet."

"I know *you'll* be quiet." Jenn was smiling now. Aaron could always make her smile.

"Yeah, it's you who's the problem," he said.

"I can't help it. You make me moan."

"That's the nicest thing I think anyone's ever said to me."

"Love you."

He sat upright again, picking a chunk of peanut from his teeth. "Yeah. Whatever."

Jenn slapped the back of his head and he jerked forward. "Ouch!"

"Ha!" Gee said. He was with Lucy and Cove by the small fire they'd started, piling on snapped twigs. "That's what you get for trying it on with a hardass like Jenn! Right, Dad?"

"Right," Dylan said. "My daughter can look after herself, Aaron."

"Oh, I know that, Pops."

Jenn snorted laughter. Dylan feigned anger, but she knew he liked Aaron's joking about him being his father. They'd never seriously talked about marriage, but they skirted around the idea like wild animals circling a camp fire.

"Spade," Jenn said, holding out her hand.

"And there I was trying to be all romantic." Aaron took the folding tool from the webbing on his rucksack and slapped it into her hand. "Watch out for poison ivy."

Jenn grinned and walked away from the fire, looking for somewhere quiet and private close by. She was soon away from the others, and she paused to look around at the shadowy woods, then up past the canopy at the starry sky. Scattered clouds high up caught silvery moonlight, and the waxing moon hung low to the south east, inviting her back the way they'd come.

There was no sense that anything was watching her from the darkness. No longer any feeling of threat. At the end of their first, strange day in Eden, Jenn allowed herself to be excited about the journey to come.

14

"Virgin Zones? Fine idea, but unsustainable, because people always screw up anything like this. And the planet's going to be just fine once we're gone. Though I guess establishing these places has given nature a glimpse at what it can look forward to, eh?"

Anonymous environmental scientist, Greenpeace

She stands on top of an isolated hill. The slopes are gentle, falling away towards a wide, endless plain, obscured here and there by drifting early-morning mists. There on the hill she is at the centre of things, and everything is more massive than her...

The weight of the hill beneath her feet drawing her down with a terrible, crushing gravity. The smothering vastness of the vista all around, nearby features discernible, those more distant offering mystery and fear in landscapes she does not know or understand. The endless sky, so wide that it seems to drown her senses, far wider than the horizons should allow. She has never seen a sky so huge, hinting at infinities that would swallow her forever if only they knew she was there.

The weight of strangeness bears down upon her, and as she feels herself crushed towards nothing—

She is on a hill she knows, but this time she is on her own. Before her lies an abandoned town she has seen before, the ruins heavy with climbing ivy and other plant growth, the slumping cranes solid and threatening as they fall forever, a constant promise of pain and destruction, as if this moment is a blink between long-ago order and impending chaos. She is the pivot between states, and the pressure is immense. It crushes the breath from her, compresses the atoms of her body towards an awful singularity that will haul her in and down forever.

Perspectives are all wrong. She stands on a low hill, and though she looks down upon the old town, the ruins rise up and around her. The deep forests and the town contain trees a mile high, their trunks a hundred metres thick, all leaning in as if seeking her warmth and goodness. But the appearance is deceptive. The trees seek to crush her.

The world is wide and awful and *deep*, and she is an unknowing speck, subject to all the tides and ripples, the waves and forces that rule the world and make it what it is.

She screams into the deep, but she makes no sound, and no one would hear even if she did.

He is running through the forest. The sky above the canopy is clear and blazing with sunlight, but down below there are wide-leafed plants and creepers clogging the space between trees, snakes hissing, spiders busily weaving webs to catch him, poisoned frogs displaying their toxic innards through translucent skins as they jump—but none of them can touch him because he's going too fast.

That's not what it was like.

He bursts through the undergrowth, ripping aside banks of foliage which should take hours to work through with a machete. A massive rainstorm crashes down on the jungle, a deluge that weighs down heavy leaves and drops gallons of water at a time from above. It strikes his face, blurs his eyes, confuses his vision.

No. I saw everything clearly. I wasn't going too fast.

He veers left and right, avoiding the great trees that support the canopy and starlit sky. He startles a big creature which flees, crashing away through the undergrowth. He can't see what it is, but he's afraid, so he turns in the opposite direction and speeds up, puts the pedal down, enjoying the speed—

No, not like this. It was never like this. He just darted out from—

The shape darts out from nowhere, and he is in a clearing now, the jungle receding as if it has no wish to bear witness. He has no time to slow down. There's not even a split second to react before he barrels into the shape, and the impact sound is something he can never forget.

A scream of brakes, his own scream, and then all motion ceases—his joyful sprint through the jungle; the ebb and flow of life watching him pass; the breath in the boy's chest; the pulse of his heart.

Stillness.

The boy lies in the jungle clearing with his toy scooter a few metres away, its rear wheel spinning to a standstill with a final, dreadful revolution. The boy's blonde hair is red. The jungle is wrong, the heat of the air, the soft carpet of grass, but all that matters about this scene, this memory, is correct.

Yes. This is how it was. The boy dead, me still alive. This is how it will always be.

He takes in a deep breath to scream and tastes the awful, squalid heat of the forest that seems to know his life.

Jenn experienced her usual brief confusion as she woke and the world reconstructed itself around her. *Her* world.

That was just a nightmare. We're in Eden, all together, apart from Mum. And she might be in here too.

She opened her eyes and it was still dark. Aaron was sitting beside her; she could feel his warmth, and it was familiar. He had one hand pressed against the side of her face. He leaned in close.

"Hey," he said.

"What's the time?"

"Four. You've had four hours."

"I feel like I've been asleep forever."

"Nightmare," he said.

"Yeah." She sat up and looked around the small camp. The fire was still burning, and Gee was crouched over a pot, the smell of coffee enticing. The others were all awake. They were sitting huddled in their lightweight bivvy bags, none of them talking. It was the moment before peace broke apart, before a rush of frantic activity would begin. They would be moving again within half an hour.

"Talk about it?" he asked quietly.

"Nah."

"It helps."

"I know," Jenn said. For a while after their relationship had blossomed, she spent occasional mornings listening while Aaron related the events that haunted his own troubled dreams. As a soldier in Jerusalem, he saw three kids killed by a sniper, while their father struggled to get them to cover and protect them with his own body. Shot six times, the father was the last to die. Traumatised, feeling useless, Aaron left the army and his country and moved to the States, leaving a brother behind. His nightmares gradually faded, but he carried the scars of that day in different ways. Moments of crippling depression stalked him, like the sniper's final bullet still seeking its mark. Jenn found it hard talking about her own vague nightmares when his had been so stark.

"I'm here," he said, leaning in and planting a kiss on her cheek. He stood and walked away between the trees.

"Get a room," Lucy said from a few metres to her left. She was making notes in the notebook she always carried.

"Writing your bestseller?" Jenn asked, hoping for a friendly exchange.

Lucy smiled. "I'm changing the names to protect the guilty." Her smile slipped. "Apart from Cove's. Him, I'm getting into trouble."

"You and he might still make up." For a while Lucy and Cove had been an item; a tentative relationship at first, but developing into something much deeper. But four months ago he'd slept with a German distance skier after they'd crossed the Husky Plains Zone in Canada, and that little dream had ended. They still worked well together in the team, but the tension between them was sharp enough to slice the air. "Don't know if I even want to." Lucy shrugged and went back to her notes.

"You can talk to me," Jenn said. They'd been close for a long time, and that's what friends were for. Jenn hoped their friendship was still strong, despite what had happened the previous day.

Lucy offered a faint smile. "Yeah. I know. I'm getting coffee." She stood and went over to Gee, then glanced back at Jenn. "Want one?"

Jenn smiled and nodded.

Aaron returned and sat beside Jenn. "Hey, your dad's off into the forest." He sounded like he wanted to say more.

"What?"

"Gee said he woke with a shout. Stood up, hurried away."

Jenn sighed. He'd had his dream, too. He told her it hardly came anymore, and that more than thirty years was long enough for the pain of such a terrible accident to fade away, its sharp edges of guilt and remorse dulled by time. But she knew that wasn't true. She also knew it was something he never, ever talked about. Aaron was aware because she'd told him, but she didn't think even Selina knew about the tragedy that had blighted her father's late teens. Something like that shaped a life whether you went with the flow or fought hard against it.

"You want to go after him?" he asked.

"No. He's best left alone. It'll fade away." *Like my dream of the deep*, she thought, and she shivered even in the warmth of her sleeping bag. Aaron hugged her close.

"Let's get our shit together," he said.

They started breaking camp. While Gee made coffee and porridge, the others rolled up their sleeping bags, checked their rucksacks and the equipment pouches on their belts, and prepared for the day to come. It had been a brief rest, but this early in an expedition it was more than enough to fuel them for a day's hard running, climbing and hiking. They all knew that rest was essential. And yet they all felt that time spent motionless was time wasted.

For a while Jenn dwelled on her dream, because she knew that to shut it down she had to face it. It left dregs of fear that probed into her waking hours, so she had to consider that fear, dismantle it, and send its constituent parts back into the chaos of sleep where they had been born. Usually she had such nightmares when she was sick, but she knew what had inspired them this time. She could not let her bad dreams taint her view of Eden, however strange their first day had been. It was a new day, and she wanted to face it with a new, fresh outlook.

It was only after a few minutes checking her gear and sipping the coffee Lucy brought her that she noticed how quiet everyone else was. There was none of their usual banter as they prepared for another hard day on the trails. Selina sketched in her notebook, but they seemed to be doodles rather than detailed drawings. Lucy tightened and loosened straps on her backpack, again and again, frowning as she sought the perfect position. Cove urinated on the fire to put it out. Usually he'd turn away from them to do so, but he seemed unaware that they could all see, or just unconcerned. Steam rose around him and stole away his expression. Gee passed out their mess tins filled with heavy, stodgy porridge and a handful of nuts and dried fruit, and though he muttered his usual quips they were lacklustre.

"Everybody good?" her father asked. He stalked back into camp, glancing across at Jenn and offering a sad smile. He knew that she knew. It made her feel close to him. A secret communication, private knowledge, broke through the tension. It was sad that it took a nightmare to lighten the weight she felt between them.

"All good," Cove said. He zipped up and kicked around the remnants of the fire, making sure every ember was extinguished before covering it with soil.

"Didn't sleep that well," Lucy said. She tugged at a strap, loosened it, cursed.

"I don't think any of us did," Selina said. "Bad dreams." Some of them nodded in agreement. Cove and Gee looked down so that they didn't catch anyone's eye. It was a brief, quiet moment, and Jenn felt it putting distance between them all when they should have been drawing close.

"Well, let's get fuelled up and ready to go," her dad said. "Dawn's close, and we can make a good start. Today needs to be a good day."

KAT

Kat wakes. For a blissful, precious second she is not a creature of memory but of the present, existing in the moment and enjoying its sensory input. She feels cool rock against her back and dampness where her right foot rests in a puddle. There is something wrapped around her legs.

I'll come to that in a minute.

She takes in a deep breath. It's shuddering, gasping, as if it is the first breath she has taken in a long time. Her chest rattles and she lets out a barking cough. The next breath comes easier. She smells the forest, and it is delicious—warm, sweet pine; scents from blooms unseen; secrets, dangers, countless untold stories that will never be heard. She hears birds chirruping in the trees, rodents scampering and screaming over a kill. More distant is the heavy, steady movement of something big forging its way through the trees. Bear, perhaps. Or a big cat.

There aren't any big cats here.

She moves her eyes, then tries to turn her head to look around. It's as if a fog is hanging over her, although she can sense the heat of a warm sunny day against parts of her skin. A crackling sound accompanies her shifting position.

That stuff over my legs. My arms pressed to my sides. Over my eyes.

The peace passes quickly, and she remembers who she is, where she is, why she came. She remembers everything, and as if conjured by that memory—or perhaps it has simply been enjoying her brief moment of ignorant bliss before truth comes crushing in—her mind is home to something else.

She cannot scream because her mouth is not her own. Control recedes, even as she feels and sees her limbs stretching. The crackling sound increases, and her body breaks out of whatever is constraining it. She can feel it scratching against her skin, taste it as the other presence uses her mouth to chew its way free. It is bitter and damp, warm and meaty. It's something that should not be.

Born again, emerging from some monstrous chrysalis, she sees and hears everything. She feels and smells it all. Her mind is afloat, buffeted from all sides by the greater presence that has taken her.

Kat wants to be strong, but wishes she could scream. Instead she hears her own low, throaty laugh uttered by something else. She feels the movement as she starts to walk. She realises that what she came to Eden for has happened; her old life is over, and this is the beginning of whatever comes next.

Then light and sense fade as she is driven down, and though the darkness is deep and awful, she welcomes the respite it might offer.

15

Captain Dane Harcourt, Dead Zone border guard: I've never killed anyone.

Carrie Daley, *NY Times*: There are four eyewitnesses who claim otherwise.

Harcourt: I've never killed anyone.

Daley: But you were a guard on the Congo Virgin Zone, more commonly known as the Dead Zone, for over three years.

Harcourt: That's correct.

Daley: A freelance guard, more commonly known as Zone mercenaries.

Harcourt: I prefer freelance.

Daley: And in your time in the Congo, how many attempted incursions to the Dead Zone were you involved in preventing?

Harcourt: I don't have a precise number.

Daley: Because you lost count?

Harcourt: (no response)

Daley: The four eyewitnesses whose testimonies I'm preparing to publish were involved in one such incursion, an attempt to gather material for an ongoing environmental study of the Zones.

Harcourt: Which is a criminal offence and strictly against the IVZA.

Daley: And they say you were part of a group of border guards who caught their team and executed three of them on the spot.

Harcourt: (no response)

Daley: They claim that you shot their friend once in the face and twice more in the chest, and then threw her into the Lualaba River, knowing that her corpse would be carried into the Dead Zone and lost forever.

Harcourt: (no response)

Daley: Have you nothing to say to these allegations?

Harcourt: I've never killed anyone.

Dylan pushed hard and fast from the off, taking the lead and setting a pace that he knew they could not maintain for more than a few hours. No one complained. When he glanced back he could see a look in their eyes which he imagined was reflected in his own. A need to work hard. A distraction from their bad dreams.

He hadn't dreamt of the dead boy in a long while, but in the dark moments after he'd awoken it felt as though those events had happened only yesterday.

Dark dreams left their residue. Running hard, sweating, challenging himself and having to concentrate on the uneven terrain all helped to clean some of the trace away.

Their first day in Eden had been troubled, and that was to be expected. Memories of the other Zones they had crossed together as a team were similar. These weren't normal places, and entering somewhere that was estranged from humanity demanded a period of acclimatisation. Each Zone was different in scope, landscape and feel, and he'd read as much as he could find about Eden to prepare.

They ran for three hours. As dawn spilled its warm touch across the forested landscape, mist rose from the tree canopy and hillsides, and in the distance to the north, snowcapped mountains came alight like sun-flaming brands. They drank and snacked while they moved, and by the time they stopped for a rest and some food, Dylan judged from the map that they'd covered almost twelve miles. It was a great start to the day, aided by the relatively gentle terrain that followed the river. For three of those miles they'd followed the route of an old road, its surface and infrastructure no longer visible, but cuttings through hills provided valuable shortcuts. In one place they saw a road sign still standing, festooned with climbing plants flowering beautiful shades of blue and purple and displaying three lonely letters, part of a name long forgotten.

They moved in virtual silence, talking only to help each other negotiate a few difficult obstacles, such as a tributary ravine with steep, overgrown sides and a slick, marshy crossing that sought to steal their running shoes. When Dylan signalled that they should stop for a rest, he moved slightly away from the group. They'd paused atop a small rise, but the views were obscured by the heavy forest growing across this low area of the valley floor. Much of Eden was forested, now that humankind was no longer there to chop down trees, concrete the ground, and stomp and drive over saplings. It was the world come to life again.

He sat on a fallen tree, unzipped a storage pocket on his belt, and took out some dried fruit and nuts. His rucksack was heavy and rubbed his shoulders, however well he packed and fitted it. They all carried high-calorie energy bars and bland dehydrated meals, and the further they went and the more tired they became, the lighter their backpacks would become.

It was more than food and equipment weighing Dylan down. When Jenn approached he looked away, feeling the familiar tension in his chest he experienced whenever he talked about the accident. It sometimes felt as if the soul of that small boy was trapped within his ribcage, and it fluttered for release whenever he gave it attention.

But his daughter knew him well.

"Ten more miles this afternoon and we're already back on schedule," she said. "You're a hard taskmaster, Dad. Trying to prove yourself to the youngsters?"

"I'm not old, cheeky."

"You're fifty-two!"

"And?"

Jenn laughed and sat beside him on the tree, nibbling on a chunk of flapjack. She made them herself, dense cakes packed with peanut butter and chilli, chocolate and butter, oats and dried fruit. She called them slabs. Not everyone was a fan.

"Don't wear us out," she said.

"We'll take this afternoon easier," he said. "This morning's terrain was relatively smooth, but we're coming up to an area of ravines and ridges that'll slow us down a lot."

"Climbing?" Gee and Lucy both carried rolls of ultra-strong, thin climbing rope and kit, just in case the group faced any slopes or cliffs that were beyond simply scrambling.

"Hope not," Dylan said. He wanted to avoid any technical climbing if at all possible because of how much it would slow them down. One hour ascending a thirty-foot cliff face could be an hour covering three or four miles of woodland on foot.

"I'm still looking," she said.

"Of course you are. So am I."

"We won't find her, will we?"

"I'm not sure what would happen if we did."

"What do you mean?" Jenn gave him a chunk of slab and he took a bite to marshal his thoughts.

"I mean, she hasn't spoken to me in six years. I don't know why bumping into her somewhere like this will change anything."

"Even if she invited us here?"

"If that message *was* an invitation, it was to you."

"And she knew I'd come with you."

"Huh. Maybe."

Jenn was quiet for a while, looking down at her trail shoes. He followed her gaze. A spider the size of a plum crawled over her left trainer, but she didn't move. He wasn't sure she even noticed.

"Jenn?"

"We won't bump into her," she said. "If Mum's still in Eden after so long, the only way we'll find her is dead."

"Maybe she liked it so much in here she decided to stay," he said. It was meant as a joke, but he knew it wasn't beyond the bounds of possibility. Crossing the Husky Plains in Canada long ago, he and Kat had lain awake one night in their tent, hot food in their bellies and a buzz of whiskey settling them into each other's arms, and they'd discussed staying. Living off the land. Making the most of somewhere so deserted. The only thing that had persuaded them to move on was the knowledge that these places weren't meant for people anymore. They broke countless laws to race across the Zones, but they were respectful of their reasons for existing.

Still, the thought was always there. Any time Dylan found himself in one of the Zones, the peace and solitude were almost overwhelming, the wilderness humbling. He could live and die in one of these places. He knew that Kat felt the same.

"Dad..." Jenn said, then she trailed off.

Dylan glanced at the rest of the team. Gee muttered something, and Lucy laughed. Selina sat with her back against a tree. It was almost perfect.

"Jenn?" he prompted.

"Nothing," she said. She stood and smiled, gave him a hug, and as they were cheek to cheek she said, "You can talk to me any time."

Dylan felt a lump in his throat. That was all the acknowledgement Jenn gave about the nightmare he'd had, and it was all that was needed. She knew him so well.

But he knew her, too. He knew that she had something more to say, and he guessed it concerned Kat. Perhaps soon the time would come for her to say it.

16

"Seven times in the last dozen years, fires set by illegal loggers in what remains of the Amazon rainforest have swept unchecked south and east towards the Jaguar Zone, and then died at its borders. In some places the Xingu River marks the boundary, in other areas a landscape of deep ravines... but these are not barriers that the fire could not cross. Whatever extinguished those flames were not geographical features. My theory is unpopular, and has made me few friends, but I stand by it—I believe those fires did not spread because the Jaguar Zone was protecting itself."

Dr Isabella Rossi, Diego Portales University

"Selina?" Dylan asked. "Some sort of plant?"

"Don't think so," she said. "None that I know, at least."

"Look like flags to me," Gee said.

"Then you're a dick," Cove said.

"Takes one to know one."

They stood along the lip of a steep ravine, looking down the treacherous slope towards a floor hidden by trees. It was maybe forty metres deep, and they could hear a stream tumbling along its base. They could descend and climb up the other side, or take a four-mile detour to the west and cross higher up the hillside. They'd already decided to tackle the ravine when Jenn saw the weird tattered shapes hanging from the trees.

"What do you think, Cove?" Dylan asked. Cove was already crouched at the cliff edge, examining options for their descent. He was sometimes reckless and gung-ho, but he was also the best climber among them. Between expeditions he spent time in Colorado and California doing casual work, and the previous year he'd climbed El Capitan over five days with two old climbing partners.

"There are ways down," he said. "It's a scramble, nothing technical, but we'll be cool. No need to use ropes. I'll lead the way." He grinned at Lucy. "You follow my lead, but please don't push."

They started down into the ravine. There were no paths to follow, but Cove used his experience to pick out the safest descent. Dylan's slight fear of heights remained at bay, though he kept most of his attention on his feet and the cliff wall beside him as they made their way down. He only felt nervous in one place, where they had to step across a wide crack in the wall that chimneyed down to its base.

As they came level with the strange things hanging from the high branches of four trees, they saw they were scraps of old material. They completed their descent, then worked their way across the boulder-strewn ravine floor, fording the stream, until they stood beneath the trees and looked up.

"Too high to see properly," Lucy said. "How the fuck did they get up there?"

"Allow me," Cove said. He shrugged off his backpack, circled the trees, chose one and started to climb. He was a big man, but he winnowed his way between branches and made rapid progress. He startled a couple of small birds which took off, circled, then landed again out along a branch, watching him climb with heads cocked. A squirrel scurried along another limb and then turned, shrieking at him instead of running away scared.

"He's keen to get up there," Jenn said.

"Trying to impress," Lucy said.

"They're too far out for you to grab!" Dylan called up. "Don't worry about it."

"Nah, it's okay," Cove said. "I can just…" He edged along a branch, holding on to those around him as it bowed beneath his weight. The material flittered and flapped as the branch moved. Dylan shielded his eyes against spears of morning sunlight penetrating the tree canopy.

"Damn it, Cove," Lucy said, too quiet for him to hear.

"He knows what he's doing," Gee said.

"Bloody showing off, as usual," Lucy said.

"Cove, it's not worth the—" Dylan called. They all heard the branch cracking, saw Cove slip, heard his muttered curse. In a moment of panic, Dylan saw what was to come—a fallen man, broken bones, concussion and a compound fracture, ineffective field dressings, making a stretcher and somehow dragging him back to the border, submitting themselves to security and being arrested…

"Got it!" Cove shouted. He was hanging onto another branch, both feet flailing as they sought purchase. In his other hand, the thin branch holding the old clothing.

"Just be fucking careful!" Lucy shouted.

Cove found his feet. "No problem, sweetheart."

"Fucking prick," Lucy muttered. "Fucking prick."

Gee laughed. "Lucy says you're a fucking prick!" he called. "Drop it down so you can use both hands to climb, prick!"

Cove launched the branch out from the tree like a spear. It snagged briefly, then flew to the ground, landing a couple of metres away from Dylan.

He stared at it for a few seconds, fearing what he would see. Kat liked Merino active wool clothing, said it was warm and breathable and didn't smell. She also liked bright colours. This had been green, once. It was faded now.

"Got it," Selina said.

"Get your ass back down here," Dylan called up. "You fall now and I'll kill you myself."

Cove descended, and the others gathered around Selina as she picked up the snapped branch and slowly unfurled the piece of cloth tied to it. It was holed, sun-bleached, tattered. It might once have been a shirt, short-sleeved cotton. Dylan was relieved to note it was not something that Kat would likely wear.

"Is that oil?" Lucy asked. The material was discoloured here and there in a random splash pattern.

"Could be anything." Selina lifted the shirt closer. "Oil. Bird shit."

"It's blood," Aaron said. None of them questioned or doubted him.

"How old?" Jenn asked. Dylan knew what she was thinking, but he didn't believe Kat would have come in with a team wearing anything like this. It was casual wear, not sports clothing.

Aaron took the fabric from Selina and examined it, pulling at it. A soft rip signalled its release from the stick. Dylan saw material fragments floating in the sunlight like dust. "Old," Aaron said. "Probably years." He searched for tags or any printing but found none. It was a rough garment. The dark spatters that might have been blood were extensive.

"Those tears," Dylan said. "Bullet holes?"

"No," Aaron said, but he offered no other explanation.

"Someone put them up there," Cove panted, appearing beside them. "That's not an easy climb, and the others are just as inaccessible, but they were definitely tied onto the branches. They didn't just blow up there in the wind, or float down from outside the ravine."

"Why?" Gee said. "Who'd go to the trouble?"

"A warning?" Jenn asked.

No one responded to that. Aaron dropped the shirt and none of them wanted to pick it up again.

Eager to leave, they started climbing up the opposite side of the ravine. Cove led the way again, and it was an easy ascent, with a profusion of trees, roots and rocky outcroppings to help them on their way.

Dylan was aware that Aaron was climbing close behind him, and when they were out of earshot of everyone else, he spoke.

"Knife holes," Aaron said, voice low. "Or maybe claws. Definitely not bullets."

"But old," Dylan said.

"Yeah. Old."

They reached the top of the steep climb around mid-afternoon. While they took a short break to drink and refuel, Dylan consulted Lucy's compass and took readings against his map, then established their direction of travel.

A few minutes later Lucy and Cove took the lead as they started across a more rugged landscape of ravines and boulder fields, all covered with the lush forest that characterised Eden. Whenever they arrived at difficult ascents or descents Cove paused to spy out a solution. Lucy stayed close to him because she had the compass, and now she carried Dylan's bound map of Eden. He'd spent some time searching for the definitive maps of their intended route from before it had been designated a Virgin Zone. Downloading these satellite maps in as large a scale as possible, enlarging some more, then printing and binding them was something he'd done for other expeditions, but this one had been the hardest to pin down. Eden was over half a century old, and when it was abandoned and closed down not all satellite mapping had been easily discoverable online. As with other Zones, one process involved in its establishment by the United Zone Council was an intentional removal of all recorded maps from public access. There was a black market in Zone information, but the older the Zone, the less reliable the data. He'd become adept at assessing the quality of intelligence on offer, though often with the black marketeers, the word intelligence was a stretch.

The fallibility of these maps had already proven itself with the confusion over the bridge location. There would be more.

They pushed on across the tough landscape until early evening. There was little chat, but the air between them was comfortable. As a team they came from different backgrounds and countries, and had diverse histories, but once drawn back together it never took long for the outside world to fade, and for them to form again into a tight unit. Even Lucy and Cove seemed to be getting on better. Indulging their individual passions melded them as a team, pushing them close in strange and complex ways that seemed to fit with a perfection Dylan had never experienced before. That's what made them function so well. Negotiating difficult terrains in comfortable silence gave them the feel of a well-oiled, quality machine.

When he suggested it was time to pause for a rest and food, Gee and Selina ran on ahead to find a suitable site. They returned a few minutes later, beaming.

"Oh, you are so gonna love this," Selina said.

"More bullets and bloodstained clothing?" Lucy asked.

"Even better than that," Gee said. "Come and see."

Selina gave nothing away as Dylan walked beside her. "Just a nice view," was all she said. They climbed a wooded rise towards a ridgeline where trees were sparse, the slope steep and rocky, sharp with dangerous edges. Cove stumbled once and cursed. Dylan could see how tired they all were. A rest was overdue, and he decided he'd suggest an hour to eat before they drove on another few hours into the night.

"Woah," he heard from up ahead. Jenn and Aaron had reached the ridge with Gee, and his daughter turned and looked for him, beaming. "Dad. It's beautiful."

The ridge ended in a sheer drop, and beyond was mile upon mile of open forest and gently rolling hills, through which the river meandered. But it was the view into the distance that made them all catch their breath.

The land rose into the first of the higher mountains twenty miles to the north, and now the sinking sun was striking them at just the right angle to set them aflame. A wind drove down from beyond the peaks, and they were shedding fallen snow and ice crystals into the air. These cool clouds caught the dusky sunlight, and a blaze of fiery colours shimmered back and forth above the whole range, pulsing and changing as the ice clouds flowed and drifted. Dylan had seen the aurora borealis several times, and this view rivalled it in colour and splendour.

"I suddenly feel so small," Gee said.

"You're tiny," Cove said.

The seven of them stood along the ridge and marvelled at the display. It occurred to Dylan that they should not be seeing this. Eden was no longer a place for people, and that was not merely because the authorities had deemed it so. It felt like a land unknown and unknowable to humankind. Not only had society consciously abandoned this place, but Eden had shrugged its shoulders and shed itself of the memory of people. It was moving on, expanding, evolving without human problems to mar its way, and this incredible display was never meant to be seen.

Gee's right, we're small, he thought. *We're so small we're not even here.* Selina slid her hand around his, and he knew she was thinking the same. He glanced sidelong at her and she was smiling at the view, all the colours of the wild reflected in her eyes.

"Like it's burning us away," Lucy said.

"This is the place," Dylan said. "One hour, refuel and rest."

"Wish I had a camera," Lucy said.

"I don't," Selina said. She was the first to sit, and by the time the others relaxed and passed around energy bars and food, she was sketching in her book.

17

"There are rumours of scientific teams living full-time in Zona Smerti, which goes against everything the Virgin Zones were established for in the first place. Observation and sampling are forbidden by the United Zone Council and the International Virgin Zone Accord, but Russia denies that anything untoward is occurring. At the same time, information that these teams gather is filtering out, and I challenge you to present me with any scientist who wouldn't give their right arm to observe it. There are also stories of some of these teams turning violent, going mad, disappearing off the face of the Earth. And that in itself offers us valuable insight into how these places are both affecting and evolving away from humankind."

Professor Amara Patel, Natural History Museum, London

The beautiful display over the mountain range almost helped Jenn forget the old clothing they had found, and the bullet casings, and the idea that there was more wrong with Eden than any of them yet knew. It wasn't the first Zone where they'd come across signs of infiltration and trouble, but this place felt less welcoming of humans than anywhere she had ever been. Creatures acted strangely around them, and though they'd seen signs of larger mammals, they remained elusive. Hiding, perhaps. Or stalking. She was starting to wonder what her mother had led her into.

Seeing the burning skies settled a sense of peace in her heart. Nature being beautiful for its own sake was calming, and it fed her natural optimism. She preferred to see the colour in things, not shades of grey.

Then came the shouting, and her heart sank, and the blaze above the distant mountains seemed to pulse and glow with the beat of Eden's mysterious life.

Gee ran back along the ridge towards them, belt unbuckled, spade swinging from one hand. The others scrambled to their feet, and Cove took a few steps towards him.

"Sorry," Gee said. "Sorry." His shout had been loud but unclear. A meaningless call.

"What the hell?" her dad demanded. Jenn stood close to Aaron. She wasn't sure, but he seemed to be shivering.

"I thought it was just more clothes to begin with," Gee said, as he clipped his belt tight and folded the spade.

"Where?" Cove asked.

Gee turned and looked back over his shoulder.

"Lead the way," her father said, and Jenn's heart sank at the resignation in his voice.

Mum, she thought. *It's Mum. That's why Gee's not saying anything.*

They followed him back along the ridge and around a bluff, into a dark, narrow cleft where a few trees grew and a stream flowed. The sides were steep but not high, and no more than fifteen metres apart. At the far end a waterfall tumbled from the higher ridge, and the sound filled the hollow with constant whispers.

Gee led them along the course of the stream past the first

few trees, then stopped and pointed up.

For a second Jenn couldn't bring herself to look. She pressed her lips tight and stared at her father's back as he aimed his head torch where Gee was indicating. Full sunset was still half an hour away, but the ravine walls cast deep shadows.

No one spoke. Jenn's life hung poised between past and future, a world with an absent mother, and one with a dead one.

When she finally looked up her knees almost sagged with relief. Then came the guilt. It wasn't her mother up there, but it was someone's son, husband or father.

The body was slumped in a black walnut tree, supported three metres above the ground at the junction of trunk and the first heavy branch. Its skeletal legs hung down like broken twigs, one foot still laced into a faded trail shoe, the other foot missing. Its left arm was pressed tight against the tree, and the head drooped down with chin on its chest. Long hair and a scruffy beard obscured much of its face, and for that Jenn was grateful.

She took in a careful breath. There was no hint of decay on the air.

Cove took a few steps closer, shining his own torch up into the corpse's face. "It's old," he said. "And it looks almost like..." He trailed off.

"Almost like what?" Jenn asked.

"Like it's grown into the tree."

"Just bleached clothes merging with the bark colour," Lucy said. "Or stuck there in its sap, maybe."

Aaron circled the tree, examining the corpse.

"Was he shot?" Selina asked. "There are holes in the clothes, I can see them from here. And stains, like on those other clothes we found. So he must have been shot."

"Not shot," Aaron said. He swapped a glance with Jenn's

father, and she resolved to ask him about that. As soon as they were away from here and somewhere less tainted.

"What's he doing up there?" Jenn asked.

"Big cats sometimes drag their kills into trees," Selina said with a shrug.

"He was killed by a fucking lion?" Gee asked.

"Jaguar, maybe," she said.

"Here?"

"It's possible. There could be all sorts of larger animals that've made Eden their home once again. We've already seen signs of wolves. Before humans, this landscape was ruled by the big mammals."

"Maybe ten thousand fucking years ago!" Gee said.

Selina shrugged. "No reason to suggest they won't have come back, given the right conditions and encouragement." She had mentioned the possibility during the expedition's planning phases, when risk was being assessed and dangers weighed. Maybe they should have paid more attention.

"But it's not recent, right?" Gee said. "We're not gonna get jumped from the shadows and eaten by a fucking lion?"

"Jaguar." Selina seemed fascinated rather than shocked, and Jenn realised that it was part of her research. To Selina this wasn't a dead person, it was some animal's kill and food store. Jenn wouldn't have been surprised if she'd started sketching it. Sometimes she came across as just plain cold.

Cove stared at the tree, looking for a way up. *He seems almost keen*, she thought. She'd seen the same concentration when he was examining the climbs they'd done that afternoon. It took only seconds—he launched himself up, hands pressed around the trunk and feet forcing against it, and shimmied his way towards the corpse. When he reached the body he moved higher and stretched his leg past the remains so that he could stand on the same branch. He crouched, and for a moment he just stared, right hand close to touching but not quite.

"Just check the clothing," her dad said softly. "Pockets. Anything like that."

Cove nodded and, with a delicate touch, began searching through the corpse's clothing.

"Just smells damp," Cove said. "Not like gone-off meat at all. It's all skin and bones. Just like Gee." They watched him search the body. He dropped a couple of items down to Dylan, then moved closer, examining the corpse's hands, shifting its hair aside.

"Cove, that's enough," her dad said.

Cove ignored him. He lifted the arms and prised open the hand, which had clawed itself closed. Jenn could hear the snap of breaking fingers.

"Cove!" she shouted.

"Just checking."

"Checking for what?"

He ignored her, shifted more clothing, leaning across the body and blocking it from view as he examined it closely. Then he sighed and eased himself down from the branch, hanging by his hands before dropping to the ground. He glanced around the group, then down at his hands as he brushed them together.

Jenn watched the corpse watching them. Its position had changed slightly, chin lowered even more as if in disapproval, head tilted to one side so that one empty eye socket was exposed.

"Cove, what the fuck?" she asked, but he acted as if he didn't hear.

"It's weird," he said.

Her dad was examining the objects he'd dropped down. "This?" He held up a knife handle without a blade. The wood was pale and holed from woodworm or some other burrowing insect.

"The body," Cove said. "It's not resting against the tree, it's almost *in* the tree. Like it's sunk into the trunk."

"Must've been up there a long time," Aaron said.

"No identification," her dad said. "Just this old knife handle and a clothing label. Made in India."

"Half the stuff I'm wearing is made in India," Lucy said.

Her dad pocketed the items, then changed his mind and placed them at the foot of the tree. "Old news," he said.

"Old news," Aaron echoed. He stared up at the remains. "We've found bodies before." Jenn knew he was trying to comfort himself.

"Not like this," Cove said. "That guy was placed there. And I don't think it was by an animal that wanted to eat him. His flesh under the skin has decayed, but he's still mostly whole."

"Apart from the missing foot," Jenn said. She was puzzled by her teammate's behaviour. Cove had examined the body, then moved it around, looking for something. He seemed twitchy and wired.

"I said mostly."

"Whatever happened to him was a long time ago," her dad said. "Let's get away from here. It's almost dusk—another hour and we'll find somewhere to camp."

"Notice that?" Jenn said. She held her breath, head tilted to one side.

"It's quiet," Selina said. "Only the waterfall."

"Dusk," Lucy said. "Most animals calm down when the sun sets."

"There are always nocturnal animals. And it's not quite dusk." Selina clapped her hands, a sharp report that echoed like a gunshot in the small canyon. A few leaves rustled, and something leapt between high branches. Something else rushed away through undergrowth and shadows they couldn't see. As her clap echoed into nothing, silence fell again.

"Ever felt like you're being watched?" Gee asked.

"It's holding its breath," Aaron said.

"What do you mean?" Jenn asked.

"Eden. It's holding its breath, waiting to see what comes next."

"You spooked, big brave boy?" Gee asked with a grin, but his attempt at humour fell flat. They were all spooked.

"Let's move," Dylan said. "West, down the ridgeline, then north towards the mountains. We'll go 'til it's too dark. Then we'll camp and break the whiskey."

"Isn't it a bit early for that, Dad?" Dylan brought a half-bottle of good bourbon on each expedition, and when they most needed it, he'd crack it open and pass it around. A couple of deep swigs each and the mood would lighten, coolness would warm, and the sharp edges and spikes of perceived dangers would grow smooth and fuzzy.

"I think it's just the right time," Aaron said.

They left the body in its resting place in the tree. All the way out of the narrow ravine, Jenn felt its hollow-eyed stare on the back of her neck.

18

"...and ran, and by then there were only two of us left, me and Rotty, and I thought we'd make it out cos I was pretty sure we were way beyond the borders already, but I heard a buzzing and whining and a drone dropped out of the sky and fired something at Rotty, dunno what, an exploding bullet or something, and... he fell and... I've still got a shard of his skull in the back of my neck. Sometimes I wonder if that's why the Zeds let me escape. Cos I can tell that story, and let you run your finger across the back of my neck. Here. Feel that lump? That's Rotty, my brother. The Zeds killed him, and everyone else in our group, just for crossing the boundary and going a mile into the Jaguar Zone."

Anon

The rain began half an hour later, just as the sun hit the western hills and clouds rolled in, turning dusk to night and whipping up a storm through the trees. The blazing display above the mountains had faded away. Darkness reduced their world to a few splashed head torches between the trees and dancing

157

spear glimmers from sheeting rain. Though the rain had not been on the long-range forecast, it was warm, so they donned their wet-weather gear and moved on. Despite the downpour the going was easier than it had been all day, with the corrugated landscape giving way to a series of rolling forested hills. Jenn's body thrummed with life, and her sore knee, aching feet, and chafed shoulders from her backpack straps confirmed her existence. She opened her mouth to take in some rain. She was used to the tang of humankind in rain, that metallic, burnt taste condensed from an atmosphere redolent with centuries of pollution. She often thought it was the waters of the world that were cursed to carry the ghosts of humanity's abuse, from the giant islands of plastic waste drifting far out at sea, to the increasing acidic content of rivers and lakes. The taste of contaminated rain was a reminder of what they were doing to the world.

This rain was fresh. Uncorrupted. She knew it was false, her senses adjusting to where she was and projecting a lie. Weather systems spanned far more than a thousand square miles, and most of the drops landing on her tongue had drifted in from hundreds of miles away.

But it tasted like hope, so she swallowed it down.

As the rain grew heavier and lightning slashed the eastern skies, Dylan called a halt. They spent a while looking for somewhere to shelter, then made do with huddling against a rocky slope, waterproofs on. Lucy and Cove attempted to light a fire but failed, so they drank water and a slog each of Dylan's whiskey, and ate dried fruit and nuts, and energy bars that provided calories and carbs but no real satisfaction. Jenn watched her father go from person to person, ensuring they were all well and fit and carried no injuries, telling them to get some rest. He waited until last to eat, and then he paced their small camp, staring out into the night. His head torch reflected splash patterns in the darkness, where wind blew rain in spirals and the light was stolen away.

"Dad!" Jenn shouted. He didn't hear. She went to stand and Aaron held her arm, trying to hug her close. His raised eyebrows asked the question. "It's fine," she said. "I just need to…" She pulled away and went to her father, surprising him when she touched his shoulder.

"Hey, sweetie," he said. He hadn't called her that for some time. His eyes were wide, and she saw her own excitement reflected there. Her wariness, too. This primeval place might only just be revealing its true wildness to them, in the unexpected storm and lightning, the raging wind and driving rain. It could provide camouflage for a greater change, a more deadly wilderness preparing to emerge when the rains ceased and a new dawn broke. Jenn was worried about what was to come.

"Dad, there's something else I've got to tell you. I couldn't say it in front of everyone else, back there with Poke. It feels too… personal. Too much about you and me." She paused and took a deep breath. "Mum's sick. She's got an illness, a degenerative thing. She's never been clear about exactly what, but she's fading. Dying. She's had it for a couple of years." She spoke loud enough for her father, but the storm stole her words away before the others could hear. She didn't know how he would react. The weight between them had never felt so massive, but something about the pure wildness of the storm gave her the freedom to tell him the full awful truth. She only wished it could wash away the grief she was bringing down on him.

"Okay," he said. "Okay." He reached for her and brought her in close, hugging her tight. Their cheeks pressed together and warmed the moisture between them.

"Is that all?" she asked. "Okay?"

"I'm not stupid," he said. "I've lost so much of what I know of her, but I knew she'd never have cut you off like she did me. And when you told me about the pictures she sent, I knew there was more."

"Just those times after she's finished a Zone," Jenn said.

"But not lately."

"Not lately. Not since '*Eden is my last*'."

"Like she came here to die." His words were a shock, harsher than the crashes of lightning. She had thought the same, though she hadn't wanted to admit it to herself. They both found it easier talking when they were hugged cheek to cheek, not looking each other in the eye.

"You think Mum is dead?" she asked, because she did not. Nothing had changed in her life; her sense of the wider world was the same. She couldn't believe that would be the case if her mother was no longer in it.

After a pause he said, "No, I don't think she is. Not yet. I think we'd know."

Jenn pulled back so she could look right at him, and both of them shed tears which the rain kept secret. "I think we'd know too," she said. "I'm so sorry."

He hugged her close again. He didn't have to say anything else. His gentle shaking was enough, the sobs that started in him and shook through to her, until neither of them knew whose were whose.

They all caught some sleep, and when the storm eased they set out again, sporting head torches and jogging through the darkness to keep warm. Jenn felt light and unencumbered of a weight that had been troubling her for years. Her father remained close, as if reluctant to be too far away from her, and she felt the solidity of the love between them. It was deeper and stronger than the troubling secret of her mother's communications had ever been.

As dawn broke they paused again and built a fire, and sat steaming as they ate, drank and planned the long day to come.

When Lucy returned from her toilet break among the trees, flustered and afraid, she said that something was following them. She had seen movement in the undergrowth, the glimmering of several sets of eyes.

Jenn felt a knot of fear in her stomach, and Eden cast a heavy weight as if she were living her own nightmare for real.

"I heard something growl," Lucy said.

19

Those seventeen people who landed on the coast of the Green Valley Zone and were allegedly killed in a "tragic sinking accident"... I call BS. That boat didn't sink in an accident. Those poor bastards—on a stag night, of all things—were taken out by the Zeds. Maybe they were boarded and got feisty, or were told to turn around and they ignored the instruction, because you know... this is Wales! Not the USA. Not Zona Fucking Smerti. They were wasted.

@PottyBonkkers

"What colour were the eyes?" Selina asked.

"I don't know what fucking colour they were!"

"Cats' eyes? Something different?"

"Selina, I don't know!"

"Doesn't matter right now," Dylan said. "Let's stay close and move on. If you see anything, shout."

"And then what?" Lucy asked.

"Nothing's going to hurt us," Selina said.

"But what if it's wolves?"

"Wolves won't attack a group of seven people."

"You sure about that?" Gee asked. "What about lynx, or jaguars, or—"

"Cats don't hunt in packs."

"Wolves," Gee said, quieter. "It's wolves."

They moved quickly, breathing hard, watching the ground but also glancing around them more than usual. The trees here grew further apart, with wide grassed clearings to cross, pools and marshy streams to skirt or negotiate, and a gently undulating landscape which meant they rarely saw more than a couple of hundred metres in any direction. It was quicker to move through, but anything could have been hiding close by. Following them. Stalking.

"Gee," Selina said, impatiently, "if I cut you a few times, slit your Achilles, broke your arms and left you behind, maybe, just maybe, a pack of wolves would take you, after watching for a while to make sure you're no threat. But seven fit adults moving in a tight group... no."

"So they're just watching until one of us weakens," Gee said. "Cool. That's good to know."

"None of you saw," Lucy said. The fear in her voice was palpable.

"You were vulnerable," Dylan said.

"Yeah," Cove said, "caught with your pants down."

"I don't know what colour their eyes were, or what they belonged to, but they were watching me *carefully*. They had intelligence."

"How many pairs?" Cove asked.

"More than one."

"And definitely not human?"

"I already said they weren't!" Lucy said.

Dylan thought it might have been nothing at all. The light was poor, plants and trees were dropping water from the recent rain, Lucy's head torch might have reflected back at her. *She saw nothing*, he thought, and with every step they took he hoped that was right.

Dawn streaked its welcome caress across the storm-ravaged landscape. They splashed through standing water and leapt over frothing streams, and after an hour moving they were warmed up and steaming. If anything followed them, it did so at a distance and out of sight.

For Dylan, the new dawn cast its light on a different world. Yesterday he had still been living with the hope that he might see Kat again, and perhaps even talk through what had happened between them. Today he knew that would never come to be. His wife was not just gone from him, she was dying, and had perhaps already left this world.

The idea that she would face death alone, without trying to contact him one last time, had struck him hard. It was so final. For years he had hoped that there would be some chance of reconciliation, if not an actual return to the way things had been, because no matter what had happened he still loved his wife. The news of her illness had put the final nail into the coffin of his hopes.

He had been mourning Kat's loss for the nine years since she had left him, and the six years since they'd last spoken. He'd convinced himself that he was as much to blame as she was, but the nature of her leaving still shocked him when he looked back on it. One day she was just gone. No discussions, no reaching out afterwards, no talk of whose fault it had been and why it had happened. Kat had always been good at forging on through their expeditions, no matter what the terrain or weather. It seemed she was also good at moving on in life.

For a while, Dylan had felt that he had been left behind, stuck in place at the moment Kat had gone, floundering. He continued his expeditions, sometimes with Jenn and the team and sometimes without, but however far he travelled he felt frozen in place in his personal life. Then recently he and Selina had started growing closer, and whatever it was between them—a deep affection for sure, something fresh that was perhaps maturing into love—helped him keep step with life once again. He was starting to feel that he had moved on as well. He still carried love for Kat, but it was old and stale like a monochrome memory, not vital and alive.

They headed into that third day filled with nervous energy. As the going became more complex and technical, with some slow climbing and scrambling up and down to negotiate a series of deep ravines, Dylan began to feel that their true journey was just beginning. The first couple of days had constituted a settling-in, adapting to their surroundings and letting Eden become more familiar to them, as they became known to Eden. The clothing in the trees, the sense of being watched, the old dried-up body, they were all vital to that adaptation. He felt that Eden was now a part of them all. Although he did not believe they were part of Eden. That would never happen.

As noon approached and the going became easier, it was Dylan who heard something moving through the forest close to them.

"Wait up," he said, and the others came to a halt. For several seconds the sounds he'd heard continued. Branches swished and snapped, something crashed through undergrowth, and a hundred metres away a scatter of birds were startled aloft. Then the noise drifted away, carried as whispers through the tree canopy.

The others watched and listened.

"Thought I saw something in that direction a few minutes ago," Cove said, pointing.

"And said nothing?" Lucy snapped.

"An animal," Cove said. "Or just an echo of our movements."

"Nothing out there now," Gee said.

Dylan thought they were wrong.

He was beginning to think Lucy might have been right.

They moved into the early afternoon, and just as Dylan began to think about stopping for a drink and some food, Cove and Aaron skidded to a halt down the slope ahead of him. After a pause Cove turned to look back up at the others, and Dylan's first thought was, *He's found Kat lying there dead.*

It was not Kat. It was not anyone. The camp they'd found was deserted.

The forest seemed silent now, and nothing kept pace with them. There was no secretive pause of movement and sound when they stopped. Whatever else was in Eden with them had left them to discover this place alone. Dylan blinked, and a shocking image flashed into his mind—exposed teeth in the shadows beneath distant trees, grinning as their owners uttered soundless laughter. He blinked again but the teeth and laughter were gone.

The river was to their right. He'd been consciously following it again for the past couple of hours, taking advantage of the relatively flat flood plain. The deserted camp was at the junction of the river and a smaller tributary running into it, and the constant whisper of the slow-moving water was the only sound. He might have chosen to camp here too.

"Stuff looks good quality." Cove led the way into the camp. "Who'd leave kit like this behind?"

"No one," Aaron said. "Not on purpose."

Dylan was scanning the place for anything he might

recognise. It felt foolish, but maybe Kat still wore her bright green waterproof on expeditions, or carried the rucksack he'd bought her in Canada, blue with grey side pockets. He saw neither.

Poke had said that the previous expedition came into Eden carrying much more equipment than them. And guns. Dylan had thought that strange to begin with. Why would Kat burden herself with heavy and unnecessary kit? And she hated guns.

"She never meant to leave," Jenn said. She was close beside him, not quite touching. They had still not told the others about Kat's illness, and he wondered if Aaron knew. Probably. That made him jealous, but also grateful that his daughter loved someone enough that she could confide in him.

"But where's everyone else?" Dylan asked.

There were two small pop-up tents still erected, though both had tears in their fabric and broken poles. The rips reminded him of the tattered clothing they had found up on those trees. *Knife holes, or maybe claws*, Aaron had said.

"Hello!" Selina called. Her voice winged into the forest around them and out across the river.

"Been pushed into a dead end," Aaron said.

"Nothing's pushed us," Dylan said. "I've navigated us here."

"Really?" Aaron asked. "Those noises in the forest didn't edge you—"

"There's nothing out there now," he said, suddenly angry. "And it doesn't matter. What matters is this." He walked past the first of the tents and into the camp.

"If something came at us, we'd have to swim," Aaron said, quieter. No one responded. Either they thought he was panicking, or they were too unnerved to consider the possibility.

Dylan wandered through the camp, desperate to see

something familiar and also hoping he would not. The tents might have been attacked, or perhaps the camp had been here so long that the elements had done their worst. Equipment was strewn at random, caught on bushes and blown against a large tangle of old branches washed onto the shore by the river in flood. A bivvy bag, colours faded by exposure to sun and rain. A torn roll mat. A plastic bag of dehydrated food, still sealed.

At some distance from the tents, nearer the junction of river and tributary, a fire pit still displayed scorched stones. A metal tripod hung over it, but there was no pot or pan. Ashes from the fire had long since blown away or been soaked into the ground.

Dylan kicked around in the pit, uncovering a scattering of splintered, blackened bones.

"Been a while," Cove said. He ducked into one of the tents, rooted around, and came out with a couple of sports tops.

"Any names in them?" Dylan asked.

"Nothing." He sniffed the tops, dropped them. It was a strange gesture. "No one would have left a camp like this."

"Certainly not Kat," Selina said.

"Unless they had to," Lucy said. She was looking out across the river, as if expecting to see a soaked and bedraggled group hauling themselves onto the far bank.

"Poke said they came in a couple of months ago," Aaron said. "This place is several weeks old, at least. Whoever camped here is long gone."

"Hopefully," Dylan said. He couldn't help thinking of that old body in the tree, probably years old rather than months. He blinked. Saw grinning teeth in the shadows once more, Eden laughing at them all.

"Doesn't look like they were racing," Cove said. Tattered

as it was, the camp didn't look like a brief stopping point. Dylan and his team carried two micro-tents, but they'd only use them if the weather grew too terrible even for waterproof clothing, and they'd rarely stop for more than three or four hours at a time. This camp even had an excavated fire pit.

She didn't come here to race, he thought, and he caught Jenn's eye. They were both thinking the same thing. Maybe she didn't leave this place at all. The river could have carried away anything, or anyone.

"Got a bag here," Gee said. He was along the tributary bank, kicking through high grass a few metres from the water. He held up a rucksack. It was red, water bladder pipe curving from its top like exposed gut. The others closed in as he undid the cover clasp and opened it. He held the bag down and away from his body and peered inside, as if afraid it might contain scorpions or spiders.

Dylan stepped closer. Gee nodded, and Dylan reached into the bag. He brought out a waterproof top, a handful of energy bars and gels, and a penknife.

"Phone?" Lucy asked.

"Hang on," he said. He dropped the contents by his feet as he brought them out—a first aid kit, opened and partly used; a notebook, swollen with moisture; a baseball cap. "That's it." He examined the cap closely, flipped through the notebook. It was blank. He didn't find a pen.

"No name? Nothing else?" Cove asked.

"Nothing."

"Someone left it behind," Gee said, dropping the rucksack on top of its contents.

Or someone didn't leave at all, Dylan thought. He couldn't understand why Kat's team would have left their equipment like this. Even if they'd come in with her intending to race, and she'd grown sick and died, they would have probably buried her in Eden and then hiked out. No need to leave the camp half-formed and equipment still bagged up.

He looked at the first aid kit again. It had been opened and contained no bandages, no sterile dressings. He pocketed the penknife.

"There's nothing to keep us here," Lucy said. She looked at Jenn. "Looks like you might find your mother yet." Dylan saw a flicker of hope in his daughter's eyes.

"We should eat now that we've stopped for a bit," Selina said. She was eyeing the water rushes growing along the banks of the river, and Dylan could tell she wanted to sketch. But he agreed with Lucy.

"We'll move on and eat somewhere else," he said. "Another hour, maybe."

"Why?" Selina asked, and he felt a flush of anger at her. *Because my wife might have been here!* he wanted to say, but that was unfair on her, and on himself. Kat wasn't his wife anymore, and if she had been here she was gone now, one way or another.

They had found nothing that resembled a grave.

"I just don't want to stay here," he said.

They checked around the camp for anything useful. Cove slipped into the tents again and spent some time searching inside. Finding nothing of interest, he began scratching around outside the tents.

"Cove?" Dylan asked.

"Yeah," he said. "Just looking."

"For what?"

Cove shrugged.

Dylan debated packing everything away and burying it

all. The Zones were meant to be left pristine and untouched, not strewn with abandoned belongings and refuse that might take decades or more to degrade and break down. In the end they decided to leave it as it was. It wasn't their responsibility, and they all agreed that making haste was a priority.

None of them voiced what Dylan felt—that they wanted to leave the camp because it left them deeply troubled.

20

"Total recorded worldwide statistics as follows (it has been assumed that unrecorded statistics are substantial, but no reasonable estimate is available):

Zone infiltrations (groups consisting of 3 or more individuals): 173
Infiltrators captured: 435
Known infiltrators not accounted for: 443 (this statistic also refers to known infiltrators not caught in the months or years following infiltration of specific Zones)
Infiltrators killed (during contact with Zone Protection Forces): 44"

Leaked document from United Zone Council
2nd Annual General Meeting

They worked upstream along the tributary until they found a place to cross. It was ten metres wide and shallow, and there was a scattering of rocks protruding above the surface. If they were careful they might be able to jump from rock to rock and avoid getting wet feet.

Gee went first, light and nimble as ever, and the others followed.

"Jesus Christ!" Gee shouted. Dylan looked up in time to see him slipping from one of the larger rocks and into the water. He splashed onto his side and kicked away, pushing back with his feet against the flow, unconcerned with the soaking he was getting and focussed only on what he'd seen between the rocks.

"What is it?" Dylan shouted. The others were splashing out towards Gee, Lucy grabbing him beneath the arm and hauling him upright. He leaned into her and edged back a bit more.

"Fuck," Lucy said.

By the time Dylan and Jenn reached them the others were all standing in the stream close to the rocks, water parting and splashing around their knees. He took a deep breath and followed their gaze.

The body was wedged low between two rocks, feet facing upstream, head tilted back far enough to face downstream. Its arms were held up against the rocks that were pressed against its ribcage and upper chest. Hands were clenched. The right arm swayed back and forth against the stone, shifted by the water, a dead wave.

The man was naked, his skin a soft pearly white. A tattoo on his right pectoral was a startling splash of colour just beneath the surface, like an exotic creature attached to his chest.

"Just what the fucking hell...?" Cove breathed.

Water pulsed from the man in spurts. His empty eye sockets, ears, open mouth, all formed jets that splashed behind his head and past the rocks, like a decorative fountain. Dylan looked at his exposed legs, groin and stomach, searching for the place where water might enter and power up and through his body. The stream's surface was too disturbed to see, and he didn't want to look closer. He didn't want to touch.

"How long has he been there?" Jenn asked.

"Can't have been long," Selina said. "A few days of that and he'd…"

"Come apart," Lucy said. "But even after days, I don't know how that could happen. It's like the river's made him part of it. It's holding him here."

"The rocks are holding him," Aaron said.

"And the river's flowing through him," Lucy said.

"We should get him out of there," Dylan said, but no one made a move towards the body. He couldn't blame them. He took the first step, and as he reached for the man's arms the right hand waved again, elbow bending slightly, straightening. Urging him closer.

Dylan's heart hammered. He focussed on the man's tattooed chest, trying to make out the design as he reached out and closed his hand around the left forearm. The flesh was as soft as foam and his fingers sank in, pink-tinged water seeping out around his hand. He cried out and stepped back, squatting to dip his hands into the stream and let the water swill the fluid away. The mark he'd made in the man's arm remained, the squeezed flesh slowly, slowly regaining its former shape.

"It's waterlogged," Dylan said.

"That doesn't happen," Lucy said. "Not like that." She stepped forward and Cove went with her, reaching at the same time, each taking one of the dead man's arms. They pulled. The limb Cove held shifted too much but the body didn't move, and he let go and stumbled back, eyes wide, slipping on slick rocks. Aaron grabbed him, saving him from a full soaking.

The arm slumped down across the man's chest, rocking there as water rolled it back and forth.

"We leave him," Dylan said. "It's not fresh, but not that old either." He turned to Jenn. "Recognise him from any of your mother's photos?"

"I... don't know," Jenn said. "His face is..." She trailed off.

"Must be one of her team," he said.

"So now we go and find Kat," Selina said. "Something's very wrong here. Something went bad, and they had to leave their camp and run like—"

"What did that to him?" Aaron asked.

"He might have fallen in upstream, maybe dead already, and been washed down," Selina said. "Water ripped off his clothing."

"But the water flowing *through* him like that."

Selina shrugged.

"We go on," Dylan said. "Maybe the others are in trouble somewhere, holed up. Cove found a clip but not weapons, so maybe they're still armed, defending themselves."

"Against what?" Lucy asked. "Those things following me?"

"There was nothing following you!" Cove said.

"What, now you don't believe me?"

"You're seeing things, hearing things," he said.

"Come on," Dylan said. "We're doing ourselves no favours staying here. Doing him no favours either." He wished he could lift the body, commit the tattoo to memory, because this was someone's husband or son. But he didn't want to touch the corpse again. He could still feel its cold, soft flesh against his fingertips.

They moved off, careful to pass the rocks and trapped body upstream.

"There's no smell," Jenn said. "Even the parts of him that are exposed don't seem to have decayed."

"Could be he's only been dead a day or two," Lucy said.

"Yeah, he's nowhere near as old as that body in the tree," Cove said.

"Maybe," Jenn said. "Or maybe the river's keeping him fresh."

Dylan felt an urgency dawning inside him, a desperate need to move forward and search for Kat. Something bad must have happened here, and whatever time her illness had left her must have been running out. Maybe her text to Jenn had been an unconscious invitation for her and him to find Kat before she died. He could no longer save their relationship or fix what had happened, but it suddenly seemed important to see her one last time. Being apart from her was bad enough. Knowing he would never see her ever again... he wasn't sure he could handle that.

His sense of urgency was increased by finding the body. If what he and Jenn suspected was correct, Kat had come here to die on her own terms. Not to be killed.

Twenty minutes after leaving the body behind they snacked quickly to refuel, then followed the river, edging west when the waterway disappeared into a sheer canyon and a ridge of land blocked their route. They could have climbed, but it would have taken too long, and any technical climb was dangerous, however prepared and proficient they were.

Dylan's elevated heartbeat refused to settle, and it was only partly down to exertion. The group was silent from the weight of what they had found. They moved closer together than usual, less than twenty metres between Lucy on point and Gee bringing up the rear. Dylan took comfort from proximity. They were friends, people he could trust, people he loved. He heard their breathing and felt their warmth, and he experienced a sudden rush of optimism. *We can weather anything*, he thought.

They moved in silence for another ten minutes until Lucy cried, "There! Another one. Oh God, another one."

The woman was dressed in bright running gear and propped

against a tree, and for a terrible moment Dylan *knew* it was Kat, it *had* to be her. Going closer, seeing that it was not his estranged wife did nothing to detract from the awful sight.

A single rose stem grew from one of the woman's empty eye sockets, its rich red bloom resting on her left cheek. A fat slug pulsed in the remains of the other eye. Her throat had been ripped out, spine exposed, skin and flesh tattered and torn, home to crawling insects. A wild rose grew around the base of the tree, and its thin stems penetrated and passed through the woman's legs, her stomach and left arm. They held her hand aloft. Her pierced skin was caught on thorns and stretched, along with the material of her running shorts and top, and blood from her mutilated throat caked her chest, hardened into a dark husk.

Gee turned away and puked. Selina stayed still while the others stepped closer. Dylan breathed softly through his mouth, afraid that if he took in a deep breath—he was panting from running, breathless from shock—he would taste her rot on the air, and he might never forget that.

"Roses," Jenn breathed, and he frowned, wondering why she was stating the obvious. Maybe she was trying to distract herself from the grotesque tableau. Then he exhaled and gasped in a deep breath, and all he could smell was the warm perfume of the wild rose. The woman's raised hand, fingers relaxed like wilted petals, might have been another bloom.

"Only roses?" Cove said. A strange comment.

Lucy was the first to approach the body. She knelt beside her but did not touch. "How does this happen? This growth? If she'd been here long enough for this she would be decayed. Like that body in the tree."

"It *doesn't* happen," Selina said. "Neither does that guy in the stream. Not in any normal place."

"Anyone know her?" Dylan asked. The racing community they came from was quite small, and they often crossed paths with the same groups on training expeditions or in planning stages of new attempts. Friendships formed. Rivalries, too. "Jenn?"

Jenn only shook her head.

Cove knelt beside Lucy, examining the body from all angles, as if trying to see behind and beneath her. He reached out, hesitated, withdrew his hand without touching.

"We need to stick together," Aaron said. "Find somewhere safe to camp tonight, get the fuck out of here tomorrow."

"We're almost thirty miles from our entry point," Dylan said. "I reckon we've come seven miles today, if that. Those ravines were vicious. It'll take two solid days of travelling to get out, at least."

"Then we put in two hard days," Aaron said. "Dylan, you can't seriously be thinking of carrying on?"

Dylan wondered if that really was such a bad thing.

"Mum's in here somewhere," Jenn said. "I know only I came because of her, but there's no way I'm leaving now." She spoke to Aaron but addressed them all.

"Babe, I care about your mother, but Eden's the size of a small country," Aaron said. "And I care about you more."

"I don't need you to look after me, Aaron. We look after each other. I'm not leaving."

Aaron sighed, shaking his head, looking at the dead woman pulled taut against the tree, with a rose plant growing into and through her in the same way the river was flowing through the dead man. It was as if Eden was eating them, or they had been fed to Eden.

But by what? Dylan wondered. Birds called in the distance. Smaller creatures rustled through undergrowth, squirrels frolicked in high branches, lizards flitted across tree trunks. He imagined Eden's grinning mouth, its teeth sharp and clogged with the meat of the dead.

"We're all in danger," Dylan said. "We have no idea what happened here."

"Someone in their group went apeshit and wasted them," Cove said. "We've heard about it happening before. The pressures, the stress."

"And threaded her corpse with a fucking rose bush?" Lucy yelled. She turned to him, eyes wide. Her shout was answered when something in the distance called back, or maybe it was an echo bouncing from an unseen cliff face ahead of them. They all froze, listening. The call or the echo faded to nothing.

"We are all in danger," Dylan said again, "but I'm with Jenn. Kat is here somewhere, and alive or dead I need to find her. If the majority of you want to leave, we'll go with that. But I'm for staying and moving on. Forewarned is forearmed."

"Forearmed with what?" Lucy asked. "I've got a pair of trainers and a fucking Mars bar!"

"We find Mum," Jenn said.

"We find Kat," Selina said.

"Madness," Lucy said, speaking directly to Jenn. "It's crazy. People are dead."

"We've seen dead people in Zones before," Jenn said.

"I'll stick with Dylan," Gee said. He was scratching his cheek with his false hand. Water still dripped from it.

"I don't do turning back," Cove said. It should have sounded ridiculous, but he wasn't being pompous or macho. It was just him.

Aaron looked at Jenn, frowning. *He's worried about her more than himself,* Dylan thought, and it was another reason to like the guy.

"Okay," Aaron said. "But this isn't the final vote. Something else happens, we get a chance to vote on leaving again."

"Agreed," Dylan said. He gestured at the body.

"We can't do anything for her, but I'll note the position of the three bodies, and when we're out I'll leave an anonymous tip."

"They'll stay here 'til they rot," Lucy said.

"I'm not so sure," Selina said.

"You think they'll send someone in to get them?"

"No, not that. I'm just not sure they'll rot."

As they moved on Dylan took a final look at the body, the wild rose bush, its stems thick and green, its blooms lush and healthy. It was well fed.

21

"It is the greatest irony that a group of radical environ-mentalists intentionally contaminated and destroyed one of the purest natural habitats on the planet, turning it into what has become known as the Dead Zone. It was a painful act, but totally necessary. Dr Hayek had penetrated the Congo Zone, allegedly discovered a mythical plant he named the ghost orchid, and performed enough field tests to pronounce it miraculous. Never seen before, it's said that it had properties that would make it priceless to the global drugs trade—a whole new form of antibiotic, as well as potential cancer-treating compounds in its roots. It was the flower that might have changed the world. But it would not have saved the world, because its home—and potentially every other Zone—would have become the focus of every fortune seeker, every corporate task force, and every group of adventurers and scientists who could get there in time. So we did what we had to do. It was painful. It was shattering. But it had to be done. And now the ghost orchid is back where it belongs—in myth."

Elise Palant, extract from Making Hell: Killing What You Love

They found two more bodies in a rocky gulley. The man and woman were half-buried in the soil, and lush plants and roots grew around and through them. The man had a tree sapling growing from his stomach, his back slightly arched where the plant lifted his torso a few inches from the ground. His head was crushed, skull shattered, brains spilled and eaten by forest creatures. The woman sprouted creeping ivy from her mouth and eyes, and bore a mortal wound in her chest. They wore similar kit—stretched Lycra holed and torn; trail running shoes; waterproof jackets which were tented by the plant growth, providing colourful backdrops to the voracious shrubs.

As Jenn edged closer, the terrible confirmation she'd been seeking struck home.

"Dad, that's Marsha Rodriguez," she said, and knowing for certain that the dead woman had been part of her mother's team, rather than suspecting, made her feel sick. She'd met Marsha a couple of times before her mother left, and had seen her on each photograph her mother had subsequently sent. Her distinguishing feature had been her ice-blue eyes, but now they were gone.

"It's her," Selina confirmed. "And the bodies appear fresh. But… that sapling through his stomach must be two or three years of growth."

"Another one here," Aaron said from along the gulley. "Not Kat." This one was also a man, twisted into the trunk of a fir tree, limbs distorted and turned a leathery brown, like old bark. His face was half-submerged in the tree, one eye glassy and staring, mouth turned down in an endless snarl. Millipedes crawled in and out of his nose and exposed ear, and a small rodent had made a home in his mouth. His long hair was hardened into the bark, set solid with leaked sap.

"I've seen him in the photos from Mum, too," Jenn said. "I never knew his name."

"This is impossible," her dad said. All of the bodies were in situations that made no sense. There was no aroma of decay about them, and when Cove pressed their flesh with a stick, it seemed pliable, not taken by rigor. Parts of their exposed bodies were weathered, skin hardened. Other parts were soft and pink like the skin had been recently scrubbed. Cove tried to lift their clothing with the stick, looking beneath. He searched the ground around them while the others stood still, shocked immobile. He seemed unable to stare at the corpses for long.

It was difficult to avoid the idea that the plants growing through them were drawing sustenance from the bodies, yet they also seemed to be providing it, keeping the corpses fresh and uncorrupted. The dead nourished the land whilst also being nourished by it.

Trying to rationalise, Gee muttered about the incorruptibility of saints, and the mummification process in some ancient South American cultures. But Jenn knew that this was neither.

This was Eden.

Jenn moved closer to her father. "Six dead, Dad."

"She's not one of them." He sounded fragile, loaded with grief.

"Maybe we just haven't found her yet."

Finding the body in the tree, and even the second in the river, might have pointed at accidents. The discovery of the woman—"the rose woman", as Jenn thought of her—made an accident a much less likely scenario. Now, with three more dead, it was more and more probable that her mother was lying dead somewhere out there, and Jenn hated the idea of rounding a boulder or climbing a slope and finding her.

"Poke never said how big her team was," Selina said.

"Probably seven or eight, same as us," Jenn said. "Mum knew the optimum size of a group."

"We've found six," Cove said. "Two definitely from Kat's team, so it seems certain the others were, too. The chance of anyone else still being alive..."

"Yeah, thanks, Cove," her dad said.

"So what do we do?" Lucy asked. "What the fuck is going on here, Dylan? There must be someone out there doing this, right? Someone gone feral. We need to turn back, get the hell out of here. Aaron? You think?"

Aaron didn't reply. He only frowned and looked at Jenn.

"I don't think so," Jenn said. She could not fix her head around the idea that this was another person or people doing this. The existence of wild people in the Virgin Zones had been mooted many times over the years, and in the Husky Plains they'd even seen distant signs of a small group following them on their crossing. It was an unsurprising idea that some people might want to live within the Zones, shedding the trappings of modern society and regressing to more basic times.

But there was no reason to believe that these people might become murderous.

And there was no way such people could have done what had happened to those bodies.

"Okay," her dad said. "Okay. Jenn, this changes things. You see that? Whatever happened here, these weren't accidents."

Jenn felt cold, empty, drained of hope. Cove was right. With six dead, the chance of any remaining survivors was slight. She only looked at her dad, and offering no protest told him everything.

"Okay," her dad said again. "We stick together. Camp, eat, drink, rebuild our strength and rest through the night. Then tomorrow at dawn we'll head back the way we came. That's the closest land border. Two solid days, eighteen or twenty hours of good hard running, climbing, and scrambling, and we can reach the boundary."

"I don't want to spend one more night in this place," Aaron said.

"Moving at night is a bad idea," Jenn said. "And we need rest."

"We have head torches," Cove said. "We know what we're doing. Maybe we should check the bodies again. Look for more clues."

"What is it with you and the bodies?" Jenn asked. He'd been first up that tree, first to prod and poke with a stick.

"Curious," he said.

"We do what I say," Dylan said. "Storm's coming in again." It was true. Heavy cumulous clouds were rolling in from the direction of the sea, darkening and thickening as they closed across the dusk. They promised torrential rain. "We could get caught in a flash flood, or washed off the side of a cliff. One of us breaks a bone and all the others are slowed down carrying them out."

"So we wait for whatever it is to—?" Lucy began, but Jenn interrupted. She could feel her own simmering panic probing the edges of her consciousness, but no one needed to *hear* it, from any of them. Panic was contagious.

"We don't know there's anything out there at all, Lucy," she said.

"Then what the hell killed those people? I heard it," Lucy said. "Or them. I *saw* them."

"No one knows what you heard and saw," Selina said. "Dylan's right. Now we've decided to go, we've got to be sensible about this. Start a fire, keep warm, eat plenty to fuel up and lighten our loads, take turns resting. Then get the hell out."

"And what about Mum?" Jenn asked. Everyone glanced at her, most of them looking away again, awkward. Lucy was the only one who held her gaze.

"Your mum knew why she came here," her dad said. "We can't put ourselves in danger looking for her, even if she's still alive."

Jenn felt a rush of anger at her father's words. *She might be lying in a fucking ditch somewhere, injured, waiting for help!* But she closed her eyes and tried to level her emotions, because she knew he was right. If she really had come here to die—and whether her team had known the truth of that or not—everything pointed to her having already met her fate.

Moving away from the bodies felt strange to Jenn. They were abandoning them, whereas the automatic reaction would have been to give them a decent burial. Yet that was her Western upbringing coming through. Burying or burning a body might not be the most respectful way of disposing of the dead. In some cultures, the dead were given to the birds. In others, mummification and retention by their families. Perhaps here, amalgamated into the place they had come to explore was paying them the greatest honour.

As it became dark enough for head torches, the clouds rumbled and the rain started again. Her father followed his old map and took them east, up into some foothills where ragged canyons cut east to west and shale slopes made the hillsides treacherous. In one such wide canyon they found a hollow in a cliff face on the westward side of a pile of tumbled boulders, and it provided good cover from the increasing easterly gales and driving rain.

Silently they set up camp, gathering wood and tucking it beneath rocks to keep it as dry as possible, starting a fire under cover of the overhang, and preparing themselves for the night to come. Her dad suggested Cove take the first watch; he nodded and disappeared for a couple of minutes. He returned with a thick branch, snapped off so that it was around his height, smaller branches removed. He hefted it in both hands, swung it a couple of times. Then he took up position facing out into the canyon, waterproof on, hood pulled up over his head. No one commented upon him having fashioned himself a weapon. No one thought it foolish.

The fire blazed in the small cave, flames dancing in the twisting breeze that still managed to penetrate beneath the overhang.

Jenn went and stood beside Cove, looking back along the canyon. Their view was blocked by boulders the size of cars and the clumps of trees growing here and there, but they would still see any shadows moving their way. She shivered. The idea of something following them was unsettling. She glanced in the other direction, and the canyon continued westward. There could be anything out there.

Darkness was falling, accentuated by the low, heavy clouds. Soon there would only be wind and rain, and the weak fire they had built against the dark.

"We'll be fine," Cove said.

"What are you looking for, Cove?"

"Huh?" He held the stick like a staff, leaning on it. He glanced sidelong at her, then out into the darkness again. Keeping watch. Avoiding her eyes.

"Out here, in Eden. What are you looking for?"

"Same thing as you," he said. "Adventure, freedom, wilderness. A place that's unfucking itself from the human stain."

"Yeah, right. We've found more than we bargained for."

"Yeah."

"But what are you *really* looking for." She saw him tense.

He hugged the stick to his chest with both hands, knuckles squeezed white. She had never been afraid of Cove, and she wasn't then, but she saw how strong he was, and how determined.

"Something rare," he said.

"Rarer than what Eden's become?"

"And what is that?" He stared at her. Rain poured down his hood and dripped across his face. It washed away whatever look was in his eyes.

"I don't know anymore," she said. "Maybe paradise, but not for people."

"Right. Maybe paradise."

"Cove, we're in danger. We can't keep secrets from each other."

A strong breeze blew a sheet of rain against the rocks. It sounded like the dark whispering.

"Ghost orchid," he said.

Jenn almost laughed. Then she saw how serious he was, remembered the way he'd searched the bodies they'd found, lifting their clothing, rooting around in the tents in the abandoned camp. "You're serious?"

The ghost orchid was a myth, a precious, rare plant that had supposedly only ever bloomed in the Congo Zone. A flower risen from nature's new-found independence from humankind, it was scented with the ghost of times before humanity, or without it. Legend had it that if the ghost orchid ever died out completely, then that would signal the end of the world's struggle, and initiate a decline towards a lifeless planet. There were rumours of a few people having gone searching for it in other Zones, but none of them had lived to tell their story. It was a symbol of everything the Zones had been created for—the recovery of nature from humankind's abuse, with humanity not figuring in its existence at all. It would only sprout and bloom in a true wilderness where nature had found itself again.

Wilder stories claimed it was a source of a powerful new strain of antibiotics, a wonder drug that might treat cancer, and a physical manifestation of the purest spirit of nature.

"You don't believe in it?" Cove asked.

"I don't really..."

"I'll bet your mother did."

"How do you know what my mother believed in?"

"I *don't* know," he said, sighing. "I'm sorry. I didn't really know her well. I just mean she seemed the sort of person to believe. A purist."

"A hippy," Jenn said, but not bitterly.

"We might still find her."

Jenn shook her head, angry. "No. I didn't ask you about her. Don't try to switch the conversation."

"Sorry. Yeah. The ghost orchid. It's something I've dreamed of for years."

Jenn was confused. Out of everyone in the group, Cove seemed the least likely person to be seeking such a legend in these places that had become almost legendary themselves.

"Hey, I've got depths," he said, but something in the way he said it made her catch her breath. He was too forced, too light. Like he was covering something darker.

"They're just a crazy myth," she said. "Made up to make us feel like the Virgin Zones are working. No one's ever found one."

"No one who's ever owned up to it, anyway."

"You really believe that?"

He stared at her, eyes bright despite the rain. "I know that," he said. "Zona Smerti, three years ago. The northernmost part, where the snow's three metres thick and the glaciers break and crack. Mountains, valleys, places people had never visited even before it was designated a Virgin Zone. A small group infiltrated and spent four weeks there, exploring. Not like us. They were there to really find out about the Zone, not just to tick it off a list."

"That's just what we do," Jenn said.

"It's not what everyone does. This team, they knew what they were searching for, and they found it. Or found eight of them, if the stories are to be believed. In full bloom deep beneath the snow, alive and healthy."

"Until they picked them?" Jenn knew what was coming. If the ghost orchid was real, people who went looking for it would destroy it. That was the way of people, and the irony of the ghost orchid legend—a plant seeding, blooming and flourishing as a celebration of the absence of humankind would be destroyed by it.

"They tried to transplant them," he said. "But the blooms died as soon as they approached the border. Crumbled away to nothing. The cold, or being handled. Who knows." He sniffed, wiped water away from his nose. "They'd have brought half a million dollars on the collector's market."

"Money?" Jenn gasped. She looked around to make sure no one else had heard. They couldn't afford a fracture in the group, not now.

"Why not? There are loads of rumours around the plant. Cures for cancer. A new antibiotic that bugs will never adapt to. Drug companies would pay through the nose for something like that." He shrugged. "And if any of that's true, it'll help people, too. You know why I'm part of the team, Jenn. I've got no job, no home, no income, and every penny I've got is invested in this lifestyle. This is all training for me, but that doesn't mean my reasons aren't as pure as yours. I love these places and what they mean, but now I'm committed to a race that means I'll see all of them, and more. I need money for that."

"And if you do find one of these ghost orchids, you'll destroy something amazing to get it."

"That's why I was searching the bodies," he said. "I was hoping they'd already done the destroying."

"I don't mean only that," she said. "You find the orchid and manage to get it out of Eden without it dying, you might set yourself up for life, but what do you think happens next? More people come, then more. They invade Eden, rip it apart. Destroy everything that the Virgin Zones were designed for in the first place. It would be..." She shook her head, feeling close to tears. "It would be tragic."

"Maybe that's what all this death's about. You think?"

"I honestly don't know." She stared into the shadows, watching rain blown in sheets across the canyon, trees waving like slow dancers in the downpour. "Maybe it's connected in ways we don't understand yet."

"Starting to think I don't want to understand," Cove said. "I just want to get out of here. That body in the tree, I knew him. Only met him once. Guy called Pez."

"You *knew* him? Why the hell didn't you say?" Jenn felt her anger rising, but she was the last person to berate him for hiding a fact from them all.

"Because he came in looking for the orchid, too. Maybe with your mum's team, maybe not. Seeing him like that has made things feel... real."

"But you'll come back next year, for The Endless."

"Maybe," he said. Cove was usually brash, confident. She'd never heard him sounding so unsure. "Depends what happens over the next couple of days, I guess."

"We'll be fine," she said. It sounded so hollow.

They stood together for another minute or two, looking out into the darkness, the rain, the wind, and seeing shadows that moved even where there were none. Jenn thought that maybe she'd get a stick too. They had no weapons other than a few knives. If it was wolves stalking them, or wild cats, they might be able to fight them off as a group.

But she didn't think it was a wolf pack or big cats. She thought it was Eden.

KAT

Kat is on the move. She's little more than a passenger, but her senses stretch further than ever before. Not only can she see the forest passing by as she runs under the impetus of something else, but she can also feel other, stranger movements, and see other sights. One moment the trees are tall, the ground close, and she can smell the dankness of soil and feel prickly shrubs stroking her face as she darts from cover to cover. With her next breath she is floating high above the tree canopy, and as the views open out around her, she gasps at the scale, the depth of the world she is becoming part of, the clarity of vision. She slithers and runs, crawls and flies, and each sense and view offered her is different—richer colours, starker outlines, visions enhanced by smell, vague shadows given form through taste. The sensations are alien and they twist and turn her mind into baffling contortions.

Whatever has intruded into her mind—a painless invasion, startling and fascinating at the same time—is also part of the land and some of its creatures. This strange consciousness has driven her down deep, compressing everything she is into a smaller, more dense whole. It welcomes the flood of different visions, signs and senses, and revels in them. It can understand and translate input from lynx and rattler, squirrel and eagle, whereas she feels her mind filling too quickly. Overload threatens. She wishes she could shut off the information, ease back on her senses.

But she is not in charge of her eyes or mouth, nose or ears. She has no control over her arms and legs. Disassociated, she runs, but the real Kat is being carried.

She knows what she is being taken towards. It has all happened before, red and wet, and for a short while she believed that she'd escaped.

Now she knows where the people are. She knows that the ones she loves are here. She wishes she had never sent Jenn that single, loaded message, wishes she had never reconnected. She wants to scream a warning at them, but she is trapped, helpless inside the wild elemental thing that has taken her. And for a while—just a short moment, when she lets go and becomes more like it than like herself—she understands its purpose.

Then she is back, and she dreads the terrible things that are about to happen.

22

"They shot my dog. His name was Boris. He thought everyone was his friend."

*Ruth Richards discussing her family's resettlement from the
Green Valley Zone,* Eyewitness: The Virgin Zone Upheaval
in Pictures and Words, *Alaska Pacific University Press*

Pressed together in Aaron's bivvy bag, sharing warmth and comfort against the storm, the sense that they were the only place of calm in a world of thunder and chaos was strong. Wind howled along the canyon like a roar from something unseen. Trees shook in the darkness, groaning together, shedding leaves and limbs that merged with the gale. Rain sheeted through the air, caught in swirls and updraughts, impacting exposed skin like hail. Lightning strobed their surroundings, and thunder boomed in the distance. As the space between flash and crash grew closer, the wind and rain seemed to grow wilder in anticipation.

Cove still stood guard in front of their small hollow, leaning against the rock for the meagre shelter it offered. Lucy had taken up position ten metres up the canyon, huddled beneath the far end of the overhang. They were both wrapped in waterproofs and wore peaked running caps to try and keep the worst of the rain from their eyes. Like Cove, Lucy also had a heavy branch in her hand.

The rest of them were gathered around the fire to try and rest. Jenn's father and Selina were close, sharing warmth, maybe asleep. Gee sat next to the fire, tending it, stoking it with a stick and dropping on snapped logs that hissed and smoked. Jenn and Aaron were deepest in the cave, bellies warmed from the dram of whiskey they'd all drunk. The elements still found them. Jenn didn't think there was anywhere in Eden where they could hide from weather like this. It probed with stark lightning fingers, seeped itself into flesh and bones. The wind passed through her core.

She was cuddled against Aaron's back, her arm around him. He clutched her hand to his chest. She could feel the tension in his back and shoulders. She pressed closer, searching for the shape and the fit that they usually had together.

Jenn closed her eyes, convinced that sleep would not come. Her body was tired. Her muscles ached from the efforts of the last couple of days, but it was a good ache, and one that she sought most days. While tiredness from inactivity was draining, exhaustion from physical exertion was enlivening. Tonight, it was aggravated by trepidation about the next day.

"Love you," she said.

"I'll look after you." His voice was muffled by the sleeping bag pulled up over his face.

"Fuck you!" she said, nuzzling the back of his neck. "I can look after myself, thank you very much. And I'll look after you, too."

"You protect the ones you love." Aaron pulled at her hand, trying to draw her even closer. He was serious, she realised, and she thought of his nightmares and the things he had seen, the father failing to save his three children. That frightened her, and she pressed her face into his hair and breathed in his familiar scent, damp and sweet from sweating and not showering. She felt his heartbeat where he clutched her hand in both of his, holding it against his chest. They had made love on expeditions before, careful congress in a sleeping bag. It meant moving gently and keeping quiet, but that only amplified their passion. She thought about it now, how she could reach down and signal her intentions, turn around and face the back of the cave while he turned around also. A warmth tingled at her core. She smiled into his hair, and he squeezed her hand as if reading her thoughts. She tried to pull her hand away, drift it down over his chest and stomach, but he held her hand tight, preferring comfort from closeness. A heavy sigh came from him. A gentle relaxation of his body. She smiled and closed her eyes.

Lightning flashes beyond her closed eyes, diffusing a red glow across her vision. Thunder crashes in, wider than before, deeper. Jenn is on top of a hill with long, endless slopes, higher than any of the surrounding landscape. Rain hammers against her, battering into her exposed skin like ice shards blown by a vicious wind. She keeps her arms up in front of her face and peers out between them. The sky is impossibly large, great rolling thunderheads boiling all around. Clashing clouds rock the sky, cracking it open with percussive peals of thunder that she feels in her teeth and bones. Lightning sheets through and behind the clouds, superheated arcs adding brief, violet exposure to the skies and hills, the awful heights above her, the terrible depths all around. The sky crushes her down. The rain is an endless weight, so heavy and close that she can hardly breathe. She is minuscule, lost in an endless landscape that she fears she can never escape.

Something moves away from her. It's the lifting of a powerful gravity, and its movement should be a relief, but it exposes her like she never has been before.

Someone shouts. Someone else screams. It might be her voice.

Cold rushes in. She is soaked to the skin.

Jenn opened her eyes and Aaron was gone. She felt a sense of loss so profound that she cried out in despair, but the storm took her breath, and there was no one there to hear.

Stars speckled the sky and floated down all around her. One of them landed on her cheek. It burnt, and she slapped it away, suffocating the sting with rainwater.

"I hit something!" Cove shouted. "I *hit* it!"

Jenn struggled from the bivvy bag, kicking it down her legs, and stood, all the while trying to make sense of what was happening, shaking the weight of her dream aside as reality came crashing in. Dregs of it remained as the deep stormy darkness crushed in around her. She blinked, took in some deep breaths. Even through the deluge she smelled burning.

Gee was still close but he was standing now, wiping at his head. The camp fire had bloomed. Swirling sparks and embers were carried on a violent gale that swept through and around the cave.

"I'm sure I hit it!" Cove was standing close to where she'd spoken to him minutes or hours before, swinging his heavy stick back and forth at the storm. It flicked raindrops, sending them spinning and splashing like errant flames where they reflected the riotous fire.

Gee stomped on the fire, sending up more clouds of sparks that were snatched by the wind and swirled around the camp. Selina was sitting up and slapping at her sleeping bag. Jenn's father crouched against the rock, watching Cove.

"Where's Lucy?" Selina shouted.

Where's Aaron? Jenn thought. Frantic, she searched left and right, trying to see past the sparking fire and into the darkness. She tried to focus, but rain ran into her eyes, and fire seemed to float on the air, sparks and flames reflected in the chaotic deluge.

A movement to her right. Lucy backed out of the darkness towards the camp, nudging up against the rock with her stick held out before her. It seemed shorter than it had been before, its end splintered.

"Lucy!" Jenn shouted. "Where's Aaron?" She seemed not to hear.

"Felt it strike home," Cove yelled. He swung his stick again. "*Felt* it!"

"Where's Aaron?" Jenn shouted again. She turned to look down at the sleeping bag, wondering for a moment if she'd woken from her dream and failed to see him as she thrashed herself awake. *He's there staring up at me wondering what the fuck I'm doing.* Lightning flashed, revealing a snap-image of the empty bag like a wrinkled chrysalis.

Thunder cracked directly overhead, smashing down and through the canyon like a visible force. It drowned out Cove's shout, and something else. Another voice screaming in the darkness.

Jenn ran a few steps to her father. She grabbed his arms.

"Where's Aaron? What's happening?"

"Cove shouted, I woke up, I was dreaming and he woke

me up, there's something out there and he's hit it and Lucy has too." His eyes were wide, never quite settling on her.

As the thunder echoed back and forth through the canyon, fading, another voice grew from the darkness.

"Get away from here!" Aaron shouted. "Away from us!"

Jenn could see Aaron now, silhouetted intermittently by his head torch as it flitted back and forth. He was out in the canyon, away from the cave and cliff face, motionless apart from the light following his line of sight... left, right, up into the canopy of a copse of nearby trees, higher towards the canyon wall. The light made a thousand spears of rain lance towards the ground.

"Aaron!" she called.

"He shouldn't be out there!" Cove said. "He's got *nothing*, and—"

Lightning flashed in a sheet directly above the canyon, setting the storming clouds aflame. This time she was looking directly at Aaron, and for less than a second she saw him standing strong against the darkness, and beyond him a shape was frozen in mid leap, a gleaming shadow illuminated for an instant by the stark white touch of lightning. Darkness snapped in again and she took a step forward, ready to run and tackle him, push him down and away from whatever was jumping at him.

As thunder rolled, its shockwave seeming to crush her down towards the ground and split the world in two, Aaron was snatched up and away, his head torch spinning in manic arcs as his voice rose into a cry, a shout, and then a terrible high scream.

"No!" Jenn cried, but her own voice could not drown out his screams. His pain was too much, agony too piercing.

His light spun around to splash across the fire, and Gee, and directly into Jenn's face. Then above everything else she heard a crunch. His scream ended, his light extinguished.

"Aaron," Jenn called. The downpour continued, unrelenting. Gee had extinguished the fire and he stood amongst a few sizzling embers, staring not out into the night, but at Jenn. "Aaron," she called again, louder.

Cove backed beneath the overhang, stick held out before him. Dylan grabbed him by the shoulders and held him still. He faced the darkness with the staff held up, and Jenn could see it shaking in his hands. Lucy came close as well, no longer carrying her stick. Her eyes were wide and wet, and she had something dark splashed on her face. Blood, spreading in the rain.

"What happened to Aaron?" Jenn shouted.

"Taken," Cove said. "It took him."

"*What* took him?" she asked. "Cove, what the fuck—?"

"The darkness," Lucy said.

"Make sense!"

"There was something out there, in the dark, coming towards us, and when we shone lights or the lightning came it wasn't there anymore."

Bullshit! Jenn thought. *I saw it, whatever it was, and...*

And she had no idea what she had seen.

She ran.

"Jenn!" someone shouted behind her. She fumbled in her waist bag for her head torch and clicked it on, slipping it onto her forehead. She sprinted towards where she had last seen Aaron. The rain seemed almost solid, glimmering curtains in the light. Lightning flashed again, and she paused to try and make sense of her surroundings. She was out in the centre of the canyon, close to the narrow stream that trickled down towards the river. It was running fuller than it had been only hours before.

"Aaron!" she shouted into the darkness. Thunder was her

answer. She tried to forget his screams, his agony. The crunch.

"Wait!" someone shouted, and she heard footsteps following. She could not wait. Aaron was out there somewhere, and she had to help him.

The unbearable weight of rain and darkness pressed in, nightmares leaking into this waking nightmare. The world beyond her weak beam of light was infinite, and dark.

She headed downstream at a run, aware that she should be taking more care across this uneven ground.

I didn't hear his scream, she thought. *I didn't hear that crunch.* Each time she tried to convince herself, the memories of both were so close and solid that she could feel them in her ears.

"Aaron!" she tried to shout again, but her voice broke with terror. She looked for his light. She looked for him.

23

"We know they call us the Zeds, and there's an implication now carried by that word—that we're a militia, mercenaries, here more because we're trigger-happy killers than to look after the Zones. And yeah, there are some guards who are like that, unfortunately. But every one of the twenty-eight men and women I've shot dead coming out of the Plains needed killing. They were changed. Damaged. Something happens to some of the idiots who manage to infiltrate, and if they ever make it out, some of them aren't really human anymore."

Extract stolen from a Husky Plains border guard's log

Dylan had dreamed of the dead boy again. Waking to shouting and chaos, and the sense that the edges could not hold, he'd shaken off the nightmare and risen into a new one.

After Jenn ran off into the darkness and Gee sprinted after her, Dylan said, "We all go after them, *now!*" He glanced down at Cove's heavy stick. Its end was splintered and torn. "What was it?"

"Don't know," Cove said. His eyes were wide.

Selina was shrugging on her rucksack. Lucy stood close to Cove, looking around at her feet.

"Lucy!" Dylan said as he started away from the fire.

"Dropped my stick."

"Lucy, what was it?"

"Big cat. Wolf. Bear. I dunno." She was blinking rapidly, breathing hard. Terrified.

"We've got to—" Dylan began, but then something growled close by. Behind the torrential rain, a wet throat rolled like distant thunder.

Cove stepped forward, shining his light into the darkness beyond the small cave, stick held out before him.

Dylan felt afraid, but it was vague, like fear remembered. It was not immediate. All he could think of was Jenn out there in the dark storm, she and Gee running blind into dangers none of them understood.

"All of us, we go after them and stick together," Dylan said, and the four of them headed away from the camp.

The growl came closer, and only at the last second did Dylan understand that it came from above, not ahead. He stepped away from the rock face and looked up, just as a shadow fell on them. Snarling, spitting, thrashing, it knocked Lucy from her feet. She shouted and rolled, her head torch describing a full circle—ground, rock, rain-filled sky.

Cove leapt forward and swung his stick, connecting with something, jarring his arms. He grunted. Lucy stopped rolling and the shadow fell from her, giving Dylan the chance to shine his light directly at their attacker. He saw wet hair, bared teeth, eyes that reflected the light as red, piercing points.

The thing opened its mouth and roared, and then Selina heaved a rock at it. Her missile struck something soft and then the shape was gone, lost to the darkness. Dylan stepped in front of Lucy and swept his torch back and forth. He caught a glimpse of something moving away, or it might have been a shift in the falling rain as a heavy breath of wind washed down the canyon.

More lightning, this time revealing only darkness.

"What the fuck?" Cove shouted.

Dylan crouched beside Lucy but Selina was already there, checking her over for injuries. Lucy waved her arms, trying to push them aside, her eyes wide with terror. Blood flowed across her face from a gash in her forehead.

"Selina?" Dylan asked.

"Don't know," she said. "Lucy! Keep still!" Lucy calmed, breathing hard. Her head torch was smashed, and perhaps the glass had cut her.

"Just what the hell was that?" Cove asked.

"Wild dog or lynx," Dylan said, though he wasn't sure himself. He'd seen hair or fur, teeth, had heard growling. He imagined that he'd smelled the thing's breath—meaty and raw, warm with fresh blood, stale with dead things—but it might have been his own fear.

Cove helped Lucy to her feet, and she slung her arm over his shoulder and held on tight.

"Keep it away from me," she said, her voice a low growl.

"It's gone after Jenn," Dylan said. "Come on!" He led the way and the others followed. He was aware that they were leaving behind their sleeping bags and other equipment, including food and water, but Jenn was out there, somewhere in the storm, and he couldn't lose her too. Not like this, and not now.

Selina ran by his side, so close that he could hear her breathing. Cove and Lucy followed behind. He searched the darkness for Jenn's or Gee's torches, but his own light reflected back at him from the rain, pulling the night in close.

Wolf? he thought. *Lynx? Wild dog?* He didn't know. He thought it might have been something else. In Zona Smerti he and his team had fought off a wild boar, a monstrous creature that had come at them when they'd trespassed too close to its young. Vicious, huge, they'd seen it away with burning brands from their camp fire, then fled before it grew brave and returned. This was too small to be a boar, but it seemed just as dangerous.

And what the fuck could carry Aaron away like that?

"Dylan!" Selina shouted. "Ahead!"

The four of them swept their head torches up from the ground and probed the night before them. Eyes glimmered back. Deep red, hellish. Two sets, then three, at different heights and different distances.

"We've got to head back, up the canyon!" Lucy said.

"No! Jenn's that way, past them, so we've got to—"

"They'll tear us to pieces!"

The eyes vanished. Shadows darted closer, and then with a roar something leapt at them again. Dylan saw it clearer this time—a big cat with wet fur, strong limbs, its teeth catching the light and reflecting a promise of pain.

Cove drove his stick into the creature's mouth, its own momentum shoving it forward. It thrashed and fell, squirming on the ground, twisting its head and ripping the stick from Cove's hands. It slinked away, disappearing into the rain.

Another shape emerged from their right and came at Cove, knocking him over sideways. He fell, cried out, and Selina snatched up a rock and jumped across him, swinging the makeshift weapon as she went. A howl, a whine, and the creature flitted away into the night.

They heard its voice, and others joined in.

Dylan moved forward, but Lucy grabbed his arm.

"They'll attack again," she said.

"That's Jenn out there! We'll get rocks, sticks, and—"

"We can't fight those things off! Not forever."

"Why the hell are they attacking in a group?" Selina said. "They don't do that. And coming at four humans—never. We're too threatening."

"Don't feel threatening," Cove said, standing. "And don't care right now. Lucy's right."

Dylan knew that she was right, but he couldn't just leave Jenn.

"Jenn and Gee are fast," Selina said. "We'll meet up with them—"

"Aaron's out there too," Dylan said.

"I think Aaron's gone," Cove said.

"We're not turning back. We stay together, move fast, arm ourselves with rocks or sticks." They were shadows in the rain, cast by downturned head torches. They were friends, people he loved. The way for them to survive would be to stay together.

"Okay," Selina said. "But stay very close, touching distance. One stops, we all stop."

"Great," Cove said. "Dog meat."

"Head for higher ground!" Dylan shouted into the night, hoping Jenn and Gee would hear. His only answer was a growl, and then a roar.

The landscape opened up around them. When lightning crashed again in a flickering sheet, Jenn glanced to the north and saw rolling hills, and realised that she and Gee had made it out of the canyon. She'd felt a rush of relief when Gee emerged out of the darkness, but there was no sign of Aaron. The storm rumbled on, and catching that brief glimpse of the expansive land around them brought Jenn's nightmare close again, so close that she wondered whether she was still asleep. But she had never felt so cold and wet in her sleep, or so terrified.

"There!" Gee said. He grabbed her shoulder and pulled her close, so that she could see where he was pointing. His false hand gleamed in their torch light, reminding her of luminous stars she'd had on her ceiling as a child. She'd stared up at them for hours.

A light flickered in the distance. Off, on, off again. It was unmoving. It cast a glow in the rain around it but illuminated nothing.

"Aaron's torch!" she said. She started running, even though her inner voice was struggling to remind her about his screams, the crunching sound, the sight of him being lifted and lowered again, as if something big was smashing him into the ground. Gee ran with her.

A roar came from nearby, a guttural, unknowable sound.

Jenn stepped in something that sent her feet skidding out from beneath her. Even though she knew she should let her behind take the impact, instinct took over and she held out her left hand to break her fall. She hit hard, landing in something that shouldn't be warm, but was. The breath was knocked from her. She slid to a halt on her side, turning to look at what she had landed in even as a shout from Gee turned into a scream.

Their torches touched something that belonged inside a body. Her hand clawed, fingers trying to withdraw from the mess like independent creatures, and they gathered a coil of something wet and meaty against her palm. It steamed as the rain hit it.

Jenn drew in a breath to scream, smelling the insides, feeling them slick and warm against her hand, and she knew what was beneath her, under her hand and smeared across her left hip and thigh. It was Aaron.

Gee grabbed her by the arm and pulled, dragging her back and away from the mess. It caught on her clothing.

Jenn's scream emerged, but it was silent. It burned at her throat as if she were exhaling fire.

She stared at the mess around her, trying to see something she recognised and hoping she would not. There was nothing. It was insides turned out, and though she had hugged and loved this body, she should have never known these parts.

"We've got to get the fuck away!" Gee hissed into her ear, leaning down as he tried to haul her upright. "Whatever did this—"

It came out of the darkness, leaping across the bloody mess with teeth bared, limbs splayed, blood around its mouth.

Gee fell across Jenn, crushing her back to the ground as he slammed his hand forward into the creature's gaping maw. It gagged and growled, and Jenn struggled to squirm out from beneath him. She had to help.

Then she was up and running and Gee was with her, his now shortened left arm held out in front as he examined the damage. His long-sleeved running top was tattered, and the stump of his arm just beneath the elbow was scratched and dribbling blood. He barked something that might have been a laugh.

Jenn slapped at her left leg as they ran, feeling slick, sticky parts attached to her that came from the man she loved. She puked as she kept moving forward. Wiping her mouth with her sleeve, she didn't let it slow her down.

Soon the rain lessened to a fine drizzle, and their lights diffused further ahead and around them. With each breath, Jenn expected to be attacked. She jumped at every shadow that moved, strained to hear any strange noises. They ran without talking, and she followed Gee across the rough landscape, not caring where they were heading. They were back in the forest now, and the air smelled of rain.

Gee led them up a small slope and they climbed a low bluff, scrambling up the uneven rock face without pause. Adrenalin drove them. On top of the rock they rested at last, just as the cloud cover parted and low moonlight shone through.

Jenn started to shiver. She was hot, not cold. As soon as a gentle breeze hit her sweat-soaked clothing the shakes set in, but it was more than temperature. She recognised the signs of shock. Her teeth chattered, jaw vibrated, and Gee pulled her in close, sharing his body warmth.

"Gee, he was... he was..."

"I know," he said. "But we're alive, Jenn. We've got to get back to your dad and the others."

"Where? We have no idea where they are."

"We're on the ridge between canyons. We'll go up, along the high ground, see if we can meet them or see signs of them."

"But if that thing got them... if there was more than one..."

She could feel blood and other fluids drying to a stiff mess on her hands. She could smell parts of Aaron on her. The stench of a butcher's shop. She curled herself in against Gee, and they sat together in the moonlight, knowing there was little defence against anything that came at them out of the shadows.

A little while later, a splash of morning colours seeped across the eastern horizon. Mostly red.

24

Cease and desist, they told me. So I moved on, cos they don't like my podcast, don't like my roving net broadcasting. And why? Cos I'm telling the truth. I have contacts, I've seen things, I *know* things. The Zeds murder people. Not in every Zone, but most. And what confuses me the most is... why this is so difficult to believe?

@PottyBonkkers

"What the fuck would have done this?" Cove said. "Animals? Really?"

"I thought Gee put the fire out," Selina said.

"I thought so too," Dylan said.

After climbing a slope they were up on the ridge, above the small cave where they'd spent a couple of hours of that long night. Down below the camp fire raged again, and they could smell the toxic tang of artificial material on fire. Dylan agreed that none of them should go back to the camp, but Cove edged out far enough to see. Sleeping bags were blazing, rucksacks popping and spitting as gels and water containers burst inside. The smoke was rank, permeating the rain and stinging their nostrils.

Dylan's map was in his rucksack. Lucy's compass. Their water bladders, spare clothing and most of their food. Only Selina had shrugged on her pack before running, and carried the first aid bag on her belt, and her meagre supplies would not keep them going for long.

"No animal did that," Selina said.

"But it's an animal attacking us," Lucy said. "Isn't it? Just an animal."

Dylan's mind was adrift, and the more he tried grabbing hold of it, the more elusive it became. He could not concentrate on any one thing. Aaron ripped into the darkness, Jenn disappearing after him, Kat sick or dying somewhere out there, their camp attacked, those things with teeth and fur, bloody and raw. It was all too much.

"We've got to find Jenn and Gee and regroup," Dylan said. "It might be more than animals out there." The four of them huddled close, finding some comfort in each other. Dylan guessed they were all thinking the same thing—*If it's not just animals, then what or who is it?*

Now was not the time for discussion. That would come. Now was the time for survival.

The rain had eased to a light mist, and off to the east they could see the fiery smear of dawn painting the horizon. Higher points of land were catching the early morning light. Behind them, the canyon was a dark scar in the landscape. Whatever haunted that place remained unseen.

"We need something to protect ourselves," Cove said. "Then we carry on looking." At the edge of a nearby stand of trees they searched for fallen sticks and branches they might be able to use. It was still too dark to move beneath the trees; anything could have been watching them from in there. A dawn chorus of birdsong filled the air, and it sounded dismissive and indifferent, a story that would continue every day whether they survived or not. It took five minutes to arm them all.

"It's not much," Lucy said, hefting her stick.

"Mine saved us back down in the canyon," Cove said. He'd found a branch, easily two inches thick and two metres long. He'd have to use it as a staff or carry it in two hands, but it was heavy and solid.

Dylan rested his own stick over his shoulder. Its weight provided small comfort.

They headed east along the ridgeline, and every minute brought more light, pushing shadows back into the deeper places of the world, forcing them beneath rocks and into the copses of trees speckling the high ridge. To the north the whitecapped mountains were ablaze again, the snow reflecting the pinks and reds of the dawn. As though Eden was bleeding.

It had drawn blood into its soil. Aaron's scream had convinced them all of that.

Dylan blamed himself for what had happened. He was the team leader, and he had brought them here. Every decision was his, and those decisions had led them to camping in the canyon, building the fire—being attacked.

He could have taken more notice of their feelings of being watched. He should have turned around and gone back when Jenn had told him about Kat's illness, or when they'd found the first bodies. Everything about Eden had felt wrong, but he had let his eagerness to succeed, and his desire to find Kat, blind him to that.

Poke told them that Eden would chew them up and spit them out. It had taken its first bite.

"Dad!"

Dylan let out a gasp, almost a sob, when he saw Gee and Jenn running towards them. They met and he and Jenn crushed each other into a hug. He felt her terror, her loss. She was warm and shivering. He kissed the side of her face and tasted tears and blood.

"You're hurt," Lucy said, and Dylan held Jenn's shoulders and stood back, looking her up and down.

"No," Jenn said. She stared at her father. "It's not mine."

He saw the mess down her legs then. Her running tights were torn on the left side, and speckled with blood and other matter.

"Aaron's dead," Gee said.

"What happened to...?" Cove asked, nodding to his arm.

"Shoved it down the thing's throat. Don't suppose you've got a spare?"

"You saw him?" Dylan asked. "You're sure?"

Jenn only stared at him, unblinking.

"We need to get the fuck out of here, Dylan," Gee said.

"We've lost our kit," Dylan said. "The camp fire spread, burned it. We've got some food in Selina's pack, a bit of water and some purification tabs."

"Spread?" Gee asked.

"Something did it," Selina said.

"So which way?" Lucy asked.

"We lost the map, too," Dylan said. "But I think back up the ridge towards the hills, then south. It's not the way we came, so maybe that'll throw them off our scent."

"Whatever attacked us can find us whenever it wants," Selina said. "Big cat, wolf, whatever, it's faster than us, better suited to the terrain. Superior in every way."

"We've got endurance on our side," Cove said.

"Right," Gee said. "We keep running, those things get tired. Right, Selina?"

"It's true of some carnivores. They're suited for the short, sharp hunt and kill."

Her final word hung in the air. Jenn exhaled and leaned into Dylan, resting her forehead on his shoulder. He put his arm around her, wishing he could truly protect her.

"I'm so sorry," Selina whispered.

"I can't believe..." Lucy said, but she could find no adequate words. "Not Aaron." She came to them, touching the back of Jenn's neck as if to draw out the awfulness of what had happened.

"So let's go," Cove said. "All of us close together means safety in numbers. Last night they were at an advantage. In daylight we'll be more even."

"So are we just ignoring everything that's so wrong about this?" Selina asked. "The fact that animals like that don't attack groups of people? Don't burn their belongings?"

"Not ignoring it, no," Dylan said. "But it happened, and dwelling on it won't help us. We're ready now, we're sticking together." *And I've got my daughter back*, he thought. The relief was a sweet, rich thing, even though the fear remained deep, the grief over Aaron's death hot as blood. He hefted his stick. "This is what we're good at. It's thirty miles or more, but it's not even seven yet. If we pick our routes well, maybe we'll even reach the border with one good long day of running. There by nightfall."

"With no food or water," Selina said.

"We'll make do. The land provides."

"Not this land," Jenn whispered, and no one responded to that.

The idea of making thirty miles across such terrain in one day, without adequate food and with only basic equipment, was daunting. But the prospect of spending another night in Eden chilled him, and he could see the same thoughts mirrored in everyone's eyes. That, and shock at Aaron's violent death.

They had to maintain some level of hope.

Lucy remained close, hand still resting on the back of Jenn's neck, forehead resting against hers. He heard Lucy's whispers, couldn't hear what she said, didn't need to. The others watched, awkward and silent.

After a minute Jenn pulled away. She stood tall and wiped her eyes. "Come on. I'll lead us out." She started running. They all followed, and Dylan felt a rush of pride in his daughter.

"Thanks for going after them, Gee," he said as the two men ran together.

"You needed to stay with the team," Gee said. "And anyway, Jenn knows I'm tougher than you."

Dylan smiled. So did Gee.

"You thinking about having to tell Aaron's family?" Gee asked.

Dylan shook his head. "Christ, I hadn't even got to that. He has a brother back in Israel, I think. But no, I was wondering what I'd have done if Jenn..." He trailed off. Gee knew what he was talking about.

"Yeah. I'd happily have lost my other hand, both legs and my eyes, rather than lose Philip." It wasn't often Gee talked about the crash that had taken his husband and left hand a decade ago, three years before he and Dylan met. It was a private, personal tragedy, spoken occasionally, and only amongst good friends.

"Thank you, Gee," Dylan said again, and Gee grabbed his arm and squeezed; he took immense comfort from the contact.

"It must be other humans," Cove said.

"The fire?" Dylan asked.

"No animal would have done that. Took calculation, forward thinking. Whoever did it is trying to wear us down, prevent us from going on."

"And why would they do that?"

"Protecting something." Cove had slipped back to jog close to Dylan. He kept his voice low, but Dylan guessed that Selina could still hear. She was so close behind that he could hear her breathing.

"And?" Dylan asked. He could tell that Cove had more to say. He'd never class Cove as one of his closest friends, but they'd known each other for over ten years. During that time, when they were together planning or undertaking races and expeditions, Dylan had got to know him well. The big man was almost transparent.

"I've already told Jenn," he said. "I'm looking for the ghost orchid."

Dylan looked at Cove to make sure he wasn't joking. "You're shitting me."

"Why would I?"

"That's just a story."

"I don't think so."

"So what's it got to do with this? With Aaron?"

"I'm not sure," Cove said. "I just feel it does."

"You don't seem like the sort to believe in something like that."

"Maybe, maybe not. But if it does exist, it's worth a fortune."

"You want it for what it's worth?" Dylan spoke louder, and the others glanced back at them. Jenn caught his eye. She knew what they were talking about, but she didn't seem to care. He wasn't sure she cared about much right then.

"I don't care about the money," he said. "I care about what I'm doing, all this, and I want to keep doing it. The ghost orchid might be a way to enable me to do that."

"But you know it's bullshit, right?" Dylan asked. "And dangerous bullshit, at that." He glanced at Cove as they ran together. Cove looked down at the ground before them, face set. "All those stories about a wonder plant that cures cancer and makes humanity happy again. It's make-believe."

"There's got to be an element of truth," Cove said. "It's a drug, a treasure, priceless... all those stories come from somewhere. Lots of people know about it, and I think that's what's happening here. I think someone might have found it, or is close to finding it, and they're protecting their claim."

"By attacking us with rabid animals," Dylan said. "Makes sense."

"Maybe it's Eden protecting the orchid."

"Jesus, Cove."

"I don't pretend to understand—"

"Enough! Don't put any more of your bullshit between this group and its survival!" At the sound of his raised voice, they all stopped running. He faced up to Cove, inches from the taller man. "Whatever shit you believe in, you keep to yourself. Our priority is getting out of here without losing anyone else." He glanced at Jenn. She was watching, blank-faced. Her eyes were red. He thought she might still be in shock.

"I'd never put any of you in danger," Cove said. "Not for a fucking moment."

"Then focus," Dylan said. He took a step back. "We've all got to focus." It was then that he realised they were looking at him the same way they were looking at Jenn—with pity in their eyes. He had lost someone too.

Kat and her team had been taken down by whatever had attacked them. They just hadn't found her corpse.

KAT

Kat is aware of herself and her memories are intact, but her world has changed. Her old world belongs to something else, a sentience that she is growing to understand is something out of Eden. It has no real personality, nor any presence she can comprehend in any logical way.

She calls it Lilith.

Lilith walks in her body. It controls her. It holds her down without effort, containing everything she was and still is. Lilith is inhuman, and looking into its alien mind is like looking into the mind of an octopus, or a lizard, or an animal still unknown. It invites madness.

If Kat pulls back, though, and allows herself to move and flow with Lilith... then her senses are freed.

She sees through the eyes of a lynx as it scrambles up a rocky slope, its big paws padding softly from rock to rock, the view low and sharp. The lynx stops often to sniff at the ground and look up the slope, then back down the way it has come. It is cautious but confident. She sees that in the way it moves. It knows these rocks, knows this cliff, and its footing is sure.

She smells with the nose of a wolf, sitting somewhere high up and testing the air with short, deep sniffs. The blood is still obvious. Its olfactory abilities are staggering, and it sets aside the scent of blood, filtering through countless other smells—a small rodent ten metres away, the whiff of decay from somewhere to the east, a fungus releasing its spores, bark fallen from a tree, mating squirrels—as it searches for the people.

She flinches back. *It's searching for* my *people.* She wishes she could distract the wolf as it smells, the lynx as it stalks, but she has no control. That is all in Lilith's hands.

She tastes fresh meat in the mouth of an eagle, and with that meat is a hint of torn cloth and deodorant. She hears with a coyote's ears—a whispering breeze, singing birds, a soft, warning growl.

Despite all this, her history is still there. Kat retains her personality, although it is a disembodied thing now, adrift from the body she once owned. She remembers Dylan, the man she once loved. Jenn, the girl she still does.

With every part of herself, Kat wishes she could fight against Lilith as it and its animal familiars chase them down.

25

"'There're ghosts out there. Dead people walking on all-fours. Plants that'll eat you alive. That place isn't here anymore. It's gone. It's there. Leave me alone. Help me. Kill me.' The ravings of Scott Mann, who emerged from the Husky Plains on his own, naked and with severe frostbite to limbs, face and genitals. He raved for three days and nights, and then bit off and choked on his own tongue. We buried him in an unmarked grave with the rest of them."

Extract stolen from a Husky Plains border guard's log

With every step she took, Jenn wanted to turn around and run back the way they'd come. Along the ridge, down the cliff face into the canyon, across the boulder-strewn floor and between trees and bushes, over the stream, and somewhere there she would find what was left of Aaron. She would hug him to her chest, find part of him she still recognised and had kissed and loved before—an outside part, not one from inside. He had often joked that she was so much a part of him that she ran right through him, and that if she opened him up and snapped off a rib she would find herself like a name inside a stick of rock. She'd found it sweet at the time, and romantic, and endearingly weird. It wasn't sweet anymore. Eden had opened him up, and now her name was on view for all to see.

Jenn had brought him here. She had brought them all, and a sick, wretched guilt threatened to suffocate her. She strove to fight it off, because she knew guilt would distract her. Consume her. Aaron would not want her to die the way he had.

Her leg and running tights felt stiff with the hardening dregs of him. She wished she could stop and wash it off, but she also relished the touch. If she could keep his blood warm against her skin, maybe he would remain with her for a little while longer.

Knowing that she must not turn around and go back, she ran faster. Her loss was raw but numbing, and she felt shock still buffering her against the full impact of Aaron's gruesome and horrific death. Knowing that did not lessen the effect, and for that she was glad. But running so fast would get her into trouble. She needed to conserve energy, because it was going to be a long day, and they had lost a large proportion of their supplies.

They could look for berries to eat, but she was no longer sure she trusted Eden enough to consume its plants.

Behind Aaron's loss was the certainty that her mother was also dead. They had found the bodies of her team, so hers was doubtless out there too, rotting in a ravine or tangled in tree roots providing food for beetles and worms. The thought made Jenn sick, a heavy emptiness in her stomach that somehow resembled the vast depths of her nightmares. It was as if she had a black hole of grief at her core, and only running would prevent her from being sucked in and reduced to nothing.

Her mother's last words to her had been "Eden is my last", and now it felt like a curse.

"We need to ease up," Gee said gently, jogging up beside

her. If any of the others had suggested that, she'd have ignored them and sprinted on ahead. But Gee had been with her when they found what was left of Aaron. He had saved her life.

She slowed a little, catching her breath and realising how hard she'd been running. Her lungs burned and her legs ached, and with the sun rising behind them her slender shadow looked ready to snap.

The landscape here was more barren than they had seen, rocky and uneven, with signs of recent rockfalls from the steep hills ahead of them. Soon the ravine to their left ended and they crossed the stream, leaping from rock to rock and managing to keep themselves dry. On the other side her father called a halt. While Gee filled Selina's water bottles from the stream, she handed out some of her rations—a handful of nuts and an energy gel for each of them.

"Look at that," her dad said, pointing across the hillside. Jenn had assumed they were trees, but now she saw more regular spacing.

"Telegraph poles," Lucy said. "So?"

"So we follow the road. Easier going."

"What road?" Selina asked.

"It's there, even if we can't see it anymore. It'll follow the easiest route across the hills, and there'll be cuttings and bridges if the landscape gets more severe."

"Fallen bridges, maybe," Cove said.

"I'm pretty sure there's a dam up in these hills," her dad said. "It's away from the routes I'd planned, but I remember seeing it on the map. The road crosses it, and eventually winds back down towards Naxford."

Jenn listened, but she couldn't concentrate. She felt hungover, drunk, her mind a haze.

"Oh, Jesus," Lucy said. "Back there. Look."

Jenn followed Lucy's gaze back down the hillside they had just climbed. Something moved, low to the ground. It was quite a distance away, too far to make out properly, but somehow the movement seemed malevolent. It was trying to not be seen.

"Keep in close," her dad said, brandishing his stick. He'd tied the penknife he'd taken from one of the bodies to the end, two knotted shoe laces holding it tight. It was the best weapon they had. It was pitiful.

"Might be a coyote," Selina said, shielding her eyes against the low sun.

"Only one?" Cove asked.

"Don't know."

"Maybe it's still got my hand," Gee said.

They moved off, and this time Jenn hung back and ran with her father. Kicking through the damp grass and feeling morning dew soaking into her shoes, she experienced a startling flash of memory that offered a brief moment of unexpected respite—she and her father running together, hitting the trails in the Scottish mountains where they hardly ever saw anyone else. Sometimes they'd run for hours without talking, and she had never felt so comfortable with anyone else, not even Aaron. The landscape welcomed them. The air was heavy and warm, the grass whispering beneath their feet, and the wildness of the place was home.

There was nothing threatening there.

"Another one!" Gee said, pointing down the slope to their left. A series of rocky mounds gave way to a woodland a few hundred metres away, and a pale creature was bounding along just above the tree line. "Selina?"

"I don't have bionic eyes."

"No, but you're a know-it-all," Gee said.

"Wolf," Jenn said, and her blood was cold. Aaron's blood

on her leg felt warm, as if he was still there trying to protect her from the chill.

"You sure?" Lucy asked.

"It's what we saw," she said. She glanced at Gee and he looked frightened.

"Yeah," he said. "I think you're right."

"This doesn't happen," Selina said. "A coyote and a wolf hunting people, together. It doesn't happen."

"Forget about what these bastards should and shouldn't be doing," her dad said. "Everyone stay close. If they come at us, we can fend them off."

"What if there's a whole pack?" Cove asked.

Jenn didn't think there was. The creature seemed to be on its own, stalking them just like the coyote or whatever it was following from back the way they'd come.

"It's big for a wolf," Selina said.

"Great," Gee said. "Just what I needed to hear. Not just a wolf, a *giant* wolf."

"Doesn't matter," Jenn said. "We run." And she ran. The others ran with her, her father by her side, Gee edging ahead, and she felt that they were closing around her, protecting her from the landscape that had done them so much harm. Though she welcomed their closeness, they could not insulate her from the terrible truth.

They followed the telegraph poles, and once they were on the old road its route became more obvious. The tarmac was long since broken up and swallowed down, but the scattered trees were younger than those elsewhere, the going easier.

She fell into a comfortable rhythm, and where the poles remained standing she started counting, an old trick she'd learned early in her endurance running career.

Just to the next pole... just to the next pole...

It ticked away the minutes and the miles, and by the time there were no more poles—fallen away to the weather, perhaps; taken down by rot and rain and high winds—she almost failed to notice that they had vanished. Her breath came in, went out, adding to the rhythm and changing with every third footfall. More tricks, more ways to pass the time and measure the distance, and then Aaron was running with her, his own breathing falling in to match her own, and she didn't dare glance to the left in case he vanished. She heard the others around her—the impacts of their feet on the soft ground, their exhalations and grunts as they tracked across the uneven landscape—and she knew that they were real. But while she ran and felt Aaron by her side, his presence was more real than anything. There was a heavy weight in her heart, and she knew it was the wretchedness of violent, dreadful loss. She would do anything to keep it at bay for another hour, minute, or even a few seconds.

Though each footfall was different, she never set a foot wrong, although she had no awareness of paying attention to the ground around her. She flowed across the land, carried by the process of running. And still Aaron moved with her, a barely glimpsed shadow by her side that was already becoming memory.

Sometimes she sobbed, but no one stopped, and no one spoke to her. They knew where she was and what she was doing. They were protecting her by not stopping—

The wolf, the coyote, if we can outrun them—

—and she felt the closeness of her group, closer than they'd ever run together before. They were a solid unit, made more solid by the loss of one. Sometimes she even closed her eyes as she ran. Daring Eden to trip her. Tempting fate—

If we can wear them out, leave them behind—

Aaron was calling her. She continued running, feeling each

impact up through her legs and body, relishing contact with the land, even though this land could never be their own.

Jenn.

She didn't want to look. Didn't want to see that he wasn't really there.

"Jenn!"

Slowing, she looked at last. Her father was beside her, sweating, keeping pace.

"They're getting closer."

"We can outrun them."

"No, they're keeping with us."

"How far have we come?"

"Eight miles, maybe ten. And they're keeping pace."

Eight or ten miles. She didn't feel like she'd been running for more than a few minutes. It surprised her, but only at a distance. She wasn't sure she could feel anything other than a terrible, consuming numbness.

She glanced back. The coyote was out of sight behind them, but the wolf was visible down the slope to their left. It followed the edge of the forest until the trees ended, then she saw it turn and come directly for them.

"Guys," Cove said, seeing it too.

"Keep running," Selina said.

"It's faster than us," Cove said.

"If it comes in close we'll stop and go at it with the sticks."

"Sticks!" Lucy said, echoing Jenn's fear at how ineffective their weapons were. The wolf was strong, fast, with claws and teeth that could rip and tear. They had soft, exposed flesh and a few unsharpened bits of wood. Maybe they could scare it away with harsh words.

It might still have Aaron's blood and flesh around its snout and on its body, she reflected. That made them alike.

The overgrown road they still followed edged upward, the incline slight but becoming sapping after a mile or so. Jenn realised how tired she had become, and knew the others were too. They'd already been in calorie deficit before losing most of their kit and rations. Coming out of her trancelike state, realising how far they'd run, allowed in the exhaustion.

To their left the hillside dropped away towards the plains beyond, the slope uneven and scattered with boulders of all sizes, clumps of trees and folds that might hide streams leading towards clefts or canyons further down. It was perfect terrain to remain unseen, and the longer Jenn went without seeing the wolf, the more unsettled she became.

They crested a rise where the elements had scored away all evidence of the roadway. A breeze breathed in from the east, sending calming waves through long grass and setting trees swaying. Every movement caught her eye.

"There's the dam," her father said, and half a mile ahead she saw a break in the land and two stone towers. They sprouted from the head of a heavy structure, an artificial dam fording the narrow valley with a road across the top. It was not a traditional concrete dam—its front face was sloping, made from thousands of large, heavy rocks piled against the core like one face of a pyramid.

"I can't make out if it's whole," Selina said. The angle was all wrong, and it was difficult to see any damage the dam might have sustained since Eden was established.

"I don't like the look of that," Cove said. "Once on there, there's nowhere to go."

"It's that or go down into the valley," her dad said.

"Or we just head downhill now," Gee said, nodding to their left.

"Towards the wolf?" Jenn asked.

"Why not?" Gee asked, shrugging. "It comes at us, or we go at it, either way—"

The attack came from above. Jenn sensed the movement and heard a low growl as the shape dropped from a tree's low branches, landing ten feet away and leaping at them.

Cove swung his stick and connected with the animal, knocking it to the side. It landed hard, a thrashing, writhing, hissing thing.

"Lynx!" Selina said.

"Here, puss puss," Cove said. He stepped forward and prodded with the stick, and the animal batted it aside with one paw. It darted to the left faster than Cove could turn and went for his legs.

Her father thrust forward with his make-do spear, catching the lynx across the hind quarters. It yowled, spinning around and biting at the stick, and he jabbed it again.

"Form in!" Selina said, waving at them to come in close. They formed a loose circle, back to back, sticks aiming outwards. The lynx eased away and padded left and right, never taking its eyes off them.

Jenn thought it was beautiful. Grey-brown, speckled, its maned face resembled that of a domestic cat, though larger and wilder. The distinctive tufts on its ears were dark as night. There was blood dotted around its mouth. Its eyes were so intelligent, and as it paced, looking for a way past their defences, she was certain it was glancing elsewhere, as if its mind was working beyond this immediate confrontation.

She could smell it, a musky, warm scent. She thought the thing that had attacked her and Gee down in the canyon had been larger, probably the coyote creeping behind them, or even the wolf stalking up the hillside. That didn't mean the lynx wouldn't be just as dangerous if they allowed it close.

Jenn looked around, and back the way they'd come the coyote was now standing out in the open. It was maybe two hundred metres away, motionless, staring at the small group with disconcerting calm. As she watched, it jumped on the spot, rearing up on its hind legs and looking downhill.

It's looking for the wolf, she thought. *What the fuck is that all about?*

"We need to go, now!" she said. The others had also seen the coyote.

"Wolf," Selina said. "Downhill, but coming closer. Using natural cover."

"Across the dam," her father said.

"We get on there and we're trapped!" Cove said.

"We only have to defend in two directions, and we'll see them coming. If that bastard had dropped onto your head instead of next to you…" He didn't have to elaborate. The lynx had backed off a little and was licking blood from the knife wound on its rump. As it licked, it kept its eyes on them. Jenn couldn't help feeling it was sizing them up.

They skirted around the lynx and started towards the dam, following the route of the old road. Cove and Selina hung at the back, watching their footing but keeping an eye on the big cat behind them. It held back, but then started keeping pace with them thirty metres behind. It stopped and started, head cocked whenever it paused, as if listening for unheard commands. Jenn saw it sniffing at the air, too. Perhaps it was smelling its mates.

It was only as they approached the dam that they saw the damage halfway across.

"Hold here," Cove said.

"That wolf's closer," Selina said. "And it's a big one. Honestly, I'm not sure I've seen one that size before."

"That's what she said," Gee muttered, and Jenn coughed a laugh. She surprised herself by shedding a tear at the same time.

I'm fucking losing it, she thought, and thinking it made her determined not to. Aaron wouldn't want that.

"Uphill looks tough," her father said. "We could try it, but it's steep and we'll be slow, and the trees are thicker up there."

"And no way of telling how or even if we can get around the reservoir," Lucy said.

"Downhill, then," Cove said.

"Towards the wolf?" Jenn asked.

"Have you seen that?" Cove pointed along the top of the dam with his stick. The earth and rock structure was straight, not curved like a larger concrete dam, and just past the first stone tower it dropped out of sight, its surface washed away. From this angle there was no telling how extreme the damage was. Decades of leaf fall had blown along the road and settled without traffic to clear it away, and grasses, shrubs and even a few trees had taken root.

"Have you seen *that*?" Jenn said, pointing down at the wolf. She'd seen wolves before, but always at a distance, little more than shapes moving on a far-off hillside. The creature closing on them was magnificent and terrifying. A metre tall at the shoulder and over two metres long, head bigger than a person's, the dark fur along its neck and back faded to speckled auburn and grey further down its body and legs. It had one pure white flash above its left eye, which gave it an almost quizzical look.

"Heads up!" Selina shouted. Behind them, the coyote was jogging close, eyes wide and focussed on them. The red tinge around its mouth might have been natural colouring, or blood. The lynx scampered aside before the bigger animal, slinking between rocks and trees above them, coming closer. It moved in and out of view, and every moment it was out of sight Jenn expected it to leap at them from behind a rock, down from a tree, or out of a fold in the land.

The coyote slowed, then kept pace just a few metres away. It was sleek, fit, well fed. Its ears were perked up. Its gaze flickered between them and the wolf approaching from downhill.

The wolf was easily twice the size of the coyote. It sat down ten metres from the group. Jenn could smell it, like damp dog. The fur across its face and down one side of its neck was dark with blood, which made the white flash stand out even more.

"We're being herded," Lucy said.

"No way," Cove said.

The coyote came closer. The wolf stood as they moved a little downhill, and kept pace with them. They could not take on either beast with the meagre weapons they had, not even as a group. The creatures seemed confident, casual, almost laid-back in their approach.

Moving onto the dam, the reservoir level gave some indication as to how severe the damage might be. It was at least ten metres lower than the dam wall. Around the shoreline lush low growth showed where the silty bed had been exposed, allowing seedlings to take root in the fertile soil and splash an array of bright green grasses and colourful blooms, a distinct border between water and land. There were only saplings growing in these areas, which suggested that the breach had happened quite recently.

With three of them facing across the dam, and Jenn, Gee and Cove facing back the way they'd come, they moved quickly towards the area of subsidence.

26

The lynx stalked them along the low wall between road and reservoir. The coyote followed along the middle of the road. The big wolf hung back, a few metres behind the smaller canine. *Like a general conducting its troops*, Jenn thought, but that was not quite right. It was a killer sending its lesser companions to the slaughter first. Weaken the enemy, wear them down. Then lope in for the kill.

The coyote's movements became more defined, less casual. Its ears pricked up, its haunches lowered, and it tensed, coiled. It feinted left, then charged.

Cove stepped towards the attack, jabbing with his stick. Jenn swung her own and caught the animal across the head, dancing back as it turned on her and lashed out with one clawed paw. Gee darted in from the other side and drove his stick into its neck one-handed, leaning his whole weight behind the blow. But it was not sharp, and the coyote simply dropped onto its side and rolled right over, finding its feet again in moments and coming at Jenn.

She stood her ground and shouted, startling the coyote enough to freeze it for a second. That was all Cove needed. He swung his stick high over his head and brought it down on the creature's head.

It yelped and fell, scrabbling with all four legs to shove itself backwards, snapping at the weapon, grabbing its end and then twisting. Cove grunted as the stick was hauled back, and he took one step with it, holding on.

"Cove!" Jenn shouted. She could smell the coyote, wild and alert, a cloying angry stench.

Cove let go and stepped back, just as the coyote dropped the stick and came at him again. Gee prodded it in the mouth and it withdrew.

The lynx was crouched on the wall ready to leap, and Jenn ran at it, swinging her stick and screaming again. It froze, eyes darting left and right, then leapt nimbly back off the wall, out of her reach and down onto the exposed ground behind it.

"Shit!" Hidden from view, the cat was now more dangerous than ever.

"Move it!" her dad said. It was a good fifty metres to where the damage in the dam's surface began, and they covered it at a sprint, Cove and Jenn moving backwards so they could keep tabs on their attackers.

The wolf still hung back, looking from the coyote to where the lynx had been, and back again. Its obvious intelligence chilled Jenn. *It's sizing up the situation, assessing what's happened and what will come next.*

The coyote was rubbing at its ear and jaw with one paw. It shook its head and a fine spray of blood misted the air around it.

"Fuck!" Gee said. Jenn glanced back and down at the broken dam. Her chill grew cooler, crawling up her spine and into her bones, into her soul. *They pushed us this way,* she thought. *They've been cleverer than us all along.*

They were trapped.

Something had cracked the dam in half. It could only have been an earthquake. The crest had slumped, and the compacted rocks and gravel that comprised the interior layers of the structure had been washed away by the resulting flood. The deluge must have been massive, and as thousands of gallons of water roared through the rent every second, it carried away more and more. The land beyond the dam's toe was scattered with countless rocks and scored with a hundred waterways. Water still flowed from the reservoir in noisy streams over and through the tumbled rocks, ranging from the size of her fist to the bulk of a refrigerator.

The slope was not steep, but it was so treacherous that they'd never choose to descend somewhere like that. It was broken bones waiting to happen.

"We've got no choice," Selina said, voicing what they were all thinking.

"We can stay and fight them," Cove said.

"No," Jenn's father said. "Look."

The coyote was advancing again, and the wolf was following in its wake. As soon as the coyote jumped, the wolf would come at them as well.

Jenn heard a hiss from her left. The lynx was slinking around from the reservoir side, padding over the uneven rock pile with a calm confidence. *We'll stumble and slip down the slope, but they're built for this.*

"Both options are shit," she said. She didn't even wait for a reply. Stick held across her stomach—partly for balance, partly ready to strike out at anything that came at her—she left the level surface of the dam's crest and started down the disrupted slope of rock and shale, mud and flowing water.

"You and me at the back," she heard her father say to Cove. Gee came with her, close behind her left shoulder. Selina and Lucy were to her right, Lucy glancing back and forth between the dangerous ground beneath her feet and the stalking lynx. It was matching their descent just a few metres away, footfalls confident and silent, its gaze glued on them.

"It'll tense before it leaps," Selina said. "Look for its head dipping down, ears coming up."

"Then I'll stick it down the fucking throat," Lucy muttered.

"Go," Cove said, and Jenn glanced back. Her father was already moving quickly down the slope, and behind him Cove was waving at them all. "Go!"

The coyote appeared above him, just a couple of steps away. It came for them. Behind it, the larger shape of the wolf stood at the crest and watched.

Cove fell, and at first Jenn thought he'd stumbled, and feared that the beast would jump on him, pin him to the ground, do to him what had been done to Aaron.

But Cove was down on one knee, steadied against uneven rocks with his stick pointed up at the coyote. It paused and growled at him. The memory of pain gave it pause.

The lynx jumped at Lucy. She was ready, swinging her staff and striking the cat across the jaw. Its head snapped back and it fell, rolling over a couple of rocks and falling between two larger ones. It scrambled up, covered in muck and spitting blood.

"Go on!" Lucy said.

Jenn and Gee hurried onward, their footsteps cautious but firm down the rocky slope. The sound of flowing water surrounded them, and she was surprised that she'd only just noticed it. At the bottom of the wide fault in the dam, several streams foamed and surged through the tumbled rocks, while higher up—where they were, and where they had come from—she heard water flowing beneath their feet, carving routes through the fractured structure.

Cove shouted. Jenn steadied herself before looking back. He was trying to back down the uneven slope, waving the stick back and forth in front of him as the coyote advanced.

It grinned a bloody growl.

Her dad climbed back up and stood beside Cove, and the two of them shouted, repeating Jenn's scream from earlier. The animal's ears flattened against its skull and its head dipped down, reminding Jenn of a dog being told off. It dropped to its belly.

Behind it, the wolf raised its head and howled.

Jenn had heard wolves before, their calls echoing back and forth between frozen hillsides, or drifting through trees, or soaring from neighbouring valleys. There was something about the sound that gripped the deepest, most primeval part of her. A howling wolf spoke of the wildest of things, in a voice that was triumphant and free.

Louder, closer, this howl was terrifying, because it was a call to charge.

The lynx came across the rocks, the coyote stood and jumped, and behind it the wolf took a huge leap that brought it down among them.

There was no time to run. Jenn and Gee stood shoulder to shoulder, sticks raised. Selina crouched beside Cove and thrust forward with her weapon, tripping the coyote as it landed in front of Jenn's father. He struck with his impromptu spear and the animal let out a high, pained whine.

The wolf landed on Selina's other side and barrelled into her, knocking her onto her back and rolling right across her body and down the slope. It squirmed to its feet, and Jenn knew that a momentary hesitation would doom Selina to die with ripped throat and torn flesh.

Jenn and Gee attacked at the same time, Gee's branch tangling with the wolf's rear legs, Jenn's stick striking its head across the flash of white fur. The impact jarred along her arm and she hoped something had broken. As Selina rolled and stood, Jenn pulled back and struck again, but the wolf had already twisted away and turned its head. It snapped its powerful jaws down onto the end of her stick, its teeth crunched through the wood. Spittle flecked the air, and its smell was stronger than ever.

Past the wolf and slightly uphill, her father was stabbing at the coyote. It thrashed away from him, falling between rocks, barking in fear rather than fury now. Cove advanced and beat at it, taking advantage of its retreat.

"Help me!" Lucy shouted. She was on her back with her foot stuck between two rocks, and the lynx fell on her legs, slashing and hissing. She had her stick held across her stomach and pressed into the creature's throat, keeping its snapping jaws at bay while its back paws scraped across her legs, again and again. Her shouting turned into a scream.

Cove ran and jumped, dropping his stick and tangling both hands into the lynx's fur, one across its shoulder, the other grabbing at its ear and lifting its head. He propped one foot against a rock and shoved, pushing the cat from Lucy and falling across her himself. He struggled to hold onto the animal.

Jenn stepped towards the wolf, not away, and it reared back in surprise, releasing her splintered stick and allowing her to draw back and prod it in one ear. It yelped and backed away. She edged towards Cove and Lucy and swung, trying to judge distance and angle, knowing that if she was wrong she might doom at least two of her friends to a bloody death.

"Head down!" she shouted, and still gripping the lynx, Cove lowered his face into Lucy's stomach.

Jenn's stick connected with the back of the lynx's neck. It missed Cove's skull by a hand's width, and one of his hands by even less.

Stunned, the animal rolled onto its side, legs moving in the air as if dreaming of running.

Cove was on his knees beside Lucy, looking her up and down and breathing heavily. Her own stick lay across her stomach, hands clawing at the air. They were covered in blood.

Jenn stepped close beside Cove and swung again across Lucy's body, catching the lynx on the head. Again, again, and on the next hit she heard a crunching impact, and the cat's legs movements sped up. It emitted a strange, almost childlike whine, and she felt a moment of intense pity. She hated killing anything. Her mother had once told her off for squishing a fly: *That's a living thing, more amazing than anything humans have made.*

Its life or ours, she thought, and one more hard swing put the creature out of its misery. The mess splashed from its ear across damp grey rock reminded her of Aaron.

"Babe," Cove said, leaning across Lucy. His arms mimicked hers, held up and out and unable to touch anywhere. There was nowhere to touch without hurting her more.

As quickly as it had begun, the attack ended. The wolf bounded up out of the slumped area of dam, back onto the level crest. The coyote followed, limping and leaving a trail of blood. Jenn's father took a step in pursuit. His spear was snapped near the tied knife and splashed with gore, with more splattered up his arm.

"Dad," Jenn said. He turned and she caught his eye. He blinked and nodded. Chasing the wounded animal would do them no good. They had to use this opportunity to escape.

Gee and Selina faced up the slope at where the creatures had disappeared. The angle meant that they might be waiting only a few metres out of sight along the crest. Or maybe they were stalking down the front face of the dam, ready to cross onto the fallen scree and come at them from below.

Lucy groaned.

"Oh, babe!" Cove said again.

Jenn crouched beside her wounded friend, afraid of what she would see, already trying not to imagine having to carry her with them. *Please let her just be cut and grazed. Please don't let me see anything I shouldn't.* Jenn had seen enough stuff that belonged inside a body to last a lifetime.

"Don't!" Lucy shouted. Cove let go of her arm.

"You've got to get up!" he said.

She pointed at her foot where it was wedged down between two rocks. Blood welled and dribbled from a dozen cuts in her thighs and across her left knee.

Jenn saw, and squeezed her eyes shut.

"We've got to get down as fast as—" her father began.

"Dad, Lucy's leg is broken." Trapped in a space between two rocks, her foot was almost at ninety degrees to her leg. It was already swollen, skin exposed below her running tights stretched and shiny across the misshapen nub of her shattered ankle.

Her father stood over them with blood on his face. It wasn't his.

"We carry her," he said. "Down there." He pointed behind him, down at where the flood had swept across the landscape below the dam. It made sense to go down, but the terrain there was as harsh as where they were now. The going would be slow and torturous, even more so carrying Lucy. She whined with each exhalation. Jenn knew the pain must be excruciating.

"There's a building," Jenn said.

"Huh?"

"There. At the far end of the dam, at the toe." She'd only just perceived the shape, and now that she saw it, it was obvious, like an image emerging from a Rorschach painting.

"Power plant," Gee said. "It'll have been flooded."

"Part of it's standing," Selina said. She hung onto Jenn's father, one hand pressed to the back of her head. Blood dribbled down her arm.

"Somewhere to hole up," Cove said. "See to her."

"Don't you dare fucking touch me," Lucy said. "I'll rip your throat out myself." She sounded angry and afraid at the same time, because she knew what was to come.

"It's going to hurt," Cove said, leaning in close. Jenn had never heard him sound so tender. Lucy pressed her lips together, put her arms around his neck, and nodded.

It did hurt. By the time her screaming had echoed away, and Cove and Gee carried Lucy between them, she had passed out.

Jenn couldn't see the wolf or the coyote, but as they made their way down and across the detritus from the broken dam towards whatever remained of the building, she sensed eyes on them. Intelligent, scheming eyes.

27

"Total recorded worldwide statistics as follows (it has been assumed that unrecorded statistics are substantial, but no reasonable estimate is available):

Zone infiltrations (groups consisting of 3 or more individuals): 776
Infiltrators captured: 377
Known infiltrators not accounted for: 1633 (this statistic also refers to known infiltrators not caught in the months or years following infiltration of specific Zones)
Infiltrators killed (during contact with Zone Protection Forces): 1880"

Leaked document from United Zone Council
9th Annual General Meeting

It might have been easier if Lucy had died.

It was an awful thought, but Dylan couldn't shake it. He wasn't sure if it was selfish, or pitiful, or right, because his mind was still running a thousand miles per hour and everything around him seemed so distant. Each step took a minute. Each breath of breeze against his skin was a long, slow exhalation. Every time he breathed, he took in more of Eden.

Somewhere deep down was a strange sense of relief that the mounting pressure had finally blown, first with Aaron being taken, and now this latest attack. It had been coming since they had crossed the river border. He'd felt it more than the others, but for a while he'd put it down to the fact that Kat had come to Eden and was perhaps still here. A sense of foreboding, an idea that her presence was a held breath ready to release a scream. He'd been stupid. Eden didn't give a fuck about him, or her, or their human thoughts or conflicts. They were nothing more than a virus.

The others would be looking to him. For now they had a destination close by, and their blood was still up, adrenalin pumping and heightening their senses. The fight or flight instinct had drawn them towards their primeval cores, and they had both fought and flown. Taking on what Eden sent against them had brought them closer to the Zone.

Soon, though, there would be a pause. Lucy required attention, Selina had banged her head, and he noticed cuts on Gee's hand from his splintered stick. Dylan's own make-do spear was snapped, gnawed through by the beast's teeth. He could still smell its breath, meaty and rank.

With Lucy out of action, they had to pause and take stock.

Fight or flight, he thought. Now, there really was no option. To stay and attempt to fight was hopeless. They had fended off three powerful animals, but what if the next attack came from a whole pack of wolves? A family of lynx? A grizzly?

They had to get out of Eden.

They kept their wits about them, expecting the wolf and coyote to attack from a different direction. But there was no sign of them. At the toe of the ruptured dam Cove took Lucy onto his back, holding her as gently as he could. Conscious again, she cried out. Blood ran down her legs and dripped from her feet, one still wearing a trainer, the other bare and swollen. They hadn't assessed the damage properly, but Dylan thought he'd seen the pale nub of cracked bone protruding from her calf.

They crossed the flood-altered terrain. Jenn and Selina led the way, picking a route across the many streams, keeping to rocks where they could to avoid the waterlogged ground between. Further away from the dam and down the valley were places where heavy silt had been laid down and plants had flourished in the fertile ground. This close, the flood had stripped away much of the topsoil to expose the harder surfaces beneath.

Cove muttered to Lucy as he carried her, and sometimes she replied. Dylan couldn't hear what was being said, and was glad. Their stormy relationship was often on show, but such tenderness should only be between them. Events were breaking down petty tensions. What worried Dylan were the cracks he saw in Cove. He was strong, confident and full of bluff and bluster, but now his eyes were wide with watery shock.

The closer they got to the ruined building, the more Dylan realised it might offer them no shelter at all. It had once been quite large, but some of the outer walls had collapsed, most of the roof had slumped down, and three huge ducts leading from its lower edge now resembled hollow, holed bones, covered in moss and home to nesting birds and scampering lizards. They approached the ruin along a wide channel, possibly a canal formed from concrete but now smoothed over by time, its sharp edges blurred by soil and shrubs, grass and creeping plants. Birds sang at their arrival, as if celebrating what had happened.

"We'll go ahead and check," Jenn said, Selina still beside her.

"I'll go with you." Gee was flanked by the two women as they neared the fallen building. They paused, and Selina hefted a fist-sized rock. She launched it overarm and it disappeared onto the roof, clattering several times as it bounced from metal and wood. It sounded like it fell inside the structure.

Something called out, high and loud. Movement to their left startled Dylan, and he braced himself in front of Cove and Lucy, broken spear held across his chest.

Birds took wing, emerging from bushes and trees alongside one half-fallen wall and fanning out above them. A few rabbits followed. Selina and Gee threw several more rocks, and undergrowth rustled and whispered as startled animals vacated the old building.

"Now anything left in there isn't afraid of us," Selina said.

"Comforting," Gee said, and he gestured with his stump. "After you."

The first part of the ruin was open to the elements and didn't feel safe. The roof had collapsed, steel purlins rusted and slumped, and they had to negotiate a network of leaning beams, cracked concrete and fallen masonry walls. Lucy was moaning now, and once when Cove nudged her leg against a beam she cried out, a high scream that faded into a long, drawn-out groan.

"We've got to see to her," Dylan said. "Selina, Jenn, go ahead and see if there's anywhere safer and defendable. For now we'll do some first aid here." He saw the fear in everyone's features.

"Defendable," Selina said. "Right."

"Over there," Dylan said to Cove, pointing into a corner. The large room they were in might once have been an open-plan office. Some scraps of furniture remained, wood rotted away, but metal legs, chair wheels and artificial coverings were scattered around. The ceiling hung low, services spewing from broken ducts resembling the innards of some vast creature. Wires dangled, with spider webs spanning between them. Copper pipes were exposed and cracked from constant weather extremes. Plants grew from holed air-conditioning ducts like hairs on facial moles.

The corner of the room was clear. Two walls remained standing, and the ceiling was mostly whole. It had once been a corner office, but glass had been smashed from the partitions, and a once-grand oak desk was green with mould. Dylan swept his stick across the desk's surface, scattering the detritus of decades. The surface beneath was solid and whole.

Cove backed up to the desk and gently lowered Lucy's behind onto it, while Gee held her leg to make sure it didn't impact the desk's side. She was frowning, concentrating on not screaming. As Cove and Dylan held her beneath the arms and pulled her further onto the desk, Gee straightened her leg and rested it on the surface.

Lucy groaned aloud when she saw the damage. The cuts from the lynx's claws were bad and still weeping, but none of them had hit an artery. They could be bandaged and sewn if needed, and Selina had one medical pack she'd rescued from the camp. The real problem was the break in her lower leg.

"Gee," Dylan said. They all had first aid training, but with Aaron gone, Gee was the most experienced.

"Gonna need help," he said, holding up his stump.

With Cove sat on the desk nursing Lucy's head in his lap, Gee went about examining her leg. After a couple of minutes he sighed.

"Chop it off," Lucy said. She laughed, but it was pained.

"You might end up losing it," Gee said. "It's a bad break—bone's splintered and snapped in at least two places, I reckon. It hasn't quite broken the skin, but there's a lot of tissue damage and internal bleeding, swelling pretty nicely. It's lucky you didn't pop an artery."

"Yeah, I'm so lucky."

"We can splint it, but you're not walking anytime soon."

"I'll carry her," Cove said.

"We can share," Dylan said.

"No. I'll carry her."

"Fucking show-off," Lucy whispered.

Gee was still looking at her, and Dylan sensed there was more to say. "Gee?"

"Those cuts from the lynx. I'll clean them as much as I can, and cover them, but an animal's claws are hotbeds of bacteria from rotting meat, mud, shit. You'll get infected. We lost our antibiotics at the camp. Selina might know some plants we can use, but…"

"That means going out there to find them," Dylan said.

"We need to just get the fuck out of here," Lucy said. "I can get fixed up and pumped full of medicine when we're out of Eden."

"That'll take longer now," Dylan said quietly. They would move as fast as they could, which was as fast as the slowest person. Cove would carry Lucy, but he'd be going at half his normal speed, and if and when they encountered obstacles—valleys, cliffs, rivers—they'd have to negotiate each one differently.

Then there were the animals. Eden's attention had been on them since the moment they entered, but now it was focussed, concentrated. They had seen what had happened to Kat's crew. Aaron had been taken, opened up, torn to pieces in the rain and dark.

The most deadly obstacles would not be inanimate.

"We need weapons," Dylan said. "Water. Food, if we can get it. We'll rest up here, but not for long. This building's pretty extensive; we can look around for stuff we can use to protect ourselves." He looked at his sad, broken spear. The knife was thick with blood and fur.

"We need to move *now*!" Lucy said. "That wolf might come back with its friends. There might be other things."

"An hour or two," Dylan said. "Splint you, treat you. And this…" He held up the spear and pulled away the snapped top portion. It made a pretty good short sword, with the knife still firmly tied.

Jenn appeared at an opening further along the wall, pushing through a tangle of ferns. "Dad. There's stuff here we can use."

"Anywhere safer to hole up a while?"

"Yeah, back here. One of the old plant rooms, I think. Big turbine in it, and we've found a tool box, mostly rusted to hell but some of it we can salvage."

"Okay, lead the way." Gee was already supporting Lucy sitting up while Cove sat on the edge of the desk. She shuffled onto his back, hissing with pain. Gee caught Dylan's eye and they both acknowledged how tough this was going to be.

"Dad," Jenn whispered. "There's something else."

28

"The forest is my world. I understand its smells and sounds, and the ebb and flow of day and night through the trees. I know its plants and animals, its rhythms and seasons. Now I live in a building a thousand miles away. My family has a room fifteen floors above the ground. I never had a choice. And they tell us we are lucky."

Yarima talking of her resettlement from the Jaguar Zone in South America, Eyewitness: The Virgin Zone Upheaval in Pictures and Words, *Alaska Pacific University Press*

Jenn led her father to a main internal corridor where the ceiling had collapsed, the floor was rotten, and the hole spanning from wall to wall was maybe three metres across and almost the same deep. There was an old body down there. It was mostly submerged in a stinking pool, the water's surface thick with oil and filth. One arm was outstretched and resting against the wall, as if still struggling to climb out.

"We cover the hole," Jenn said. "Anything coming at us along here will fall in."

"We won't be here long enough for that."

"Maybe, maybe not," Jenn said. "She's bad, isn't she?"

"It's a bad break, and Gee says she'll get an infection."

Jenn stared down into the hole for a while, silent.

"It's not your fault."

"That's not one of Mum's team," she said, ignoring his comment.

"No, much too old."

"There's lots of death here."

"Yeah."

"We don't belong here."

"No."

"Mum..."

"I don't know," he said, "but there's nothing we can do about it. We can't go searching. We'll be lucky to get out in one piece ourselves. Something's happened here, something we don't understand."

"Eden has turned against us."

"I think it was against us from the minute we entered," he said. "It just took a while to let us know."

"Don't tell Cove," she said.

Dylan frowned. "Tell him what?"

She stared at him, then nodded down into the hole. The open roof allowed in some light, but she plucked her head torch from her belt pocket, switched it on, and pointed it down. The body's raised hand was not grabbing at the wall as he'd first thought. It was holding something up, as if to protect it from the impact as it had tumbled through the rotten flooring and into the stagnant pool below. It was a shrivelled, pale thing, slumped around the skeletal hand like a melted ice cream.

"What, you think that's...?"

"Ghost orchid."

"It's just a flower," he said.

"That body's years old. It would have rotted away to nothing by now."

"But it…" *It has rotted away*, he was going to say. Then he realised that the paleness was a bloom, milky white in the poor light. Its stem curled around and through the body's bony fingers, hand and wrist. Beneath the light, the orchid already appeared to be raising its head.

It was beautiful and mystifying, and looking at it gave Dylan a strange sensation, as if he was seeing something not meant for human eyes. He felt uncomfortable, like an intruder on a private moment. When he caught Jenn's eye, he knew that she was feeling the same.

"Don't tell Cove," she said again. "We'll cover the hole. Help me."

They found a spread of stiffened carpet in a nearby room, shifted rotten furniture from it, and by folding it in half they negotiated it through a doorway. Easing it over the hole, Dylan was relieved when the corpse and its clasped orchid were obscured from view. He kicked dust over the carpet, stood back, and wiped his hands on his shorts.

"We should block up the way we came in," he said. "Anything that comes at us along here will hopefully end up down in the pit."

Jenn stood beside him and rested her head on his shoulder. At that moment when his dear girl needed comforting and reassuring and a loving word, he couldn't think of a single thing to say that wasn't a lie.

While Gee patched the cut on Selina's scalp and then got to work on Lucy, Dylan, Jenn and Cove searched for anything they could use as weapons. There were screwdrivers in the toolbox, rusted and dulled but still strong enough. They took a hacksaw whose blade was still relatively clean, and set to work sawing copper tubing and metal struts from the turbine and associated equipment. By the time an hour had passed they had a collection of pipework, lengths of steel framing and various small tools. They went about attaching tools to the longer lengths with electrical wires stripped from the walls, fashioning a spear for each of them and some smaller, stabbing weapons.

"Can't you build us a tank?" Gee asked from where he cleaned Lucy's leg wounds.

"How about a helicopter?" Lucy asked. She was sweating, pale. She winced every time Gee touched her.

"Fridge full of beer," Cove said.

"Trust you," Lucy said. "Although, I wish we still had that whiskey."

"I'll check outside, see what's going on," Dylan said.

"Need company?" Cove asked.

Dylan shook his head. "I won't be long. For now, you make sure we can defend this place if we have to." He smiled at Jenn then left the ruined office, pushing his way through the plant-clogged doorway into the wide corridor beyond.

He liked ruined buildings. As a teen he'd been into urban exploring with friends, visiting dilapidated or forgotten structures, breaking in if necessary, then taking pictures or souvenirs to prove they'd been there. It was a dangerous pastime, with the risk of injury and arrest always overshadowing their exploits. But they'd *liked* the shadows. Risk was part of the buzz, and cuts from broken glass or chases through deserted hallways and corridors were part of the adventure.

Over time his fascination with these old places had faded, to be replaced with a love of the wild. On the surface they were very different, but Dylan understood why both such places appealed to him—there were no people there.

He moved along the main corridor, edging carefully past the carpet-covered hole. He had to hug the wall, testing his footing on decayed joist ends before stepping along, holding onto false ceiling brackets screwed into the walls. Damp plaster fell away from the fixings, the remaining floor dipped beneath his weight, and he imagined plummeting into the hole, splashing down in the stinking water next to the dead body residing there.

The building ended ten metres beyond the covered hole. Whatever cataclysm had damaged the dam might have collapsed half of the turbine station, or maybe the flood had undermined the walls and washed it away. The corridor was roofless, and where the walls and floor ended, Eden began. What was left of the power station was a small holdout of humanity, like an embassy in a hostile foreign land. Dylan paused inside the ruin, hiding behind a bank of bushes, and looked out.

The dam loomed above him to the left, its fallen section further along. He could just make out the treacherous slope they'd descended—the other side of the breach—in the distance. He could not see the dead lynx. Maybe it had been snatched away already, stored for food. That made him think of the old body in the tree, and the newer corpses of Kat's team. They looked as if they'd been fed to Eden.

What had done the feeding?

He hefted his new weapon, two lengths of copper piping wired together for strength, and topped with the knife he'd rescued from his wooden spear. It felt heavier, stronger, and he hoped he would never have to use it.

It was mid-afternoon, and the sun was behind him and

dipping to the west, casting him into shadow. The flood plain was covered with lush green trees, tumbling streams, glimmering pools. It was sobering, how something picturesque could become so dangerous. They were exhausted, injured, hungry, thirsty. The speed at which things had turned bad was shocking.

A movement caught Dylan's eye. He held his breath, ducked down, and parted bushes with the spear.

Another movement. A shape was making its way across the flood plain, dipping down into gulleys and streams, leaping over higher ground briefly before finding cover again. He squinted, trying to make out what it was. The wolf? Coyote? Maybe even a bear? He couldn't see, and as if it had sensed his eyes upon it, the shape remained out of sight. It reminded him of a soldier crossing no-man's-land, darting across exposed terrain and dropping into cover whenever it presented itself.

And then to the left, close to the toe of the dam, a dark figure appeared on top of a mound of rocks and dried mud. It was the coyote. It limped, and although Dylan couldn't make out any detail from this far away, he knew that he'd wounded it. It was a wild animal, but something about Eden had made it wilder. It followed instincts that had been deformed. Even though he couldn't make out its eyes he felt its unnatural intelligence focussed on him, burning brands he would never unfeel.

As if it knew him.

KAT

It watches, she watches. It sees the human invader, she sees the man she once loved. She is an island in a sea of strangeness, and beyond that sea—distant and hazy, like the man—is a world she once knew. The strangeness surges against her, eroding her fragile shore and reducing the space she has to survive. She knows it could sweep her away and then she would drown, opening herself to its unknown depths and, perhaps, glimpsing some of its infinite truths and mysteries before she died.

It does not do that. The threat is always there, but for some reason it leaves her intact—sentient, surrounded, and with no hope of escape.

It lets her see beyond.

She wants to call to him, warn him that this is more than he thinks and more than he can possibly understand. She has no voice. Trying to feel sorry for him, she feels a remoteness reflected in the distance around her. She struggles to retain herself. *Kat, Kat, Kat. I am Kat.*

The distant man draws closer, although he is not moving.

It is moving towards *him*. Kat tries to shout again. Concentrating, forcing herself forward as hard as she can, she imagines her mouth opening, her lungs filling, and with every shred of body and soul she has left, she calls his name.

29

"From an early stage, it was agreed that the International Virgin Zone Accord would not only be signed by sovereign states. The document amounted to over six hundred pages of content, but a more basic three-page version was sent to every household in every country involved, and everyone in those households was asked to sign, children as well as adults. Everyone—some estimates put the number of documents that were electronically signed and returned at over two billion—*everyone* was asked to take responsibility for their future. And for the planet's future. It was a statement of intent the likes of which the world has never seen. We can only hope the Earth was watching."

Common Ground, a History of the IVZA

The coyote pointed its nose at the sky and let out a shuddering howl. As the beast sprang forward and raced towards him, another movement caught Dylan's eye, from a different direction across the debris-strewn flood plain.

Wolf, he thought.

And then he turned and ran back into the ruin. It felt darker in the enclosed hallway, even though the fallen roof let in some sunlight. The walls felt closer than they had before. There was only one way for him to run, no other escape, but that was what they'd intended.

Even so, he felt the heat of breath on the nape of his neck, the boring of strange animal eyes into his back, and he smelled the meat and rot of it. The brief spell of pity he'd felt for the injured creature dissipated beneath the burgeoning fear—he was being hunted, like those prehistoric people whose memories he shared.

Skirting around parts of the fallen roof structure, jumping a pile of twisted, rusted ceiling grid and tiles, he saw the open span of the hole covered by the stiffened carpet a few metres ahead.

Behind him, something entered the building. Claws skittered on the degraded floor covering, accompanied by the soft slapping of padded feet. He had no time to turn around.

"They're coming!" he shouted, then he took in one more deep breath and leapt.

For a horrible moment he feared that he had not jumped far enough. Eyes still adjusting to the shade after staring out at the bright day, he had trouble making out where the solid floor ended and the carpet began. If he stepped on the carpet and it crumbled beneath him, he'd fall down there with the water and the corpse, and whatever else the pit contained. Things in the water. Rot and bugs. Sharp edges.

His leading foot struck solid ground and he dropped into a roll, striking the ground on his right shoulder, holding the spear away from him so that it did not snap. His head hit the wall. Pain drove through his skull, a brief, bright light that faded into dazed darkness.

"They're here!" he yelled again.

He heard the sound he had been waiting for. A crunch as the old, stiff carpet gave way. A crack, and then a high-pitched shriek as the coyote fell into the hole. A splash. Brief silence, then a long, low howl.

Footsteps approached, and he felt hands beneath his arms.

"Dad!" Jenn whispered. "Come on, up, quick!"

Quick? he thought. *Why? We got it!*

Selina and Gee appeared beside Jenn, and they pulled him up. He swayed a little, leaning against the wall for support. Then he looked back along the corridor, across the open hole, to see the coyote pacing back and forth at its far edge, looking down into the pit.

"I heard it fall," Dylan said. "It must have been the wolf! I thought the coyote was ahead of it, but—"

The coyote howled, and in the confined space it was painfully loud. It continued pacing, howl reducing to a whine, and then it looked up at them. Its ears flattened back across its head, but in fear now, not fury. It crouched and backed away.

Gee snatched up a broken ceiling tile and threw it across the pit. It struck the ground close to the coyote, and the animal skittered around, leapt over the debris in the corridor, and in seconds it was back out into the open and gone.

Water splashed out of sight, down in the hole. Deep, heavy breathing echoed from the rough walls. Snorting.

Gee approached the edge of the hole. The carpet had crumbled and fallen in, so the broken edge of the floor structure was visible.

"Careful!" Selina said. "It might be able to jump out of there."

"I think it's hurt," Gee said. "Listen."

A whine, whimpering, a wet cough.

Gee edged closer and peered down into the pit, a spear made

from a shelving strut raised in his good hand.

"Holy fucking Christ," he said.

Dylan and the others edged forward, and the four of them stood shoulder to shoulder, looking down.

At first Dylan thought he'd banged his head harder than he'd realised. He was seeing things. Seeing something he wanted to see, something he'd been searching for.

"Mum," Jenn breathed.

Kat was naked, her skin scraped and filthy, her hair knotted and tangled with twigs and leaves. She was wading back and forth, kicking the skeletal body aside, ignoring the dead. It was the living she was focussed on.

"Kat," Dylan whispered, but something was very, very wrong. Even though he had not set eyes on his wife for nine years, he knew that this was not her. She could never have changed so much—despite being sick, despite everything that might have happened to her in the meantime. She could never have become so different.

"Mum?" Jenn said again.

"That's not your mum," he said. He could not tear his eyes from the figure down in the hole. Jenn squeezed his shoulder, and he knew that she thought the same.

Kat crouched, and Dylan thought of the coyote preparing to leap. She was low to the knee-high water, legs bent and hands clawed by her sides. Beside her, the body's skull rested against her leg. Its hand still clutched a drooping orchid.

In her hair, Kat wore a similar bloom that was lush and alive.

She jumped. It was so fast that Dylan didn't have time to think. None of them did. The hole was almost three metres deep, but she made it close to the edge with one leap, reaching for Gee and Selina, grasping Selina's tee shirt and the waistband of Gee's shorts, and then she braced her feet against the edge of the pit and pushed back.

Selina fell, diving head first over Kat without a sound. Gee managed to half-turn as he overbalanced, kicking out and connecting with Kat's face, and he grabbed onto the edge of the floor. His eyes were wide, petrified. He swung into the side wall of the pit and hit hard.

Kat fell back into the hole, and she was still glaring up at Dylan and Jenn when she landed on Selina.

"No!" Dylan shouted. He crouched and grabbed Gee's stump. Jenn fell to her stomach, reached down and clasped a handful of Gee's tee shirt. As they started to pull, Selina began to scream.

Kat was up on her feet, standing astride Selina while she struggled to surface in the stinking water, lashing down with both clawed hands, again and again. The disturbed water released a stink that made Dylan gag. What he saw also made him sick. Each time Selina tried to stand, Kat stomped on her chest or head, driving her back down beneath the surface. She spat blood and water. Kat's hands scratched across her throat, her face, sometimes fists, sometimes spiked fingers. Her nails were long and sharp and they slit skin as easily as a knife.

"Pull me up!" Gee shouted. They pulled, and as he started to rise, Kat saw. She jumped again and Dylan and Jenn tugged, dragging Gee up over the edge of the pit just as Kat smashed against it. She reached for him and clawed her fingers into his lower legs, nails biting in. He shouted in pain.

Dylan let go and punched Kat in the face. She was grimacing, growling, and her eyes were not Kat's eyes. They were wide and black, the pupils dilated so much that her beautiful green irises were no more. The whites of her eyes were pink with burst vessels.

When his fist connected with her left cheek, her skin was searingly hot.

She fell back into the hole and Jenn hauled Gee away, leaving Dylan on his hands and knees looking down.

While Kat had been leaping for Gee, Selina had risen to her knees. She held both hands out in front of her, grasping at the air. Her left eyeball was pulped, blood and clear fluid leaking down her cheek. Her right eye was swollen shut and bleeding. Her mouth was open but she made no sound. Her only scream was an exhalation of blood, misting into the air as Kat splashed down beside her and started attacking again.

"We'll get you out," Dylan said, but he was frozen, unable to help, unable to flee. *I should run, I should jump in and help her, I should drive a spear through Kat, I have to jump down there and—*

"Dad!" Jenn shouted.

Dylan felt around for his dropped spear, unable to tear his eyes away. Selina's arms rose in a pathetic attempt at defence. Kat's fingers clawed into her throat and ripped it open. Blood splashed, breath hissed.

—and I have to stop Kat being this thing. His hands closed around the metal spear and it was cold against his palm.

"Dylan, we gotta fucking go!" Gee was tugging at him. Jenn stood behind him, coiled, ready to run.

"Dad! She's dead!"

Dylan took one more look down into the hole, at the woman he had loved in the past murdering the woman he was growing to love now. Kat's arms swung back and forth, and when Selina began to slump down she held her up by her ragged throat and slashed and punched with the other hand. Skin split. Bone cracked, crunched.

Dylan stood and backed away from the hole, hoping that

Selina was already dead. Hoping she did not sense him leaving her down there.

They ran. Back in the office, Cove already had Lucy up on his back, poised to flee ahead of the shouting and turmoil he'd heard. He said nothing as he jogged before them, weaving through the turbine room, kicking aside the rotting door they'd placed on its side to block the way they'd entered, and out through a fallen wall.

When the sun touched his skin, Dylan felt a flash of confusion. *It must be night. Things like this only happen at night.* He could still hear the wet, sickening impacts of Kat's fists and claws against Selina's corpse, even though that was impossible. He would always hear them. They were sounds as wretchedly familiar as the impact of a car against a child's body.

They headed away from the old power station and down the flood plain, following a water channel worn into the layers of deposited silt. Kicking through low bushes, looking for the fastest route, Cove led the way with Lucy clasping onto his back. She didn't make a sound. Her agony must have been huge, and they'd not had time to splint her leg. And now Selina was gone, Selina who had been special to Dylan, who had loved nature and animals, who had recently said, *Don't you think it's time you came to Madrid to meet my mother?* She was gone.

Dylan blinked and saw her falling into the hole, heard her splash down. He smelled her blood mixed with the rancid stench of the pit.

Now he'd have to tell Selina's mother about her death without ever having met her.

Gee was grunting with every footfall, and Dylan eased back and glanced down at the back of his friend's legs. They were torn and bleeding from where Kat's claws had dug in. His right calf was open, pink and fresh and oozing blood as his muscles warmed and his heartbeat increased. He had a pronounced limp, and however hard and gnarly he was, a torn muscle could not be fooled or ignored.

They had no time to worry about it now. They had to put distance between themselves and whatever Kat had become.

She wasn't there, Dylan thought, remembering his wife's face, her eyes. *Kat wasn't there at all.*

Running, watching his footing, he risked a glance back to make sure that Jenn was okay.

Jenn was not with them.

30

"Total recorded worldwide statistics as follows (it has been assumed that unrecorded statistics are substantial, but no reasonable estimate is available):

Zone infiltrations (groups consisting 3 or more individuals): 1543
Infiltrators captured: 744
Known infiltrators not accounted for: 3876 (this statistic also refers to known infiltrators not caught in the months or years following infiltration of specific Zones)
Infiltrators killed (during contact with Zone Protections Forces): 3066"

Leaked document from United Zone Council
22nd Annual General Meeting

Jenn left the remains of the building, started running with her father and the others, then slowed to a halt. She could not leave her. Guilt built upon guilt. She had just lost Aaron. Whatever she had become, leaving her mother would be too much.

She turned and went back into the building. It already felt

stranger, more alien, as if in the few minutes since they had left all memory of them being there had been wiped away. The power station was part of Eden. Like an old sunken wreck that becomes home to corals and crustaceans, fish and plants, the dilapidated building was merging into the land. All she heard as she stalked back through the ruin were the sounds of the wild.

Grunting and sighing. Wet sounds. If she closed her eyes they could have been sex or horror, creation or destruction.

Holding her spear, Jenn went to her knees and crawled the final few metres to the edge of the pit.

It took her several seconds to understand what she was seeing. Her naked, gore-covered mother was holding Selina's corpse against the pit's wall. Selina was clearly dead—her throat was torn out, head misshapen, clothing tattered and soaked with blood—but Kat held her almost delicately, the wet sounds coming from her own mouth as she opened and closed her lips, strings of saliva and blood stretching and popping. No real words emerged. She stood up to her knees in water now turned oily with spilled blood and body fluids. The old skeletal corpse had vanished beneath the surface.

The ghost orchid from the corpse's hand was now in Selina's hair. It no longer drooped. Lush and luminescent, it had found strange life once again.

She moved Selina back and forth, only a few inches in either direction. The wall was rough concrete, but over the years it had cracked and broken away. Behind, solid earth and rock swallowed most of the weak light filtering down into the pit.

As Jenn watched, the soil behind Selina appeared to be softening, flexing, as if her leaking blood was permeating the hard surface and breaking it down. A few crumbs dropped into the water with tiny splashes. A small stone tumbled, then a larger clump of material, striking the water's surface and breaking apart.

Her mother leaned closer to the body, the moist chattering from her lips growing more insistent. At first Jenn thought she was examining Selina's broken face, but then she realised her angle of perception was wrong, and she was actually staring at the surface beside her head.

Roots extruded from the wall. Pale white things, wormlike, barely thicker than a hair, probed out of the earth and stone and shrivelled a little in the weak sunlight. One, then three, then a dozen more, until countless small roots protruded from the dirt.

They turned towards Selina's corpse like flowers seeking sunlight.

A few heartbeats later, Jenn's mother let go of the body and stepped back. Selina remained with her back pressed against the wall, feet off the ground. A creaking sound grew, and the fresh corpse vibrated with some unseen force. Her head rested back against the earth, as if searching for sunlight with blind, dead eyes. Her heels drummed against softened soil.

She was hauled partly into the wall by roots that curled around and through her torn body.

Jenn gasped. Kat looked up at her.

I came back to kill my mother, Jenn thought, and despite the wet red horror of what lay before her, and the shock and grief at seeing what her beloved mother had become, she felt grim determination as she stood and raised the spear.

She came much faster than Jenn was prepared for, faster than was possible. One second she was half-crouched in bloodied water in front of Selina's clasped corpse. A blink later, she had scrambled up the pit wall and stood before Jenn.

"Mum!" Jenn shouted.

Her mother stank of raw neglect. Her hair was clotted, body covered in scrapes and cuts, rashes and growths. Gore from Selina glimmered all across her skin, blood and flesh. Her lips were split and bleeding, teeth pink with blood. Her eyes were red and black, no sign of those striking green irises. In that blackness Jenn saw and felt the unknowable depth of terrible, familiar nightmares. As a counterpoint to the darkness, the ghost orchid in her mother's hair was pale and alive, yet just as disconcerting.

Fear thrummed in Jenn's bones as she stepped sideways and lashed out with her spear.

Her mother knocked it to one side, tugged it from her hands and threw it over her shoulder into the pit.

"Mum," Jenn said again, injecting all the love, wretchedness and fear she felt in that moment into one single word. She had memories of this thing's hands nursing her up from terror and tucking her into their warmth, seeing away dark, heavy nightmares and guarding her against the dangers in their depths.

Kat changed. With a jerky, broken movement she froze to the spot, head tilted to one side, limbs splayed at impossible angles. Her hair hung across her face, oily and slick. From flowing and threatening, she became impossibly still, so much so that Jenn wondered if she had died.

"Mum," Jenn whispered one more time, and it was a word of strength. Summoning every ounce of strength and courage she could find, she took a step towards the bottomless blackness of those eyes. The orchid caught her attention again, plump and alive as if planted in Eden's fertile soil. It was unlike any bloom she had ever seen: full and lush, beautiful, its sheer white petals so thick and heavy that they seemed like flesh.

Her mother made a sound that did not belong to her body

as it was. Not quite a word, more of a whine, a moan, and for the briefest moment something about her changed. She slumped, the sharp angles of protruding bones smoothing as muscles relaxed and unknotted. Her shoulders dropped and fingers unclawed, drawing together, still dripping blood.

Her eyes were almost her own.

Jenn gasped as her mother looked at her. The whites of her eyes were still bloodshot, but the pupils had shrunk, and her pale green irises were those that Jenn recognised. She could not read their expression.

I came back to kill her, Jenn thought once again, and even now that seemed the most merciful act she could undertake. She had lost her spear. She had no other weapon.

Jenn heard a noise behind her and her mother glanced past her shoulder, changing in an instant back into that snarling, animalistic thing that had slaughtered Selina so horribly.

"Down!" her father said, and Jenn dropped to her knees, feeling an object hurtle past her ear. The rock struck her mother in the face, a sickening thud against her left cheek and eye socket. She growled and stumbled back, losing her footing, arms pinwheeling.

She's on the edge, Jenn thought, and everything was clear in that moment, represented by the monster and her dying mother balanced on the lip of the pit.

She fell.

As Jenn heard the splash, her father stepped past her with his spear raised in both hands, ready to leap down onto his wife and pin her to the floor.

"I saw Mum!" Jenn shouted. She grabbed her father's arm and pulled, turning him around. There was so much in those three words, and she saw in his dawning expression that he understood. His grief and rage fought his confusion and the sense of loss that had been plaguing him for years. "Let's go, Dad."

They ran, and as Jenn led the way back out through the ruined building and onto the flood plain beneath the broken dam, she was already wondering if leaving her mother alive had been a mistake.

Behind them rose a scream of anger and fury. There was nothing recognisable in the voice, but Jenn knew where it came from. Contained, blurred with echoes, it bled from the ruined building.

From further away other voices rose up. The howl of a wild dog or coyote, the call of a wolf, the roar of something else, myriad wild voices mimicking her mother's sickening song.

No, not mimicking, Jenn thought. *Replying. They're talking to each other.*

As the implications sank in, she exchanged a glance with her father as the two of them ran for their lives.

Mum killed Aaron, Jenn thought, and although she wasn't yet certain about the accuracy of that, she knew that she must have been involved. Aaron's death was so sickeningly fresh that it seemed almost surreal, a terrible nightmare, something she had yet to absorb and process. Seeing what had happened to Selina, and what her mother had become, brought it in close once again. And what relationship might exist between her mother and the animals that had attacked them? Coyote, wolf, lynx—they had been acting together. Was that terrible thing her mother had become somewhere behind them as a driving force?

After hearing their voices calling together, Jenn was convinced of that. She also had no doubt that their plight was far from over. The pain of her friends and loved ones snapped her back into the moment—Gee's cry of agony when his gashed leg twisted; Lucy's whimpering as her shattered ankle and foot bounced against Cove's thigh.

Her father, running before her with the make-do weapon in his left hand that he had almost used to kill her mother.

"I can't run for long like this," Cove said, and his admission was another shock. Jenn berated herself for hearing it as failure, but she feared what would happen to them if they stopped. *We have to keep running. We need to keep thinking until we find our way out of this.*

"Let me help," her father said, but Cove shook his head.

"I'm okay for now. Just… a bit slower."

"We'll try to get back to Naxford and hole up there," her father said. "It's seven, eight miles, I reckon." He kept glancing back the way they'd come, and she could read his face. At the moment they were not being followed. He was holding it together. She wasn't sure how long that would last. She felt her own sense of outward composure growing brittle, and it wouldn't take much for it to break. She took strength from her father, and when he glanced at her she knew that he also took strength from her. They had always been a good team. She smiled. He returned her smile. There was nothing at all to smile about, but they told each other, *It's okay, we're here together, everything will be all right.*

Gee stumbled and fell, crying out as he hit the ground. His spear skittered into a pile of rocks, throwing sparks.

Jenn crouched beside him and helped him to sit up. She grasped his arm and tugged at his tee-shirt sleeve, ripping it away with a few hard tugs. Then she shoved it over his foot and, as he bit his lip and groaned aloud, tugged it up and over his gashed calf. He was shaking, sweat beaded on his skin, and he gripped her hand hard, hauling himself back to his feet.

She felt his pain vibrating through his grip. Blood coated his right leg from knee to foot, and his left was also spattered with red. She'd seen that the wounds were bad, and the temporary bandage would do little good. They needed cleaning and binding, but not here, not now.

She glanced at Lucy's leg. It was much worse than Gee's wounds, the bone broken, skin torn, swelling stretching the remaining skin and causing the wound to pout. They'd need more than a torn sleeve to tend that.

"Selina had the last first aid kit on her belt," Gee said.

"Doesn't matter," Jenn said. "We're good at making do. Once we find shelter—"

"Shelter?" Cove asked. "Like fuck. Shelter against that? Against them?" He nodded back towards the dam spanning the valley behind them, and Jenn twisted around, afraid that Cove had seen shapes chasing them. But there was nothing. Only the ruptured dam, the fantails of flood plains and gulleys and piles of scattered rocks and lush plant growth. And hidden at the toe of the dam and smothered in undergrowth, the ruin where Selina had died.

Seeing nothing didn't mean they were not there.

"Dad's right," Jenn said. "We can get to Naxford and hole up if we have to. We'll find stuff there to use—"

"After fifty years?" Cove scoffed. "You saw that place when we came through. There's fuck all left there. Eden's taken it, eaten it and—"

"Cove!" Jenn said. She remembered her mother pressing Selina against the wall, those roots growing through and pulling her tight, hugging her into the earth, and being eaten by Eden didn't seem so ridiculous. But they had to hold it together.

"Keep chill, babe," Lucy said into his ear. Her expression of affection calmed him.

"I'm sorry," Jenn said, looking at them all, then focussing on Lucy. Her teammate's weak, pained smile gave her the courage to continue. "I'm so sorry. But I've lost Aaron, and Dad just lost Selina." Her voice grew steadier, stronger. "We've both lost my mother, and we're holding it together. You all have to hold it together too." Cove blinked and looked down at his feet. Lucy nodded.

Gee managed a smile. "We'll sort ourselves out once we're safe in Naxford. Yeah. Come on."

It felt like only an hour ago that she had slipped and fallen in Aaron's insides, spilled on the ground in the dark and the rain. It was not raining now, but it would be dark again before long.

Jenn feared what this new night would bring.

Staying closer together than ever before, the five of them made their way down the valley towards what was left of the old human town.

KAT

Trapped deep down in the body that is no longer hers, Kat is still afforded access to the senses, the experiences, and the gloriously alien thoughts of those creatures beyond. Some of them she has grown to recognise, in an instinctual sense that is strange but which she does not question. The cautious lope of the wolf. The similar, but more erratic scampering of the coyote. There had been something else but it is gone now, and she will always remember its pain—the agony of wounds being inflicted, and the desperation as it sensed death's approach. Her own death had been a full stop in her future for some time, drawing closer with each heartbeat, but this was different. Violent, unexpected, shattering. She mourned the loss, a dark place within whatever remained of her.

She scurries through low plants, seeing little but sensing everything in smells and sounds. She soars high over the landscape, letting the winds carry her as if she were little more than an errant thought. The texture of the ground below is heavy in detail, and she discerns every moving thing like a map of now and the future. Sometime soon, those she seeks will form part of this map.

She senses an intense effort on Lilith's part to control these beasts. It takes time, concentration, and it weakens with every element of control it projects outward. Its reach can only go so far. It chooses those few creatures that will fulfil its intentions most effectively—the fast, the intelligent, the vicious.

There is something else. It feels dark but its colour is red, deep red, warm tangy red. It hides beyond these sensations, a secret she probes out towards. It's a memory of something very recent, and she remembers enough of how she got here, and the wet redness that preceded her transition, to recognise what it is.

She has to know *who* it is.

Though helpless and somewhat carried away from whatever petty concerns drove her before, she cannot bear to think that she has harmed...

The one I left.

The one I gave life to.

Lilith presses back, holding her down deep and trying to prevent her from seeing and remembering what just happened. But Kat is nothing if not tenacious, and smart. She eases back beneath its pressure, allowing herself to soar with the birds and scamper with the lizards once again. When the pressure eases she pushes again, hard and fast.

She sees.

And wishes she had not. She has no eyes to close against the sight, and no mouth to rage at the terror and grief she feels. The senses that she knew, and some she did not, are overloaded with that brief, awful memory, an intense assault that threatens to shatter the tenuous hold she has on herself. She sees a face she knows coming apart beneath her clawed hands, tastes blood like toxic warmth, hears wet screams and lost shouts, smells shit and rot, feels cool and warmth, sharpness and meat. She senses frantic despair, and it reminds her of the creature's thoughts facing violent death, only this is a thousand times more intense because it acknowledges terrible, final loss as well as pain. A sickening hopelessness vies with a sense of base, primeval joy for supremacy in her mind, and the mind of Lilith, the thing carrying her. It is her hands doing the slashing and whipping and killing, but she does not drive them. She is nothing more than a witness, a mute observer.

That makes it all so much worse.

Kat believes that the elemental can't block her out completely because it needs her to persist in this body, however driven down and constrained she is. Kat is the life source. Perhaps that is why the thing fled Philippe and came to her, because Philippe gave in, died and faded away. Lilith is a parasite, its psyche encompassing hers like a blooming fungus growing around its host.

Like all parasites, it is drawing from her to survive.

31

"Creatures that have emerged from Scott Preserve have been found frozen to death in conditions much less harsh than they would have endured inside the Zone. It's as if when they leave their natural home, and enter the wider world of humankind, they lose the will to live."

Extract from National Geographic: Virgin Zones: The New World

I was going to kill her.

The thought played on a loop in his head. It was so alien that, as he ran, Dylan struggled to recall whether he had left Kat alive or had actually killed her. His reality was uncertain, unsettled by those words offering one possible past.

I was going to kill her.

The memory of what had happened to Selina was so fresh and terrible, the things he'd seen, heard and smelled at that moment confirming the sick reality. Kat had killed Selina. It seemed impossible, yet it was already a solid part of him.

I was going to kill her, but Jenn stopped me.

He imagined jumping down into the pit and driving the spear through Kat's throat. He heard the sound she would make, the feel of the rough metal piercing her skin, flesh, cartilage, and scraping and jarring against bone. He felt the blood pulsing around his hands, smelled it, tasted it misting into the air as she coughed her final few breaths.

Jenn stopped me.

He'd resolved to kill the monstrosity she had become; an act of kindness, an ultimate compassion. But Jenn had stopped him, preventing him from losing both the women he loved in one day and in one place.

Every reality about Eden was strange, and memories and events were clouded and merged.

"Kat killed Selina," he said. "That's right, isn't it? That's what happened?"

"Yeah, Dad," Jenn said, jogging close beside him. "I'm so sorry. But she wasn't really Mum when she did it. I'm sure of that."

"Maybe it's her illness," he said. "It's got into her brain."

"No, Dad."

"It's this place," Gee said. He was hobbling, wincing, no longer offering tasteless quips.

"How close are we?" Cove asked.

"I lost the map."

"Your head's a map, Dylan!" Gee said. "You spend hours reading them."

Lucy rested her cheek on Cove's shoulder, looking back at Dylan, face clouded with pain but lightened by hope. She was waiting for him to save them all, when he wasn't sure he could even save himself.

"I think we're going the right way," he said. They were back into the trees now, but the landscape was still marked by the dam burst, the forested valley floor scoured here and there from the roaring waters that had carried rocks, soil and other detritus. More established woodland was disturbed here and there by these newer areas of growth, where saplings and shrubbery smoothed the terrain and took advantage of the fertile ground.

"East has to be right," Cove said. His breathing was heavy. He used words sparingly.

"The river that passes through Naxford was in the next valley to the north," Dylan said. As they moved—their well-oiled machine, now with creaks and groans from injuries, and losses that were too awful to dwell upon—he found that concentrating on their location, and his memories of the map, helped sharpen his focus, and drew in his scattergun thoughts, fears, and memories. As the map reformed as a textured image in his mind, so reality settled around him.

"The river fed a small tributary, which fed into the reservoir behind the dam. Now that the dam's breached I guess the small streams through here have rejoined the river at some point south and east. Follow them, and we'll either come to the river that passes through Naxford, or find the town itself."

"And then what?" Lucy asked. Her voice sounded too composed, almost flat.

"And then we decide what's best," Dylan said. He was already thinking ahead, expanding the map in his mind to plot out their easiest route out of Eden. In theory, the simplest way would be to follow the route they'd taken in. But that was a dozen more miles across tough terrain, in the dark with a river crossing, and with injuries slowing them down.

Slowly, another plan was presenting itself.

"We should spend the night there," Jenn said. "Take stock of what we have between us—"

"Fuck all!" Gee said. "I got a water bottle, but it's empty. Food? Kit? Anything else?"

"Jenn's right," Dylan said. "Naxford. That's where we'll make plans."

"Or make our stand," Cove said.

The words hung in the air, a promise of more grief to come.

Dylan led the way, and his memory proved accurate. A couple of times he thought he saw movement through the trees, and his heart started hammering as he imagined Kat coming at them, naked and covered in blood and screaming in a voice that was not hers. But nothing came for them. Once, Gee said he saw the wolf stalking across the hillside. But the trees were growing thicker, and if he did see movement that far away, it could have been anything.

One step at a time, Dylan thought, and the flash of memory that phrase inspired brought a tear to his eye, a smile to his lips. Kat had said it to him many years before, when she discovered she was pregnant with Jenn. They'd gone on a long hiking holiday together, travelling through the Peak District in England, staying at small guest houses and walking fifteen miles each day. It was their way of having some private time to come to terms with looming parenthood. It had not been planned, but neither of them had ever called it a mistake. It was a natural result of their love and marriage, and while they'd not consciously started trying for a baby, they agreed that it was something they both wanted.

On that hiking holiday, Dylan had started talking about how being parents would change their lives. In truth, he was worrying about how it would affect what they both loved doing, where they would live, how they'd make ends meet, and a dozen other concerns that expanded the more he thought about them.

One step at a time, Kat had said to him one evening. It was a phrase she'd used before, when they'd faced a particularly steep and treacherous ascent in Patagonia and one of their team had despaired of ever reaching the top.

She'd been right. Rather than doomsdaying ahead about how much a child would change their lives, they had lived day by day, tackling the mountain of parenthood and succeeding.

Until she left. Perhaps that had been her own personal summit.

Guilt prodded at him for thinking of those old memories, but his newest memories were too bad. They would hobble him. If he dwelled on Selina too much, and for too long, he might not be able to take one more step.

"Wolf," Jenn said.

They were climbing out of the valley, heading up a steady incline of loose rocks and small trees towards a ridge from where he hoped they would look down upon the river.

"Where?" Gee asked.

"Above and ahead."

She was right. The creature's silhouette stood out against the late afternoon sky, sharp and familiar.

"Just one," Dylan said.

"Same one?" Cove asked, but none of them replied. It would be impossible to tell one wolf from another, especially at that distance. And of course it was the same one.

They switched direction and headed across the hillside. The creature kept pace with them; Dylan thought it was limping, but he wasn't sure.

"How do we get over the hill with that thing up there?" Jenn asked.

The wolf had vanished.

"Preferred when I could see it," Cove said.

"Could be coming down towards us, hidden by trees or behind folds in the land," Gee said.

"Could be anywhere," Dylan said. "We take control. Uphill again." He grasped his metal spear so tight that his hand hurt. *We'll go through it*, he thought. *Through anything that tries to stop us.*

He blinked and imagined Kat coming at them through the trees, bloody and horrific. The wolf, coyote and lynx might even have been acting with her. That seemed impossible, yet after the howls and roars he'd heard in response to her scream, he couldn't help believing it. Kat had become something else, and however much Jenn was sure she'd seen her mother in that creature's eyes, Dylan had seen only something that had torn Selina to pieces.

I can't fall apart now. I won't. Selina won't let me.

"I'll feel safer when we get to Naxford," Gee said. Dylan remembered the fallen buildings smothered with plant growth and overtaken by trees, the roads vanished over time, the cranes at the river, every sign that humanity was gone and nature had taken that place for its own. He looked around for the wolf, and instead saw a bird of prey circling high above, a colourful lizard skittering across a nearby rock, spiders nestled in the centre of webs caught in low sunlight. He wondered which creatures were mere observers, and which were antagonistic, siding with the wolf and coyote, and with Kat.

It could be that they were already doomed, and their attackers were toying with them before rushing in for the kill. A glimpse of wolf here, a coyote's bloody trail, a call from the trees. A sliver of hope given and then snatched away again. None of them knew the nature or extent of the threat facing them, but two dead people in the space of twelve hours indicated how serious it was.

Dylan's idea was forming with every step they took. It relied on chance and a good deal of luck, but looking at Gee's torn legs and Lucy's flapping, broken foot, he knew that pure luck might create their only escape from this place.

"It's not Naxford we need," he said. "It's the river."

32

"They tell you about the generous resettlement fee. We spent that in two years, then we started struggling because in that time only my wife managed to get a new job. They talk about the sensitive way in which our belongings were transported, the reintegration efforts for our children in new schools and new communities, and how each family was assigned a support officer from the UZC. What you won't hear them discussing are the suicides. The mental health issues experienced by many of those uprooted. The abuse suffered by some of the orphaned kids fast-tracked into new foster homes. Uncomfortable truths aren't called truths at all."

Bradley Leonetti, resettled from the northern extreme of the
Eden Zone, Eyewitness: The Virgin Zone Upheaval in
Pictures and Words, Alaska Pacific University Press

They moved along the hillside, having to stop every half an hour to rest. They were thirsty but had no water except what they could drink from the occasional stream; hungry but had only a few energy gels between them. But with a destination in mind, the miles moved past, slowly, too slowly.

After several offers, Dylan took Lucy from Cove's back onto his own. He was fifteen years older than Cove and fifteen pounds heavier, but Lucy was light, and Dylan prided himself on his levels of endurance. He was afraid that if they kept following this valley they might miss the town altogether, and then they'd cross the route they'd taken into Eden only a few days before. That might put them within a dozen miles of the border, but it might as well be two hundred miles.

Dylan was starting to doubt his memories of the map, but he didn't want to voice that to the whole group.

"We going the right way?" he said to Lucy in a low voice.

"Think so," she said. "Feels right." She was the best navigator among them. "South-west, then south as soon as we can."

"Yeah, that's my thinking."

"I'm sorry," Lucy said, but Dylan wasn't sure what she was sorry for, and he didn't want to ask. There were too many possibilities, and he had to keep focussed.

Leading the small group, he switched direction slightly and started following a narrow gulley up the hillside. He kept out of the gulley, not wanting to be trapped inside it, and made high ground wherever he could, using elevated positions to keep watch around them. It was all but impossible. Trees and wrinkles in the landscape obstructed their view. The slopes were fractured and broken, and most of the time creatures could be hiding thirty steps away without them knowing.

With both arms supporting Lucy's legs, he kept the metal spear nursed across his stomach.

Gee was starting to really struggle. He didn't complain, but Dylan knew him well enough to recognise the fact. He was quieter, face more determined, and sweating from pain and exertion. His right trainer and sock were soaked with blood, and made a squelching noise with every step he took. Even wrapped in the shirtsleeve, his wounds were wet, torn muscle and flesh attracting flies and infection.

My wife did that, Dylan thought. He remembered her painting her nails one day when they went to a posh wedding, frustrated when it went wrong because she hardly ever did it. Three weeks later she'd ripped one clean off on the lower slopes of Mont Blanc, shaking her hand and signing the snow with her blood.

When they reached the hilltop, Gee with one arm flung over Jenn's shoulder, they carried on past a rocky outcropping and looked down into the next valley. The sight came as a relief. The river snaked along the next wide, shallow valley, and nestled a couple of miles to the east was the dark stain of Naxford. Dylan could just make out the cranes hanging out over the river, and the slightly different shade of foliage that had made the abandoned town its own.

"Home sweet home," Gee said, and Dylan was glad to hear a quip from him.

"It might be safer, but not safe," Jenn said.

"If they even let us get there," Cove said. He nodded along the hillside. The wolf emerged from beneath a copse of trees, its shadow long. Back the way they'd climbed, the coyote was making a careful ascent. If they could see it, it could surely see them, but it sniffed at the ground as it came, scenting Gee's blood, their fear.

The bird of prey Dylan had seen circling was lower now, making graceful swoops across the hilltop, a pale grey and white flash. It was huge.

"Harpy eagle," Lucy said. "Beautiful."

It came lower and lower with each pass, barely moving its wings, silent and powerful.

"I think we should—" Jenn said, and the bird called out and

dropped towards them, claws extended.

"Down!" Dylan shouted. They dropped, and Dylan made sure he hit the ground on his side so that Lucy's bad foot was not crushed beneath him. Still she grunted in pain.

Jenn knelt, snatched Dylan's spear from his hands and held it in front of her. As the bird spiralled up and then fell towards them again, she prodded outwards with the spear. The eagle plucked it from her hands and flew past them, dropping the weapon before drifting out over the valley. Dylan was hypnotised by its size, beauty and the power it radiated, such a magnificent beast snatching away several pounds of metal as if it were a stick.

"Fuck," Jenn muttered, and when he sat up beside Lucy, he saw his daughter looking down at her hands. Blood pooled in her palm and dripped to the ground; having the makeshift spear ripped from her grasp had slashed her left hand across the fingers.

"It's coming round again!" Cove said. He stood and edged in front of them all, gripping his own spear and facing it at the eagle. It flapped its wings twice and came at them from out over the valley, head lowered, claws hanging beneath its body, ready to stretch out at the last moment.

"Swing it like a club!" Lucy said, and Cove did not hesitate. He crouched down and lowered the spear, then swung it up and out as the eagle came close. His timing was off, but the bird's claws closed on nothing, and it spun and flapped away with a loud call.

"Let's go," Dylan said. He knew Jenn was in pain, but they didn't have time to address it now.

"Wolf's closing in," Gee said.

"Keep close together," Dylan said. He dashed to the dropped spear and snatched it up. Cove and Gee were still carrying makeshift weapons, and Cove handed Jenn an old screwdriver wired to a shorter length of wood. Gee could hardly walk, Lucy was pale and sweating, and Jenn held her bleeding hand to her stomach, blood soaking into her top. They were hardly a fighting band. "We'll hold them off as we're going downhill. Once in Naxford we'll find somewhere to hole up; an old building, walls, maybe doorways we can block."

"And then the river," Cove said.

"I'm thinking there'll be a paddleboat with a bar, casino and some good Cajun food," Gee said.

"Yacht," Lucy said. "Jacuzzi on deck. Champagne."

"Let's go," Dylan said again. He knew that the chances of finding a boat still afloat and seaworthy were minuscule, but that was a problem for later. Measuring day by day, hour by hour, was long in the past. Their future was minute by minute.

They started off down the hillside towards Naxford, and whatever tenuous safety that old settlement might offer.

33

"Total recorded worldwide statistics as follows (it has been assumed that unrecorded statistics are substantial, but no reasonable estimate is available):

Zone infiltrations (groups consisting 3 or more individuals): unknown
Infiltrators captured: 434
Known infiltrators not accounted for: unknown (this statistic also refers to known infiltrators not caught in the months or years following infiltration of specific Zones)
Infiltrators killed (during contact with Zone Protection Forces): unknown"

Leaked document from United Zone Council
43rd Annual General Meeting

It was as if whilst trying to kill them, Eden also wanted to hold them close.

"Cove, no."

"But you can see them, Jenn!"

"Up a cliff."

"I've climbed harder faces in my sleep."

"With a fucking huge eagle trying to attack you?"

"You'll be on your own," her father said to him. "We won't wait for you."

"I can't believe you. Any of you. Do you know what that is, what it might be?"

"It might be the reason all this is happening," Lucy said. "It's not ours, babe."

A day ago the idea that Eden might have turned against them because of a flower would have been preposterous. Now, Jenn wasn't so sure.

"You'll die," Jenn said.

"That a threat?" Cove asked, voice raised. The words were bullish, but she could see that they merely hid his own doubts and fears.

It was Gee who'd seen the speckling of ghost orchids across a rocky bluff as they descended the valley. If he'd been quiet no one else might have noticed them, but Jenn could not blame him for his gasp of wonder. The blooms were of the purest white, like fresh snow, and even from this distance there was a life and vitality to them exuded by no other plant they'd seen in Eden. There were maybe two dozen individual plants, sprouting in cracks and holes twenty metres up the sheer rock face. An easy climb for Cove.

"Of course it's not a threat," Jenn said. "It's something none of us wants to happen, Cove. You're my friend." She thought of so much else to say—*Don't be greedy, don't be stupid, don't be blind to everything that's happened.* She could already see that Cove knew the truth, but she wondered if this was the point where their team came apart.

It was Lucy who brought him back.

"You can't leave me again," she said.

Cove crumbled. He held out his arms and took Lucy back from Jenn's father, and together they continued on down the hillside.

Jenn did glance back, just once. The ghost orchids were hypnotic in their simple beauty, and everything they might mean and promise. They were proud and brash, so solid in their presence, as if Eden grew from them rather than the other way around. She wasn't sure she would ever see anything so beautiful again, and that more than anything was reason to leave them behind.

That, and the eagle perched on the ridge high above the orchids. It stared down at her, head dipped as if ready to swoop from the cliff at any moment.

Her hand throbbed where she held it pressed to her stomach. It was a centre of pain, the burning heart of her concentration. She'd taken a quick look and seen the severe gash across the base of her fingers, skin pouting, flesh dark pink, blood seeping. The bird seemed to sense her weakness. It called out, and she turned away and followed the others.

She imagined the patterns her blood would make spattered across those perfect white blooms.

The wolf howled behind them, a glorious exhalation of the wilderness that now only meant danger. The coyote trotted downhill from them, keeping pace but coming no closer. It was limping, but its ears were still perky, as if listening to commands they could not hear. The eagle drifted down several times, its claws extended, but Cove's attempts to knock it out of the sky with his spear were fruitless. It flapped by just out of reach.

Although Naxford had been her father's idea, Jenn now felt that they were being herded that way. She wracked her brains for other alternatives.

"Dad," she said, and he nodded.

"I know. But I don't know what else to do."

"Hit the river somewhere else," Cove said. "Go against the animals, not with them. Fight our way past the coyote and find the river further east, past the town."

"And then what?" Lucy asked. "Make a raft out of your trainers?"

"We can build one," he mumbled.

"We've got no tools," Lucy said. "No rope or axes, only a couple of crappy knives and a few rusty screwdrivers. And no time."

"Then we can float downriver on logs," he said.

"It's miles to the sea," Jenn's dad said. "And there could be anything in that river."

"It has to be the town," Jenn said. "But it doesn't have to be on their terms."

"What do you mean?" her father asked.

"I'm the fastest runner here," she said.

"No way." He shook his head.

"Dad, it's a couple of miles away. I can get there first, find somewhere safe, guide you in."

"But… if your mother appears," Gee said.

"I don't think she'll hurt me." Even as she said it, she wasn't sure. She might have seen something of her mother in that mad thing's eyes, but her father had arrived, and there was no telling how events might have gone if he hadn't launched a rock into her face.

"She killed Selina," her dad said. "And somehow, maybe Aaron too. I can't let you—"

"I'm not asking you to let me." Jenn snatched the spear from Gee's hand, lobbed him her shorter weapon, and started running.

"Jenn, please don't! I can't lose you too!" Her father's words cut into her, more painful than the wound across her fingers, but Jenn would not stop now. She still felt responsible for bringing them here. No one had forced any of them to come, because Eden had been on their minds for years. But the seed of this expedition had been planted by her, all because of that message from her mother. She was scared, but also felt that she had to do something other than simply go along with the group, letting the animals—and her mother—corral them towards whatever awaited them in Naxford. She had to take control.

She put her foot on the gas and sprinted for three minutes, leaping rocks and holes and tucking the spear beneath her arm so that her technique was not too compromised. If her father was coming after her she'd already be putting distance between them, but she didn't think he would. He led this expedition, and he'd stay with his injured teammates, aware that he could not catch up to her, knowing too that she had made up her mind.

Stupid decision or not, she was stuck with it now.

Heathers gave way to grassland on the valley floor, with copses of trees and a network of small streams to ford or leap. Birds took frightened flight from undergrowth like seeds cast to the breeze, their startled singing filling the air. Though scared, Jenn also felt an exuberant release at running so fast on her own. It was something she'd felt a hundred times before, but now—with pain scorching her hand, grief burning her heart, and fear setting the world around her aflame with the promise of unseen dangers—it meant so much more. She leapt a stream. Landing on the other side something tripped her and she went sprawling, releasing the spear and landing on her good arm. She managed to hold her injured hand up to prevent more damage, and the jolt gave her a brief, shocking image of ants swarming across her cut hand and into her wound, beetles clawing the skin wider to reach her meat, millipedes supping her blood. She stood and picked up the spear, and saw what had tripped her.

A length of rusted wire wound between two concrete posts. The wire was curled with delicate green creepers along most of its length, the posts cracked and crumbled. She was closing on Naxford.

Moving again, she thought back to that moment beside the pit. The blood-filled, horror-filled pit, where her father's lover lay dead by her mother's hands. And in her mind's eye she tried to recall the flash of clarity and recognition she'd seen in her mother's face. It was the fleeting memory of a dream.

I'm betting my life on that, she thought, and something moved ahead and to her left. A patch of ground seemed to shift; she saw the shadow, and she knew that this time the eagle was dropping in for the kill, claws extended and held forward, the nape of her neck exposed, and she had to wonder whether she had made an awful mistake.

Jenn fell forward, and at the same moment she swung the spear ahead and then back over her head, using its weight to give it momentum and keeping hold of one end. She felt the impact and heard a loud cry, and then she rolled to her right, taking the spear with her. With a flurry of huge wings the eagle rolled across her and thrashed into a copse of ferns and brambles. One wing lashed at the plants. Dust filled the air from its feathers, and a smell like burnt orange, sour and old. It turned to face her, and on the ground the creature was even larger than in the air, a metre tall and with a wingspan of almost three metres.

It screeched, head lowered and hooked beak aiming at her. The feathers behind its head stood up like a huge splayed hand. It flapped one wing, and Jenn made it up onto her left knee, crying out when she grabbed the spear with both hands, trying to bring it up and forward to defend herself against the vicious, beautiful bird.

The harpy eagle jerked around in a quarter-circle. It paused, lifted its other wing, and Jenn saw the damage. The wing was wounded, perhaps broken. There was a vivid flash of blood on light grey feathers, and a dozen large feathers littered the ground where it had fallen.

"Got you," she said, and the bird's reply was another loud call. It jumped at her and Jenn rolled, kicking out with one foot and connecting with the bird's raised right claw. It was larger than her foot, talons two inches long, and she kicked five times, six, before scrabbling away and finding her feet.

Even standing she felt dwarfed by the bird. It was beautiful, regal, terrifying, defiant with its injury. It came for her again.

Ignoring the agony in her hand, Jenn gripped the spear in both hands and swung it high over her head. The eagle saw the metal falling towards it and looked up, and in that last second Jenn agonised over what she was doing. But though killing something wonderful, she was also sending a signal to whatever sought to destroy her and her friends.

The spear struck the eagle's head and it went down. Jenn heard and felt the soft crack of its delicate skull giving way. It hit the ground on its front and its wings flapped, broken wing as well as the good one. One claw scraped at the ground as if still trying to haul itself towards her. One eye was gone, pulped along with that side of its head. The other fixed on her.

She stared into the dying bird's eye. She sobbed, one heavy exhalation of grief at what she had done.

A final strike from the spear put the magnificent creature out of its misery.

Panting, Jenn backed away. She felt a mixture of shame at killing such a beast, and relief. *I was protecting myself. It tried to kill me. I saved myself.*

Even so, the land around her suddenly seemed even more

threatening than before. It grew quieter, more dangerous, as if holding a breath in shock at the travesty she had perpetrated with the eagle, and the lynx she had killed so recently. She imagined the eagle as a king in this land, and the lynx one of its subjects. It was a servant to the land also, guided by Eden and now sent to its death. She had never killed such wonderful animals, and no part of her had ever wanted to. Fish and rabbits and grubs for food, yes, but never anything so beautiful, so graceful.

Confused by her feelings, Jenn gripped the spear, pressed her wounded hand to her stomach once more, and set out for Naxford. The riverside cranes were just visible across the rolling landscape. She had made her choice, and now she had to see those actions through.

Heart still pounding from the kill, she glanced around her as she ran. She felt alert and attuned to danger, the adrenalin pulsing through her heightening her senses, slowing the world down so that she could discern the threats closing in all around her.

The shape she saw, the shadow, might have been from another world.

Mum! she thought, but it was not her mother. It was too large, too deep and black. Deeper than her worst nightmare. It stood uphill from her, regal and utterly motionless. Even so she knew that it was something alive. She was the subject of its regard, and her skin crawled as if it were already drawing its claws across her.

It was the largest bear she had ever seen. Standing on its hind legs, its three-metre frame silhouetted against the sky, it watched her run towards the town. It might have been a sculpture placed there by Eden, a guard intended to view the wide, wild landscape.

But it had not been there a few moments before.

Jenn did not pause. The bear remained standing, watching her go, and it was only when she glanced back the third time that she saw it drop onto all fours and come for her.

As she approached Naxford, the wolf raised its voice far behind her, and in its howl she imagined she heard her name.

34

"Yeah, I went into four Zones. No, I was never caught. No, I'm never going into one again. Why? Cos they're unnatural. And that's all I'm saying on the matter. Unnatural."

Patrick Slater (pseudonym), British extreme sports enthusiast

Until recently, the worst moment in Dylan's life had been when Kat left him. He'd been aware of the growing distance between them, but had still been shocked when she'd left. It was an absence that had marked a period of loneliness in his life. Her lack of communication ever since had made his memory of that time even worse. He had grieved over her as he would for someone who had died, and in the same way his world had adapted and changed to fit around that loss. He had always told her that his world had never been the same since his parents had passed away. Kat leaving had effected a similar change.

He'd done his best to move on, but everything was different.

Now his life was changing again, scarred by terrible events. Aaron's death had been devastating. Witnessing his wife slaughtering Selina, the woman he had been growing to love, was even worse.

Watching as Jenn ran away from him hurt almost as much. Every shred of him had demanded he run after her. She was the best thing in his world, and the idea that this would be his last sight of her was unbearable. But Dylan was analytical; he followed reason and logic above desire and emotion.

That was why he had not run after Jenn. First, he knew that she was right: she was the fastest among them. He would never catch her. Also, the others needed him, and if he abandoned them they might well die. As team leader, he already bore the weight of Aaron's and Selina's deaths on his conscience. He would not be able to weather any more.

He had to trust Jenn to keep herself alive. He had to believe that he would see her again. No other outcome was thinkable. Every step he took towards Naxford, every breath of Eden's pristine, alien air, was a step towards their reunion.

"Wolf, above us again," Gee said. Grasping Jenn's short screwdriver weapon, he swung his arms as he moved, endeavouring to put less weight on his most severely injured leg.

"I see him," Dylan said. "Cove, you okay?"

"I'm good."

"Why not ask if I'm okay?" Lucy asked.

"'Cause you're sitting there looking pretty while I carry you," Cove said. "Go to sleep. Have a rest."

"Condescending shit."

"There," Dylan said, pointing down a slope towards a woodland filling a small depression in the land. Beyond, he hoped they would find themselves on the approach into Naxford. There was no sign that Jenn had come this way. She had only left them ten minutes before, but already it felt like she had never been here at all.

They headed down the slope, Cove and Lucy in the lead. Gee gasped with every step. Whenever Dylan caught a glimpse of the back of his legs, he saw fresh blood leaking around the makeshift bandage Jenn had put in place. There was no way he should still be on his feet. Sheer bloody determination kept him going, because the alternative did not bear thinking about.

The wolf kept level up the slope from them, moving fluidly, one moment visible, the next disappearing behind a rocky outcropping or stand of trees or undergrowth. It was watching them. The white streak on its head was a raised eyebrow saying, *I have you already, I'm just playing with you.* Dylan felt his gaze locking with the wolf's. It bore a terrible intelligence.

As they entered the woodland, the coyote sprang at them from shadows beneath the trees.

Cove staggered and lashed out with his spear, catching the creature with a clumsy blow across its flank.

Dylan went to leap in front of Gee, bringing his spear up to protect himself, but the animal was faster. It ducked beneath the spear and barrelled into him, taking his legs out, growling, biting at his left leg, but missing as Dylan twisted in the air and hit the ground hard. The wind was knocked from him and the spear jarred from his hand.

The coyote rolled and leapt up, turning and coming at him again before he could even catch his breath. He could smell its dank animal scent, could almost taste it on the air, and its viciousness was shocking, its hatred for him a cool, hard fist inside his gut.

With Lucy still hanging onto him, Cove swung his spear around and down, slamming across the coyote's back and knocking it to the ground. It rolled again and stood, turning and hissing at its assailant.

"Cove!" Dylan shouted, because he saw movement past him and knew what was to come.

As Cove turned to swing Lucy away from the incoming

wolf, the coyote came for Dylan once again. He was ready this time, plucking up the spear, getting up onto his knees, jabbing. The weapon sliced across the animal's shoulder but it didn't seem to notice or care, weaving past the spear's sharpened point and opening its mouth.

Dylan brought his arm up to protect his face. Instinct drove him now, the same instinct that would make him hold out his hands if a train was coming towards him at a hundred miles per hour.

The coyote never hit him. Gee knocked it aside and fell on top of it, his shortened left arm tightening around its throat, right hand rising and falling as he stabbed with the screwdriver. He squirmed astride its back, using his weight to pin it down and keep its gnashing mouth from his face. He stabbed again, some strikes piercing its hide, others skimming off as the creature thrashed and struggled.

Dylan edged forward, spear at the ready. The coyote squirmed beneath Gee, held down by his greater weight but never still, never submissive. Dylan couldn't find a good angle to stab at it.

"Bastard!" Cove shouted, his voice deep and loud, and for a second the wolf paused in its attack, ears flat against its head, head lowered. It looked uncertain, perhaps confused by this roaring creature with another attached to its back.

"Now!" Lucy said. Instead of retreating from the wolf, Cove charged at it, still roaring. Lucy added her voice, and the startled beast leapt back and away from them.

"Gee, hold it still!" Dylan said. He was poised with the spear, yet fearful of striking Gee by mistake.

"I'll roll to the left!" Gee said. "Ready?"

"Ready."

Gee tensed, muscles coiled and ready. The coyote relaxed

and grew still, panting. Dylan held his breath, surprised by its momentary stillness.

It twisted beneath Gee, threw him off balance, turned its head up and back and bit into his right thigh.

Gee shouted and punched the animal in the back of the head. The movement only drove it harder against his leg, and it started gnawing, twisting its head from side to side, and Dylan was sure he heard the deep vibration of teeth against bone. Gee's shout rose into a roar.

The wolf noticed, slinking around them and then leaping at Gee.

Dylan jabbed with the spear and caught the wolf in mid-air, slashing its side but not affecting its trajectory in the slightest. Cove came at it from the other side, prodding his spear and losing balance, Lucy's weight pulling him down.

Gee pummelled the coyote with his stump, jabbing the screwdriver at its eyes, his own eyes wide with pain and terror.

The wolf hit him beneath his shorter arm, teeth clamping into the side of his chest and trapping his limb, raised and even more useless than before.

He screamed and dropped the short weapon. Dylan had never heard him scream. He'd seen him in pain, witnessed controlled fear when the smaller man had saved his life on their first race in Bolivia, but he'd never seen Gee not in control. The pain was obvious, a scent on the air of blood and wet dog and something sweet and more primal. The terror was fresh and stark. Gee's eyes were wide.

Dylan darted towards his friend and the attacking canines, but Gee's shout brought him up short. "Go!" he shouted. Then he let go of the coyote chewing the flesh of his thigh and gripped the wolf's left ear, twisting, turning, rolling sideways onto the animal and shaking as the beast bit deeper. He curled his legs around the coyote and squeezed tight.

"No, Gee, we can—"

Gee's shout cut him off. Half scream, half bellow, it was accompanied by a splash of blood that painted the air red and fell in an arc across the ground. The shout ended in a gurgling, bubbling sound, and blood foamed at his mouth.

He caught Dylan's eye, hand still full of the wolf's ear.

The wolf gnawed and burrowed. The coyote fought free and came in again, biting at Gee's stomach, exposed now that his tee shirt was torn from his torso. Cove was on his feet, Lucy holding onto him and standing on one leg. They stared in horror at their friend being eaten alive.

I can't leave him, Dylan thought, but then he remembered Jenn running away from him, risking herself to help them all because she knew she was fastest, knew she could get to the old town and find somewhere safe. Gee was making a greater sacrifice. He knew that he was finished, even if they did manage to fight off the wolf and coyote attacking him. His wounds were too bad. He would slow them down too much.

"Fucking *go!*" Gee shouted again, louder and higher pitched, and it was a scream wet with blood that misted the air and spattered down across the coyote's back. The animals were shaking him now, and somehow he'd managed to snatch up the screwdriver, drive it down into the wolf's shoulder. The animal growled but did not let go. Instead it ground down with its powerful jaws, and they all heard bones cracking.

Gee's head lolled back, his eyes wide and sightless. His legs locked around the coyote. His hand clasped the screwdriver handle, point buried in the wolf's shoulder.

Dylan turned away. It was another worst moment of his life. If he'd heard Gee shout, or cry, or scream again, he might have gone back and fought the beasts to his own inevitable end. But as they fled the scene, if Gee managed to fight on in silence, he did so with relief, not despair.

Cove moved as quickly as he could with Lucy hopping beside him, one arm slung across his shoulder, useless foot flapping. Dylan took her other arm and she was slung between them, all three of them in close contact as they made their way into the cover of trees. It was cooler in there, quieter. The trees swallowed the sounds from behind them.

None of them spoke. They saved their breath, and Dylan thought the decision they had made was killing them all. Even if they survived Eden, their deaths were already approaching. Gee's sacrifice was a poison of guilt and horror in their veins.

Trampling through undergrowth and across old fallen leaves, he listened for a final shout or scream, but heard nothing. His old friend was quiet to the end.

If Selina had been with them, she might have told them enough about how wolves and coyotes hunted alone to keep the group alive.

But Selina was dead, and these creatures weren't hunting naturally at all.

Nothing about this is normal, he thought. *And now I see Kat's touch in every move they make, feel her eyes on me when they look, smell her when they attack.*

They emerged from thick woodland on the outskirts of Naxford, Dylan and Cove still carrying Lucy between them. They could hear each other's heavy breathing, smell each other's body odour and breath, feel clothing rubbing against skin, yet the space between them felt immense. Dylan did his best not to catch Lucy or Cove's eyes, petrified that his own sickening guilt over Gee would be reflected there. He had never judged himself a cowardly man. He wasn't certain how he should view what had just happened.

I left a friend to die, he thought. *But if we'd stayed to fight and died as well, his sacrifice would have been for nothing.*

Sometimes he ran to clear his head but this staggering run into Naxford cleared nothing. With every footstep his perception of what had happened changed, and in Lucy and Cove's grunts and sighs he thought he heard the same feelings.

The edge of the old town was marked with a series of depressions in the ground that reminded him of surface mining, necessitating a slowing of speed and caution as they negotiated the dips and ridges. Most holes were overflowing with low, thick ferns, and now and then they slowed to a virtual walk so that they could probe forward to see the lie of the land. An old building to their left had fallen into ruin and become home to several large trees, three of them holding aloft the skeletal remains of part of the roof, like victors holding up the corpse of a vanquished foe. If they fell into a hole, something might be waiting in there to rip them apart. If they moved too close to the fallen building, creatures might leap out at them sharp in tooth and claw, or perhaps Kat would be lying in wait somewhere, Selina's skin and blood drying beneath her long fingernails.

Still none of them spoke. Lucy must have been exhausted, but she did not complain. *I don't know what to say,* Dylan thought. They'd left Gee behind ten minutes before, maybe fifteen, and the longer their silence persisted, the harder it was to break.

They emerged into open space, punctuated here and there with banks of undergrowth and swathes of waist-high ferns. It pushed the horizon out and made it easier to make out the lie of the land—the plant-smothered skeletons of cranes and the river to the east, hills rising to the south. They'd descended those hills only a couple of days ago, fresh and excited, unsettled perhaps by the strange feel of this Virgin Zone, but determined to make a good attempt at an unassailable crossing time.

Kat had been on his mind, a vague shadow somewhere close by that might shine a light on what was then the most uncomfortable moment of his past. Now, her shadow loomed over all the bad moments that had passed.

"Dad!" Jenn's voice, quiet and urgent. She appeared beneath a tree to their left, standing in front of what might have once been a wall. "Mum's already here. And there's a bear. Come with me." She must have noticed that Gee was no longer with them, but she said nothing.

With the silence broken, Dylan glanced at Lucy and Cove as they headed for Jenn.

"We have to survive," he said. "For Gee."

Lucy nodded. Cove looked away.

"Hurry!" Jenn said, and now she sounded scared. "I've found somewhere."

KAT

Her consciousness resides in a mind that has gone truly, comprehensively wild, and yet with a level of control and purpose that is chilling.

The thing inside her, Lilith, is nature. Kat has never believed in spirit or soul, but she has to believe in the elemental that has possessed her body. It is pure spirit of nature, pure soul of the wild.

She tastes blood, smells fresh meat, feels the slick warmth of insides turned out. Bones grind and splinter between her teeth. Hair strokes across her face as skin tears. She hears a gurgling cry, a gasped breath, a scream. No pleas, no begging. She is grateful for that, at least.

She tries to see, but the eyes she looks through are not human. Vision is blurred with hunger and rage, splashed with blood. She cannot make out who has come apart beneath the creatures' assault.

Please not her, she thinks, remembering her daughter's sweet voice and the smell of her as a child, baby warmth and sweet breath. *Please not him*, and she feels a soft, warm hand against her hip, a word of love whispered against her neck.

It might be either of them. She can't tell. And if it isn't now, it will be soon, because Lilith's intentions are obvious.

It is pushing out with its own alien senses—those Kat can recognise, and some she cannot—and insinuating itself into other creatures. She feels that it is an extreme effort on Lilith's part, that it is still young and not yet fully formed. Its strength is still limited. But it has a reason to project itself and control these other animals. They provide their own strength and power, which she can steer.

And Lilith will not let things stand as they are. Not while the invaders are still alive.

Not her, Kat thinks. *Not him*. There is no reaction from Lilith, though she is certain that it can hear and even understand her thoughts. It does not mock. Cruelty is a human conceit.

35

"It's said that if you stand on the eastern border of the Scott Preserve, and it's a still day, and the air quality is just right, you can hear the cries and roars of creatures unknown to humanity from the ice floes across the bay. It's a haunting idea, but more an example of the way we have come to view these wild places than a valid scientific observation. Although in truth... who knows?"

Extract from National Geographic: Virgin Zones: The New World

"Where is she?" her dad asked. He looked different. Cove and Lucy did, too. They looked haunted.

"Down by the river," Jenn said. "At least, I'm pretty sure it was her. A person, walking through the trees. There's no one else it could be."

"And the bear?"

"It followed me down into the old town, then I lost sight of it. It was huge, but it didn't run at me. Maybe it's just a normal bear."

"You think this is the safest place?" Cove asked.

"For now," Jenn said. "I went down towards the river, saw

Mum, doubled back. I looked in a few other places, but I think we can hide here for a while. And make a stand if we need to."

"What about a boat?" Lucy asked. "That was the idea, wasn't it?"

Jenn shrugged. "My mother was there."

"Your mother," Lucy said.

"Kat would never do anything to hurt us," her father said. "So whatever's happened, that thing's not her." But he didn't sound confident, and Jenn wasn't sure either. Everything was confused.

"Tell that to Selina," Lucy said.

Jenn tensed. Her dad drew in a sharp breath, but he didn't respond.

"Gee," Jenn said. She thought she already knew the answer.

"Let's get somewhere safer," Cove said without meeting her eyes. He was still carrying Lucy, her arm slung over his shoulder. They were exhausted, and Lucy was looking down at the ground as if to disown what she'd just said.

"There's a basement," Jenn said.

"It's called a crypt, and it's full of dead people," Lucy said.

"It's isolated, cut off, and there are a couple of other ways in and out," Jenn said. "Narrow ways a bear couldn't access. It'll do for now."

She went in front. They'd seen the ruined church from a different angle when they'd entered Naxford a couple of days before. Coming upon it a second time, she'd been drawn by walls still upright, banks of bushes and heavy trees, and it was only while standing directly behind it that she'd seen the stained-glass window held aloft in the arms of a young oak.

"Gee?" she asked again.

"They might follow us here," Cove said to Dylan.

"The wolf and coyote?" Jenn asked.

Her father nodded.

"He made us go," Lucy said. "Held onto them while they were…"

"He was dead," Cove said. "Dead, but still able to help us."

"Oh, Jesus Christ," Jenn said.

"He's no help here," Lucy said. They were within the embrace of what was once the church, but now the roof was gone and so were most of the walls, other than a few remnants here and there, smothered in plant growth. Trees were their temple now.

"Follow me down," Jenn said.

She led them to the route she had found into the old church's basement. She didn't know if it was a crypt or not, but right then it was somewhere to hide, tend their wounds and plan what to do next. She couldn't help feeling that the creatures had been steering them up to now, edging them this way and that, herding them towards whatever her mother wanted for them.

That's not my mother, she thought. Her father was right. She wouldn't have hurt any of them, not if she had a choice. *Which means she has no choice. And that means we really might have to kill her.*

She pulled aside a heavy swathe of climbing ivy and other tangled plants and pushed through the gap between it and an old, crumbling wall. Her father and the others followed. She ducked down and crawled beneath a tumbled stone column, then turned to guide Lucy through after her. They headed down a set of stone steps, the stairwell clogged with old plant growth. Pale stems were crumbly to the touch, and there was newer growth that almost hid the stairs from view. She had to press tight to one wall to force her way down.

"You're sure it's safe?" Cove asked.

"I've been down, looked around," she said. "Long as you don't mind a few creepy-crawlies."

"We'll be trapped down here," Lucy said. She was hanging onto Cove as he helped her hop slowly down the steps, injured foot held up as much as she could.

"Like I said, there are two other ways out."

"They'll smell us," Lucy said. "Find out where we are, smell us out, come down and—"

"I'm trying!" Jenn said, almost hysterical. "You can hardly stand, let alone walk, and we can't carry you forever! If we just hobble up and down the riverbank looking for a boat, we'll be out in the open. Vulnerable. You want to fight off a ten-foot grizzly? At least you can rest down here, and me and Dad can go looking for a boat. I'm *trying*." She could barely make out the others in the fading light.

"Sorry," Lucy said. "I don't blame you, Jenn. This is no one's fault. Let's go."

"Hey," Jenn said, and she squeezed Lucy's shoulder and smiled. "So, my head torch has smashed. Dad?"

"Lost mine," he replied.

"Ours were strapped onto our backpack straps," Cove said.

"Great. Great." Jenn took out the small penlight torch she carried in the zip pocket of her running trousers. The batteries wouldn't last long, but she hoped they wouldn't need long. If she and her father couldn't find a boat, they'd have to start walking again. It would be dusk soon.

They continued down the steps, and soon the plant growth became thinner where sunlight never touched, and the darkness that closed about them was complete. Jenn shone her penlight down and around.

It might once have been a subterranean room, with defined lines and comfortable furniture. Time had smoothed sharp edges, and the furniture had rotted away to almost nothing, swept up in the tides of rainwater that had entered and dried again and again, a process which wore away signs of humanity as decisively as the sea scouring pebbles along a shore. The erosion of humankind from Eden was not a passive process. Even here, in a place that had once been entirely human and artificial, nature held sway.

"There's a sort of hatch over there, in the corner," Jenn said, pointing with her torch towards where the floor rose and the ceiling fell, and an opening led up and out of the room. She aimed towards a far wall. "And there, a narrow ditch leads beyond the remains of the church's outer wall."

Jenn handed Lucy the penlight. They touched hands briefly, forefingers locking in a clumsy, secret squeeze.

"Won't be long," Jenn said. "Don't get frisky down here, the two of you."

"Awww," Cove said. Lucy raised an eyebrow.

They checked their weapons. Jenn left her spear with Lucy, and took a short metal chair leg from Cove, its end split and sharp. Cove still had his spear, as did her father.

"We'll give two whistles when we come back," her father said, and he demonstrated two quick, soft whistles. "Don't want you to stick us—"

"Shit!" Cove shouted, and he pushed away from the wall he'd been leaning against, almost spilling Lucy to the ground. Jenn caught her. Cove stomped his feet and danced away, brushing at his shoulder.

Jenn saw movement, and when Lucy aimed the torch they all saw the shadowy shape scurrying for cover. It disappeared into a pile of old, wet leaves.

"I thought you liked spiders," she said.

"Not when they creep up on me." Cove took a couple of deep breaths and shivered, rolling his shoulders.

"That was a big one," Jenn said, and she was quietly pleased that she and her father weren't staying down there. "Come on, Dad. Sooner we leave, the sooner we can come back."

"Don't be long," Cove said. "I mean it." He spoke to Jenn but was looking down at Lucy.

"You all need rest," Lucy said.

"No time," Jenn said. "Maybe we'll find a stream, even something to eat, but if we stop…"

"They might find us," her father said, completing her thought. "We can't just wait for them to come to us."

"Right," Jenn said. "Come on. That way." Lucy shone the penlight towards the opening in the slumped ceiling at the corner of the room. Jenn went first, and she heard her father close behind.

36

"Look at the state of the world today—flooding, extreme weather events, rise in sea levels, species extinctions, contagions from melting permafrost, population explosion, and it goes on and on—and how can anyone doubt that the Zones were the right thing to do? We owed them to the world. Sometimes I wish they'd expand and become the world."

Anon, United Zone Council

Once outside she was surprised at how quickly the daylight was fading. It was almost sixteen hours since Aaron had been lured from the camp and slaughtered, and sometimes it felt like sixteen minutes. They had been running for their lives, and now two more of them were dead. Eden had taken them, and Eden was still coming for them.

A surge of anger rushed through her. She remembered that strange look in her mother's eyes, a vague recognition, and the anger became even greater. She'd tried not to judge her mother for leaving, but deep down she resented her selfishness, and the way she'd cut off the ones who loved her to suit her own needs. Now, those needs had led to this.

They waited in the shadows beneath some trees, listening, watching their surroundings for signs of movement. If the wolf and coyote had followed them to Naxford, they might even now be stalking through the post-human landscape searching for them. The bear she had seen might still be here too. Jenn knew there might be more. She'd killed a lynx and eagle, and there could be other creatures connected somehow and trying to kill them.

Spiders? Jenn thought. But that was ridiculous.

"I don't want to split up," she whispered. She was afraid, but more for her father than herself. She couldn't lose him too. She didn't think she could bear that.

"We should," he said. "It'd be much quicker. But no, I don't want to either. Besides, I've got this." He wielded his spear. It looked so puny, so human. They were weak.

"We're going to be all right, Dad."

"We're going to be all right," he said, and he cupped the back of her head as he had when she was a child, bringing her close and kissing her cheek. When she was a kid she'd found comfort in that, because he was her father, the strongest man in the world and the person who kept her safe.

Jenn didn't believe that now, and she didn't think her father did either.

They went towards the river, moving quickly but cautiously from cover to cover. They used trees and bushes, and old fallen buildings subsumed and overgrown by nature, funeral mounds for human civilisation. Birds sang and flitted through the dusky air, and anyone could have been spying down on them, ready to guide larger, more dangerous creatures in for the kill. Small mammals scurried away through dense undergrowth. A lizard scampered beneath a broken section of concrete slab. Squirrels ran up tree trunks.

From somewhere farther away, they heard the solitary howl of a wolf.

They froze, staring at each other. *That's howling through Gee's blood*, Jenn thought, imagining the animal's mouth wide, its teeth pink and clotted with cloth and flesh.

"Where did you see Kat?" he asked.

"Further along the riverbank. Towards the south of the town."

In the fading light the stark shape of an old crane loomed over them, reminding Jenn of an old, dead *War of the Worlds* tripod. Beyond, she saw the silvery flow of the river. The half-sunken ship in the middle of the river was little more than a silhouette. Whatever warehouses and service buildings had once lined the river were fallen now, taken down by decades of deterioration. Perhaps some of them contained boats, but they would be impossible to find. She was beginning to regret leaving Lucy their only surviving torch.

Her father tapped her shoulder and pointed, and she followed him along a narrow walkway between banks of bramble, poison ivy and other tangled plants, once an open space between buildings.

The river's flow was a steady hush. Once, Jenn would have found it comforting, but now it masked other sounds. If something stalked towards them, she would not hear it. If someone called her name, the voice would be lost to the river.

The bulky dock structure had been washed away in places, forming a jagged bank of bare concrete and exposed reinforcement. It was more visible than many other parts of Naxford, great grey swathes exposed to the elements, cracked and holed through decades of weather exposure.

"There'll be nothing in the water," Jenn said. "Any boats left behind would have rotted or been swept away ages ago. We'll have to look in or around the shore buildings."

"Or out there," her dad said. "A lifeboat on that sunken ship, maybe."

"Swimming out there is a last resort," Jenn said.

He was staring at the river, hypnotised by its flow.

"Dad?"

"Okay. I'm okay."

They started along the river, keeping away from the edge in case crumbling concrete spilled them into the water. They were both good swimmers, and the flow was not too strong, but Jenn's concern was with what might be in the water. With wolves and coyotes on land, there could be anything in there ready to drag them under.

She watched out for movement, listened for sounds of pursuit. They kept to cover as much as they could, lifting plants, delving into shadows, looking and feeling for any sign of a small boat that might be their salvation.

After a few minutes of careful moving and searching, it wasn't a boat that they found.

"Holy shit," her father said. They'd reached a small dry dock area, the heavy wooden gates still somehow intact. Decades' worth of flotsam was piled outside the gates, forming a solid mass of tree trunks and branches, and broken human things, which Eden had taken apart and washed into the river. Water birds nested in this tangled mass. A pair of otters scampered across its lower edges. A larger shape moved and slipped into the water, barely breaking the surface. At the other end of the dock farthest from the river stood a crane, fifteen metres tall, its skeletal metal framework home now to creeping plants and several large clumps of what looked like birds' nests. The dock was half-filled with plant detritus from the past few decades, rotted down into a rich, fertile soil. It gave life to the beautiful blooms now flowering there.

"There must be a hundred," Jenn breathed.

The ghost orchids were almost within reach. Two or three metres down, the uneven surface of the dry dock's bottom was mostly in shadow. Even so the flowers were easily visible, almost luminous in the dying light. They didn't look real. They looked *more* than real.

"I never really believed in them before we came here," her father said. "They're beautiful. They're horrifying."

"They could be washed away at any time," Jenn said.

"Maybe they only grow in treacherous places."

She wondered if that was possible. These orchids clung to precarious life, at risk at any moment of the old dry dock's gates rupturing and giving way, thus flooding the dock and drowning the wondrous blooms. The others they had seen had been growing high on a sheer cliff, exposed to wind and rain and blazing sun. Perhaps they only grew in places where life existed on a knife edge. On one side, a quick death. On the other, exultant existence. It was as if they represented the fragile nature of these Virgin Zones, which could at any moment be invaded and trampled by humanity. They celebrated nature's fine line between purity and corruption by humans.

In Eden, that nature was defending itself.

"We can't let Cove find these," her dad said.

"Mum had one in her hair."

"I don't like them. Let's go. Past the dock, along the other side, and—"

"Down there." Jenn squinted, kneeling close to the edge of the dry dock as she tried to make out the shape she saw below. It was pressed close to the far wall, half-submerged in decades of rotted vegetation.

"Boat," he said.

"Yeah."

The orchids grew around it but did not touch it, as if loath to grow close to anything artificial.

"It's buried," he said.

"We can dig it out."

"You really want to go down there?"

"No," Jenn said. "Not at all. But I think we have to."

"I don't think we can. I don't think we should go anywhere near those orchids, or—"

"Or what? Eden, or Mum, will kill us?" Her father knew what she meant. It, or she, was killing them already. He moved from foot to foot, looking around at the old town taken back by nature, along the riverbank where green cranes stood sentinel. Life surged, pulsed and raged all around them.

"Okay," he said. "You and me. We can't let Cove see those blooms."

"I'll go down and—"

"No," Dylan said, and he leapt down into the dock. He landed on his feet, bent his knees and rolled, standing quickly and turning to look back up. "It's soft," he said, prodding at the ground with his spear. "Should be able to unearth it pretty easily."

"Stubborn shit," Jenn said, and he smiled.

"You keep watch. Lie low, maybe over by the crane, under cover. I'll be as quick as I can."

Jenn saw the sense in everything he said. He'd never been impulsive, always the one who calculated risk rather than plunging headlong into danger. Even now, when danger was coming headlong at them.

"Just don't trample any of them," she said, thinking again of that bloom her mother had slipped into Selina's hair. Her death had given it life.

37

"Actually, I think some of the Zones have been far more successful than anyone ever thought possible. That's not necessarily good news for humanity. But it's great news for nature, and that's what it's all about."

Anthony Keyse, Green World Alliance

Jenn hurried along the side of the dry dock and reached the foot of the crane. Close up, its metal framework was more visible, regular struts and cross bracings mostly smothered by creeping and climbing plants. Here at the bottom shrubs and bushes grew all around, seeded by decades of birds roosting higher up. It loomed over her, threatening and yet also offering cover. She hunkered down in its shadow and kept watch while her father worked.

Most of the orchids were closer to her end of the dock, while the part-submerged boat was at the gate end. If he was careful, he wouldn't have to come near them.

As soon as he gets it free I'll go and drag it up, she thought. She forced herself to look at her surroundings. She checked along the riverbank in both directions. Back the way they'd come, all was still. This was the first crane, and to the south she scanned the base of several more, looking for movement or anything that might constitute a threat.

Her father's safety depended on her seeing any such danger before it arrived.

She's here somewhere. Maybe she's found the church, smelled us out, and is making her way down into that basement room...

Jenn tried to master her thoughts but they were loose and wild, her imagination creating sickening scenarios.

Her dad whistled softly. He'd loosened the boat in the mud and was working it back and forth to break it free. He gave her a quick thumbs up with one hand, then got to work again.

Jenn broke cover and crept around the other side of the dock. She held the chair leg in one hand, low to the ground, trying not to present too much of a silhouette. The sun was settling into the hills to the west now, sinking into the heart of Eden and lighting the cloudy skies aflame. It was beautiful and intimidating, like spilled and diluted blood.

She drew level with her father and crouched down.

"I think it might work," he said. "Too dark now to see much, but it's fibreglass, not wood. Old rowboat."

"We'll have to paddle with our hands."

"River's flow will take us." He grunted, pulled left, pulled right. "We'll only have to steer."

They hadn't even discussed what would happen once they reached the sea. The coast was miles away, and that was where Eden ended. Even with Eden attacking them, anything outside felt remote and unreal as a dream, fading away with every moment that passed.

What if we reach the sea and everywhere is Eden. What if the whole world has become a Virgin Zone?

It was a foolish thought, but it chilled her. Fear gave it credence and weight.

"Keep looking around," her dad said. Jenn did. There was something strange, and she couldn't pin it down. She'd let her focus drift, and now something had changed. The sun was setting. Shadows grew out of the old town, like dead memories of humanity's time there. They spread across the ground, probing, slinking.

It's the quiet, Jenn thought, and she realised what had happened. Birds had ceased in their song. Insects and flies no longer buzzed in the air. Even the river seemed quieter, as if dusk could muffle its flow. Nowhere fell silent so quickly. She'd spent long enough in Eden to tell the difference.

"Dad, something's—"

She heard the growl, the padding footsteps, and she rolled to the right and came up kneeling, lifting the chair leg just as the wolf appeared. It seemed to emerge from close by, a shadow given form and features. The white streak across its head was sunset-pink. Its muzzle was dark with Gee's blood.

"Jenn?"

"Wolf," she said. "Keep going. I'll hold it off." If the wolf leapt into the dry dock, he'd be trapped down there, nowhere to run or hide. It would corner him and tear him apart.

Without thinking about what she was doing, Jenn stood and ran at the wolf. She shouted, screamed, roared, swinging the sharpened metal before her. She must have startled it as the metal point skimmed from the wolf's teeth and caught in the corner of its mouth, turning its head as the beast backed away. It yelped and shook free. Jenn continued her attack with another stab of the leg, but the wolf was ready now.

It crouched ready to jump, just as the coyote barrelled into her from the right.

Jenn grunted and fell, dropping the chair leg and wrapping her arms around her head. She kicked and rolled, expecting to feel teeth at any moment.

The coyote stood close, one front paw raised, one eye a bloody mess. Blood caked the fur around its jaws. Its teeth were red. It kept turning its head to look at her, whining softly. Gee had done some damage before being eaten alive.

"Crane!" she heard behind her, and she wanted to shout at him to shut up and hide. Maybe he could crouch beneath the unearthed boat. Maybe if the ghost orchids really were linked to this he could run into them, threaten them with destruction in the hope that the beasts would hold back.

Jenn snatched up the metal spike and ran. She swung it behind her with one hand as she did so, hoping to ward the beasts off when they came at her. In seconds she reached the crane, searching ahead for any way she could reach the lower struts. The undergrowth around the structure was too thick to simply step around or through. She had two seconds to decide what to do.

She could hear no sounds of pursuit. She didn't have time to wonder why.

One second...

She dropped her weapon and jumped, reaching out with both hands to grab the metal structure, and to protect herself from impacting it if she'd jumped too far. She landed across the top of the mass of undergrowth, fingers skimming something hard. Feeling herself sinking down, she spread her weight and grabbed for the metal, fingers closing around something cold and flaked with rust.

She pulled, trying not to thrash her legs in case she sank deeper and became trapped in the plants. Her gashed hand scorched with pain, but she ignored it. Thorns spiked all across her body, sticking in, scratching. Most of them simply stung, but she felt herself pierced across her stomach and chest. She cried out at the pain.

Stuck like a fly on paper, she would be a sitting duck if the wolf and coyote came for her.

Pulling herself forwards and up, Jenn risked a quick glance behind her.

The animals were pacing back and forth along the edge of the dry dock. She couldn't see her father—it was growing dark, and the angle was all wrong—but they knew he was there. They knew, and that meant they'd stopped caring about her.

He's trapped down there! She pulled harder, got a good grip on the metal, used her upper body strength to haul herself across the top of the clawing plants. She hissed as thorns and brambles scraped and poked, then her right trainer found purchase and she pushed herself forward so that her other foot found metal.

Standing on the crane structure at last, she turned and looked down into the dock.

Ten metres away, her father was crouched beside the now unearthed boat. It was a dark, regular shape in the fading light. He was looking up at her.

"Now what?" she said, hoping it was loud enough for him to hear.

"If I climb the gates, haul the boat up after me—"

The coyote growled. The wolf barked. It was shockingly loud, and Jenn almost lost her grip on the crane.

The coyote turned its head and saw her, as if noticing her for the first time. Reaching the base of the crane, it leapt at the plants, seemingly unconcerned at any scrapes and other injuries it might receive. It growled and slavered, and soon it had both front paws on a metal prop.

Jenn climbed, ignoring the pain, moving quickly. After a few seconds she paused and looked down. The coyote was below her, growling but unable to come any higher.

The wolf was now braced at the edge of the dock. Tensed. Ready to jump. Her father had backed slightly from the boat, and stood with the spear held in front of him. Stalemate.

Jenn slipped. Her wounded hand skidded through something soft and stinking, and above her a shadow broke the sharp, firm edges of metal. She was beneath a scattering of small nests, and her hands slid in shit. It mixed and merged with fresh blood. She edged sideways.

Something jabbed at her leg. She looked down and saw several small birds flitting around inside the open structure, angry at her disturbance. They were taking it in turns to drift in and peck at her legs. If she moved one hand to wave them away, the other might lose its grip, sending her falling into the plants below. They'd soften her fall, but she'd become tangled within them, pinned and held at the coyote's mercy.

Panicking, breath coming faster, Jenn climbed higher, edging at a diagonal away from the nests. Above her the bulk of the crane's overhanging arm was a shadow against the sunset sky. It had no straight edges, the whole arm smothered with plant growth.

Something caressed her left hand. A piercing, bright pain bit in and she shouted out.

"Jenn!"

"I'm okay," she said. It was a snake. She couldn't see what kind, and she didn't know if she was at all okay. It reared back ready for another bite. She snatched at it, closing her hand behind its head, tugging and throwing it over her shoulder. It made no sound as it landed.

She climbed some more. Her heart hammered, and she

wasn't sure whether it was fear and panic, or the early signs of some terrible toxins from the snake bite.

"Jenn," her dad said.

"I'm okay." She climbed higher. Something drove her up. The height made her feel safer, further away from Eden and what it had become. The coyote growled and whined below, and she could hear its claws scratching at the metal and feel it through her feet. Her hand tore through a spiderweb and a spider dropped onto her arm. She panicked, shook, banged her arm against a metal strut and crushed it. She felt the creature's body pop against her skin.

"Jenn."

Something in his voice gave her pause. She pressed herself against the crane structure, letting go with her right hand so she could turn and look down.

Her mother stood at the edge of the dock, looking down at her father isolated below. The wolf was beside her, still coiled, still ready to leap. She stroked the back of its head.

"Mum," Jenn whispered.

Kat growled.

38

"The Chinese guard the Wang Dayuan Zone with utmost dedication. It is perhaps the purest, most untouched of all the Virgin Zones. We all have lessons to learn from China."

Dr Hilda Trechman, United Zone Council

I should have killed her at the dam, Dylan thought. *There's nothing of Kat there. Jenn was wrong. There's nothing of my wife, and if there is, she's in pain.*

The makeshift metal spear in his hand felt useless. He held it across his waist, not yet pointing up at Kat. He was afraid to make a move. She'd appeared without a sound, and now each breath she took was a growl, like a big cat grumbling deep in its throat. She was naked, scratched and cut. Dried blood smeared her body and was caked in her hair. Very little of it was hers. Kat had always been lithe and fit, but now she looked leaner than she ever had before, muscles knotted beneath her skin, limbs strong. He had kissed that skin, run his hands through that hair.

It was too dark to see her eyes. He was glad.

Still, he tried.

327

"Kat," he said. "I don't know what's happening, but we can talk. We can come to an agreement. We're leaving, and we'll never come back."

Kat moved and flexed and the wolf growled, as if in response to a silent signal. It had been acting on these commands all along. The coyote too, still scrabbling at the base of the crane in an unnatural attempt to climb after Jenn.

I can't let Jenn see this, he thought. *She can't see her mother killing her father.*

"Get out of here," he said, still looking at Kat but talking to his daughter. He wanted to see her one last time, hold her and hug her close. There were never enough hugs. He'd tried to show her how much he loved her, especially since Kat had left. He wished he'd shown her more.

He glanced to the right without moving his head. Jenn was two thirds of the way up the crane now, almost at the point where the lifting arm was cantilevered out from the tower.

"Go!" he said. He wasn't sure that she heard.

Kat crouched and sat on the side of the dock. The wolf edged forward, ready to leap. He only had seconds left. It was all about buying time for Jenn now, giving her as long as he could so that she could get back to Cove and Lucy. He'd give her a chance to survive.

The wolf grunted as it leapt, and he heard Kat's skin brushing against stone as she dropped down into the dock. He didn't even look. With the fibreglass rowing boat between him and them he turned and ran, and within ten paces he was standing amongst the spread of ghost orchid blooms.

He stepped deeper, picking his footing carefully. Then he turned and raised the spear, ready to bring it swinging down in a scything motion. *It's all about these, isn't it?* he thought. He held his breath, because he had no idea if this would work.

Maybe they had been wrong about Eden and the orchids. Maybe Kat was simply mad.

She was closer than he'd expected, less than three steps from him. The wolf was to his left, pressed to the side wall of the dock and slinking closer. As Kat's eyes went wide, the wolf froze. It became a statue, less than a shadow. Above and behind him, the sound of the struggling coyote also ceased.

"I'll do it," he said. He was talking to Kat, but nothing could convince him he was talking to his wife. There was no recognition of him in her stance, her face, or her eyes, and in turn, he did not recognise this creature in front of him. A hint of the smell was her, perhaps, beneath the stench of filth and neglect. That was all. Jenn had believed she'd seen a flash of her mother back at the dam, but it must have been wishful thinking.

Dylan would not make that mistake.

"I'll do it!" he said again.

The orchids were barely as high as his bloodied and scratched shins, but standing amongst them, they seemed so much higher. He had never believed in them. Now he could feel them around him, heavy, solid blooms with a heft and a weight he'd never have imagined. The flowers were the size of his closed fist, but he believed if he knelt and held one it would be as heavy as a brick. They were the most solid, real things about Eden.

If the wolf and coyote were beholden to whatever drove Kat, she was in thrall to the ghost orchid.

She was looking down at his feet, eyes wide and darkened with no irises showing, only deep black pupils and pink eyes. She seemed possessed both with a need to spring and tear him apart, and an urge to remain as still as possible. The conflicting desires thrummed through her, and he could feel the power coiled inside her ready to burst out. Her skin rippled. Her limbs shook. Her eyes seemed loaded with violence, like windows onto a storm.

Dylan sensed Jenn watching, as still now as the animals and her mother. As still as him.

Something's got to give.

"We can talk," he said.

It's not a stand-off, it's violence waiting to burst.

"Kat. Honey."

Nothing in her eyes. *I didn't call her honey for years even before she left, but if she's there Kat will hear it now and remember.*

The wolf growled and shifted, and from his right Dylan heard a deeper, heavier grumble. He glanced up to the edge of the dock and saw a huge grizzly standing there staring at him, its size dwarfing them all.

Dylan gasped, flinched. He overbalanced and started to fall back and to the right, so he shifted his foot slightly to counter the weight. He only moved it six inches.

The orchids were so delicate that he didn't feel anything through his running shoe, or even across his bare leg. He sensed it, though. A shifting of tension, a flow of sadness and loss through the air as if the world itself had sighed with intense, shattering grief.

He glanced down and saw the crushed plant beneath his shoe, pale white blooms wrinkled and torn in the mud.

Kat made no sound as she came for him, primal fury blazing in her eyes.

When she reached the crane arm Jenn climbed up and sat on it, resting for a few seconds, letting her tensed muscles settle.

The air froze around her. The sun stopped sinking. Even the mass of creeping and climbing plants that smothered most of the crane's superstructure seemed to pause, stuck between one moment of life and the next. She held her breath and looked down.

Her dad had backed into the spread of ghost orchids growing at the end of the dry dock almost ten metres below her. He stood with metal spear raised, her mother just a few steps from him. She couldn't see the wolf. It must have melted into the shadows.

I have to get back down to help! she thought, but then she glimpsed movement close by. A snake emerged from within the latticework structure of the crane arm, much larger than the one that had bitten her. Its motion was smooth and full of intent. It tasted the air, smelled her. Came for her.

She shuffled out onto the arm to escape it, keeping as quiet as she could, careful on the open metal structure. The coyote no longer watched her. It looked down into the dock and seemed to have forgotten she was even there.

She could hear her father speaking in soft tones, but couldn't quite make out the words. She caught a sense of movement in the dry dock, a shadow leaving the shelter of the wall and looking up at her. The wolf. And then the grizzly appeared from the shadows, as if emerging from out of nowhere, standing close to the edge and ready to leap down.

Her father moved. He stepped back and to the right, and Jenn felt a huge held breath being released, but not with any sense of relief or calm. Rage filled the air.

The snake struck at her foot. She kicked and it coiled back into a tight ball.

She looked down.

It's too far, she thought, but her mother was going for her father, and the wolf was there too, and she knew what she had to do. There was no way she could simply watch her father torn to pieces, like Aaron and Selina and Gee before him.

It's way, way too far.

But she would have fallen a hundred times further if it would save him.

There was barely any thought process involved. One moment she sat on the cold, rusted, overgrown skeleton of the crane's lifting arm. The next she was in freefall.

She had time to draw up her legs and tuck her chin into her chest before she hit.

39

"We were turning the air toxic, water levels were rising, average global temperatures were increasing year on year, the oceans were turning acidic, we were discovering plastic pollution in the deepest parts of the oceans and on the highest, remotest mountains. We were burning, degrading, deforesting, depleting, destroying, and even the most optimistic scientists would admit, in private, that the Zones were little more than an indulgent long shot. But in our arrogance, there was something we didn't take into account. And that was nature's eagerness to move on."

Professor Amara Patel, Natural History Museum, London

Even now, Dylan wasn't sure he could plunge the metal spear into the thing that had been his wife. He held it up and out, but it was half-hearted, a gesture more than true intent. *If it gives Jenn another few seconds*—he thought, and then Kat was no longer there.

Something struck her and drove her into the ground. She collapsed with the sound of breaking bone and a soft, terrible crunch as she was forced over onto her front and into the soft soil. Beneath her, a dozen orchids were crushed.

He fell back and dropped the spear, right hand splaying out as he destroyed another flower beneath his palm. It felt soft and moist, its sap as warm as fresh blood.

Jenn grunted, rolled, and knelt with her forehead pressed to the ground. That was when Dylan's shock gave way to a sick realisation of what his daughter had done.

"Jenn!" He scrambled to his feet and went to her, skirting around Kat. She was motionless, face pressed to the soil, back curved like a giant beetle curled into itself in death. "Jenn?"

He reached her and pressed a hand to her back. She was shivering. Her left arm trailed by her side, hand twisted at an unnatural angle. He glanced back at Kat. She was writhing slowly, arms and legs moving independently of each other.

The wolf! he thought, and he crouched and turned, expecting it to be leaping at them. It stood three metres away close to the edge of the dock, ears up as it watched Kat. It wasn't moving. It no longer seemed threatening, but confused. It lifted a paw and looked down, whined, unable to step in between the orchids.

Jenn gasped in a huge breath, then another. Perhaps she'd only been winded, but he feared that when he moved her he'd find ribs shattered, lungs and other organs punctured.

"Jenn, please, please, sweetheart, just tell me you can stand."

"Fuck, Dad," she gasped. "Fucking hell."

"Come on," he said, and he grabbed her under each arm and tried to pull her upright. She was still gasping for breath, and she cried out as she tried to raise her left arm. She looked at it as if it didn't belong to her.

"Oh shit."

"Don't worry about it."

"Won't be juggling any time soon," Jenn said.

"We need to leave."

"Wait."

They paused together and looked down at Kat. Her limbs were slowing, and though she'd turned her face out of the ground, it was covered with mud and torn, broken petals from crushed orchids. There was soil in her open mouth, blackened with drool and blood. Dylan could smell the blood on her.

The wolf leapt at the side wall of the dock, clasping on with its front paws, scrabbling with its back legs as it hauled itself up and out. With a blink it was gone. The coyote had vanished from the base of the crane tower, and the grizzly had melted away into the dark. Other creatures fled—rats and spiders, beetles and a few birds that had been nesting or roosting in the plants scattered around the uneven base of the dry dock. They ran into shadows, climbed or flew away from Kat, as her movements slowed into eventual, terrible stillness.

"I killed her," Jenn said, her voice barely a breath.

"You didn't kill her, you saved her. You saved me."

"I didn't think about it. I just fell."

"Can you walk? We need to get out."

For a moment she did not move, staring instead at the pale shape in the scattering of ghost orchids.

"Jenn?" Dylan asked. She turned and looked at him, her eyes filled with so much grief that he took a step back.

"What have I done?"

Jenn felt sickness rising in her, not from the pain from her arm and her ribs and elsewhere across her body, but from the knowledge of what had occurred. Her mother's corpse was stark and pale against the dark soil. She could only remember falling, not hitting, and she wished she were falling forever. She thought perhaps it would give her time to think.

Around her mother, pale ghost orchids seemed to be fading away as dusk led into night.

"She called me here, and I killed her."

"Jenn, we have to go," her dad said. He held her right arm and steered her towards the side of the dock. She had no idea how she could climb out. Right then, the centre of her world was her dead mother, splayed across a carpet of broken flowers. Jenn didn't know what it meant for her or for Eden. It was a sadness heaped on deeper sadness, and she felt dizzy, nauseous and scared. The depths pulled her down, threatening to crush. It was only her father's touch that kept her from falling into the void.

More movement caught her attention. A shape appeared above them at the side of the dock, and her heart jumped. But it was Cove. He fell to his knees and bent over, and for a moment Jenn thought he was going to tumble in.

"Lucy…" he said. "Bitten. Or stung. She's gone." He kept looking behind him, breathing hard. "And I ran, and something was in the shadows, something big."

"Where is she?" Dylan asked.

Cove looked down at them, taking in the scene. When he saw Kat's body and the orchids he froze.

"No, Cove," Jenn said.

He switched on the penlight, and though the beam was weak, when he played it across the orchids they seemed to bloom as if luminous.

"You okay?" Dylan asked.

"Got bit. Thing went for Lucy, I knocked it away, and…"

"*What* bit her?"

He was still looking at the flowers. He took no notice of Kat's body. "Look at them all."

"We need to get the boat out," her father said. He held Jenn close, hugging her like he hadn't hugged her for years. She felt tears pressing at her eyes.

"We have to check on Lucy," she said. She nodded up at Cove. He was sitting now, swaying, the light hanging from his fingers.

"He says she's dead."

"We have to, Dad."

He nodded. "Okay. But you're getting out first." He bent down against the dock wall and Jenn stood on his cradled hands. She shoved gently down, and with one huge lift he had her up against the wall, her good arm levering on the ground above. She pushed her toes into the rough concrete, found a hole, and heaved. Her ribs hurt as she bumped against the concrete, and her left hip shone with a grinding agony.

Cove dragged her up. He looked terrible. He was sweating and shaking, his eyes wide and wet.

"I saw her die," he said. Tears spilled but his expression didn't change.

"Where were you bitten?"

He raised his right hand. It was swollen, the skin tight and hot.

"What was it?"

"Something small. What happened to you?"

"I fell off a crane." Jenn turned his hand this way and that, locating the puncture mark. It might have been from a snake's fangs, or a double strike from a scorpion. If the toxins had been powerful he'd have been dead by now, but she still had doubts about trying to suck it out.

Her dad appeared behind her and took in the scene. He rooted around on the ground and picked something up.

"Those ghost orchids," Cove said, pointing into the dock with his bad hand. Dylan grabbed it, held it still, and sliced something across the bites. Cove flinched, but then relaxed, knowing Dylan's intent. He bent and sucked at the wound, spat, sucked again.

"I'm checking on Lucy," Jenn said.

"No, I'll go," Dylan said. "Cove, we've got to make sure. Kat's dead, and the animals have gone. I think we have a little more time."

"I saw the wolf running away," he said. "I was afraid he was chasing one of you. And something else in the dark, something bigger."

"Grizzly," Jenn said. "It chased you?"

"Only until I saw the wolf running. Then I didn't hear it anymore."

"We found a boat."

"You did?"

Jenn stood and started stripping off her running belt. It was difficult with one hand. She held it up. "We've got one good hand each. We can use this to pull it out of there."

"I'll be quick," Dylan said.

"She's still inside the church," Cove said. "I tried to drag her away. I tried, but she was already..."

"Help Jenn," her father said, but he was looking at Jenn when he spoke. She nodded.

"Be careful. Please, Dad."

He smiled and then ran into the silent darkness.

Dylan felt a sickness of the soul, an emptiness at Kat's strange death, but Jenn was still there to keep him whole and grounded. He wished he'd had time to tell her none of this was her fault.

He could not leave Eden without checking on Lucy. Cove

seemed confused, and the sting or bite he'd received might have skewed his senses. Dylan had to make sure.

He ran across the old ruined town, through the falling darkness and the shadows bleeding out from their daytime hiding places, and for the briefest moment he revelled in the simple act of running.

That brief moment refired his confidence, saw away some of the darkness, and made him determined to survive. Eden was doing its best to kill them, but they were fighting back. He hoped Kat had fought back as well, as much and as ferociously as she could.

Naxford was a different place without daylight to illuminate the human elements. He was aware of the bulk of old buildings around him, but they might have been mounds of rocks and soil, or something older. When he was younger, before Jenn and even before Kat, he and a group of friends had hiked through a region of the Amazon where ancient ruins hid away from sight, echoing with stories that would likely now never be told. Passing through these sites had filled him with a sense of wonder and dread, and the feeling that these old places were observing from the past. He felt the same now. He ran, he was on his own, yet he felt the focus of an unreasonable, unknowable intelligence.

Closing on the old church, he realised his mistake. It would be pitch black in there now, and he'd forgotten to take the penlight from Cove. A few steps closer, he knew that he would not need it.

"Lucy!" She was a pale shape in the grass, pushing weakly with one good leg, pulling with her arms, movements that reminded him of his dead wife. He dropped down beside her and grabbed her arm to roll her over. She was burning hot, her skin slick with sweat. He pushed her onto her back and she let out a long, gargling sigh.

Dylan caught his breath and flinched back. Lucy's face was swollen, eyes puffed up and almost closed, and she was bleeding from the nose and mouth. Her breathing was wet and uneven, short, desperate gasps.

"He... he..."

"Keep quiet, keep still," Dylan said. He'd seen people stung and bitten, and knew that some poisons worked incredibly fast. Cove had said she was dead. He'd lied, but she would be soon. Dylan didn't know what had stung her, or where, or how long ago.

"He... left me... for his... flowers?" Lucy posed it like a question, her difficult words said in disbelief. "Flowers..."

Dylan didn't know what to do or say. He reached for her and went to pick her up, but knew it was already too late. Her breathing was shallower, her body twitching, contorting as she tried to draw in breaths past her swollen airways.

"I'm here," he said, leaning low over her and making sure she knew he was by her side. "I'm here, Lucy."

"Fl... flowers," she said again. It was her last word. She struggled some more, grunted a few times, and then lay still.

Dylan sat back on his heels. Her death felt unreal, a shock piled upon shocks. Perhaps he was going mad.

He stood, looked down at his dead friend one more time, then turned and ran back towards the river. The wolf, coyote and grizzly might have fled when Kat died and her control over them faded, but Eden was still inimical to them, and it always would be.

A hundred metres from the dock he could just make out Jenn standing at the edge, silvered by moonlight emerging from behind a bank of clouds. She was leaning down and holding onto something. She stiffened and hauled the front end of the boat up into view.

Then she grew still and shouted, "Cove, no!"

The darkness surrounding Dylan tensed as Eden watched.

40

"Yes, of course I've heard about the orchids. Fairytales. Wish fulfilment. Nothing more."

Professor Amara Patel, Natural History Museum, London

Jenn knew it was a stupid idea to let Cove down into the dry dock. But he insisted, and before she could protest he'd slipped over the edge and landed in a roll. Standing, he glanced around, gaze lingering on her mother's body splayed in the spread of orchids.

"Cove!" Jenn said. "Hurry."

Lying on her stomach, grimacing through pain that almost made her puke, she dangled her belt down to him. He grabbed one end and she held on tight as he tied it around a bolt in the top end of the boat. They'd still not inspected it properly— it might be holed, cracked, ready to fall apart as soon as they shifted it—but one step at a time.

"Okay, pull gently," he said. With only one good hand it was tough, but she stood, braced her legs and started pulling. She turned her body slightly, trying to position herself where the pain bit in least. Still, her head swam and sickness threatened. Her ribs hurt like hell, and her hip was ablaze. *I did that killing my mother*, she thought, but she could not dwell on it. That awful deed would haunt her forever, adding a weight and depth to her nightmares that might make them inescapable. For now she had to keep it at a distance. Time enough for new nightmares once they'd escaped this one.

Cove pushed as she pulled, and the boat barely moved. It was too heavy.

"Hang on," he said. His voice sounded light and weak, but he seemed more in control than he had when he'd arrived. Perhaps he was averting the settling of his own nightmares.

While Jenn hung onto her stretched belt, Cove scooped soil from the boat with his good hand, easing its weight. With every movement she felt it growing lighter.

"That'll do it," she said. "Push, Cove. I've nearly got it."

Nothing. She leaned over and looked down. Cove was still standing by the upright boat, but he was no longer looking at her. He was staring at Kat and the orchids, the blooms somehow still easily visible in the darkness, possessing their own strange luminosity.

"Cove!" He didn't move. Jenn frowned. The flowers looked different now, grouped closer together around her mother's body. It must have been an effect of the darkness. "Cove, we need to get—"

He started walking towards the body and the ghost orchids he had come here seeking.

"Cove, don't!" she whispered. She was afraid to shout now that he was within touching distance of her mother. She wasn't sure why.

Perhaps she was afraid of waking her.

"The flowers," Cove said, kneeling, reaching. "The flowers are in her."

Jenn didn't know what he meant, and didn't wish to know. The air thrummed as he reached lower, as if charged and ready to unleash a surge of lightning. The hairs on her arms stood on end. Her scalp tingled.

He reached across her mother's corpse and closed his hand around an orchid's stem.

"Cove, no!" she shouted.

He plucked it from the ground. Then another, and another, pressing them into his injured, bleeding hand and holding them tight while he picked with his good hand. He groaned, a wretched sound, almost inhuman, and it sent a spasm of fear through her.

When he froze, Jenn realised it was not Cove who had groaned.

Her mother's limbs were moving.

Jenn felt intense relief that she had not murdered her after all, and crippling terror that she was still alive.

Cove started backing away as Kat placed one hand on the ground, delicately, ensuring it was not touching any of the plants. She pushed herself up. Her other arm hung loose, shoulder dipped and misshapen.

"Get out of there," Jenn whispered, and her mother's head lifted and turned almost too far on her neck. She stared upside down at Jenn. Jenn could not see her eyes, but knew that they were dark and deep.

Cove reached the boat and started pushing again, grunting as he shoved with one hand and Jenn pulled, digging her heels into the ground and lifting with all her strength. Pain flashed through her arm and shoulder, her torso and hip and hand, making her dizzy and nauseous. But she did her best to shut it off and concentrate on the effort. She was good at closing off pain. Pain was just weakness leaving the body.

Her mother was standing now, swaying back and forth as she staggered in a half-circle so that she was facing them. Everything about her was broken. She hung like a fractured marionette, her limbs moving in a jerky, pained motion as she began to walk.

Cove placed the orchids he'd picked into the boat and braced his shoulder beneath it, crouching and heaving upwards. Jenn took a step back and continued pulling, and the craft pivoted on the dock's crumbling edge and fell towards her. She stepped aside as it struck the ground, then went back to the edge.

Her mother was moving faster now, making shambling progress. As she moved Jenn heard pounding footsteps behind her. She crouched, ready to fight. Her father skidded to a stop beside her.

"Lucy's dead," he said.

"Mum's still alive!" Jenn said. She fell to her knees and reached in and down. She grabbed Cove's bad hand and he cried out, but there was no time for pain, or for subtlety. She started to pull. "Dad?"

He was looking past her and down at Cove.

"Dad, what?"

He knelt and grabbed Cove's good hand. Together they pulled, and with Cove helping with his feet they hauled him out of the dock.

Below, Kat hissed as she scraped claws across the pitted concrete.

Jenn and her father grabbed the front of the boat and Cove pushed from the rear, and in a few seconds it was close to the river's edge. It was a six-foot drop into the water.

"It might just sink!" she said.

"It might." Dylan pushed it parallel with the river's concrete edge. It was difficult to tell exactly where the edge was because of plants hanging over and the old concrete having broken and crumbled away over the years. Jenn was sure he didn't mean to push it too far, but the boat slipped off stern first and splashed into the river.

Then he turned to Cove.

Cove didn't hesitate. Eyes wide, staring down at the orchids in the boat, he ran past them and leapt into the water.

Beneath the splash Jenn heard excited yelping in the distance, and then the wolf's howl. Further away, exultant, the spine-tingling roar of the brown bear.

"They know she's not dead," her father said. "They're coming back."

The old town was now silvered by bright moonlight, so it was easy to see the grey shapes of the wolf and coyote. The wolf was around the other side of the dry dock. It paused at the edge and looked in, then started around the far end, past the crane and towards them. The coyote was approaching from deeper within the old town, the larger shadow of the bear following close behind. Most days the creatures would be sworn enemies. Now, they served a common master.

"Dad, what happened with Cove and—?"

Kat appeared over the edge of the dry dock. She moved like a spider, broken arms scrabbling for purchase, legs rising up and toes digging into the ground, pulling and dragging herself upright. She stared right at them. Her head was tilted to one side, shoulder dropped and broken.

The wolf and coyote were only metres away, and they paused and watched Kat. The coyote limped. The wolf was still bloodied, the white streak above its eye bright with moonlight. The bear held back close to the crane, pacing, guarding their retreat.

"That's not her," Dylan said. "We both know that." He

grabbed Jenn in both arms and hugged. It hurt. She did not complain. "Watch Cove," he said. He squeezed her even tighter, kissed her neck, whispered his love into her ear.

Then he let her go and ran at his wife.

"Oh, Dad, no!" Jenn said. Her grief and guilt were too raw, her nightmares too deep, she couldn't face this as well. She took one step after him, but he was already there.

Kat hissed as Dylan embraced her with both arms. His momentum carried them back, then down into the dry dock and out of sight.

The wolf and coyote switched their gazes to Jenn.

Behind them, the grizzly stood on its hind legs and roared at the moon.

Jenn balanced on a knife edge sharper than she had ever known. Forward, and she would die. Backwards, and perhaps her father might have saved her. Like a ghost orchid blooming in a precarious place, both destinies beckoned.

She took three steps back and fell into the river.

They landed on their sides, his arms still wrapped around her. The wind was knocked from him, and he heard a grunt from Kat in a voice that he recognised. There was a time when they'd been so close that they could have identified each other in the dark from the tone of a sigh, the movement of a foot over soft ground. They had been aware of each other and attuned to the tones and frequencies of their love.

The sound surprised him, and he flinched back to look into her face.

She was already struggling in his grip. He held tight, pulling her close again and pressing the side of his face to hers. Her teeth clacked together close to his neck so he pulled even tighter, not giving her room to move around for a bite. She was snorting breath through her nose, growling. He wrapped his legs around hers and clenched them together.

There was no longer any smell about her that he recognised. The contours and angles of her body were sharp and strange. Her hair seemed thicker than before, her movements much stronger. There was no sense that she recognised him, yet Dylan was doing this for Kat as much as for Jenn. And he was doing it for himself.

As she struggled to break free, he knew that soon she would succeed. She was much too strong for him to hold onto for long. Her teeth clacked again, grazing his ear, as loud as two bricks being slammed together.

"Kat," he said, and he drew back so that he could look at her face. The movement surprised her, and for a moment all her struggles ceased, and she looked at him. "I'll never let you go again."

It might have been wishful thinking, but in his final seconds of life he thought that she was there.

41

"Humanity will never tire of playing God"

Pope Benedict XVIII

Cove grabbed her arm and pulled her close. Spluttering, trying to see past the pain as she kicked closer to the boat, she flung both hands up over the side and held on. Cove was gripping on with his bad hand. The boat was drifting, caught in the river's flow and edging out from the bank. The water was cold but the initial shock had faded. The river was full of debris— branches, small trees, soft islands of leaves spinning in the current. The heavy rainfall from the past couple of days was washing out of Eden.

"Where's Dylan?" Cove asked.

Watch Cove, he'd said. Jenn could not answer. She looked back towards the bank, and the large pile of flotsam crushed against the dry dock's angled gates. The silhouette of the crane faded into darkness, and a taller one came into view as the river carried them away. To their right was the shadow of the beached ship.

"Jenn? Is he coming?" Cove was looking as well, searching the shore.

"No, he's not coming. He held onto Mum, took her down into the dock so we could get away."

Cove continued looking back where they'd come from. A shadow moved on the shore, too low to be Dylan, too sleek. One of the animals was following their progress.

"I'm sorry," he said. He sounded wretched.

"Fuck that," Jenn said. "Fuck sorry." She let go of the boat and started kicking for shore. She couldn't leave him like this. His final hug and words remained with her but she wanted more. She wanted the elderly father recounting stories to his grandchildren, telling them tales of tall adventures and distant lands. She wanted his grey hair and weakening limbs, his failing health as time caught up so she could look after him as he'd looked after her.

Something grabbed her foot. She kicked out but it wouldn't let go. Surfacing, spluttering filthy river water, she heard Cove calling her name.

"Jenn, look!" He released her and she drifted with him and the boat, looking back towards shore.

Her mother was standing close to the edge and watching them go, glimmering in the moonlight, wet with blood.

She dived into the river.

"Oh shit!" Cove said. "Into the boat, now!" He hauled himself up and over, slumping into the boat and reaching for Jenn. They grabbed hands and he pulled, both of them crying out at the flaring pain from their injuries. She rolled into the boat with him, splashing down into the fluid muck that swilled around its base.

"Scoop!" he said, and they set about throwing handfuls of wet mud out, again and again. Jenn kept her attention behind them as she baled, focussed on the splashing that was edging ever closer to them.

The river had them in its main pull now, the boat spinning slowly around until it faced downstream.

Her mother swam, a furious splashing shape throwing up water that caught the moonlight in graceful arcs. On the shore shadows followed them along the bank. The wolf howled. The coyote barked. The bear grumbled and growled as it ran. Other creatures made their own noises, roaring and singing and calling into the night. Eden sang a song of darkness.

She glanced at Cove in the stern of the old boat. He'd stopped baling and was gathering up the orchid blooms and holding them against his chest.

"Cove, are you fucking crazy?"

"We can't just let them go."

"Of course you can! Throw them over, now. Let them float away. Maybe she'll leave us alone then, let us go."

"I can't," he said, and he looked at her helplessly. He was shivering, and she could tell he was telling the truth. Nothing in his make-up allowed him to cast these wonders aside.

"Dad told me to watch you. Why's that, Cove? What did you do to Lucy?"

"Nothing," he said, but he glanced away from her, back down at the orchids he held close. "I did nothing to her."

"You said she was dead."

"She is."

Jenn baled. With every handful she threw out the boat felt lighter. There were leaks, but as she reduced the weight of the mud they moved faster.

Her mother seemed to be falling behind them. Perhaps she was tiring. Maybe her father had injured her more, or pierced whatever was left of her heart with his final words.

"Priceless," Cove said, and he rocked lower in the boat with the luminescent flowers clasped to his chest.

She was shaking from the cold, shock, hunger and thirst. Her body was damaged, the pains merging into a steady blaze. She couldn't remember the last time she had eaten. She wondered how long it would take the boat to drift to the coast, and if Eden would allow them to go that far. She thought not. Especially with Cove gripping onto those orchids. If her mother couldn't catch them in the river, she'd reach them another way.

"Throw them away, Cove."

He no longer even answered her. He was curled up, sweating and quivering, his eyes watery.

She tried to paddle with her good hand, but it didn't seem to make them move any faster. She continued baling instead, cupping her hand to throw out as much water and silt as she could. The old boat was in surprisingly good shape, with only a few small leaks. If she kept working, she thought she might be able to keep them afloat. If Cove helped they could do it for sure.

His knees were drawn up, hands cupped close to his face. The ghost orchids seemed to emit their own glow. She saw them reflected in his bloodshot eyes, like distant stars.

As they approached a curve in the river, she heard a splash. Something moved close to the boat, ripples catching starlight and stroking against the hull. Jenn opened her mouth to call a warning, but the words died in her throat. The boat was small, but Cove was much further away than he should have been. Holding the orchids, he was unreachable.

I can't let him leave with them.

Another splash, closer. Cove heard the noise and raised his head. He and Jenn looked at each other, and his eyes widened.

Watch Cove, her father had said.

The shape burst from the water beside the boat as if propelled by something powerful from below. She almost left the river completely, and as she reached the apex of her lunge she closed her arms around Cove's neck. His eyes and mouth went wide.

Jenn could only watch as her mother fell back, tipping the boat and rolling Cove after her into the river. He did not make a sound. Neither did she. The second splash was much larger, and then the waters began to settle as the boat drifted on.

Jenn knelt up and stared back at the disturbed surface. There was no sign of Cove or her mother, other than a few scattered air bubbles. All she saw were several ghost orchids floating on the surface. Their path seemed different from hers, and they spread out in the darkness, their glow eventually vanishing in the night as she drew further and further away.

She watched for the wolf and coyote, but saw neither. The bear followed her along the bank, but soon it came to a halt, standing on hind legs and watching her go. It did not make a sound. She expected water creatures to slink and slide into the boat and attack her with teeth or toxins. She waited for her mother to return, as she had waited for most of her adult life. But she never did.

She kept baling through the night, hoping that the monotony of the movement would afford her some sense of peace. It did not. Around dawn, the estuary opened up wide, banks receding, and the distance and space above and around her pressed down and in. Her heart started hammering, but not with exertion. Its beat echoed through the hollowness she felt inside.

The love of her life was dead. Her father was dead, and her mother was gone, more distant than she had ever been. The loneliness and crippling grief were smothering. In the vastness of this place Jenn felt smaller than she ever had before. Ahead of her, beyond Eden, was the stink and pollution of the human world, and now she would face it alone.

But something inside her clasped onto the hope her father's sacrifice had provided.

I'm going to live, she thought, and then she spoke those words aloud with a surprising strength. They saw away the weight of the wildness closing around her, fending off the looming nightmare. She started baling faster, faster. Her injuries burned, pulsed, the pain pinning her to the moment and reminding her of everything that had happened.

When both shores were far away and the surge of the tide caught the boat, she stopped baling, and saw a single petal in the mud where Cove had been sitting. She brought it close to her face and stared at it, relishing its strange beauty. Sniffing its mysterious scent. Knowing it might change the world. For a long while she simply held it, two uncertain futures resting in her muddy hand. Then she trailed her hand in the water and let the petal float away.

Several hours later, with the sun high above the curve of the ocean's horizon, Eden was gone, and Jenn allowed herself to cry.

KAT

There is no sense of cruelty about Kat's incarceration in what was once her body. The elemental is not offering punishment or torture. Her body is cured of its illness and injuries, and she senses that it is more powerful and fitter than it has ever been before. Yet neither is she offered any hope of release. Lilith is indifferent, and over time Kat has learned to exist with that. Sometimes, she even enjoys this symbiotic relationship.

The single time when she gathered herself, pushed to the fore, and urged Lilith to take no action is a long time in the past. She can hardly remember how she achieved such a feat. She thinks perhaps Lilith allowed it. She also accepts that she will never know for sure. There is one remaining memory of this time that she holds dear, and which gives her a faint glow of pride.

Seen through the eyes of a bear, the memory is of a woman in a boat, leaving.

Lilith spends long, long periods motionless. Sometimes it sits beneath a tree and grows still, allowing day and night, moon cycles and different seasons to pass it by. Other times it finds somewhere deep and dark, and the passage of time is even more difficult to discern.

From time to time it moves across the ever-changing

landscape of Eden, visiting sites where ghost orchids bloom and sitting within their glow, like a proud parent watching its children grow. As time goes by the places where the orchid grows become easier to reach. From clifftops and ravine slopes, to meadows and hillsides, the plant experiences a calmer, more peaceful life.

Occasionally there is a need to take action. As time passes and both Lilith and Eden grow stronger, the creatures it calls on to serve it grow more numerous and diverse. But these periods of intervention are few and far between, and they are becoming less frequent. Maybe the people are learning. Or perhaps the world outside is experiencing a change, and those who would seek to infiltrate Eden, damage it and make it their own, have more urgent needs to attend to.

On very rare occasions, the elemental travels back to the place where it killed the man Kat used to love. A long time has passed. His body is buried deeper now, given back to the land. She and Lilith sit there for a while, and Kat thinks about the past.

These visits are the elemental's only real acknowledgement of her continued existence. It is almost an expression of humanity.

Kat considers it a kindness.

THE END

ACKNOWLEDGEMENTS

I started scribbling notes about this novel in a hotel in New York, days after having spent time on the set of *The Silence* in Toronto, and I'd like to send a big thanks to everyone who made that film a reality—Alexandra Milchan and Scott Lambert, John R. Leonetti, Robert Kulzer, Carey and Shane Van Dyke, and everyone at Netflix. And special thanks as ever my most excellent agents Howard Morhaim and Michael Prevett, who guided me through the whole amazing process with superhuman patience. Also a huge thanks to Cath Trechman and the whole of Team Titan.

THE SILENCE
TIM LEBBON

In the darkness of an underground cave system, blind creatures hunt by sound. Then there is light, there are voices, and they feed... Swarming from their prison, the creatures thrive and destroy. To scream, even to whisper, is to summon death. As the hordes lay waste to Europe, a girl watches to see if they will cross the sea. Deaf for many years, she knows how to live in silence; now, it is her family's only chance of survival. To leave their home, to shun others, to find a remote haven where they can sit out the plague. But will it ever end? And what kind of world will be left?

NOW A GRIPPING NETFLIX MOVIE
STARRING STANLEY TUCCI AND KIERNAN SHIPKA

"Lebbon develops a believable and intense narrative that is certainly a must have for any horror enthusiast to add to their collection" *We Love This Book*

"*The Silence* is a chilling story that grips you firmly by the throat" *SciFi Now*

"A truly great novel with a fresh and original story" *Starburst Magazine*

SOON

LOIS MURPHY

On winter solstice, the birds disappeared, and the mist arrived.

The inhabitants of Nebulah quickly learn not to venture out after dark. But it is hard to stay indoors: cabin fever sets in, and the mist can be beguiling, too.

Eventually only six remain. Like the rest of the townspeople, Pete has nowhere else to go. After he rescues a stranded psychic from a terrible fate, he's given a warning: he will be dead by solstice unless he leaves town – *soon*.

"Lois Murphy's *Soon* is an exquisitely written, atypical post-apocalyptic/horror story that smartly focuses on the characters/survivors without sacrificing story/thrills/scares. Like the nightly mists, *Soon* will linger."
Paul Tremblay, author of *The Cabin at the End of the World*

PHANTOMS

The brightest names in horror showcase a ghastly collection of eighteen ghost stories that will have you watching over your shoulder, heart racing at every bump in the night. In "My Life in Politics" by M.R. Carey the spirits of those without a voice refuse to let a politician keep them silent. In "The Adjoining Room" by A.K. Benedict a woman finds her hotel neighbour trapped and screaming behind a door that doesn't exist. George Mann's "The Restoration" sees a young artist become obsessed with returning a forgotten painting to its former glory, even if it kills her. And Laura Purcell's "Cameo" shows that the parting gift of a loved one can have far darker consequences than ever imagined...

These unsettling tales from the some of the best modern horror writers will send a chill down your spine like someone has walked over your grave... or perhaps just woken up in their own.

KELLEY ARMSTRONG
A.K. BENEDICT
M.R. CAREY
JOHN CONNOLLY
GEMMA FILES
HELEN GRANT
MURIEL GRAY
JOE HILL
MARK A. LATHAM

TIM LEBBON
ALISON LITTLEWOOD
JOSH MALERMAN
GEORGE MANN
LAURA PURCELL
ROBERT SHEARMAN
ANGELA SLATTER
PAUL TREMBLAY
CATRIONA WARD

TITANBOOKS.COM

For more fantastic fiction, author events,
exclusive excerpts, competitions, limited editions and more

VISIT OUR WEBSITE
titanbooks.com

LIKE US ON FACEBOOK
facebook.com/titanbooks

FOLLOW US ON TWITTER AND INSTAGRAM
@TitanBooks

EMAIL US
readerfeedback@titanemail.com